JUST THIS ONCE

Scott French

A BIRCH LANE PRESS BOOK
Published by Carol Publishing Group

A Birch Lane Press Book
Published by Carol Publishing Group
Birch Lane Press is a registered trademark of Carol Communications, Inc.
Editorial Offices: 600 Madison Avenue, New York, N.Y. 10022
Sales and Distribution Offices: 120 Enterprise Avenue, Secaucus, N.J. 07094
In Canada: Canadian Manda Group, P.O. Box 920, Station U, Toronto, Ontario, M8Z 5P9
Queries regarding rights and permissions should be addressed to Carol Publishing Group,
600 Madison Avenue, New York, N.Y. 10022

Carol Publishing Group books are available at special discounts for bulk purchases, for
sales promotions, fund raising, or educational purposes. Special editions can be created
to specifications. For details, contact Special Sales Department, Carol Publishing Group,
120 Enterprise Avenue, Secaucus, N.J. 07094

Manufactured in the United States of America
10 9 8 7 6 5 4 3 2 1

Library of Congress Cataloging-in-Publication Data

French, Scott R.
    Just this once / Scott French.
      p.   cm
    "A Birch Lane Press book."
    ISBN 1-55972-173-1
    I. Title.
      PS3556.R443J87   1993
      813'.54 — dc20   92-39500
                                                                   CIP

"Five Miles Out," words and music by Mike Oldfield, copyright © 1982 by Virgin
Records, Ltd.

I would like to dedicate this book to Robert Stone, Jim Harrison, and other wordsmiths who realize that madness is hopelessly intertwined with great writing.

WHEN I AM GONE AND DEAD
I HOPE IT WILL BE SAID
HIS SINS WERE SCARLET
BUT HIS BOOKS WERE READ
— Hilaire Belloc
I think Jacqueline would have liked that

"She works for the great proletariat machine.
In the novel writing section"
— George Orwell, 1984
I like that one.
sf

ACKNOWLEDGMENTS

Because this project has spanned some eight-plus years from inception to finished manuscript, a wide selection of people must be thanked for their input, guidance, and direct help.

The project would not have been feasible without the introduction of the artificial intelligence shell NEXPERT, which dropped the price of a top level AI program, a software program that actually let's a computer "think," from the $100,000 range into the $5,000 area, numbers which gave me the opportunity to stop fantasizing and actually begin work on the project. The founders of Neuron Data (makers of NEXPERT), Dr. Alain Rappaport and Patrick Perez, must also be publicly thanked for their encouragement and allowing me the use of need facilities including attendance at users' groups and conferences. Dr. Rappaport's papers were also quite valuable in formulating my front end strategy.

Bechtel Engineering provided valuable training in the use of my specific AI program, NEXPERT.

The task of defining style and natural language programming was introduced to me by the works of Robert Wilensky and Wendy Lehnert (*Strategies for Natural Language Processing*), Sergei Nirenbug, who edited the book *Machine Translation,* Terry Winograd, *Language as a Cognitive Process,* Robert Simmons, *Computations From the English, Beyond Style,* Gary Provost, *Characters and Viewpoint* by Orson Scott Card, *Fuzzy Sets, Uncertainty and Information* by George Klir and Tina Folger.

Special thanks to Kenneth M. Ford from the Institute for Human and Machine Cognition at the University of West Florida for graciously sharing his work in knowledge acquisition, Jack R. Adams-Webber, Brock University, for his input on the psychological side of things, and, of course, John Boose, who pioneered the strategies and acquisition tools for rating and inputing data in the repertory grid system, and, even though he was working on a proprietary system for Boeing, returned my calls, provided me with the direction, and supplied his papers that effectively distilled the earlier works of Dr. Kelly and others.

Next would come my instructors and students in the various courses and seminars I participated in at the University of California Berkeley, UC San Francisco, UC Santa Clara extension, and especially at UC San Diego, where several gentlemen from RAND Corp. found my project intriguing enough to spend many hours dissecting my methodology and offering suggestions.

And all my friends who, although considering me crazy for spending maybe $50,000 and a major part of what could have passed for my social life on a rather, uh, novel project, never wavered in their support.

INTRODUCTION

How did *Just This Once* come about? I'm glad you asked that...

Break the rules.

Once in a lifetime someone writes a book that blows away conventional book buyers. Jacqueline Susann was one such person. *Valley of the Dolls* became the best-selling book in history *(20 million plus)* because *she broke the rules.*

Valley attracted not only traditional readers but millions of people who had never purchased a book in their lives.

Jackie S. was the best at what she did, no question about it. Her books plunged the reader into an amazing world that few people ever get the chance to experience. Her early death saddened millions of loyal fans, myself included. Secretly I hoped someone had frozen her, à la Walt Disney, waiting for that magical time in the future when doctors could thaw her out in the microwave, cure her cancer, and put her back in front of a typewriter.

A number of years ago I decided to do just that... Lacking a cold storage device, I opted for a resurrection that was more philosophical in nature. I began studying an advanced form of computer programming known as Artificial Intelligence. One branch of AI, Expert Systems, was invented specifically to allow *a computer to think like a human being.*

Expert Systems apply the thought processes of a certain "expert" to a new problem, solving it in the same manner as would the human model. Computers that think diagnose diseases in hospitals, help fly the space shuttle, and set your credit line at American Express.

I spent nearly eight years and $50,000 of my own money studying computational linguistics, natural language programming, and Artificial

Intelligence, in order to program the best Expert System on the market to *think and write* like Jacqueline Susann. The seminars and courses I attended consisted of me and the guys from the think tanks; they were teaching their computers to predict how world leaders would react under pressure and track missile launches. I was trying to make mine create a dynamite novel.

Mine worked.

Just This Once is not a rehash of another book — instead it's the novel Jacqueline Susann would write if she were still alive.

I broke all the rules on this one. And damn, it was *fun*.

— scott french

THE
DOLLHOUSE

Silent vibrations of power emanated from the four men who occupied the plush velvet chairs surrounding the antique cherry wood table supposed to have once been owned by Napoleon.

Actually, the chances were good this meeting was more than the result of an idle rumor. Nick Salerio was a man with a flair for class.

The irony of this meeting was not lost on Mr. Salerio; although worth millions, he was very much at the mercy of the other members of this select gathering.

A fact he was not used to dealing with.

The main threat was by a small, nerdy-looking man. He was dressed in an ill-fitting, off-the-rack suit, his face was both framed and diminished by too-heavy horn-rimmed glasses. However, he was known to be the right arm of the governor of California and rumors had him already selected to be the next candidate for state attorney general.

Nick had instantly picked up that the act of the suit/glasses was nothing more than a diversion, designed to hide the graduate degrees and force most observers into a weak, premature appraisal. Nick held no such illusions about the power this man wielded.

The other guest of note was a senior member of the Nevada Gaming Commission, a CPA who controlled the state's main source of income. He was the closest thing to a god in this state.

The final knight of the round table was Nick's long-term lawyer and sometimes friend. His pudgy appearance notwithstanding, this man was entirely at ease in meetings where the fate of a thousand people and billions of dollars would be decided.

"We're all here," the man from California stated as he rattled his thick document file to effect authority, "let's get down to it. The basic issue is that the ACE corporation, the majority stockholder being one Mr. Nick Salerio"—he glanced up to let this sink in—"has been operating an illegal gaming establishment within the state limits of California for almost eighteen years."

"Uh-huh," Nick's attorney commented neutrally. "It should be pointed out that eighteen years ago we were informed by the surveyor California employed that we were operating in the state of Nevada. To what do we owe this sudden revelation that moves the state line a hundred feet into our territory?"

The man from California laughed. "Lasers! Ain't technology great? The magic of modern science. The first survey was apparently in error, but this one would stand up in any court in the land. We can even tell you which ferns are yours and which ice plants are ours. No screw-ups this time.

"As the direct representative of the governor of the esteemed State of California, I see no alternative but to ask the Nevada Gaming Commission to issue a cease and desist order for this establishment, effective at once."

For the first time during the meeting the Gaming rep asserted his presence. He shrugged as if to say, "What else?"

The silence ran towards a full minute. Nick spent every second studying the California man for any sign of weakness he could use.

He found none.

"Suppose"—Nick was the first to break the quiet—"an acceptable compromise could be reached?"

"Like?"

"Well"—Nick leaned back—"as I see it, we are in violation of the gaming laws, nothing else." This was followed by three silent nods.

"What if we rearranged the internal layout of the building so the show arena was situated in California, and the gambling section in Nevada? Of course, the corporation would pay our esteemed neighbor some sort of entertainment tax on each show."

"I like it. I think the governor might just go for it, with certain guarantees, of course."

"It would certainly be a legal first," Nick's lawyer chimed in. "However, I can foresee no real problem."

"Gentlemen, if you are both ready to follow through with that suggestion, I would be happy to put it before the gaming committee for a vote. And I feel certain I can predict acceptance of such a logical deal."

He stood up. "And now, if you will excuse my rudeness, I have several other matters to attend to today, but again, I feel I can almost assure acceptance and will give a positive answer within the week."

The Gaming commissioner left the room.

Nick faced the California representative. "You want a drink...or anything else?"

"I'll take a Martell Blue, Nick," he answered. "You don't mind if I call you Nick, do you?"

One thing Nick Salerio prided himself on was his ability to control his outward emotional responses. To smile now took every ounce of that training. At least the man has taste in booze, he thought. That's something. Too bad he didn't want a broad. I'd love to hear the report.

"Scotch and soda," Nick's lawyer called. He had never quite learned to differentiate between well and call brands.

Nick pressed a hidden button of his belt transmitter and a tuxedo-adorned waiter appeared within seconds to take the order.

After a few moments the drinks arrived and the man from California sipped his after first swirling the amber liquid around to feel the warmth of the preheated glass.

"I'm glad this whole affair went smoothly," he said, pretending the meeting had been anything more than a carefully scripted scenario. "The governor sends his personal regards and asked me to convey his deep appreciation that you have taken such a personal interest in his re-election campaign. It's always good to know you have friends in other states." He gulped down the remainder of his expensive cognac. "You won't forget that little campaign contribution we discussed, will you?"

Even at this brazen break in protocol, Nick managed to summon up a laugh. "Tell your boss the check is in the mail."

The other man nodded, as if the thought of a million dollars in cash being entrusted to the U.S. Post Office was not in the least unusual.

"Good, he'll be pleased." He also rose as if to leave. "Perhaps we will meet again. The winds of politics do blow in strange directions."

"You know"—Nick stood up to see him out—"I like you. If you ever want a real job, give me a call."

The attorney seemed taken aback by this suggestion. "Thank you. I don't believe in burning bridges. We'll see." He bowed from the waist and left.

Nick's lawyer did up his Scotch in one fell swoop and slammed the empty glass down. "I miss the old days. We would have had no problem. That smart ass hyena would have woke up planted in the desert face down with his feet sticking up like one of those modern art exhibits, and that would have been that."

"No," Nick said, "times, they change and we must change with them. He would have been replaced with some other double-knit shyster armed with the same instructions. Besides, I liked him. I really did, he had balls. That's rare now, you know, really rare. I think doctors cut them off at birth these days."

He stared at the now-closed door.

"Are we really going to pay? It'll just be the first in a line of 'requests.'"

"Yes, pay it, and then put the casino up for sale. We're going to do something I've always wanted to do—move the operation into the big leagues. We are going to build the only high class operation in Las Vegas. No slots, no cheap food, a dress code, the best shows. A place that will draw heavy hitters like flies to honey.

"The DollHouse will become a legend in this business and that's all that matters...

"That's all."

IN THE
BEGINNING

CAROL

It was a normal summer day. The mercury was stuck at 106 degrees in the non-existent shade. The sudden air-conditioned atmosphere inside the building struck her like a small hurricane, almost knocking her off her feet with the unexpected man-made wind, both the artificial coldness and the indoor acres of brilliant gold-and-black furnishings grabbing her senses unexpectedly.

Somehow she made her way to the cage. The girl inside smiled and said, "Can I help you?"

For a long moment she remained stunned by the artificial world swirling around her. Finally Carol found her tongue, "I'll need a room and I want to talk to someone in charge." Even as she said this she realized it sounded like a complaint. "I mean about a job."

The other girl cocked her head at an angle, sizing Carol up. "Well, as to the room, you're in luck. We're sold out of regular rooms, all booked up."

Carol grimaced. "That doesn't sound very lucky."

The cage girl laughed, "First time in the big city, huh? It's good because we have orders to give a suite when we run out of rooms. For the same price, I mean. You'll love it. Trust me." She handed over an embossed key.

"The other one may be a trifle tougher. What kind of a job are you looking for?"

"Well, anything, I guess. I really don't have too much experience, but I really want to work here." Oh, oh, she thought, this isn't going the way it should. She slid her credit card over the transom with shaking hands.

"Uh-huh, it suddenly becomes clear." The girl leaned forward on her elbows. "You're here on the Nevada plan, right?"

"I'm not sure I know what you mean."

"I figure you're doing time on the six weeks to life installment setup." When there was no reaction the girl leaned forward to whisper the punch line. "The blue plate special: a divorce."

"Does it show?" She glanced down at her coordinated outfit.

The other girl put a hand on Carol's arm, "No, I'm naturally psychic about some things. I can pick out several a day. I rarely miss. Don't feel conspicuous," she giggled. "Most look a lot more desperate than you do. Listen, I'm on break in ten minutes. Why don't you pull up a table at the bar and I'll join you for a quick run-down of the scene?"

Carol looked at her luggage and the other girl seemed to pick up on it at once. "Don't worry, I'll have a bell captain take them to your room. Go sit down." She picked up the credit card and read the name embossed on it. "Oh, by the way, Carol, I'm Lisa. Welcome to the DollHouse." She grabbed Carol's hand and shook it.

Carol was into her second white wine when Lisa plopped herself in the chair directly across from her. She immediately waved to the bartender and shouted, "Perrier, John." The bartender nodded his head in response and lowered the glass beneath the bar to pour the drink. Lisa winked. "We're not allowed to drink on duty but it's been a bitch of a day. I deserve a little pick-me-up."

The bartender delivered the "Perrier" personally. "Who's your friend?" He raised an eyebrow in Carol's direction.

"Johnny, this is Carol and vice versa." Lisa took the glass in both hands. "She's doing the sit and split and looking for a gig."

"Yeah," he paused to study Carol, "she'll score wherever she tries. Great face." He picked up the empty ashtray and made a show of pouring invisible ashes into a tray.

Lisa waited until the bartender had returned to his station. "So. Your idea or his?"

"Pardon?"

"The divorce, is he home pining away for you or out screwing your replacement? If he is, she must be an amazing lady, 'cause you look like a hard act to follow."

A good question: Whose fault was it? Four years of what seemed like a great relationship followed by only three months of a very rocky marriage. Did he change with the pressure of the wedding band or did she? Was there one problem or was it just a mismatch? Why had Glenn suddenly seemed so different, so alien? "Quit your job," he said. "No wife of mine is going to work. I can support both of us."

Give up her career? Admittedly it had been only a minor position as a reporter for the local newspaper, but she quit, and for what? To wait around every day for him to come home and start in with the martinis? To sit around waiting to get pregnant like some medieval lady-in-waiting? After a couple months even their lovemaking seemed to lack interest for him.

She had disappointed both him and his parents by not getting immediately knocked up. Carol laughed to herself as she thought of that phrase. God, what would my mother say to language like that? Not only have I become a fallen woman, I'm here in Sin City.

And then there was the final day when she had caught him in "the act." Looking back at the scene that followed, she realized that Glenn had almost seemed relieved to have been caught. Even during the tear-filled fight afterwards he really didn't put his heart into it.

"It's not all my fault. I can't reach you. I don't think you even enjoy sex. Maybe that's why we don't have a kid. I feel rejected every time we're together. Maybe I just needed to feel that someone wanted me. Did you ever think of that?"

Carol had to laugh, feeling as if she had read it all before in a cheap novel.

She had wanted him, hadn't she? After all, she had married him. Maybe it wasn't love like in the supermarket romance novels, but she had tried damn hard. He had no right to say those things to her. No right at all. Perhaps there was no fault involved. Kismet. Perhaps it was just never meant to be. Whatever the reasons, it still felt like someone was plunging an icicle into her heart whenever she played it back. It felt like failure.

"I guess it was pretty mutual. There was nobody else involved." I like this girl and I've just told her a lie, she thought, moodily.

"It doesn't make any difference. Men are like busses in this town. A new one comes by every five minutes. With your looks you'll land a hot one in no time. Just be sure to look for the telltale tan." Lisa held up her left hand and pantomimed a ring around the fourth finger. "It's easy to take off a ring but it's not so easy to hide the evidence."

"I'll remember that."

"Or take my advice and date only married men. It's easier in the long run."

"No, I don't think that's me. I couldn't foul up anybody's marriage." Silently she told herself, because someone fouled up mine. I don't want to stoop to that level, but I can't tell anyone that, not yet.

"Suit yourself. I prefer to be the other woman. Then I get all the good times and they go home to their wives to bitch about their jobs, money, and life in general. Besides, they always feel guilty and I'm here to assuage that problem by accepting any little gifts they might have in mind." She shrugged. "All the good stuff and none of the problems."

"Don't you ever feel guilty?"

"Nah, I'm no hooker. I never take money. Besides, if the wifey is so hot, how come they're out with me. I kinda consider myself a public servant." Lisa lit a cigarette.

"Well, I'm not in the market anyway." Escape, Carol thought, that's what I want to do. Just escape into this ozone and blend in with all the happy faces. Make it legal and then start all over. There's just got to be more to love than sitting around a heavily mortgaged house reading the latest novels.

At least that was one positive thing that marriage had brought. I can discuss any of the *New York Times* best sellers over the past year. It was almost an addiction, waking up every morning and jumping back into the world of spies, police stories, and mysteries. Reading until two A.M. with a tiny book light while Glenn slept on. Feeling more like one of the characters than herself. Looking forward to the release, the more exciting world of popular fiction, where things were always happening and time was condensed instead of stretching on and on into the void.

"Is there really a chance for a job here? I don't have enough money to last the six weeks in a hotel." And whose fault was that? True, she would get some money when the house and furniture were finally sold, but she could have asked for a lot more. Put Glenn under the forever thumb of the alimony court. But why? He really didn't owe her a living. If they had children it might be different...

"Well," Lisa answered, "you could go to school for three weeks and come back as a blackjack dealer, or you might land a change-girl job now, but that pays less and no tips. It's too bad it isn't a couple of months from now. I've got a part dancing in a show across town. It ain't the DollHouse but it's a start and if I can land another gig I'll quit here, but I gotta make sure there's something else out there."

"You work a show at night and this job in the daytime? When do you sleep?"

Lisa shrugged. "Show biz, you know? I just give up the little things like eating and having any social life. But it's worth it. I ain't going to be a clerk all my life. Anyway, if I was leaving I could suggest you for the job, but it's just too soon and I can't give up the DollHouse. I could end up back on the strip in one of the tourist traps."

"Is there really that much difference? I mean, they're all casinos..."

"Oh no, this is the only casino with any class. It's a whole different world out there. I mean, I've never been to any place really fancy like Monaco or anything but everybody says this is the next best thing. Pretty much high rollers, no slot machines, you don't have to take a lot of grab-ass shit from drunken construction workers, and the management actually treats us like humans. Believe me, if you are going to work in Vegas it's the DollHouse or nowhere. That makes it pretty tough to get a job here but with your looks you might get a waitress job or even be a shill. That's fun for a while, until it gets old. The turnover is high, but for God's sake don't tell the man that you are only here for six weeks. If he suspects you are here for a divorce, he won't hire you."

"The man?"

"Oh, that's the house name for Nick. He runs the place. I guess he owns it but nobody knows for sure. Anyway, he interviews everyone personally, no matter what the job. He can be really rough or really easy. Just be your innocent self and lie about the divorce. You'll do okay.

"Listen, I have to get back to work. Use your room and he'll probably call you before you check out. I'll see you later." Lisa walked back to the check-in area.

Carol walked over to the bank of elevators and got in the first one available. "What floor?" the only other passenger asked her, poised to punch the correct button.

Suddenly she realized she didn't have any idea where she was going. Hurriedly she looked at her key. "The penthouse floor."

The man raised his eyebrows, "A heavy hitter, huh? Unfortunately this car only goes to the first seventeen floors. You'll have to take one of the elevators across the way. They go the VIP rooms." The car was already rising.

Feeling suddenly stupid and obvious, she studied the speaker. He was tall, at least six-two, and dressed in a well-cut suit. Then she noticed the black bow tie and the finely creased white shirt.

"Do you work here?"

He clicked his heels together. "Taylor Stevens, house flack, assistant manager, and chief bottle washer at your service. I only double as the elevator operator when we're short of hands."

When they reached the fourteenth floor he started to exit, turned, and held the door open. "You really don't fit the image of a fast lady. Why the penthouse? Do you have a rich boyfriend or were they out of regular rooms?"

She was irritated with both the man and his insight. She tried to be very cool. "I'm here to see Nick." That should do it. Put him in his place.

But he laughed, "Looking for a job, huh? Well, mention my name to Broadway. Say you are a long lost cousin and I'll vouch for you. For whatever good that endorsement will do." He released the door and stepped out into the hallway. "If you want some inside advice, I'm in 1412 and still free for dinner."

"Thank you, no." She tried to be stiff but this brash, good-looking character seemed to possess some hidden chemistry. It was as though he could see right through her act. As if he had been there before.

"Suit yourself, but I'm a man of my word. Mention me and I'll back you. Besides, I never rape anyone on the first date. House rules."

The door shut behind him with a hydraulic whoosh.

Carol punched the up button and tried not to think about the strange encounter. She was not successful.

The door to her room opened with almost no effort and she gasped out loud at the view. The suite utilized the same vivid black-and-gold color scheme as the casino area, reminding her of a high-class whorehouse in some turn of the century novel. It was overwhelming: a large living room with white couch at least eight feet long, a small kitchen, huge bathroom that included a separate tub area, and telephones everywhere, even next to the bathtub.

I wish I had someone to call, she thought, just to try out that phone while lying up to my neck in bubbles. Is this how the rich and famous live? She walked into the bedroom and stopped. Vivid gold everywhere—carpet, walls, ceiling—except for the huge canopied bed. White.

And the mirrors. All over the place, folded in right angles on every wall, as well as a huge one-piece mirror on the underside of the canopy, directly over the bed. Good God, what if there is an earthquake during the night? I'd die, buried in a million glass shards. I've never watched myself sleep before.

The phone rang. Rather, all the phones rang. It sounded like high noon in a clock repair shop. The first ring had already died into infinity before she was able to place the offending noise. Who could be calling? It was either a wrong number or they had discovered an unused room and were kicking her out of her glorious lap of luxury. Should she answer it?

What the hell, they'll just keep calling back until they get someone. Her suitcases seemed to be glaring at her. I didn't even get a chance to unpack. Oh well, no one could expect this king's castle for thirty-five dollars a night. Life just isn't like that. "Hello?"

"Settled in?" The vaguely familiar voice asked.

"Who is this please?" I should have asked what number he was calling.

"This is the house welcome wagon. And elevator operator."

"Oh." What a great comeback. Really impressing him.

"Listen, now that you're relaxed and enjoying your good fortune, I'm trying again for a dinner invite."

"Well, like I told you, I'm tired and..." She let it hang. Why can't I say a simple "no"?

"You have to eat, right? If you go alone chances are you'll have to stand in line for the worst seats in the house. If we go together I can throw my weight around and get us anything we want. Even a counter seat. Good service, good food, and I'll try to be good company. Remember the house rule. You're perfectly safe."

"Listen, I need to shower and…"

"Great. I'll swing by in an hour. See you then."

The line went dead. *Did I agree to anything? Or was it just a case of no opportunity to refuse? Well, at least I can get some suggestions about applying for a job.* She walked into the oversized bathroom and turned on the scalding hot water.

Taylor was as good as his word. They went to a restaurant in the casino specializing in aged steaks and were seated at once, earning envious glances from the long line of customers waiting for a seat. Any seat. He waved away the menu the subservient waiter brought. "Jimmy, bring us whatever is fresh and good. Plus a bottle of Dom Perignon."

"At once, Mr. Stevens." The man seemed about to fall over from his departing bow.

"Flack, huh? I'd guess you are fibbing just a little. You have to be pretty high up in the pecking order to get that kind of treatment."

Taylor shrugged. "It's all relative. I'm high on the list to waiters and bus boys, but others seem high to me. At least I've got the pencil."

"The pencil?" Carol asked.

"Say, you really are new around here, aren't you? I thought it might all be an act, you know, the Miss Innocence bit." He watched her angry reaction. "No offense. It's just that we see them all and I've been taken in before.

"The pencil means that I can sign off anybody I want. Usually that translates into big spenders, winners or losers, they deserve a free room and meal at least. It's amazing how a hundred-fifty-dollar freebie can satisfy someone who just blew ten thousand on the craps table. Some people never learn." He shook his head.

"Do people really bet that much in a night?" She thought of the eight dollars in quarters that had served her for almost one and a half hours on the slots when she first arrived in town.

"Many, many, that's how we survive, my lovely friend. The DollHouse and this state thrive because hope really does spring eternal. The stick and the carrot. It could be you; after all it has to be someone, right? The ads never show the losers, you'll notice. They go home quietly."

"Doesn't that make you feel bad?" She watched his face closely.

"Not at all. This is the land of free choice. Take it or leave it. Quit while you're ahead. Nobody makes you stay at the table. Of course, it is my job to entice you to remain there until you pay for the privilege, but it's gentle persuasion at most. No cheating, no leg breakers and any good gambler knows exactly what the odds are at any game here. It's no secret. You places your money and you takes your chances. Isn't that what life is all about?"

The tuxedoed waiter brought their dinner. Poached salmon, asparagus with Hollandaise sauce, and fresh greens. Taylor opened the champagne and poured for both of them. "By the way, I've comped your room. You're set for five days."

"Oh no, I can't do that. I mean it's nice but I really can't accept. I mean I hardly know you and I want..."

He waved his hand. "Don't feel obligated. We had a paid-up room for a certain roller who dropped fifty thousand last night trying to play out-count the dealer. I set him up and he left with someone I, ah, arranged for him to meet. The room is already covered. Enjoy it."

"So pimping is included in your job description?" As soon as she said it she was sorry, even though she felt the need to bring him down a notch.

He laughed. "That's one way of looking at it. Damn, you are direct, aren't you? That's refreshing. Nobody uses that word around here. I just did him a favor. He's happy, we're happy, I'm happy. Eat your fish."

When the meal was finished he rose abruptly and apologized. "Duty calls. Sorry, but you'll have to see yourself back to your room. I enjoyed it."

She was waiting for a polite kiss, but he only shook her hand. Am I really that cold? Carol wondered. A sense of disappointment crept in spite of her efforts to stop it. "By the way, you have an interview at ten A.M. tomorrow with Nick. Try and be natural. You will stun him." He waved and walked off.

Right on schedule all the phones rang at nine-thirty the next morning. "Mr. Salerio would like to see you in half an hour in his office. Can you make it?" the impersonal voice said.

Could she? "Certainly, I'll be there." Then as an afterthought: "Exactly where is his office?"

"Go down your hall to the end and turn right. It's P, number one."

"Fine, I'll—" but the line was already dead.

Her heart was doing double time as she entered the office/suite. Although she had expected something fancy, this exceeded her expectations.

"Please, do come in," the man who opened the door into this crystal and chrome wonderland said and gestured to a white leather chair. He was impeccably dressed in a custom-cut, dark blue pinstripe suit and a brown tie complete with an embossed emblem of pure gold. Carol recognized it for what it was, the crest of the DollHouse. He was probably in his mid-sixties but had the piercing stare of a thirty-year-old.

"Carol Davis to see Mr. Salerio." *If he pays his assistant enough to cover that wardrobe he can surely afford me...*

"You're expected." The man watched her sit down and proceeded to look her over from toes to head. She decided he was visualizing her sans clothes.

"Could you tell him I'm here, please?" This came out a bit sharper than she had intended. *No use alienating the hired help...*

"My pleasure." He bowed formally and disappeared into the back office.

A moment later a muffled voice called out, "Come in, Miss Davis." She took a deep breath and opened the door.

The mahogany desk was the largest she had ever seen; behind its polished face sat the same man who had opened the door. Carol was thrown off balance for a split second. Recovering her poise she said, "I was expecting to talk to Mr. Salerio personally."

He smiled like an errant child. "And so you are. And so you are."

"Oh, I'm sorry, I just assumed..."

"Therein lies your first Las Vegas learning lesson. Never assume anything. Here things are rarely what they appear to be."

He picked up some papers from the nearly bare desk, "It's quite an interesting résumé. I see you haven't actually worked for nearly two years." He looked at her with the bare minimum of a smile. "Independently wealthy?"

"Not exactly." *Right, another sharp comeback.*

"You have a Harvard business master's and some of the best legs I've seen in years. Which do you plan on using here?"

A damn good question...

"Dancers do okay, and you're tall enough. Now, I am assuming you have no real experience, of course. A few weeks in dancing school and you could probably kick with the best of them.

"Or there's change-girl duty. Not bad. Not bad, if you don't mind working for minimum wage and getting varicose veins at thirty. Or you could be a shill. With your looks and cool exterior, you would do wonders. How does that sound?"

"What's a shill?"

· "Come here a minute." He walked over to the panoramic window at the rear of the room and opened the curtains. Carol looked out onto the entire casino floor, stories below. The unexpected sight made her gasp involuntarily. "Don't worry. It's a one-way trip." He laughed at her lack of response. "We can see out but there's nothing but a mirror for anybody who chances to look upward."

"It feels like we are some sort of gods, peering down on our helpless subjects."

Nick did a slight double take and narrowed his eyes. Then he laughed. "Taylor said you were a direct one. Yeah, that's it, we *are* sort of gods to those below. The only time they look upward is to pray, 'Please, God, let me break even. I need the money'..."

She moved over to glance down into the organized partying stories below. "So what is a shill?"

"Miss Davis, do you really think all those beautiful people down there are having as much fun as they appear to be, losing their hard-earned money to us? Look closely. Every third person, one out of three, is working for me, and only me."

"What?" Carol looked back up, startled.

"Oh, yes, it's true. One out of three is working for the house. They are either security or shills, people hired to make it look like they, and by association, you, are having a good time. Each shill is betting with my money, and win or lose, it all comes back to the DollHouse." He shrugged and turned back towards the window. "No one wants to party alone. It's much easier to bet if you think someone else is riding along with you. The only problem is when the not-so-casual customer starts to recognize the shills. And then there's the burnout factor. It's rough trying to be overjoyed when you can't win. Or lose.

"The turnover is quite high. Here," he put his arm over her shoulder and guided her vision. "See that redhead in the designer gown?"

Carol peered along the extended arm. "The one betting the hundred-dollar chips?"

"Yes, that's the one. See how happy she is? Almost like she's got nothing to lose. Which, of course, she doesn't because that's our money she's playing with. Not hers..."

"What if she wins?"

"By the grace of God, it's still our money. Come hell or high water, it's still property. So is the dress she's wearing, by the way, and I'll take it back after the shift. Along with everything in the pockets. A philosophy that helps keep the workers honest..."

"You mean she is just betting DollHouse money? Entirely?"

"That's about the size of it, along with thirty-three percent of the rest of the people on the floor. Nobody parties alone in the DollHouse."

"It must be very boring."

"Boring it is. Most of our shills last it out for about three months. Can't blame 'em, after a while it's easy to remember only the times you've 'won' and forget the losses. Then they start to think it could have been their money... Part of my job is to detect that syndrome before they start to cheat the house."

"How do they do that?"

"Several ways. Usually they team up with a dealer and palm chips, turn in a five-dollar chip and get change for a hundred, even work with the dealer and a friend to tip off the hole card—you'd be surprised at some of the amazing ideas that get their start out there." He waved at the floor. "Creativity runs rampant." He looked at her with an intense stare. "So what do you want?"

"Well, I thought I could work into some sort of accounting or even management trainee position. I mean I don't have a lot of ex—"

Nick waved his hand to cut her off. "Let's skip the games today. I'm not in the mood. You have a Harvard MBA. No work in two years and suddenly here you are. Honey, it's obvious you're sitting out the six-week divorce period and I'd be a fool to hire you for anything except a change-girl, right?"

Carol did not respond.

"On the other hand, there is always the chance you might fall into the glitter life and not go back to Illinois."

"Connecticut," Carol said quietly.

Nick laughed. "Whatever. The point is I am a gambler. I'd be willing to bet you'll never use that return ticket if you have the right job."

"And what would that be?"

"I'm tired of answering my own door. I need an assistant. It's a strange job, more than just a secretary, not nine to five."

"Thanks anyway." Carol stood. "I'm not looking for extracurricular activities."

"Sit down, sit down. Look out there. I can have any broad in this town I want. Showgirls, pros, hopefuls, wives looking for a credit line. I don't need a mistress. I need a sharp backup. Someone who can be my eyes and ears, provide some real input. Everyone here is too jaded; you're still, well, innocent.

"Besides, I happen to think the greatest ideas come from people outside the field. People who take what works in one area and apply it to another. I'd expect you to study our system and make suggestions for improvements. You might be detached enough to pull it off. Starts at sixty K a year," he hesitated, "and you can have a room here if you want it. On the house."

"Ah, well, I'll have to think—"

"Sure, sure," he waved her out, "take a day and get the feel of the DollHouse. I'm betting you'll like it. And Carol, I rarely loose…"

She was still dreaming. She had to be… The plush four-poster brass bed and the veiled canopy were definitely out of some Arabian Nights dream. Maybe she was an exotic princess being made desperate love to by a handsome sheik…

Carol willed the dream to continue and then her eyes absently focused on the gigantic mirror directly overhead. Her heart leapt into her throat and she jumped involuntarily as the stranger appeared in front of her. Then it all came back in a rush. No wonder she thought she had been dreaming, she had… Yesterday seemed no more far-fetched than any other dream. She risked one more look at her life-sized reflection and smiled. *I wonder if men ever shave in bed? It would be easy enough with a set-up like this.* The reflection vanished as if a cloud had crossed the moon.

Carol showered and dressed and realized she was famished. For a fleeting second she was tempted to pick up the bathroom phone and call room service. *My gosh, one night in the palace and I've become* decadent! She shook her head and headed for the elevator bank at the end of the hall.

Carol was still thinking about the mirror over the bed as she leisurely walked into one of the downstairs coffee shops. Mirror, mirror on the ceiling... Who's the fairest... Hmmm, the only rhymes available didn't quite seem to fit somehow. Peeling just wasn't a very poetic word. Carol was jolted out of her thoughts by the sound of someone calling her name.

"Over here! Come on, sit with us." It was Lisa and she was sitting next to one of the most gorgeous men Carol had ever seen.

"You look like you're lost in space, what were you thinking about?"

"Trying to find a rhyme for ceiling," Carol muttered.

Lisa cocked her head at this response and then ignored it. "Well, are you going to take it?" she asked.

"Feeling." The man spoke with a voice belonging to a large jungle cat.

"What?" Carol realized she was staring at Lisa's breakfast companion.

"Rhymes with ceiling."

"The job!" Lisa raised her hands towards the sky. "Are you going to take the job?"

"How did you know about that already?" Carol felt like she was nearly stammering under the weight of the stranger's gaze.

"The DollHouse is like a small town." He was blond and his eyes were Paul Newman blue. "A very small town. Gossip travels fast."

"Oh." It seemed to be her time for clever responses.

Lisa watched the interplay and then suddenly giggled. She reached over and pinched the man's cheek. "I'm sorry, Carol, this is my friend, Leon. Isn't he cute?" She shook the captured cheek back and forth while she talked and the man laughed indulgently. "Leon is a big-time director. He's going to make me a household word someday, aren't you Leon?"

"Tide is a household word Lisa."

"That's really funny Leon." Lisa said in a very flat voice.

Leon shrugged. He faced towards Carol. "Are you?"

I'm missing something here, I know I am, she thought silently. "Ah, am I what?"

"The job."

"I, I'm not sure…" She was interrupted by the waitress. After they ordered Leon continued.

"Think it over!" Carol was sure Lisa was talking so loud the entire restaurant must be listening in. "Think it over! What's to think over?" She leaned forward, "Listen, you've got to stay here anyway, what else are you going to do, work as a temp in some dreary office shuffling papers all day? This is the easy way, you'd be right where the action is!"

"Not to mention, of course, that Lisa would then have a friend who would be able to put in a good word with the boss as well as get all the latest dope on everyone."

"Leon!" Lisa *was* now yelling, "That's not fair. It would be a great job, you know it would be."

"Maybe. And maybe Carol could even handle Nick. She looks like she's got a real backbone underneath that pretty exterior."

Carol felt herself blushing.

"Well, anyway, I do have to think it over." Even as she spoke Carol realized Lisa's reasoning was probably on the mark. After all she did have to stay here…

"Come on, Carol, I think we need to go to the powder room." Lisa pulled Carol from her chair and led her off towards the back of the room.

As soon as they were inside the door Lisa grabbed Carol's arm, "Listen, don't say no. I mean, I know we hardly know each other and all but I often get these hunches, see, and they're almost always right, and if you do take the job you've got to have a place to live, right?"

This delivery was so intense Carol had to laugh. "Listen, even if I did stay on I don't think I'm ready to live with any man especially your boyfriend."

"Boyfriend? Oh, oh, I get the picture, sweetheart… Ah, see you really don't have to worry on that score. Well, really on either score." She raised one eyebrow and smiled slightly.

"You mean—"

"A faggot." Lisa released Carol's arm and cocked her wrist. "As queer as a three-dollar bill. Oh, don't get me wrong, he's my best friend, but no boyfriend."

"But he's so—"

Lisa giggled again. "Beautiful is the word you're searching for. Ain't it a bitch? Not only does all that go to waste but he's actually the competition too."

"Gosh, he doesn't seem, I mean are you sure—"

"Believe me, I know what you're thinking and it ain't true. I don't know why mother nature fucked him up, but fucked up he is. One night I got really blasted and decided Leon had just never had the right offer, you know? The ultimate challenge, who could resist this? Love and desire." Lisa cupped her hands under her breasts and pushed up her cleavage. "Boy did I make an ass out of myself that night. He's gay through and through."

When they returned to the table Carol felt that she was blushing from head to toe. She turned her entire attention to her food but the silence seemed oppressive. How do you suppose Leon actually did—?

"It's okay, it's not contagious." His voice broke through her thoughts.

"Pardon?"

"Being gay. Scientific studies have proven it's not a virus. You're safe."

"Oh, no, I wasn't thinking…"

"Of course you were." Leon said. "I think you're the type that is always thinking, but it's okay. I like to be up front with people. That okay with you?"

"Sure," Carol said, more positively than she felt. "Sure."

"Think of it, it would be just like a movie. The Three Musketeers. We'd be great roomies." Lisa put two fingers into a hot fudge sundae and scraped the top layer into her mouth. "It wouldn't be boring, I guarantee it." Lisa dug back into the ice cream. "God I love this stuff. It's like sin."

No matter what else might happen, Carol felt that it wouldn't be boring was indeed a safe statement.

TAYLOR

Carol showed up for work at eight-thirty-five Monday morning. She wasn't due until nine, but she had awakened at six-thirty and the clock hands seemed to move so damn slowly. A new job, a new city, new roommates and a whole new world. It still seemed a bit too good to be true. Carol could feel her anticipation growing as she picked over her wardrobe.

Every dress seemed too East Coast, too conservative, for Vegas, and besides she had no idea of what she would be doing for Nick. Finally she picked out a mid-length dress that she figured would pass. Come on clock, move it along!

Able to wait no longer, Carol pushed open the office door to find Taylor sitting at the big desk instead of Nick. She was momentarily flustered but recovered quickly.

"Good morning."

Taylor looked up from the papers he was studying. "A bit early aren't you? This job doesn't pay by the hour you know, nothing extra for overtime."

"It's my first day on the job, trying to make a good impression, all that sort of thing."

"Well, apparently you did make an okay first impression. Two days ago I was pushing buttons for you in the elevator, now I'm practically working for you."

"Pardon me?"

"Special assistant to the chairman of the board." Taylor waited for a reaction. "Your job title: you report to no one except Nick himself. He asked me to give you your first assignment but you're officially outside the system, even I can't give you orders. Pretty slick."

Carol couldn't decide if Taylor was laughing at her or a bit irritated with the idea.

"So give it to me, what is my first assignment?"

"To learn—to study, to find the soft spots in the operation." Taylor pushed a package across the marble desk top that included several books, a pile of papers and a sealed envelope.

"Should you decide to accept it, your assignment is to learn the difference between the DollHouse and the rest of the system. Also to learn about gaming and how it works. You might want to start with this." He pushed the envelope towards her.

Carol carefully slit it open to find a stack of new one hundred dollar bills. She looked up at Taylor. "Thank you, but I hardly know you well enough for gifts."

"Five thousand bucks," Taylor ignored her comment. "You are to take it and gamble. Only a couple of rules; one is that you have two days to play. Two, you must bet at least ten bucks a throw, and three, you have to play every game in the house."

"And if I lose it all?"

"A cheap education at the price."

"What if I win?"

"Damned if I know. I guess you get to keep it." He watched Carol's startled reaction, "or give it to your favorite charity, whatever. But I wouldn't call United Way quite yet. Give it a day or two.

"Have you gone to any of the other casinos yet?"

Carol nodded, sheepishly.

"Okay, that's good. Let me start your job off by showing you the way we see the customers. Let's go to the Eye."

"What?"

"The Eye in the Sky. We've got the latest in video technology employed at nothing but letting me see every player, every dealer and every hand in the house. I'll let you in and show you the inside story." He flipped a plastic ID card onto the desk in front of Carol.

"Put that on, they don't like strangers in the Eye."

"I see it," Carol said, "but I don't see it. Why do they come to Las Vegas to spend their social security checks when they can't afford to pay the rent?" She looked out of the Eye in the Sky's two-way mirror. "I still can't believe the end of the month rush at the other houses, all the little old ladies cashing in their checks to play the slots. Hour after hour... I'm glad the DollHouse isn't like that. And they cash their checks so willingly."

"If one didn't, the next one would," Taylor said, but she could sense a hint of something behind the words.

Suddenly a new insight dawned on Carol, "Did you ever gamble?"

He looked at her sharply, "No, I don't believe in gambling." And just as he said those words, Carol disappeared, the DollHouse disappeared, and Taylor was someplace else. "However, I did used to play a bit..."

Stanford University, Palo Alto, California, 1985. Taylor Stevens watched a girl bicycle past, late for class. Her skin was so tanned she

appeared to be some sort of Indian. Only her sun-bleached blond hair
and her bright liquid blue eyes effectively blocked that impression.

Taylor watched her thigh muscles contract and then extend, pushing against the tight cuff of her white shorts as she pedaled her two-
thousand-dollar BMX mountain bike up the asphalt bike path that
paralleled the road.

A native, Taylor thought. Indigenous Californians. Specimen
Perfectus. Nurtured on sprouts and non-red-meat protein. The end
product of a most unusual genetic pooling—some Midwestern farmer
who had the wherewithal to look for something better, coupled with
high-checked Scandinavian women who came to look for the promised land.

Mother a lawyer, daddy a successful software developer, Taylor
thought. Riding on a California Porsche...Some day, after the great
quake levels us, her remains will drive future anthropologists crazy; a
bent BMX, crushed Walkman, tennis shorts, one diamond earring and
no bra. What will they make of it all? An offshoot of yuppie Homo
sapiens? A branch of the family tree that disappeared as surely as the
dinosaurs. What killed them off? The quake, the post-nuclear dust
storm, or the simple lack of non-hothouse tomatoes?

Like the dinosaurs before them, gone in a universal nanosecond...
And I happen to know she's not only a gorgeous specimen of womanhood, she's a bright med student, already picked to go places in a tough
field. And she's so damn cute. Taylor raised his hand and waved back at
a flirtatious wave from the girl in question. He settled back, sliding the
book so it was in the shade of the eucalyptus tree he was relaxing
under.

Where are the Beach Boys when you need them?

Sometimes it just seems too easy. Here I am, full ride at what's just
gotta be the best college in the entire free world...Oh sure, Harvard,
Yale, all that crap, but it's not the same. This was Stanford, all the good
stuff with none of the hassle. Prestige, a laid-back atmosphere and
none of the yuppie-dink crap that goes on at the Eastern schools. Shit,
here I can do my time, go surfing after class, borrow a turbo 911,
smoke dope with my professors on the green in front of the library,
have my pick of gorgeous, bright ladies, eat clams, drink beer at the
Dutch Goose and slide right on by.

Good chance I'll end up teaching Lit to a batch of kids just like me, lazing, grazing, and learning the better things in life. An endless progression of social grace, BMWs and blond shiny faces. And gorgeous California tanned tits. What a great life. No classes scheduled before ten A.M., endless theoretical arguments while picking the top brains of my generation.

So why am I so fucking bored with it? A mind is a terrible thing to waste...

Taylor walked slowly across the campus, occasionally acknowledging a hello from classmates or a friend. I can picture my life washing out in front of me like a well-mapped road; smooth and predictable. Is this what I really want? It's like an old Chinese proverb—don't depend on your dreams because they might come true. He opened the room of his small apartment and tossed his books across the ten feet of open space directly onto the bed.

"Jesus!" a voice responded to the airborne attack. "Is that you, Taylor?"

He stepped past the door and glanced at the slightly comic figure of his roommate in his usual position—bent over a dimly lit computer terminal rapidly punching information into the keyboard, his long unwashed hair swept forward in a rude imitation of a mad scientist's. His sweatshirt was on inside out and a roach burned in the crudely formed aluminum foil ashtray next to the keyboard.

Straight out of a Disney cartoon, Taylor thought. I'm rooming with the mad professor. No doubt that he was one of the ranking computer geniuses, even in a hardware-rich atmosphere like Stanford.

"Wow, you wouldn't believe it. I've got an AI program running in Turbo Prolog that will forward and backward chain."

"Uh-huh," Taylor grunted, "have you eaten anything today, Rob?" The other man paused at his task and looked up thoughtfully at Taylor. "Today?" Like that was the important part of the question. "No, I don't think so."

"Let's go get something. My treat, Japanese," knowing full well that Rob wouldn't know the difference between Japanese and Italian, but he felt like company tonight. No heavy thoughts. Just some company.

"Sure, ah, that is, I don't know. What time is it?"

Taylor responded, understanding that something else was going down besides dinner. He could see the quandary of losing a free meal etched across his roommate's face.

"I've got this, ah, meeting at six o'clock, and I can't miss it. See it's, well, it's really important, but I would like to go to dinner with you."

Taylor sighed. "Life is full of choices, Rob, make up your mind." He had already discounted the possibility of dinner together and did not feel like getting involved in a long discussion about it.

"You could come to the meeting. I mean it's supposed to be a secret but if I vouched for you it would be cool."

"Rob," Taylor looked at him and exhaled a long sigh. "I enjoy your company on a one to one basis but I ain't going to waste another evening on one of your 'nerds take over the world' programming conferences. I'm just not that interested in operating systems and the care and feeding of viruses.

"Life is full, the world consists of more than programming and I, for one, am not going to contribute to the gradual decline of mankind due to monsters masking as dumb lumps of silicon."

"No, no!" Rob leapt up from his chair and began searching through some loosely piled papers. "It's not that kind of thing. It's something you'd get off on."

"Are they programmers, Rob? Just tell me that."

Rob looked at Taylor blankly. "Well, sure, I mean everybody programs, that's not the point. It's not about programming or anything like that."

Rob shrugged, "Okay. Too bad." He started out the door. "They probably would have been pissed off at me anyway. It's a bunch of guys who are paying for school by ripping off roulette games at some casinos..." His voice faded as the door shut behind him.

Something inside Taylor clicked audibly. "Wait," he said. "Rob! Wait a minute, I'm coming..."

It was the most fascinating thing Taylor had ever seen. The programmers, after the initial period of hostile vibes had worn off at having a stranger in their midst, were only too proud to show off their system.

Ego, gonna be the death of us all, Taylor thought as the team leader strutted his stuff. A regulation roulette wheel and table took up so much space in the small room that the spectators had to crowd into the odd corner, forcing Taylor to stand on someone's bed to see, but no one complained about his manners.

"See," the man spun the wheel and launched the tiny ball in the opposite direction. "You can still place bets until the ball actually falls onto the wheel so every time it passes one of these halfway markers, the current watcher simply clicks the transmit button on this VHF transceiver.

"We, the follow-up contingent, enter it into the computer like this," he punched a button, "and after a couple of consecutive passes we have enough input to load the knowledge base and run a super-quick simulation. Then we flash it back to the table people who then place a bet. Easy, huh? Any questions?"

"Wait a minute," Taylor was surprised to hear himself speaking. "Where are you?"

"Upstairs in a rented room, of course."

"And you can predict the winning number?"

The leader rested his stare on Taylor and then looked at Rob, who shrugged as if to say, "Yes, I know he's simple, but he's a friend."

"No, man, we don't predict any numbers. We can just localize which arc of the wheel it's going to land on. We bet that."

"And you win?"

The other man seemed half amused and half ticked off at Taylor. "All we got to do is be right fifty-three percent of the time and, believe me, we do far better than that." Several of the other team members let out spontaneous cheers attesting to this fact.

"You see, it's all a component of this parabolic program. It was first used to predict when a particular satellite orbit would degrade enough to drag it into the atmosphere. Quite simple, really, just a question of quantum mechanics. You knew that, of course." The man was now smiling openly at Taylor.

"Uh-huh."

"Okay, the problems to date have been attributed to security picking up unusual behavior in the watcher's act when operating the transceiver. Our next update is here, people." He reached into his briefcase with a show of secrecy and withdrew a small radio with a number of wires and pads hooked up to it.

"*Voila!* These modifications will allow the players to operate the transmitter by the use of toe switches, the receivers will alert their wearers through these vibration sensors."

Taylor felt like he had fallen onto the set of a James Bond movie. "Toe switches?" He muttered out loud, receiving a distinct glare from the lecturer.

"We foresee a time when we will be able to send teams into several different casinos at once and, by mixing and drifting the members and the bets, operate within a circular area of probability large enough to drain substantial resources without detection."

"Ambitious son of a bitch, ain't he?" a man next to Taylor whispered into his ear and handed him a lit joint.

Taylor looked the speaker over and was surprised to find he was at least ten years older than anyone else in the room and dressed like some small town police department's idea of an undercover agent. Brand new denim jacket, a large flashing emerald ring, and expensive snake boots. Little warning bells began to go off in the back of Taylor's mind.

"They're going to get their legs broken within the next thirty days. I got a hundred bucks that says I'm right."

Taylor shrugged noncommittally.

"No bet?" the stranger said. "You're a smart man. What do you think of all this?"

Taylor looked the man in the eye and said, "I think they're too easy with their idea of security."

The other man choked out some smoke. "Loose lips sink ships. You going to join Robin Hood and his merry band?"

"Don't think I'd tell you if I was." Taylor turned back away from the stranger.

"Ah, but admit the idea of organized larceny stirs your bones a little bit. I'd bet a thousand bucks you're thinking about how to get in on the take."

"You're quite a betting man, aren't you?"

"No," the man said very seriously, "I never gamble. I do, however, play a little bit. And these are two very different things. Do me a favor," he switched the smile back on. "Read a book for me. Just one little paperback book. Okay? Might expand your horizons."

"Why should I?" Taylor tried to remain detached but he knew he was interested in spite of himself.

"Why shouldn't you? Come outside for a second.

"Here," he tossed a book into the air and Taylor almost dropped it, staring at the brilliant red paint on the man's new Ferrari 580. Never knew paint could look so deep, he thought as the door shut behind his friend.

"I'll talk to you in a few days."

"You don't even know my name." Stupid thing to say.

"Don't bet on it, Taylor, when I play I never lose." The car roared off and Taylor looked at the book in his hands for the first time.

Beat the Dealer, by Edward O. Thorpe

"The choices are two." Taylor tried to concentrate on the saying as he watched the other two team members casually seat themselves at the green table. One had to rather rudely elbow an elderly man out of the way in order to secure the third-base position.

Taylor had arrived, according to plan, twenty-five minutes earlier and positioned himself behind first base, the seat on the far left of the dealer, in order to grab that particular stool before the hourly shift change. He had ignored the hostile looks of the seated player as he peered over the man's shoulder, chuckled occasionally at inopportune times, and physically forced his presence into the game.

The original player had left several minutes ago, glaring at Taylor, who pretended not to notice the hostility. The important thing was to secure first base before their "pet" dealer came on duty.

In fact, Taylor had been nursing a rapidly diluting Scotch and soda preparing himself to "accidentally" spill it onto the man occupying the position if it had become necessary to force him off the table. To Taylor's delight that particular escalation had not been necessary; the man had become irritated enough by his pressure to move to another table.

This had left the first-base chair open for Taylor's occupation. He had been placing minimum ten-dollar bets since then, letting the ebb and flow of the game wash over him. Not caring if he won or lost. After all, it was just a game.

Taylor made a conscious effort to appear anything but what he was. He slurred his words, flirted with the dealer, talked to the neighboring bettors, insulted the waitress and generally made a point of not watching the cards.

"When you enter a casino the choices are two, you steal from them or they steal from you." The words kept racing through his mind. And we aren't stealing, he reminded himself. Just pressing our luck—

taking advantage of the natural lay of the land. Much like any other pioneer group; nothing strange about it…

Out of the corner of his eye he watched the other members of the team take their places at the table. They sat at the third- and fifth-base seats, not acknowledging the presence of Taylor or each other.

We probably represent the cutting edge in taking-the-house technology, he thought. It had taken him only a few days to absorb the statistics involved in counting.

Dr. Thorpe had kicked it off by using a computer to simulate a couple of million blackjack hands—us versus them. The player against the house. The good doctor discovered what happens when the deck ran hot: when the small cards were played out leaving only mainly 8's through the 10's—giving the player the advantage, allowing him to bet two hands, double down on marginal adds, expect a 9, 10 or ace. Go for 21. Effectively shifting the odds from the house to the player. Sometimes. When the deal went right.

Radical. When the cards went radical. Only then could a conscientious player/counter push the bet—double up, draw down. But then the odds were *there*. The downside was the accuracy involved. All the major casinos freaked out after *Beat the Dealer* was published. Pit bosses trained to watch for counters—eyes that reflected too much concentration, lips that moved, anti-social players, anything that even hinted that the player was counting.

Throw them out—that was the rule. Never mind if they were winning or losing—never mind the score. Ask them to leave or simply harass them into going elsewhere. No one needed to be positive; any suspicion on the part of the pit boss, or even the dealer—toss 'em.

Very few people in any form of management took the time to investigate the nuts and bolts of card counting, they simply decided anybody that was too serious was to be 86ed.

Taylor had learned, painfully at first, that the truth was quite different from the concept. One overlooked card in a fifty-two card deck could screw up the running total to the effect that his bet would not only be ineffective but actually counter the odds.

Never bet your initiative. Never bet your ideas. Stay with the count, stay with the tables. Anything else blew all your efforts. Don't talk to the shills, don't joke with the dealer, never, never take a "free" drink (they got progressively stronger as he won).

Stay on the ball. Bet the odds as they changed. Never vary, never screw around. Bet this hand, double down here, bet two hands now, take a hit against the odds (but of course, the real odds were in your favor), try to look stupid and/or drunk so the pit boss wouldn't notice the seemingly unusual play.

Be disciplined. Don't fuck around. Keep the running total and the odds charts lodged in your mind at all times.

Taylor spent long days practicing both on the blackjack table in his instructor's luxury apartment (in the nook, off the atrium, next to the marbled hallway). Working against a real Vegas dealer recruited to put the prospective team members through their paces in her off duty time.

"Think about it, man, you don't want to hit that." The woman looked at Taylor and shook her head. "Think, the deck is ten rich."

Taylor realized his mistake as soon as she started talking. Stand on the stiff, let the dealer take the bust card. But it went so fast. It was so hard to keep the count straight and play the game. Register each card as it was turned over—plus one, minus one, neutral. Ace. It flowed like a river, a river of cards. He could see why the casinos had relaxed their vigilance against counters—it was, quite simply, too complicated for ninety-nine percent of the betting public to handle.

Taylor sharpened his skills at night, after "their" dealer went off shift, by using a slide projector to flash three cards "hands," both his and the dealer's, on a white screen.

What I did on my summer vacation, Taylor thought, as the bright cards rushed by. Plus two, minus one, plus three, two aces down, deck two-thirds done, finishing factor is... And there's the lovely Mrs. Stevens and the twins enjoying the surf at Laguna Beach, the king of diamonds, a two of clubs, dealer holding the four of spades.

Plus one, one ace down, deck new. CLICK. See the kids trying to body surf on the gray waves, beautiful Laguna sunset in the background?

Two fives and a jack, plus two, still three aces waiting. Don't think, don't show you're counting, smile at the dealer, see little Julie disappear under the building water, mom laughing with joy, plus six, the deck half under and running radical. Three aces in waiting, play two hands, triple the bets, watch those tens and aces appear like magic and pay two and a half to one...

Oh gosh, little Julie is being tumbled head over heels by a big wave and knocking the little boy next to her into the maelstrom, and it's plus seven.

Plus seven! Watch the tens come up and the dealer gets a stiff. She has to hit and the odds hold true as she busts. Time to shuffle, but it's an easy thousand bucks in thirty seconds. Sort of.

See mom pick Julie up from the receding water line and scrape the sand from her suit. First hands are all face cards and the count plunges to a minus three. CLICK! And another ten bites the dust.

Minus five, cut the bets, back off the hands. What I did on my summer vacation...

And how to make a fortune in your spare time.

TAYLOR

He must like me. The redheaded dealer peeked at her hole card and smiled at Taylor. Cause he sure doesn't play blackjack very well. You'd think he would get tired of losing night after night.

True, he only bet the minimum, play after play, never varying his wager, but he still did the dumbest things. Hitting a hard 17, standing on a soft. Adding wrong, drawing more than 21 and still not flipping the cards over...

It was, well, almost pathetic. He couldn't make too much money, the way he dressed and those two-dollar bets, and he was losing a chunk every night. Susan peered back at the hole card and thought, let him read my thoughts, I've got a stiff, don't draw to that 15, I'll bust. Just wait.

Involuntarily she smiled at Taylor, willing him to stand. I'm not on commission, honey, don't give your money to the house to impress me.

A sudden electric shiver ran down Taylor's spine as he caught the telltale smile. That smile. The I've-got-a-bad-hole-card smile. Jesus, he realized, Wilson is right, she's trying to be nice to me. Casually he touched his right index finder to his temple as if in thought.

Let them pick that one up on the tapes. He visualized the poor slobs hunched over telescopes in the Eye in the Sky, laughing at his indecision, all of two dollars riding on the outcome.

Except Taylor knew it wasn't only his measly two bucks riding on his decision. As soon as the other two team members saw his fingers touch his temples, they would stand on their bets and then bet a thousand bucks apiece on two different hands on the next deal.

About six thousand bucks riding on a casual finger touch to the temple. But it wasn't even a bet. Taylor knew that smile. Good old Susan is trying to tell me something. Watch the face cards fall.

Taylor didn't look up at the other two team members. Ever. They were as different as any three people could be; a bleached blonde who looked just like what she was—twice divorced, mid-fifties, big tits and a low cut dress. Swirling "free" Scotches as fast as the waitress could bring them. Rainbows of light flashing off her two-carat diamond ring. Matching those from her earrings.

God, how can she put those Scotches down and still keep her mind on the business at hand? Taylor laughed inside as the loud woman in the loud dress with the loud voice yelled to the world, "Hit? Hell no, I don't want no hit, honey, my momma didn't raise no fools!"

The final team member sat on fifth base shaking his head at the blonde's antics. He was wearing a two-hundred-dollar Stetson hat with a band made from real rattlesnake skin, a custom-tailored Needless Markup suit and ostrich-skin boots.

He never drank, rarely talked, and when he did, always managed to mention Austin, Texas, and this terrible depression that had affected both the oil business and his family's wells.

Shit, he was down to betting $500 a hand. Sometimes.

Taylor knew the closest the man had ever been to Texas was Ann Arbor, Michigan, where he had flunked out of a liberal arts program. Oil wells, my ass, Taylor thought.

Not in a million years would anyone ever connect the three of them. Taylor played stupid, appeared barely aware of what was going on and bet his two bucks as steadily as the north wind.

Ms. Williams drank like a fish, swore like a whore and pinched men's bottoms when they sat next to her.

John walked like he had a ramrod up his ass, spoke with a noticeable drawl and was fully comped by the casinos because: A, he obviously had money, and B, his luck couldn't last forever.

Both team members had been carefully watched and put into the "bets carelessly, the odds will catch up with them" category. Neither could have possibly been counting cards, they just didn't pay enough attention to the play.

Taylor? Who cared? Two-dollar bets? Let him go wild. Besides, he always lost... Poor sucker.

Oh, but the blood was running high in Taylor. It was all he could do to smile at Susan-the-dealer and not move his hands. Make an accidental gesture that would cause his teammates to blow a couple of thousand bucks on a real ear itch...

Not only is the count running at plus 7, good old Sue just gave me that never-fails smile. The one that says, "Please don't waste your money, Taylor, I'm going to bust."

The pity was that she didn't even know she was doing it. A freebie. She's just being pleasant. An involuntary reaction to a set of circumstances beyond her control. I almost hate to do it...

Taylor watched Susan grimace as his bet went to the house. She hardly even noticed the $1,800 she paid out at the other end of the table.

The men in the sky shook their heads. Some people had all the dumb luck. And there was nothing you could do about it. Life wasn't fair.

Susan wasn't the only target. They pushed their advantage whenever they could take it. There was a male dealer with a facial tic that told Taylor stories, and then there was Chantel, an aging, embittered career dealer who felt her back pains starting up two hours into the shift and thought only of her chiropractor. She hated her job and the slobs who sat at her table.

She hated everything so much that she began to bend the cards up a bit at the corner when she looked at the hole. Just enough so that the first-base player, if he scrunched his shoulders and hunched down in the shortest chair in the house, could see the number.

Taylor loved taking her down. She took the losses personally and the madder she got, the more she turned the corners up and the madder she got.

Counting was good and Taylor was hot—he didn't make mistakes anymore, not one in a four-deck shoe. Sometimes he could even name the burned card after two-thirds of the deck was played. He was hot. They could bank on any count Taylor did, but the edge, that tiny fraction that made the nut and slid the game into the Twilight Zone was, quite simply stated, cheating.

First they had worked with gimmicks, rings that would prick an ace (not so that anyone would notice, mind you, unless you knew where to look) reflecting surfaces, even infrared paint and tinted contact lenses. The cutting edge of technology...

But there was always something screwing it up—the more sophisticated it got, the more room there was for error. The bigger the chance that somebody—an unusually astute pit boss, a tape operator in the Eye in the Sky, even a dealer looking to make good with the house—would notice something slightly askew. Something amiss. A tiny hole in a card, a contact lens slipping out of place.

Hell, they didn't even have to notice anything concrete—just vague suspicion was enough to open Pandora's box and bring the demons down on everybody's head.

Thrown off the table, being escorted to the front door of the casino, to the parking lot, not-so-subtle handshakes from a large "pit boss" asking how the day was going and suggesting that they play some other game besides 21...

Here, try roulette for a change of pace...

Several team members had been burned so badly they had quit out of fear, nerves or been dropped from the organization because they had made the book.

The little black book. Actually it should have been called the Little Black Books because a new one was published every month. Researched and compiled by a local private detective agency, the book held names, photographs and pertinent data on about four hundred cheats, counters, or "suspicious" winners.

And the book was law. You made the book, you didn't play in Nevada. Period. No questions, no appeals, the jury was not out. You lose.

Every pit boss studied the book, every manager had it memorized. The first time you were caught on the premises it was a polite "goodbye." The second time it was not so polite, and the third, ah, the third time was the charm.

Suffice to say most people didn't come back for a fourth time.

Several condemned counters had taken their cases before the courts. The outcome had been quite predictable, even the Nevada Supreme Court had come out on entirely one side of the decision.

Why didn't the state have an income tax? Why was the sales tax the lowest in forty-nine states? How were the roads maintained, the judges paid?

Greed, pure and simple. Greed and gambling. The casinos footed the bills and the courts never bit the hand that fed them.

Wilson was a prime example of the system's inequities—a bit too much ego, a few too many winning hands, one thing led to another. Suddenly no casino would let him play blackjack. It was as if he had suddenly contracted the plague, and it was published in the local paper.

Some house turned him away at the door, others were only too happy to let him inside, just don't go near the 21 tables please… The situation got so bad that Wilson began to affect various disguises in order to break into the game.

These worked for a short time at best. The size and pattern of his betting soon drew unwanted attention, incognito or not. These experiences did not tip the situation in Wilson's favor.

The straw that broke the camel's back fell at the Sahara. Wilson had just sat down at the table, THE LOW RENT TABLE, for God's sake, when the pit boss whispered into the dealer's ear and the next thing Wilson knew he was talking to the casino manager at a suddenly completely empty blackjack table.

"You want to play 21 Mr. Wilson?"

Try not to show any surprise at the use of his name. "Thought I might."

"Well, I'll tell you how it goes then. Okay, we'll each put up $25,000 cash and we'll play—just you and me and the dealer, until somebody has $50,000 and somebody has 0? Okay?"

Wilson nodded carefully. The proposition was too good to be true.

"Oh, and just one or two other minor things," the manager said, watching Wilson unfold a wad of hundred dollar bills from his pockets. "It's a one-card deck and we'll shuffle every four hands. Right?"

The man smiled.

Wilson saw his advantage folding onto itself and disappearing like a tule fog on a hot summer day. Single-card decks, while easier to count, ran far less radical, the numbers almost always favored the house.

And even if they started to run one way or the other, the four-hand shuffle would reset the odds much too often to be successful.

Unless. Unless, one played every card just perfectly, doubling down whenever the winds of luck changed, playing as many hands as possible when the deck was 10 rich, backing off and not letting ego get in the way when the deck ran shallow.

"Sure," he said, smiling. Twenty-five thousand bucks was a lot of money in those days. The loss would more than dent his playroll. "Let's do it."

Plus three, all four aces still in the deck, go for it. Wilson spread a thousand dollars each over four hands and watched the tens fall onto the green felt. One more hand, God, give me one more hand. He smiled at the manager, watching the line of sweat beads breaking out on his brow.

It had been twenty-two minutes since the man proposed the wager and Wilson could see the regret in his eyes.

Only two hands had fallen by the wayside since the last deal. The manager couldn't shuffle now and save any face. Plus three and four aces left, Wilson spread $5,000 between two hands and smiled.

Eat my dust, asshole.

And two 21's fell directly onto his outstretched hands.

Wilson left with the fifty grand but not until the manager had pulled the book out, shown Wilson his entry and then circled his name and photo in red ink, swearing he would never "play in town again."

"You don't know how long I've waited for someone to actually say that to me." Wilson picked up his winnings and carefully folded them under the irate manager's nose. "You've been watching too many late night movies."

But even as he left he knew the other man was right. He would move to the top ten in the book and he would never play in Nevada again. It was little satisfaction to know the manager probably wouldn't work in the state again either. It was the house's money he had carelessly offered, not his own.

That was then—this was now. Wilson spent six months every year touring the world and plying his trade in casinos in England, Africa, France and Monaco. Casinos that didn't subscribe to the book...

The other six months he devoted to putting together crack teams to take down Nevada casinos on a scale never before seen.

Hit 'em fast and hit 'em hard was his new motto. By training the right people he was able to make and mix three to four teams one weekend a month and take down almost a quarter million bucks at a shot.

Wilson had a series of rigid rules concerning the play. Never play more than one hour at a shot, never take a drink, don't ever acknowledge the other team members in any way, if you lose count back off, and never, never bet a hunch.

Always, always bet the count. Bet the rules, bet the cheat, but never bet your feelings. No place existed for feelings in this game. No room existed for error. It was not a demonstration of freedom of choice.

And never, never, let them see you sweat.

Lately Wilson had been, well, pressing, if not breaking, his own rules. He stretched counters past the hour limit and left teams intact longer than he would have a few months ago. Something was going on that Taylor couldn't quite pick up on—it was there, just out of reach, hovering…

Taylor felt someone touch his shoulder and he jumped without thinking. It was his dealer, Susan, and she was saying something to him.

"I'm off shift. You want to go and get a bite to eat or are you going to play all night?"

"What?" My god, I missed a shift change. How long have I been playing? Taylor glanced at his watch, two and a half hours without a break. Oh, my God, I'm losing it here.

"Well?" the woman asked.

Taylor opened his mouth to give a standard brush off and saw the telltale smile appear on Susan's lips. She was a cute lady, and, shit, he hadn't had dinner…

"Come on, I'll buy. I owe you that much." If she only knew, he thought, if she only knew…

It was halfway through the meal when Taylor began to visualize the quicksand he was becoming mired in. It wasn't as if Susan wanted to dig too deep into his personal life—but she did want to make polite conversation and establish a few pertinent facts.

Like his last name. And where he was staying, why he came to Vegas so often ("To see his, uh, friends"). Little things. The kind of things people used in a polite conversation; or with someone they were interested in. More than politely.

somebody sees us hanging out together and starts asking questions,
I'm fucked.

If I lie to her or brush her off and she finds out, I'll burn our best
asset. What do you figure she's worth to us? How much has one or
another team member carried from Susan's table? How much can we
walk off with in the near future?

And what happens when that telltale smile is gone, replaced by a
"where were you the other night" glare? She thinks I'm cute and she
feels sympathy for me...

"And I could teach you..." Taylor shook his head to clear it and took
another bite of his steak. He was suddenly glad Susan had chosen a
small, dark, out-of-casino restaurant. She obviously thought it was
more romantic, but Taylor was glad for another reason.

He was starting to sweat.

"Teach me?"

"You know, how to play blackjack. I mean, I couldn't make you an
expert or anything, but I could teach you how to cut your losses, and
then if you just play right and follow your hunches when you get a
strong one you can, you know, maybe win a bit."

Oh, God, no! She wants to improve my blackjack game. She wants
to smarten me up, change my style of playing. Taylor could see a very
lucrative job evaporating before his very eyes.

Get me out of here, God. I'll never kick another cat, I'll show up for
church on Sunday, I'll never tell another girl I love her unless it's the
real thing. Get me out of here intact.

"Oh, I don't lose that much. It's sort of a hobby with me. I figure,
lose a few bucks, it's like going out for the night. Like going to a movie,
I get entertained, have fun, sometimes I win, sometimes I lose."

"It's only money," he attempted to smile. Great, now she thinks I'm
rich and crazy. So why do I always bet two dollars a throw?

"God, that's a cool attitude, Taylor. You're so different from most of
the people I have to put up with every night. It's really nice to meet
someone who's human for a change."

"Uh-huh." He was beginning to feel beads of sweat staining his
shirt. Got to get out of here. Get sick? What would that fix? She
probably has a mother instinct.

"Listen, Taylor, in two hours I could teach you how to really play
blackjack. You could still think of it as entertainment, just that it would

cost a lot less. You could come over to my place and I'll bet I could teach you the basics in an hour or two." Susan gulped another glass of wine down.

"We could even go over tonight. My boyfriend and I broke up a few weeks ago and I have the place to myself. It would be fun to show you how to play, and besides," she giggled a little tipsily, "I think you're kind of cute."

Kind of cute... Kittens are cute, Taylor thought, guppies are cute, puppies are cute. God, I hate that word. Cute. I don't feel cute. I feel trapped. Help.

He smiled, unable to think of any response whatsoever. I guess I should just go through with it, take advantage of that smile and then ask Wilson to shift me to other casinos and hope Susan never works anyplace else and doesn't have any friends that are dealers that she commiserates with about cute assholes who take advantage of girls who just lost their boyfriends...

Or that she never dates a pit boss and starts talking about this dumb guy who was too stupid to learn the basics but always sits at the table where these incredible lucky streaks happen...

Or that. Or that. Or that... Damn it all, anyway, the world's full of cute women with telltale smiles. What am I doing here? A momentary lapse of reason? Overactive hormones? God, get me out of here.

Susan was waving to the waiter. "Can I get the check, please. Oh, and two cognacs, please? You don't want coffee do you, Taylor?"

He shook his head.

When the drinks came, Taylor slammed his back without a second thought. He felt Susan's hand cover his. "I'm shocked, Taylor, I thought you didn't drink." She giggled again. "I guess there's quite a bit we don't know about each other."

Taylor stared into the now empty snifter. "Could we have one more? That one seemed to go so quickly."

"Sure, you're not stalling are you?" She laughed again.

Who me? Taylor shook his head. What, me stall? At least it can't get any worse... Then he looked up and saw Wilson enter the restaurant.

At first Taylor couldn't believe his eyes. He was wearing small town sheriff sunglasses, a leather WW II bomber's jacket and tight designer jeans, but it was definitely Wilson.

I've got to get out of here, Taylor realized. If I tell her the truth and

Oh, my God, here it goes. Wilson walked straight to Taylor and Susan's table. He stopped, smiled directly at Taylor, lifted the new cognac and drained it in one swallow.

"Aren't you going to introduce us?" He raised his eyebrows at Taylor. Without waiting for an answer he reached his hand out towards Susan. "Hi, sweetheart, my name's Norman, I'm Taylor's roommate."

Susan shook his hand as Wilson pulled a chair from the neighboring table and sat down. He looked at Taylor like a cat looks at a mouse. "Imagine meeting you like this. Small world, isn't it?"

"Small." Taylor repeated, waiting for the axe to fall.

Wilson leaned forward on his elbows and looked directly into Taylor's eyes, "Boy she's cute. You changing horses in mid-stream?"

Suddenly it snapped into place. Like an out-of-focus image suddenly pulled into perspective, the entire scenario crystallized in front of Taylor. He saw the open road stretching before him.

"No, no, she's just a friend. Don't be a jerk. Susan is nice people."

Wilson turned to look at Susan. "Oh, I'm sorry, if I seemed bitchy, it's been a long day. I'm sure you're a very nice person." Wilson reached over and pinched Taylor's cheek playfully. "And so's Taylor, he just sometimes forgets that not everyone he meets picks up on his preferences at first."

Susan looked from Wilson's hand to Taylor's cheek and then to Taylor. Her eyes widened in recognition. "Oh, my God, you're gay!" Her hand flew over her mouth, "I'm sorry, I don't mean to be rude, it's just that I thought…" She left the rest of the sentence unspoken. "Oh, my God… I sure can pick 'em, can't I?"

"Susan I… I like you. And I thought we could be friends. I didn't mean to, ah, lead you on, or anything. We can still be friends, I mean I would have to have told you anyway, wouldn't I?

"Nothing against you, I like your company, it's just well, for a long time it hasn't really worked with a woman."

"And to think I might have been the first, now we'll never know, will we?" Susan laughed and swallowed the rest of her drink in one gulp. "Taylor, my luck with men is a lot like your luck at the tables… Short and bad, in that order."

She got up and kissed Taylor on the cheek, "Well, we'll still get together someday and talk blackjack. Maybe we can still be friends." She turned and walked out.

Taylor watched her leave with mixed emotions. Neither he nor Wilson spoke for some time.

"Old joke," Wilson said, "farmer marries a woman, they drive off from the wedding in the buggy. Horse stumbles, farmer says, 'That's one,' they go on. Horse stumbles again, man says, 'That's two,' and they proceed. Horse stumbles a third time, farmer takes out a gun and shoots him dead.

"His wife screams, 'That's terrible, how could you do that, you're a horrible person, what have I married?'

"Farmer looks at her calmly and says,"

"That's one..." Taylor filled in the punch line softly. "Right?"

"Let's have another drink." Wilson smiled and waved at the waiter...

Taylor walked into the room of the biweekly meeting and stopped in mid-step. Instead of the usual eight or so team members, the room was packed with at least twenty-five bodies, some of whom Taylor recognized but many of whom were unfamiliar to him.

He sat next to a man about his own age with whom he had played on and off several times. The man was a top-notch counter and seemed to be as nervous in this new situation as Taylor was.

"Tupperware party?" Taylor asked as he sat down. "Someone we know getting married? Was I expected to bring a gift?"

"It's not funny," the other man said. "Too many people, too many potential problems. I thought the idea here was that you couldn't roll over on anybody you didn't know."

"You've seen too many gangster movies," Taylor said, but inside he agreed with the other counter's opinion.

"The narc principle applies here. You get too many people who think they're clever in any small space and at least one of them is bound to be a narc. I wish I knew what was going down here. You suppose Wilson is retiring? Maybe this is an outlaw gold watch ceremony."

The door opened and two of the most extraordinarily beautiful women Taylor had ever seen breezed into the room and began handing out manila envelopes to each of the room's occupants.

Taylor accepted his without taking his eyes from the messenger. Amazing, he thought.

"Likes to make an entrance, doesn't he?" Taylor's neighbor was turning his packet over in his hands and shaking his head from side to side. "Sealing wax," he rubbed his fingers over the monogrammed closure. "Pretty corny." He began to slit the envelope open with his fingers and then paused as Wilson strode into the room accompanied by a number of random gasps from people in the audience who had opened their packages and discovered that the first thing to fall out was a paper-clipped pad of hundred dollar bills.

"It's been a good year." Wilson held up one hand in a "black power salute." "Hasn't it?"

A chorus of howls and hand clapping answered his call as more envelopes were opened.

"Just a little thank you for all your help. And," he reached inside an identical envelope from the ostrich skin briefcase in front of him and withdrew an airline ticket. "A little invitation to a last get-together."

"Last?" someone called out.

"We've done well but it's time to walk away winners. One more weekend and I'm officially dismantling the organization. If any of you wants to keep playing on your own, that's your business, but I would suggest everybody take a vacation. Personally, I've always wanted to spend some time in Brazil."

"Boo," the older blonde Taylor knew only as Williams called out. "Why quit now? We haven't had any problems. Nobody's been made. I say if it ain't broke, don't fix it."

"No, we walk winners. A time for everything, and I think the time to quit is at hand. But first let's make a monument, go out with style, leave 'em something they'll remember for a long time to come."

"Oh, oh," Taylor's neighbor muttered, "here it comes."

"This weekend, in a little over forty-eight hours, we are going to take the combined casinos in Las Vegas for the sum of two million dollars."

"Can't be done." Taylor said directly to Wilson. "Not safely. It's stupid to try. We'll stand out like sore thumbs."

"You're wrong, Taylor." He uncovered a large professional-looking chart with people's names, house designations, table numbers and times in military time.

"Each of you has a duplicate of this in your envelope. If you follow your color you can see where you've got to be every minute of the day, just like a huge monopoly game. We'll shift the teams around and turn them inside out so no one catches on to anything.

"Everybody has meal times and rest periods. Even eight hours of sleep, all plotted with a magical computer to avoid error. We can do it!"

Taylor waved his chart to get attention from the again cheering crowd. "Too many rules gone by the wayside here. Too much time, too many people who have played together before, too much money on the table.

"Shit, you've even got us staying in the casino hotels. That's the first thing you taught me to avoid."

"We can do it, Taylor. For one weekend and one weekend only. In and out, we'll take the town for more money than anyone has before and be out long before anything is discovered.

"It's not the money. It's the winning. We are going to make the *Guinness Book of Records*. In future years we'll be known as the Great Train Robbery.

"Think of us as a plague of locusts; fly in, strip everything clean and then we'll be gone. No tracks."

"Why this particular weekend?" Taylor asked, knowing his arguments were falling on deaf ears.

"It's Bastille Day, of course."

Taylor could feel his shirt sticking to his back and beads of sweat threatening to drip into his eyes as he stifled a yawn and tried to concentrate. The best laid charts of mice and men... He signed for a hit and then felt a rush of panic as he tried to remember if he had added his hand to the count.

Unsure of himself, he rubbed his left arm, the signal to hold all bets until the next deal. He could feel the eyes of the other team members glaring at him. He felt like throwing the cards down on the table, "I'm sorry, I'm fucking sorry but you see I played for over ten hours today alone, including three on this table and half the time my relief hasn't even shown up."

In fact his replacement was nearly a full hour overdue at this very moment and he knew it was getting to him. Ten more minutes, Wilson has exactly ten minutes to get me out of here or I'll just get up and walk away. He stared morosely at his dwindling stack of two-dollar chips.

The dealer picked up the shoe and emptied the remaining cards out into her hand. Thank God, a shuffle, at least we can start playing again.

But instead of shuffling, the dealer spread her cards out in a fan on the felt and stepped aside to allow a new dealer to step in.

That was quick, he thought. It didn't seem like it was time for a dealer switch.

The outgoing dealer stood directly in front of Taylor, leaned towards him and pointed her forefinger directly at him. One of his personal nightmares unfolding right in front of his eyes.

"Him," was all the woman said. Taylor could feel everyone watching him. The pit boss, the other players, his partners collectively holding their breath.

He started to protest, thought better of it, grabbed his chips from the table and stood up. He looked at the silent crowd of people and something snapped. He knew the best thing to do was bow and scrape his way out of the casino as if he didn't grasp what was going down.

Instead Taylor reached into his pocket, took out a gold money clip and casually tossed a C note onto the table. "For you," he said. "Play it or take it. Thanks for the game."

Then he turned and walked off.

Taylor had walked about fifty feet when he felt someone fall in step on the sidewalk next to him. "That was an asshole thing to do." It was Mark.

"How true," Taylor commented and kept walking.

"Okay, I'm beat too. I'm sorry I'm late but I didn't get relieved until a couple of minutes ago."

They walked on in silence. "We gotta have a little talk with Wilson. This isn't working out. Something's going to crash."

"He's eating dinner at that French place over on Palm," Mark said, waving down a taxi.

Wilson was not happy to see them. His eyes flashed fire as they sat down at the table next to one of his blonde "helpers." "This better be good," he chewed a bite of steak without taking his eyes from Taylor and Mark.

"No, actually it's bad. I was burned. Before Mark could take over. We decided to give it a break."

"Give it a break? You decided?" Wilson shut his eyes and clenched his mouth. "When did you take over command? Do you know how far behind schedule we are?"

"The odds aren't holding. I think the MGM slipped us a mechanic a couple of times. Took us down hard."

"Sometimes it just runs against you—you of all people know that." Mark said. "It doesn't always go exactly according to schedule and besides, we're exhausted. Everybody's making mistakes."

"Okay, you two rest for an hour and hit it again."

They looked at each other. Taylor spoke slowly, "You're not listening. I was made, I can't go back in there. I shouldn't go in anywhere. Let's call it."

"NO! One more day. That's it. We're going to finish what we've started. We've got to do this! It's what I've worked for the entire year. Everything's planned out to the last detail. It will work if you just do what I tell you.

"Mark will take over the rest of your shift." Wilson inked out a name on one of his multi-colored pocket charts and wrote Taylor's in. "Taylor you go over to the DollHouse, table three, first base, and play there until the end of your shift. Then get some sleep and I'll revise tomorrow's schedule to minimize your exposure."

"Minimize my exposure," Taylor repeated to himself. "I feel like an F-16 going into a dogfight."

"God damn it all anyway," Wilson rudely spit a piece of his beef Wellington onto the table cloth. "These fucking pretentious waiters speaking their phony French can't find the time to get the fucking food to the fucking table before it's stone ass cold and then they have the nerve to act like they're doing me a favor.

"At these prices you think those faggots would be hustling for tips instead of jerking us off. Why can't I find a goddam restaurant that gives a shit about the people paying their goddam salaries?

"WAITER!" Wilson shouted and rubbed his thumb and forefinger together to indicate he wanted the check. Across the room two waiters who were having an animated discussion pointedly turned their backs to Wilson's signaling.

"Do you believe those assholes?" Wilson seemed amazed by the response. "This is why I left New York. I can't handle this bullshit.

"HEY YOU, with the tux, I'd like some service over here! If you can fit it into your busy schedule..." The entire clientele looked up from their dinners to see what was going on.

"Oh, yes, this is not cool," Mark mumbled. "We'll see you at the next break," he started to rise from his seat and was stopped by Wilson's hand.

"No, no, wait a minute, it'll be worth it." He turned back toward the waiters. "Come on man, bring the check, I haven't got eternity to waste here."

With an obvious air of reluctance, one of the waiters eased towards their table. He placed the bill face down and sniffed, "Everything is acceptable, I presume."

"Just dandy." Wilson picked up the check and folded it carefully. Taylor could see the storm coming from a distance.

"You know," Wilson began in a conversational tone that included the whole room in its radius. "We have a problem here. A very specific problem. You know what that is?"

The waiter shook his head, a trifle less cool than he was a moment ago.

"No speak the English?" Wilson inquired a bit louder. "My problem is that this was going to be your tip." He unrolled a new $1000 bill and flashed it theatrically.

"But you see the food sucked and your service was non-existent at best. So, now what?" He paused for a moment of quiet reflection.

"If I don't tip you anything you'll just go back in the kitchen and have a good laugh at my expense. Just another cheap motherfucker with no class, you'll say…"

"Sir," the waiter attempted an interruption. "If—.

"No, no, please, bear with me. And if I do leave you the tip every single person here will know I wimped out and paid for something I didn't receive. A bit of a conundrum, isn't it?

"At first glance one might think it's a no-win situation." Wilson stood up and peered directly into the man's eyes.

The waiter took a step backwards.

"But, no—there is a way out we haven't considered. A single path leading from this Zen-like jungle. A plan whereby nobody loses." He leaned over and stuck the corner of the bill directly into the flame of the candle that graced the table. The paper caught fire and burned with a vengeance.

"But you…" Wilson tossed the burning bill onto the table, turned in an arc, smiled at everyone in the room and walked out.

"What's wrong with this picture? Call me paranoid, but I think he's lost it," Mark commented, watching Wilson's back as he left.

"Maybe we should go into something less risky—like importing cocaine," Taylor said.

"Finish the weekend out. That's all he wants... Almost seems like the least we could do under the circumstances," Mark sighed. "I guess, anyway."

"Man, the weekend has gone on too long already. I got a bad feeling about this whole scene."

"Feelings come and feelings go," Mark said. "Let's do it."

For some reason things began to swing the other way. Taylor experienced a strange calm—like being in the eye of the hurricane. As soon as he slid into the new table, he felt a warming glow of confidence.

His teammates were returning from a sleep period and were all hungry to get back on a streak. The dealer was nearing the end of her shift, she was tired and inattentive, her mind already home and cooking dinner.

Twice in the first twenty minutes Taylor had managed a glimpse at the hole card and he was starting to read her glances. The count had followed exactly according to the laws of probability; not only were the bettors ahead several grand, Taylor was up about twenty-five two-dollar chips.

It was embarrassing. I can't even give these buggers away, Taylor thought as he hit a soft 17 and the four of spades appeared as if summoned for the occasion. Silly stuff.

Taylor laid a chip out for the dealer and looked up as if unsure how to give a tip. The dealer took it, shifted her weight to the foot that was hurting the least, and gave him a much bigger smile than the meager tip deserved.

All right, Taylor thought. I was wrong to doubt Wilson. We're really pulling this one off. Two million bucks—home free and tax free. Taylor began running his cut over in his mind. A used 911—well, not too used—he could easily afford that and still have next year's tuition in the bank.

His grades had slipped a bit since he'd taken up this hobby, but, hell, what did he need a scholarship for?

For that matter what did he need college for? He already had a profession that paid more than most doctors earned, and this one hadn't taken five years of medical school.

Sliding right by. The matron playing next to Taylor chuckled, gathered in her top-heavy stacks of five-dollar chips and got up. "For once in my life I'm going to quit while I'm ahead. Good luck, son." With that she patted Taylor on the arm and left the table.

Her replacement was of the male persuasion and his smile seemed forced. Besides that he looked hauntingly familiar to Taylor. I feel like I'm going through déjà vu all over again. Taylor laughed to himself and realized he was starting to drift away from the count.

Pay attention! This is life, we can't change the channel, Taylor mentally kicked himself. Probably a regular, I've played with him ten times before and just never saw him. Tonight's different, that's all it is, put your mind back where it needs to be…

Half an hour later another player joined the table who also rang a little bell inside Taylor. A heavyset, plain looking woman in a sloppy sweater and wrinkled skirt. No reason I would recognize her, I'm just getting tired, it's all starting to catch up, it's been one hell of a long day. How much longer do we have?

Without thinking Taylor looked at his watch and with a start realized he had just signaled the bettors to double their already substantial bets. On top of that the count was running as bad as it had been all day — minus 6.

Oh shit! This one quadruple loss would effectively wipe out the last thirty minutes of play. Forty minutes to go before the end of the day and I had to screw the bitch…

Taylor felt himself tensing as all four hands in question drew stiffs. The entire range between 12 and 15 carefully illustrated in this work of art—four losing hands in full color, each detail painstakingly hand painted by our aging artists—not sold in any store… The dealer turned a queen.

Taylor wanted to laugh in spite of himself as both players read the numbers and involuntarily glared at him. It's only a game, friends, win some lose some—but he knew that particular homily would not go too far when he was debriefed by Wilson.

It's only money.

Both team members were forced to draw in a vain attempt to strengthen their hands. Let them break even, Taylor thought. Just one hand apiece, that's not too much to ask, is it, Lord? Cut us some slack—one apiece… Even though he knew it was against all reason.

Amazingly none of the four hands busted—one even drew a rare five-card 21, the rest fell between 17 and 20. Not bad. Taylor felt the luck running on strong. Not too bad.

The dealer turned her hole card over. It was the four of diamonds. The entire team watched with bated breath as she spun the next card onto the table. Taylor quickly calculated the new odds—they had drawn out enough small cards to run the count to just about even— then the king of spades grinned back at him from the table as a reward for his diligence.

Twenty-four! She had gone bust! All four hands—well, actually all five, counting Taylor's—instantly became gold. Both teammates' mouths fell open as they looked toward Taylor with a renewed sense of appreciation.

Nothing to it, he thought. Just a healthy dose of blind luck... Then something flashed at the edge of his consciousness. Shills! The other three players at the table—everyone who wasn't part of the team— were shills, house players filling valuable seats for no reason! That's where he had seen them before—they were all inbreeds!

Good God, something was badly out of phase. This had never happened before and the odds against it in prime time were good. Taylor gave the "chapter 7" sign to his amazed team, grabbed his chips, stood up and pushed his chair back.

Only to find two very large men standing directly behind him, blocking his path to freedom. "Sick," Taylor mumbled, grabbing his stomach, hoping he looked as pale as he felt. "Just got back from Mexico," he tried pushing his way through the human fence.

Only he couldn't. "We'll help you, don't worry about a thing." He felt a vise-like grip dig into the nerve center on the inside of both of his elbows. Taylor straightened up as if an electric shock had passed down his spine. He felt as if his feet weren't even touching the floor as the pair of behemoths force marched him through the casino floor.

Kidnapped, I'm being kidnapped in plain sight of a thousand people. He tried to fight down the panic he felt at his helplessness. Shit, scream, do something!

He opened his mouth and one of his escorts punched him directly in the solar plexus. The man hadn't moved his arm more than three inches but Taylor felt all of the air rush from his lungs and his knees sag, all in a split second. He realized that if it wasn't for the gorillas he couldn't stand upright.

"Excuse us, our friend's sick." One of the men shouldered a path through the crowd of craps players. Taylor could hear sympathetic chuckles at his condition.

A self-fulfilling prophecy—he *was* about to be sick.

At first it appeared they were indeed headed for the rest rooms, but his two new "friends" veered off at the last moment and guided Taylor towards a small elevator at the end of the corridor.

He noticed that there were no buttons on the wall to summon the car. How bloody inconvenient Taylor thought, how bloody inconvenient. The man holding his right elbow produced a magnetic card and pressed it into a recessed space in the wall.

As if waiting, the elevator arrived with a small, theatrical "whoosh." The men tossed him inside with no visible effort. He started to protest, but one put up his hand. "We don't want to hear it. Mr. Salerio would like a little chat with you—upstairs."

Both guards turned to face the now-closed doorway, leaving gray suitbacks blocking Taylor's only avenue of escape. It looked like the great wall of China.

Inside the suite there were a number of gray-suited apes virtually identical to the ones that had delivered Taylor. My God, he thought, I've stumbled onto some sort of prehistoric island—creatures unknown to modern man, running amok...

Another group of older men were also present, their attention focused on a television set in the middle of the huge suite. It took Taylor a few seconds to realize the picture was actually a video tape, obviously filmed from inside the Eye in the Sky.

He could see anxious players and bored dealers acting out a soundless charade. Occasionally the camera would zoom in for a closeup of a certain hand and then go back to a wide angle shot. Then the unseen cameraman would focus in on a dealer's face, or his hands, picking up every slight motion that could be indicative of anything but honest play.

In spite of himself Taylor was fascinated by the candid camera film unrolling before him. He watched several minutes before deciding to speak up.

"Excuse me..." he began in a plaintive tone.

One of the seated men turned towards him, "Oh, hello there Taylor. I'm glad you could join us." The man smiled like somebody's father but Taylor was shocked into silence by the use of his name.

"Please, sit down here," he patted a spot on the deep sofa. "There's a piece coming up I really want you to see." Taylor felt a heavy hand on his shoulder forcing him to sit where he had been directed.

Suddenly the focus pulled and Taylor realized he was watching himself and his team playing at a DollHouse table. By the composition of the team he knew it had been filmed several months ago. He watched as the video dissolved into what was obviously part of today's play.

Taylor felt like he was looking into a magic mirror as the shots professionally captured his physical signals, froze at the crucial moments and then cut to his partners' betting patterns.

The video was extremely well edited—special effects and all— freeze frames of Taylor touching his ear, cut together one after another, so it became only a question that he had some major fungus of the right ear or that something else was going down—hard and fast.

Stacks of chips being played—and won—by Taylor's partners were narrated by a professional sounding announcer explaining how they were varying their betting with no apparent grasp of reality—unless they had some sort of inside information...or unless someone was counting.

The tape cut back to an extreme closeup of Taylor's eyes looking every bit like they were following every card on the table; which, of course, they were.

Taylor felt himself being convicted without the benefit of judge or jury.

The man who had asked Taylor to sit down began talking, his eyes glued on the monitor. "Quite professional, isn't it? We actually hired a top director to cut it together. Amazing how he was able to bring the plot out of all that superfluous tape, isn't it? The man has a future, no doubt about it."

He turned towards Taylor. "Almost an epic, wouldn't you agree?"

Taylor didn't respond.

"By the way," the man said casually, "my name is Nick Salerio—and I figure you owe me $168,012—what the hell, round it off, say a hundred and fifty even. We'll forget the change."

"Do you do this to all your winners?" Taylor slid his eyes over to the window, calculating his chances. It was closed but that seemed like a minor consideration at the moment. If he could bet a two-step head start...

Nick laughed loudly, "No, no, we do this to all our cheaters. Winning's fine, you just went about it the wrong way."

Taylor sucked his breath in and committed himself. He tried to remember how they did it in the movies—head first or feet first.

He felt cold metal pressing into his temple. Oh, God, I don't want to see this. One of the musclemen was holding a 9 millimeter pistol directly over Taylor's eye.

The hole seemed so large...

"No, no, let him go." Nick turned and moved the gun away with his hand. "It's five stories straight down. Not to mention the mess window glass can make of one's face. But I realize you have your priorities. Go ahead."

He raised his hands and waited. "No, huh? That's funny, your pal Wilson took the chance when he was offered it, three years ago. Of course, that was only two stories, and still he broke his ankle pretty good. I'll just bet he never told you that little tale, did he?

"Well, don't worry about not having the cash on you, I'll take a check. Of course, you're going to sit here until it clears, no disrespect intended, you understand?" The older man leaned back in the deep couch and watched Taylor closely.

"Rough decision, isn't it? Maybe one of my friends here," he indicated the armed apes, " will have to help you make it."

Taylor felt a block of ice forming in his stomach. He really means it...

"After all," Nick continued in a conversational tone, "nobody would ever know. Tired and depressed, another gambler decides life isn't worth the trouble involved. Not exactly a new story, probably wouldn't rate more than the back page of the local paper.

"Maybe I'm being too harsh on you. You think a good beating would do it? A couple of ribs, two fingers and one knee, would that impress the gravity of this situation on you, Taylor?"

Taylor tried to swallow but found his mouth was too dry to spare any saliva.

"Or maybe we could work something out—you pay half, we just break a thumb and a couple of ribs. Sort of like a negotiated settlement. Just to show you we can play fair.

"Come to think of it, that concept may be a bit alien to you."

A heavy silence fell over the room. Taylor tried to evaluate his chances at escape. They seemed to check in right between nil and none. One of the guards smiled slightly and winked as if there was nothing he'd like better than to help dispense a little frontier justice.

"Okay, everybody outside. Wait in the hall. I want to talk to Mr. Stevens alone."

The guards looked startled by this order. "Uh, you sure, uh, that you should..."

"I don't think Taylor is going to try and throw me out the window and fight his way through the entire DollHouse. Besides you'll be right outside."

Nick waited until the door had shut behind the departing crew. "Did you really think you could get away with it forever?"

"No, not forever," Taylor replied, still waiting for the axe to fall.

"Oh, yes, that's right, this was going to be the weekend to end all weekends wasn't it? Everybody goes home a millionaire." He bent over and took a file folder out of a briefcase at his feet. "Oh, don't look so surprised, you must have figured out why we aren't asking you for names."

"Somebody else talked."

"Several, in fact. You'd be surprised just how conversational several of your teammates can be when there's incentive involved." He opened the folder, put on a pair of glasses and began reading to himself.

"So what are your present plans?" He didn't look up from the folder.

"Live," Taylor said in spite of himself.

Nick laughed and looked up from his reading. "Pretty funny. I meant now that you've fucked up your scholarship and generally let your life go down the slats. Figure you'll transfer to state, graduate with the other displaced yuppies, become a junior partner in some ad agency...

"But at least you'll always have this wonderful night of excitement to tell the other drunks about over Monday Night Football. Assuming, of course, that we come to some sort of agreement that includes a future for you."

Taylor was too shocked to reply.

Nick slammed the folder shut. "Man, that was our money you were stealing. *My* money you were stealing, you ever think about that?"

"It wasn't like we were stealing, exactly..."

"Never con a con man, kid. You're no dummy. In fact, I happen to think you've got a rare streak of brilliance—well, perhaps that's too strong of a word. I think you have a rare aptitude for common sense and a fair talent for the written word.

"I thoroughly enjoyed your paper, *Luck: Fuzzy Sets, Probabilities versus Horseshoes.*"

"You read my paper? The paper I wrote for…" Taylor rubbed the sweat from his forehead—things were happening too fast. "I don't understand."

"Read it? Shit, I've made it mandatory for all our managers and pit bosses. Real solid stuff." Nick looked off into the distance.

"How do I know all this?" He tapped the file folder. "Kid, we've got an intelligence set up most countries at the UN would envy. I know a lot more about you than Stanford ever will…

"Well, enough idle conversation, let's get down to it. The choices are three. I can turn you over to the cops, and believe me, you'll do time, even if we have to fudge the story a little bit—a counterfeit chip here, a witness there, a couple of years in the joint.

"Door number two, I pack my bags and leave the room. You take your chances with the gentlemen outside in the hall, but I gotta tell you a couple of them think they're real cowboys. You know, the Mafia, honor, all that kind of stuff that they see on television nowadays. It warps 'em. They'd like nothing more than to kick the shit out of you. However, I promise you won't die or anything. Just take a while to heal."

Taylor shut his eyes. "What's the third choice?"

"Ah-ha, I knew you were sharp. The third choice is the Nick Salerio fellowship for underprivileged students. To sum it up, you go back to Stanford, keep a 3.0 average or above and we wipe out your debt.

"We also pay your tuition and a modest living allowance."

"I don't get it. What do I do for you, find other counters?"

"Snitch? Nah, we don't need informers in Palo Alto. The deal is that when you graduate you come to work for me. For at least two years. At the DollHouse."

"Doing what?" Taylor was trying his best to follow the sequence of events.

"Whatever I want, kid. Whatever I want. Think of it as an ROTC scholarship, you do school and then you owe a couple of years. You might even grow to like it. I can hire all the muscle I want," he waved towards the door. "Raw talent, that's a bit more difficult to recruit."

"What if I take your money and then don't come here. What happens then?"

"It's a gamble I'll take. And Taylor, I never lose." He looked Taylor straight in the eye and didn't blink. "You have any questions?"

"Wilson?"

"Vacation. He finally landed that South American trip he'd been planning on. I doubt you'll be seeing him again." He said it with a perfectly straight face and Taylor realized whatever the truth of the matter was he probably never would see his tutor again.

For better or for worse it was obvious that one segment of his life was over and another was about to begin.

Taylor carefully put his right hand out. After a second's hesitation, Nick shook it. "Wise choice."

Nick walked Taylor into the hall and the waiting group of "security personnel" snapped to attention. "Mr. Stevens, is leaving us now, and we won't be seeing him for a couple of years. I know you all wish him well."

The man who had winked at him earlier shook his head as if he couldn't believe Taylor's luck.

And when I do come back, asshole, the first thing I'm going to do is fire you.

But he didn't say it out loud.

Taylor hugged his mother and turned to slap the backs of two of his nearby friends. They had done it! Graduated from Stanford! And in Taylor's case with honors.

He hadn't quite breezed through it as easily as he thought he would—some of the courses had really demanded his full-time attention and he had found himself actually enjoying the challenge of learning once again.

He didn't miss the weekend games—not *too* much at least; maybe he missed the excitement a little bit, but all in all things had worked out pretty well.

He had been amazed when the first check actually arrived from the DollHouse—just as Nick had promised. It wasn't enough to let him live high off the hog, but it did pay his expenses, and soon he found he was taking the monthly envelopes with the gold crest for granted.

The lack of personal contact seemed strange—there was never any correspondence from his benefactors, just the check. He had kept up his end of the deal by working his ass off, but now it seemed stranger than ever. Was he expected to get on the next bus for Las Vegas?

Taylor stumbled forward as a classmate hit him on the back and failed to catch his balance until someone reached up and steadied him. "Thank you…"

It was Nick.

Taylor stared, his mouth open in surprise. I guess I should have expected someone, he thought, but I didn't expect Nick.

"You did good, kid. Congratulations." He handed Taylor an envelope. "It's not much, a couple of weeks in Mexico, but I figure you need a break."

Taylor looked at the tickets. "Thanks, uh, thanks for everything." He read the agenda. "Return ticket to Las Vegas. Okay, then what? I start at the DollHouse?"

"Not quite. You're going back to school. It may be a step from Stanford but I think you'll learn something.

"Dealer's school. Six weeks on your feet with hairdressers and waitresses trying to move up in the world. You gonna love it.

"If you do well, we'll put you to work." He shook Taylor's hand. "Enjoy Mexico. And Taylor—try and stay out of jail…"

LISA

"So tell me what you've learned," the voice came from behind Carol's shoulder and she knew immediately who the owner was.

Without lifting her eyes from the green felt of the craps table she replied, "I've learned never to bet the hard way or press your luck. You new in town, sailor, looking for some action, just got paid, wanna get married?"

This was tossed out without taking a breath.

"Christ," Taylor said, "you're starting to sound like your roommate. I was hoping it would work the other way, maybe some of your breeding would rub off."

"Which roommate are you referring to?" Carol turned around and looked directly into the flint steel eyes.

Taylor shrugged, "I can't think of any major differences between the two." He smiled, "Offhand."

Carol stepped away from the table and silently bit down on her tongue.

Taylor laughed quietly, "How much?" he said.

"Okay," Carol said, "I'll be the straight man, how much what?"

"Why, money of course. How much have you made off the five grand? Enough to give up the job, go live in Hawaii? Live a life of carefree luxury? Leave the salt mines and never look over your shoulder?" He waved his hand to indicate the main floor of the DollHouse. "Never look back."

Carol reached into her purse and carefully withdrew a yellow and black hundred dollar chip. She looked at it for a minute, sighed and placed it in Taylor's hand and then curled his fingers around the plastic marker.

"I'm surprised."

"Don't be, it's fake, I saved it out to impress you. The rest is gone. Foolishly wasted."

He flipped the chip into the air and watched it tumble end over end. "Ah, but did you learn anything for your tuition? Or was it spent in vain like so many liberal arts educations?"

"I can play any game in the house. I can tell you the odds on every play. I can even tell you how much you'll lose per hour, per level of play. I can tell you almost anything you want to know."

He laughed, "Except what?" He tossed the solitary marker up into the air again and quickly caught it with his other hand in a swiping motion. "How to win?"

Carol found herself enjoying the conversation in spite of her efforts to the contrary. "That too..."

She turned to watch two elderly women arguing violently over a Keno ticket, grateful for the distraction and the chance to catch her breath.

One of the women began to shriek loudly. Suddenly she pushed her opposite number with both hands.

The other woman fell backwards and sat rudely on the floor.

"Why they do it? Why two women with thousands of dollars worth of jewelry between them get into a public fist fight over fifty dollars in quarters.

"Why people eat dog food every day so they can show up here on the first of every month, social security check in hand, just to endorse it over to a casino.

"Why some crazy person walks in here with his life savings and risks it all on a roll of the dice.

"Why they stand in front of a slot machine for hours at other casinos on end pulling on that handle.

"Why they do it all. Why they play."

"Tell me Ms. Davies, what's your favorite, secret, personal fantasy? Do you have one? One so much fun that you never share it with another human being?

"Something you can use to get you through those really lonely times?"

Carol felt her blood rising to her face. She struggled to control the reaction. Be cool...

"Oh, good, I see you do have one. That's probably the first blush to take place within the city limits of Las Vegas since Bugsy Siegel was planted in the desert."

"If we're suddenly on close enough terms to discuss my sex life, I guess you can drop the 'Ms.' routine. My name's Carol."

"May you never lose that bite, Carol, you're going to need it just to survive around here, believe me." He placed her elbow in his hand and starting guiding her towards the center of the bright room.

"The point I was trying to make is that most fantasies fade with time. They get shopworn, we update them with new nuances, new twists. That's why *Playboy* sells month after month. Thirty days is about the life span for most dreams.

"That's why people come here day after day, month after month. This particular fantasy never pales. That's our main job—keep the fantasy alive."

Carol didn't move into the small cottage that Lisa and Leon occupied, but she did allow herself to be convinced to take a larger place where the three of them could all live. She found that friendship with Lisa was growing as suddenly as it had begun. Almost in spite of herself she found she thoroughly enjoyed Lisa's stories of backstage squabbles and petty jealousies among the rich and famous as well as her obvious enthusiasm for what she called "the life."

When they ran into each other late at night after Lisa got out of rehearsal, or found time to have the occasional lunch together, Carol found her to be a glowing, street-smart, fresh-looking girl.

"You know I was invisible when I was a kid, I had two brothers and my old man broke his back putting the fenders on Chevrolets for thirty years to send them to college. Get 'em a better life, all the advantages he never had.

"Now one's a sleazy lawyer and the other's a stuckup doctor—not a surgeon, though, he couldn't stand the sight of blood. He has a stuckup bitch of a wife who fucks her golf pro at the Grosse Point Country Club."

"That's pretty good, your father must be proud."

Lisa arched her eyebrows. "Yeah, I suppose he's real proud. The visible siblings make good. My parents never even knew I existed.

"My dad wanted me to quit school at sixteen and go to work. I was allowed to finish high school in lovely downtown Hamtramck only because it was assumed I would meet some nice up-and-coming Polish factory worker and settle down and start my litter.

"You know, he wouldn't even acknowledge my presence at the dinner table. If I asked to have the potatoes passed, he would just look through me until my mother would finally risk it and hand me a fucking potato.

"You could see he considered it a wasted potato. I was a big disappointment. Why spend good food on a girl? Why was I taking up space in his household? Why didn't I go and marry some loser, that's what I was there for anyway.

"Get it over with.

"It used to pain him that the State of Michigan was wasting a good high school education on a girl. College? Hah! That was a joke. One of the few times that he ever spoke directly to me was when I asked about attending the local junior college after graduation.

" 'College degree?' He laughed until he shook."

Carol felt like she should add something to the conversation. "I've never heard of Hamtramck, what a strange name."

Lisa giggled, "The Polish-American capital of America. I was a PAP: a Polish-American Princess. Just like a JAP except I was expected to keep my mouth shut, never question anything and land a good job cleaning houses until I could marry into the assembly line.

"My real name is Rachel Lewalski. Ain't that a gas? Everyone except my teachers called me Lisa 'cause I would refuse to respond to my name. I used to go to school for a half day and then work until supper so I could pay for my dance lessons.

"That's the only thing that freed me. Dancing. God, I used to love those times. That was all that kept me from succumbing to the pressure and getting hitched to some downed-out welder. Looking in the mirror and watching myself dance.

"I was so afraid my father would find out about the lessons and forbid them... Shit, he probably would have kicked me out of the house. He was always looking for an excuse to do that.

"Looking back, I can see that it was a silly fear. My old man didn't even know that I existed; the thought of me doing anything on my own just couldn't have entered his head.

"After graduation it got worse. I worked as much as possible to stay out of the house. To... to... feel like I was alive. Like I was visible. At lunch time I would watch daytime television. Even the stupid commercials were interesting because they were about people who were real. People who were doing something with their lives, not just surviving behind a closed door.

"They gave me a burning desire to go to school, to become somebody, like a welding-bartender." Lisa laughed at the recollection.

"To do something, to be someone, but Hamtramck was sucking me back all the time. Carol, it was like being in quicksand, always tugging at you, always pulling at you: Get married, have some kids, make something of yourself."

"What about your mother?" Carol asked.

"She was a good Polish housefrau. Never went against the old man. Her father was an alcoholic who split when she was three years old. Do you know, when she was growing up she used to dream that she would marry someone rich enough to be able to go out to a restaurant every Sunday?

"That was her biggest dream. Eating at the town coffeehouse once a week. Having more than one dress to wear to school. Hell, she made it. Her dreams came true.

"But there was once, one time she stuck up for me. I had decided I wanted to go to business school to become a glorified secretary. I thought it would be my ticket out of that dismal town.

"I saw it on television," she added sheepishly.

"You can imagine what the old man said when I finally got the nerve to bring that up. My mother stuck up for me and said I should be able to go to school. She prevailed, although her idea of a higher education wasn't exactly business school..." Her voice trailed off.

"So what happened?" Carol prodded.

Lisa jerked back to the present. "What happened? I'll tell you what happened. I compromised my high ideals and when to dental hygienist's school."

Carol laughed, "You're kidding!"

"For six fucking long months I learned about bicuspids, molars, overbites and how to please your boss." She shuddered visibly. "You can't picture the scene. All these weird girls in direct competition to get that great gig. End up elbow to elbow with an ORAL SURGEON.

"Wearing starched whites every day and pretending we were attending Harvard Medical School while some bored old fart looked up our uniforms and explained about gingivitis."

"Why did you do it?"

"Because I was desperate. Mom figured it was my one shot at the good life. Find some nice eligible dentist to nest with." She leaned across the table towards Carol.

"Do you know what dentists are like? In real life? Depressed, cornered motherfuckers whose wives sent them through school and now they don't 'understand' them.

"They've all got a uniform fetish. Most are fucking the receptionist, the hygienist and trying for the bookkeeper. They've all got two kids. I think they come with the job. Always rubbing their hands over your starched ass, wrinkling your uniform.

"Spend the day listening to the Bee Gee's and people named Barry and Barbara on the elevator music station. Watching yourself get older... I could picture a day when I would be the one trying to get some middle-aged cavity filler to call his wife and lie about dinner so we could spend a couple of hours bouncing around in the bliss of the Hamtramck Motor Inn.

"Scary, Carol, you can't know. Really scary...

"At least I kept dancing. It was all I had, the only thing I enjoyed. And then one day it dawned on me that I had an okay face and big boobs. Guys went out of their way in order to hit on me and all the other chicks hated me for it. And my dance teacher told me I might be good enough to have a shot at the big time.

"I think it was her idea that finally convinced me. I know she never did what she could have and I think she wanted to live through me. What do they call that?"

"Vicarious," Carol answered in spite of herself.

"I knew you'd know, princess. Anyway, she convinced me that I could do something else with my life besides handing picks to pricks. One day I saw an ad for some sort of gamblers' charter to Vegas and I thought, 'It's now of never.'

"I left the next day. One suitcase. That's all it took to move all my life's possessions twenty-five hundred miles away. Fly the friendly skies..."

"Have you ever been back?"

"Back?" It was as if Carol had asked if Lisa if she was planning on visiting Mars.

"Back? You mean to Ham Town?

"Good God, it took me nineteen years to realize that I was free to leave! I thought it was like Berlin or something... Why else would those people stay there?

"Go back? No, no... Never..."

"Don't you miss your family at all?"

"My mother used to force me to take piano lessons with my grandmother. At the time I hated it, but it's weird, sometimes I miss those times."

Lisa brightened, "She went through Juilliard."

"Your grandmother?"

"Oh, yes, poor but talented. Our family story. She's dead and I don't care if the rest of them are dead or alive. Let them rot in Polish heaven."

"I don't know, it sounds like you're too hard on your family. At least they didn't pressure you to always be the best in everything you ever tried." Carol flashed back to her upbringing.

"At least you had the room to do what you wanted."

Lisa wrinkled her nose. "Look, Carol, you and I are different people. Your old lady may have been a little uptight asshole but it's... hell, it's a whole different concept than where I'm coming from.

"I'm not a citizen, I'll never be one. That's the basic difference between you and me. I've got to be *somebody*. I've got to make it. I'll do anything, *anything* to get there.

"You and I..." She exhaled loudly. "Well, the truth is, Carol, I'll never know what it's like to love a child, or drive a station wagon with wood on the side..."

"Actually, I think it's a Volvo or a BMW now," Carol said with a touch of sarcasm.

"Oh, I didn't know they put wood on them. The point is, Carol, you're not one of the great unwashed"—Lisa indicated the rows of slot machines outside the restaurant—"but you're still a citizen.

"You'll always be a citizen. Check them off, Carol: Maternal instinct? I don't have one. Nesting urge? I like hotels just fine. Paternal feelings? I love children, just as long as they're someone else's. Show business is my life. I would rather hear applause than my kid crying for me. Maybe I live for cheap thrills, but that's better than living for no thrills at all."

"What would you do if you made it big?" With a start Carol realized how much she would miss Lisa if she suddenly left.

"Whatever it took, princess. And I'll do whatever it takes to get there. I've gone down on dentists to keep a job, how can it get worse?"

She rubbed her hands over her body, emphasizing the curves. "This is a gift, I'd be a fool not to use it. Those high sounding ethics are going to get in your way, Carol, mark my words. You only go around once in life. Use it, don't let it use you."

Carol felt herself blush, much to Lisa's amusement.

"When I first hit town I worked as an 'erotic' dancer in a topless bar. You don't know how scummy those cheap clubs really are. But it was that or back to the white bread world of dentistry. There was really no choice involved." She brightened. "Then I met Leon. He's really a great guy. He was working in an ad agency at the time, and I guess I fell in love with him. It's just too damn bad he's gay, you know?

"Anyway, he got me a job in a commercial. It was really neat and we sort of, uh, helped each other through some things and Leon convinced me I could do better than that stupid bar. He helped me get on weekends with the show and we're sorta like family now. It's really great to have friends that you know will stick with you and help you out. I think all three of us will be like brothers and sisters."

She paused for a second. "It's still too damn bad that he's gay, though. I wonder how that happened. Maybe if I'd met him first. Oh, well...

"Maybe I still dance with my tits uncovered but it's *show business*, and that's what counts. It's like rolling the dice; I've still got a shot at it. I've still got a chance to make it big. And people respect me. Half the broads in this town would give their eye teeth to trade places with me.

"How many secretaries, real estate agents, aerobic instructors or dental hygienists can say that? *I've still got a shot at it.* I may be dancing in the shadow of the leads but still got my dream and *it's going to come true.*

"Whatever it takes. Carol, whatever it takes." She looked into space.

LEON

He was never sure why it happened but he would always remember when. He was fourteen years old. He had a comfortable, if small town life in Billings, Ohio, "The Glass Container Capital of the World."

At thirteen Leon discovered girls, or rather his lack of concrete interest in them. Every month one of his classmates whose father owned the local liquor store would bring in the latest issues of *Playboy* and *Penthouse* for after-school perusal. Leon would admire the newest examples of prime American womanhood along with everyone else— even if he didn't always understand the terminology.

On certain occasions he would be lucky enough to be singled out for a special favor and would get to take the magazine home for a night or two where he would carefully wrinkle up the pages to give the illusion they had been dutifully studied.

Frankly it bored him stiff. Big tits reminded him of cows and no matter how firm they looked in the photos, he pictured the roll of fat around his mother's stomach and the way her breasts hung like pendulums when she fixed dinner in her bra and slacks.

There had to be some redeeming value that was slipping by Leon. it didn't particularly worry him—sooner or later it would catch up and he would spend half of his class time trying to peer down Susan Lee's blouse like the rest of the boys—but until then it was no major inconvenience.

One afternoon the art appreciation group was more excited than usual. The shopkeeper's son had gotten a copy of *Hustler*. It was suggested that they all enjoy the purloined copy together, as it was "loaned out" at great risk and had to be returned before its absence was noticed.

Besides, the pages couldn't be all stuck together...

The boys watched the store owner's son as he carefully flipped past the few introductory pages of print.

"Jesus! Look at that!"

"Talk about a split beaver!"

Someone giggled. "They must have shoved the camera up her cunt to shoot that!"

Leon could tell from their expressions that some of the kids found the photos very revealing. Leon found them very revolting. Gross. Ugly. Even the girl's faces seemed less than attractive, but he could sense that no one else felt quite that way; in fact, no one else seemed to even notice their faces...

"Let's do a circle jerk." Ritchie looked at the rest of them with a mocking smile, "Unless you're all chicken." He was almost sixteen, had been held back last year and was obviously experienced in the biblical sense.

"Listen, my mom might come home early." Steve looked from face to face.

Yes, Leon thought, let's agree with him. However, the tide was obviously shifting away from the safe point of view. A couple of guys snickered. "Ah, don't be such a little shit, we could hear the car in the driveway if she came home and she won't be back this early anyway. Come on." Ritchie unlooped his belt and slid his jeans down to his knees. "Man just shut your eyes and think about that pussy sitting on your face."

Leon could see the bulge in Spencer's underwear. He looked again at the magazine and thought of that hairy, greasy slash actually sitting on his face. He wanted to throw up. Around him other zippers were being rapidly unfastened. "Come on, you two chicken or just faggots?" Several of the boys laughed and Leon realized only he and one other boy were still buckled up.

He looked at the other holdout hoping for support. Their eyes locked for a brief moment and then the other boy reached down and unzipped his pants. Leon looked back at the glossy magazine and did the same.

About two heated minutes into the procedure Leon cautiously glanced around the room. No one was speaking and all eyes were riveted on the glossy centerfold. Everyone had a hard on. Everyone but Leon.

Oh God, no… He shifted his hand to enclose his entire penis to hide it from view. Luckily nobody was looking anyway. Maybe if he shut his eyes and thought about…

Thought about what? He got hard ons in his sleep and sometimes when he was awake, but what was he thinking about during those instances? Susan Lee's breasts? Looking into the girl's shower and watching… watching what?

Oh, come on God, don't do this to me. He felt sweat breaking out on his forehead and around his shirt collar. Fear sweat. Now he could smell it. He tried to concentrate on the photograph, think of women everywhere, anywhere. Women with their soft, fatty…

"What's the matter Leon? Isn't she your type?" Ritchie, the leader was looking directly at him with that same irritating smirk/smile. "Got a problem?"

Leon felt the gaze of several others tear away from the pussy shot and fall on him. He covered his penis and silently begged God not to let this happen. Anything, do anything, but this, don't let him—

"Oh shit! That's my mom!" The sound of car wheels on gravel and eight boys stumbling over their cuffs, trying to zip pants over swollen flesh. "Christ!"

"Hurry up! Get your pants up! If she sees us I'll get grounded forever." Leon realized he was just sitting like a statue holding onto his cock and listening to a car door shut.

Finally he was upright and moving. His zipper stuck on his underpants just as the front door opened.

"Hello boys, how come you're inside on such a nice afternoon?" Leon faced the wall and pulled with all his might as the rest of the group mumbled greetings and filed out. With a final tug the errant zipper closed and Leon turned to face Steve's mother. "Hi, Mrs. Fletcher, how are you?"

As she replied his eyes glanced over the copy of *Hustler* which was still lying opened on the floor next to the couch. Everyone else had left the house by this point.

He turned and placed himself between the offensive magazine and Steve's mother. Then he walked over, shut it and rolled it into a small tube. When he turned back Mrs. Fletcher was watching him intently.

"Homework," he said and raised the magazine towards her. "Almost forgot it."

She smiled and he walked out to join his friends.

"Man, that was cool, another second and we would have been dead meat."

"Yeah, you really handled that cool."

Leon handed the magazine back to the librarian. He noticed that Ritchie was still smirking at him, "Yeah, that Leon, he's really cool, nothing get's to him."

A few months later Leon was showering in the school locker room. He had just taken two first places in a track meet and was still feeling the glow.

Not bad. Not bad at all. Leon looked around the locker room, he had just beaten several of the other boys in the room and the hot needle spray of the shower felt so good... He shut his eyes and drifted with the water.

When he opened his eyes Leon had the vague feeling something was wrong. He heard a giggle from the boy next to him and suddenly Leon realized he had a conspicuous hard on. A complete, blue veiner. He stared at it like it belonged to someone else, like he had no connection with the gorged member.

The locker room got very quiet.

"It's about time." It was his old friend Ritchie. "Been thinking about that *Hustler* cunt shot for half a year and old Leon finally get's his boner. Just had to work on it a bit, huh Leon? The best things in life take time."

Leon felt his face burning as he walked by Ritchie to reach his locker. He dressed as fast as possible and then ran from the locker room with laughter ringing behind. Without a doubt the story would be all over school tomorrow.

The walk home was a complete daze. How could that happen? Don't I have any control over my body at all. Why the hell did it have to happen there?

By the time he got home Leon was in a complete panic.

Maybe he should cut school for a couple of days until things died down. He went to the wooden cabinet over the stove and withdrew a partially filled bottle of gin that his mother used to get through particularly rough days and poured half a water tumbler full. Stale tomato juice was added to fill the glass to the brim and Leon gulped about half in one swallow.

Shit! A raging fire burned from his mouth into his chest. What the hell was he thinking of anyway? Another huge drink that didn't burn quite as much as the first helped him think objectively.

He tried to mentally recreate the scenario. Had he been thinking of some girl and just forgot? All he could remember was a locker room full of naked boys...

Oh God! It suddenly hit home. He hadn't been thinking of anything, there was just a room full of... No! That couldn't be true! He drank the last swallow and then the pain seemed to condense into a small point of light and disappear.

Leon spent the evening in his room, he couldn't face his mother. By morning he had a plan worked out, a plan that did not include humiliating himself in front of his classmates.

Every morning for the next two weeks Leon dutifully left for school, waited until his mother left for work and then holed up in his room sipping from the gin bottle and replacing the contents with water (luckily his mother and her "friends" weren't too observant when it came to the strength of the booze) and reading movie magazines.

After two weeks the high school attendance officer decided the phone calls to Leon's home (talking with his "uncle") were no longer sufficient excuse, a personal visit was in order.

Leon saw him coming. Literally. Before the third knock he was prepared.

As the front door opened a crack the truant officer found himself taking a step backward involuntarily. The apparition peering out from the dimly lit house was definitely the boy, but there was something severely wrong.

In a breathless voice Leon explained about his rare skin condition... At least the movie mags were good for something. Leon offered a hand to the official for examination, but he refused; one glimpse of the face had been enough to convince him of the severity of the condition he was dealing with.

The school enforcer departed, shaken to the core, and Leon went inside to scrape off the green tinted Noxema smeared over every inch of exposed skin.

The skin cream disease ran strong for nearly six weeks, then it collapsed in one fell swoop.

"How was school today, honey?" His mother inquired one evening after the daily charade. She seemed to be smiling just a trifle too much...

"Uh, fine."

"That's nice dear," she was frowning at the level of liquid in the gin bottle, "because I got this very interesting letter from the principal today inquiring about your skin condition." She snatched up a sheet of paper from the counter in front of her, "Six fucking weeks! Where the hell have you been for six fucking weeks! Are you playing house with some little chippie?"

If she only knew, Leon thought, if she only knew...

"Well?" She waved the letter in front of her, "what the fuck is going on?"

Leon looked up at her and his soul cracked. Tears flooded from his eyes and he ran to the sanctuary of his room. Stunned by this release of emotion his mother gave Leon several minutes to compose himself before she knocked on the door. "Listen, I don't know what's going on here but we've got to solve it. You're only fifteen years old, nothing can be that bad."

Leon looked up from his mussed bed. Fourteen, he thought, I'm only fourteen. I'm not going back to school. Not for anything. I'll kill myself first. I really will.

Leon's mother finally came to accept the situation. She left him alone for several months and then lied about his age in order to enroll him in a trade school for commercial art.

To everyone's surprise, including his own, Leon excelled at the new school. He had a natural talent for drawing and, most important, he discovered other boys, older boys, who had much the same attitude on sex, love and womenkind as did Leon.

During his second year at the school three important things took place. Leon discovered how pleasant sex could actually be with the help of a twenty-one-year-old fellow student who also introduced him to the pleasant high of marijuana. "It helps you relax, gets you a little loose, you draw better, it's *goood* for you..." His tutor also got him a part-time job in the mail room of a local ad agency where he worked.

Within two years Leon was putting in sixteen hours a day as the assistant art director of the agency. He was doing well; he was also using little pills to help him relax from the stresses of the job.

Then he got an offer to move to Las Vegas as the art director of a major agency. He also learned that just a taste of heroin relaxed you far, far better than a little pills, booze or grass.

Just a little, not like he was mainlining. Just chipping. Completely under control. It was good for you.

LAS VEGAS

Somewhere along the way a vague line had been crossed and the truth of the matter was that Leon had no clear idea exactly when he had crossed it. But crossed it he surely had.

It wasn't that he had anything against getting high, mind you. A good healthy high was still the equal of staying young, having great sex and writing a novel—well, at least a good short story—all in one fell swoop.

No. The problem wasn't getting high, the problem was *in* getting high. He couldn't quite do it any more. The same amount of high quality horse just didn't kick it loose.

He could shoot up and still feel a buzz, but he found himself always waiting for the rest of the high. The good part, that incredible body rush that felt like a constant orgasm that left his body singing and his mind in a very pleasurable corner, wasn't there anymore.

He found himself constantly thinking back to other times, other highs, always trying to match the quality of his memories. Without success...

When Leon mentioned this to the man he was buying from, he found little solace was to be had. "You questioning the product? You can buy somewhere else man—the joys of a free marketplace."

"No, no," Leon said quickly, "it's not that. I just don't feel as good as I used to..."

"Welcome to the real world. That's why they call it chasing the dragon. He can be such a slippery little bastard." The dealer left his packet and walked away.

The little plastic bag looked so promising...

But that wasn't the worst of it. No, the real problem was he didn't seem to be functioning quite as well when he wasn't high. In fact, it was starting to feel more normal to function with a bit of heroin than it was to try and function without it. Even work seemed to slide by better with a little taste. It wasn't as if he was getting high. Shit! He was just trying to stay straight.

Really strange…

Deep inside Leon knew very well what had happened. One day with no warning a chemical process inside his brain had changed: A molecule formed that had never existed before and now he needed it just to get along—just to be himself—and it wouldn't come into being without a little help.

But knowing the truth did not set him free, emotions were not so easily manipulated as were thoughts. An invisible hand had grabbed hold of his soul and it showed no promise of letting go…

Not today, Leon thought. I'll just not do any today. So it'll bug me a little bit, so what? I'll just keep a handle on it. Maybe I'll have a bit of wine with lunch if I need it—or even a drink. But no drugs…

He sat at his desk and watched the black clock hand edge ever so slowly towards the twelve o'clock position. God damn, what was going on? He held his hand out and watched it shake back and forth.

Just a little bit. Maybe just snort—a taste, not to get off, just to stop this fucking feeling, of, of, what the hell was it? Something beyond control, some sort of evil being that had…oh fuck, this isn't funny.

He tucked his hand back into his lap and held it immobile with his other hand. His nose was running and his back was aching beyond belief and time was moving so fucking slowly…

Fuck this! Ain't nothing in charge of me but me! I don't need anything else to get through the day. This is my life. He bit his lip and tried to concentrate on the pile of papers on his desk.

It was a very important pitch meeting; he *had* to concentrate. The client's voice seemed to be some sort of buzzing like an errant mosquito you couldn't swat. Twice he found himself begging excuses and asking for things to be repeated. He couldn't quite understand what was being said.

It all seemed so unimportant compared to the dull ache in his soul and the goddam sick feeling that was—Suddenly he realized everyone was staring at him. He'd missed something else.

"I'm sorry," then he shut his mouth to prevent being physically sick as an unexpected wave of bile leapt into his mouth. What the *fuck*? Leon stood up and pushed his chair back.

"Are you okay?" He felt several hands reach out to steady him.

Get out of there. "No, not good. Excuse me." He stumbled over a rolled-up chart and tore into the hallway heading for the bathroom.

Not a moment too soon, Leon puked into the toilet. He felt terrible, and getting worse by the second. Sweat was pouring from his forehead, he felt dizzy and the neck of his shirt was far too tight.

Another wave of nausea washed through him and he choked on the mass trying to force its way from his constricted throat into his mouth. Holy shit! Sweat seemed to be bursting through his skin; his shirt was soaked and he couldn't stand up anymore. Leon knelt over the bowl and gagged. This couldn't be... He must be coming down with something, maybe the flu. He threw up again just as the door to the rest room opened.

"Leon are you all right?" It was his boss.

"Had oysters for lunch," he managed to choke out. "I think they were bad. Oh, Jesus." His stomach was cramping. "I'll be okay as soon as I get them out of my system. I'll be back, give me a few minutes." There had to be a logical explanation for this.

"You sound terrible, maybe I should call a doctor." The other man hesitated.

"No! No doctor." He gathered his strength together. "It's getting better already, just give me a few minutes.

"Okay. If you need help just yell." The other man left the room.

Help? Christ do I need help. Leon sat on the stained toilet seat. His shirt was stuck to his body and his hair felt like he had just shampooed it without drying. He slammed his briefcase on the tile floor and it popped open. He grabbed a little case and searched for the catch. There it was.

Leon breathed a sigh of relief as the lid flipped open revealing an eye dropper that ended in a hypodermic needle, a silver spoon and a packet of gray powder.

His hands seemed to be shaking less as he melted the chemical over a burning match and watched it disappear into solution. I can't believe I'm sitting in the executive washroom with a fit...

He squeezed the rubber bulb and then let it go, sucking the liquid up into the glass dropper. He slid his belt from around his waist and looped it around his arm just above the elbow touching the rolled-up French cuff of his shirt. Leon took the end of the belt in his teeth and pulled it tight. The veins in his arm popped from the pressure and stood out like little hoses.

A part of him watched in stunned disbelief as the other part slid the needle into the main vein on the inside of his elbow. He released the pressure on the bulb a fraction and the spike pulled a red flag of blood back into the dropper. Then he squeezed down on the rubber bulb and pumped the mixture directly into his bloodstream.

The result was immediate. A wave of pleasure broke over his head and washed down to his toes. He gave it a second to take hold and then stood up and unrolled his shirt sleeve. He held his handout and studied it.

Steady as a fucking rock.

Oh, Jesus, that was not real good news. Not real good news at all.

Leon washed his face in the sink and then held his upper body under the hot air dryer for three full cycles drying his hair and shirt as best he could. It was time to go back and face the real world.

With a little help from a friend...

That night Leon made a decision. It was time to get off drugs—while he still could. *If* he still could. He was a commercial success, life was going good, except... Time to go.

He rubbed his hand through his hair. He could swear he could already feel the shakes coming back, but that couldn't be true. It was too soon. It should be good until at least morning.

But it wasn't. Leon was starting to hurt.

I've got to get clean. I've got to kick—but how? If I stick around here I can always get more and I probably will. God, how did I get here?

He opened his briefcase and took his stash out. I'll start by throwing this away. His hand was shaking so badly he could hardly hold the fit. Maybe just one more hit would help get him through the process of giving the shit up forever.

That's stupid. He held the glassine envelope over the toilet, but his hand had a will of its own and flat out refused to take the final step.

Compromise. I'll take off, leave town. Go someplace where I don't know anybody—back off for a few days and relax. Just cool out. I could phone in and leave a message at work, they think I'm near death anyway. Nobody will question a couple of days off. He could feel the sweat starting to pop out in miniature rivulets on his forehead. It was going to be a long night, unless... Compromise, that was the key.

Leon took the spoon out of the case and tipped some smack into it. He watched it for a second and then tapped the bag in order to spill more onto the pile.

After all it was going to be the last time. The moment of reckoning.

He faced the woman at the ticket counter and thought, I'm glad I did that last hit. It would be miserable to get sick on a plane.

"Can I help you?"

"Next plane out." I've always wanted to say that.

"To where?" The woman's pasted-on smile seemed to slip just the tiniest little bit.

"You choose. Anywhere domestic, I didn't bring a passport."

The woman began punching buttons on her computer keyboard. "Is this like, ah, a vacation?" she asked.

"A working vacation." Leon was enjoying the woman's perplexity.

"Is this a joke? I'm too busy to—"

He cut her off by waving his American Express card in the air. "Nope, put it on here. In fact don't even tell me where I'm going. Just pick someplace I can get to in a couple of hours and write the ticket."

She appeared to make a decision. "Smoking or non?" she asked.

Leon smiled and took the ticket face down so he couldn't read the destination. "What gate?"

The agent told him and he started to leave.

"You're not going to tell me what's going on are you?"

He turned back towards her. "Bank." He said. "I just robbed a bank. A small bank, not worth a trip to Brazil, but definitely worth leaving town for."

She looked at Leon like he was some sort of insect, then shrugged her shoulders. "Have a pleasant trip."

That was really a stupid thing to say. He watched the gate numbers as he walked past each one. All I need to top off a perfect evening is for her to call the airport cops and turn me in. Then he was in front of his gate.

She won't call the cops, Leon realized. She's managed to send me to someplace worse than jail all by herself.

"If you're going on this plane you'd better get aboard." The gate agent waved took his ticket and waved him onto the idling jet.

Leon lay on the too soft mattress and contemplated his choices. It was too late to go back, even if he wanted to, there weren't any more flights out of this town to anywhere tonight. He also doubted if there were any organized tours of downtown Redding, California, after ten o'clock at night.

He could probably find a bar, but God only knows what he would find in the bar. Somehow he really didn't feel like defending his masculinity or lack of accent this evening.

Why kid myself? I'm just lying here waiting for it to begin again. Maybe I should get drunk. Room service—they could send up a bottle. He reached for the phone on the night stand.

The front desk clerk laughed for what seemed like quite a long time at the suggestion of room service. At least someone is getting a kick out of this, Leon thought as he wrote down the directions to the nearest liquor store.

He poured a water tumbler of expensive Scotch from the bottle, turned on the television and took a huge swallow. It had been some time since Leon had drunk alcohol and the burning took him by surprise. He choked and spit up part of the drink. Maybe just a little bit slower. He took another drink and managed to keep it down. This wasn't going to be as rough as he had feared. He took another drink and lay back down.

It had been a long, hard day and he was already exhausted. He could feel a numbing effect as the alcohol slid right through his empty stomach and entered his bloodstream. One more glass and he could sleep, probably all night. By morning he should feel better. Take a day or two to kick back and let the rough edges smooth themselves out.

He shut his eyes and let the heaviness of the day take him down…

It was a white ceiling but it wasn't his white ceiling. That much was for sure. He licked his dry lips and tried to lift his head from the pillow to take stock of the surroundings. Then things all came back in a rush. He sank back into the bed and tried to make himself sleep.

It wasn't going to happen. He got up and ate some potato chips. Breakfast, the most important meal of the day. Maybe a hot shower would help the world look better.

It didn't.

By mid-morning Leon was pacing back and forth in the small room to the backdrop of television cartoons. He was starting to get sick again.

I've got to get out of this room—take my mind off my problems. But his stomach was already cramping so badly Leon couldn't get off the bed. He tried to take a drink of warm Scotch for inspiration but couldn't force his throat to take in the bitter-tasting brew.

Shivering began in spite of the oppressive heat clothing the small room as gut-wrenching cramps began to slice through his stomach. A metallic taste filled his mouth. It refused to be washed out.

Just sit it out—there was really no option. How bad could it be—he hadn't been doing smack long enough, or at least steady enough and long enough… Leon bent over double and held his stomach as the worst cramp yet knifed into his stomach.

He wiped his nose and climbed under the blankets in a vain attempt to stop the insane shivering. His entire body was in pain from his hair to his toes. Was it possible to have a full body toothache? He shut his eyes and sweat into the already damp blankets.

It has to get better soon—just ride it out. *Relax and ride it out.*

It didn't get better. It got worse. By mid-afternoon Leon thought he might really be dying. Something else was definitely wrong with him. Perhaps he had cancer and just never noticed because he was high too much of the time. Maybe he should try and get to a doctor, and see what was really wrong, or maybe it would be better to just explain… No, that was stupid, not only would a doctor not have any sympathy, he might even call the cops.

On the other hand jail couldn't be too much worse than what it was he was experiencing right this very second—and maybe they would give him something to ease the fucking *pain*… No, no, that was a stupid attitude. He'd just have to let it pass.

Leon rolled to the other side of the bed, bunching up the wet sheets in the process. He looked out the window. God it was dark already and he wasn't feeling better—in fact, he was feeling really, really bad. The legendary death of the 500 cuts. Knives and needles dug into every square inch of his skin. One second shaking like it was winter in Ohio but then sweating profusely, Leon was past wanting to get straight. He fucking needed to get high.

Anything was better than this.

Wait a minute—that was it! Even here in bum fuck California people still had to get high. Just a dime balloon would cut him some slack, then he could get straight later, when he felt better, maybe even check into one of those hospitals where they eased you through this shit with downers.

Yeah, that was how to do it. This Lone Ranger act was for the birds. How could he have been so dumb? Leon got up and pulled his pants on.

It couldn't be that hard to score, even here. The immediate neighborhood was pretty run down. It was bound to turn up a dealer or even a hooker who would turn him on to a taste. He felt better already. At least he had a course of action.

It was not as easy as Leon had predicted. The only two hookers he had been able to identify lost interest in him as soon as he brought up the subject of drugs. Fucking amateurs anyway. One even had the effrontery to chant "narc, narc," as Leon walked off.

And that was several hours ago. He had passed the rest of the time in two different all-night doughnut stores, but even these usually fertile breeding grounds of sleaze were running dry.

Leon was getting real sick again. He couldn't stand another cup of coffee or one more goddam doughy cake doughnut and the late night crowd was starting to thin out.

He still hadn't picked out any likely prospects in this location and it was getting late. Shit, I look so bad you think somebody would come up and ask me if I want to score. What's the matter with these people?

Actually he was lucky to have gotten out of the first shop with his life. As soon as he had said "hello" to some asshole who looked like he might have been in the business, the fucking homophobe had jumped down his throat calling him a faggot, threatening to do various things to his body.

Leon held no desire to go back to that shop but the pickings here were really slim. He was hurting so bad he wasn't sure if he could find his way back to the hotel.

A young man in a denim jacket slinked into the shop. While he ordered he kept tugging at his long, greasy hair. He had to be told the amount of the bill two separate times before digging through his pockets and coming up with some change.

The man shuffled over to the table next to Leon only to be called back by the smirking clerk because he had forgotten his coffee. He looked back blankly, grasped the situation and went back for his order. Leon recognized him at once, for here was a kindred soul. The man was loaded, stoned, blessedly, blessedly high.

Leon nodded a polite hello across the table. A subtle attempt at letting the man know that *he knew*, and more important, that they were on the same side.

The man looked right through him.

Leon fought back a quick bit of panic. This time he raised his coffee cup, "Nice night, isn't it?" More so for you than for me…

The man seemed to focus on Leon's coffee cup for an inordinate amount of time before he shrugged, "Uh-huh."

This is going to be harder than I thought. "Do you mind if I join you for a second? I just want to ask you something."

The man watched Leon warily as he changed tables. "I don't have any spare change."

"No, no, nothing like that."

"I'm also not into religion and I think L. Ron Hubbard is a total asshole."

"I can live with that," Leon said. "I got no trouble with that, see, what I do got some trouble with is I really, really would like to get high and I'm from out of town and I don't know anybody, see, and I thought maybe you could tell me where I might go to score."

The man looked wary again.

"I really need to get straight, you know? Please, if you can help me, I've got money."

The man shook his head.

"Come on, at least tell me where I should go. I'm not in good shape here."

The other man held his hand open on the table. "Give me your wallet."

"Huh?" But at the same time Leon reached into his back pocket and removed it. Then it dawned with a sudden clarity what was happening.

He felt giddy. Leon flipped the wallet open on the fly. "See, no badge, out-of-state driver's license and money…"

"Let's go outside."

Yes, Leon, thought, hot damn, let's go outside…

"What do you want?" the man asked when they had reached the parking lot out back.

"Whatever you got. A couple of dimes, even a nickel would ease the pain."

The other man stared at him. "Huh?"

"Horse. You know, smack, heroin, whatever the fuck you people call it here. Please don't screw with me, I'm not in a good humor."

"Heroin?" The other man repeated dumbly.

"YES, YES! What did you think I was talking about? Buying beer for me? Come on man, I can tell you're high."

"Oh, yeah." The man pulled two little blue pills out of his pocket. "On these."

"Demerol?" Leon peered through the darkness, looking for a shred of hope.

"Acid. Really righteous acid."

"Acid?" Leon was mentally searching through a long list of nicknames.

"LSD man. Four-way tabs. Really nice."

Leon took the two tiny pills into his hand dubiously. "I don't think anything this small is going to do me much good. I'm really hurting."

"Suit yourself." He started to take them back.

"Wait, I'll try it. I'll try anything." Leon handed the man a twenty dollar bill.

"Far out." He was backing up. "I'd take it easy on that stuff."

"Uh-huh." Leon turned away to look for a taxi.

At least the little fuckers dissolved easily. He swirled the spoon around and watched the mini-pills disappear into a couple of drops of water. Didn't even have to heat them.

God, I should've got some more—this is just too little and too late. Christ, that couldn't have been a thirtieth of a gram, even if there wasn't much cut…

The fact was the entire thing was probably a burn. That asshole probably just made twenty dollars on two cake decorations. In fact, the more he thought about it, the more they resembled two of the tiny blue decorations from a doughnut.

Too late to call the Better Business Bureau now. I might as well go through with it. Leon sucked the water up into the dropper, tugged the band around his arm tighter, then inserted the needle while simultaneously squeezing the rubber bulb.

The result was instantaneous. Leon fell over backwards grabbing his elbows, clamped in a fetal position. The needle was still sticking out of his arm like some grotesquely wounded insect quivering in its death throes.

The chemical was burning his brain with an intensity he had never before dreamed possible. Leon was no longer in a cheap hotel room in downtown Redding.

He was in hell.

Sometime before dawn the evil hand that was squeezing his soul let loose just enough for Leon to have coherent periods of thought. Or, if not coherent, at least close enough that Leon could remember where he was and, sort of, who he was. The telephone was dangling free, he vaguely remembered trying to call for help at least once in the night.

Obviously the operation had not been successful.

There was no denying he was still high—or whatever the condition was that the pills had induced—and far worse, he was still hallucinating madly. Bugs—little, black, evil, eight legged, edgy, crawly bugs—covered everything. The sight made him sick but when he tried to throw up it came up empty. It had been a long night. Nothing was left. Leon stumbled upright, something crunched under his foot. Sometime in the night he had stepped on the dropper/needle outfit and little shards of glass lay scattered about the cheap rug.

Involuntarily he caught sight of himself in the mirror—and tried to vomit again. The image was stretched, ugly, red and fucking evil. Leon heard someone moan. Suddenly a lightening bolt of reason struck him. In order to exorcise the demons, he would have to go back to their source.

Wildly Leon looked about the room until a jagged steak knife from an earlier dinner came into view. He held the knife in his hand and started out the door. If he could just find the son of a bitch that sold him that poison and cut him open from one end to the other, maybe, maybe, things would get back to normal.

Leon walked out into the growing dawn with murder in his heart...

The next two hours were vague at best. The one clear image was when the policeman kicked his feet out from under him, knocking out two teeth in the handcuffing process.

The terrible sound of the teeth cracking against the cement sidewalk would stay with him for quite some time...

Jail was not a place where they kept civilized people. Although parts of the booking process remained quite vivid in his mind, set apart like individual black and white photos with incredibly jagged edges, most of it seemed to have blended together in the form of one long nightmare which Leon wouldn't mind forgetting. If he did try to play the scenes over again in his mind they seemed disconnected, reappearing in no particular order. Sort of like watching a Fellini movie with every other script page missing...

He did remember the terrible tension that accompanied the entire scenario. The most accurate description Leon could come up with was biting into a ball of aluminum foil, for thirty-six hours straight.

The pushing, shoving, with some asshole cop tightening his handcuffs far past the point of reasonable pain for a minor verbal infraction; trying to explain the terrible reality of bugs on everything; asking for a doctor—no, begging for a doctor—and then getting thrown in a solitary "rubber room" cell for two very long days.

He was also fairly certain he bit at least one cop—maybe two. That would probably also explain the amazing black bruise covering most of his chest and possibly also what he felt was at least one broken rib.

His entire body felt as though it had been fed into a giant blender, free running on the "liquefy" setting. He was bruised, battered, and beaten. One eye was swollen almost shut and he still grimaced every time he ran his tongue over the stumps of his front teeth.

It would be funny if it wasn't so real...

As the drug wore off the physical pain grew more and more intense and the generous jailer's dose of two Tylenol every eight hours really didn't quash it all that well. The up side was that Leon was pretty sure he had kicked his habit. The acid had been so intense and now the pain from his beating was so bad he wasn't one hundred percent sure, but... It was really secondary to his other problems.

Perhaps he would start a new treatment center for drug abuse—give you an overdose of LSD, kick the shit out of you, lock you in a small room with a million bugs, bad, bad food, and zero human contact.

Couldn't fail. Make a million dollars.

At least today the human contact problem was about to be a thing of the past—they were going to move him into the population. Of course, he could try to reach out and touch someone. He hadn't used his obligatory phone call yet—partly because he was too fucked up to properly use the instrument and partly because he was too embarrassed to call anyone.

Maybe he should just drop off the end of the earth, stay here until some judge took pity and cut him loose in his old age and send for his few possessions. It was a pitiful scenario but then again so was calling the agency and explaining that he was in a dirty jail cell in Redding because he overdosed on LSD to help kick his heroin habit and then assaulted a major force of inner city police officers.

Might not go down too well with the more stodgy clients...

Oh, Jesus, how did I get here? This can't be my life... Change the channel, cancel the series, let me loose... he groaned aloud and held his throbbing head in both hands.

If he could just survive a few more days in this shithole—he really hadn't done anything too wrong. No drugs of any sort were still in evidence by the time he actually got popped—and he really didn't' knife anybody. With any luck at all the cop with the bite marks might just be too embarrassed to press the case. If Leon's recollection of where the marks were actually located were true, court would be a most revealing experience...

Leon had never felt so alone in his entire life. Did anyone really wonder where he was or why he was here? He pounded his fist against the padded floor. Was this what life added up to in the end? Bouncing off the walls in a rubber room...

Suddenly Leon heard a key slide into the lock. The door opened and two deputies stood there slapping their palms with their Mondock batons, just like in the movies.

"Come on, killer, time to check out. We need the room." The man pointed with his stick and smiled. "You're going to love the guys in population. They like to goof with the nut cases."

"Phone call," Leon mumbled.

"What about it? Little boy needs to use the telephone?" The two cops laughed. "What do you want to say?"

"Fuck your mother," Leon said clearly.

"In here asshole." One of the deputies shoved him forward along the steel tier whacking the back of his legs as he fell forward. The pain shot up his entire body and for a second Leon regretted his smart mouth.

A hush fell over the hundred or so prisoners who were witness to the drama. Leon could feel blood trickling down his already split lips onto the front of his khaki jail shirt. He tried to stand up—his knees went watery.

If I wanted to feel this bad I would have gone into pro boxing and made a fortune, Leon thought.

A single voice rang out, "It's the cop killer, the guy who bit Kosinski. Get up man, just get up," someone urged. Leon felt his legs lock as he uncertainly stood straight.

"Alright!" Spontaneous applause surrounded him like a warm hand. He was shoved into a cell as a multitude of people began to scream from every direction, "Fuck the pigs—assholes—bite 'em again."

Someone reached out and helped Leon to a bunk. "Way to go man, you couldn't have bitten a bigger jerk." A huge black man gave Leon a high five to which he responded uncertainly.

"Sit down my friend, ain't nobody gonna bother you here. Right, guys?" The other figures in the cell nodded assent.

Great, Leon thought, I'm finally a hero—wrong place, wrong time, for the wrong reasons—but at least I made it...

His first night in population was eventful: A tall, gangly, insecure and genuinely scared boy on the second tier slashed his wrists just before the lights went out. He did a remarkable job. Blood flowed like a river. Then just as the final cut was finished, he underwent a common occurrence in suicide victims—he changed his mind.

"Oh, God, I'm going to die. Please don't let me die, God, please don't let me die." The boy's screams were interspersed with frantic cries for help.

Leon looked out between the bars and down into the second tier, where he could see the boy's arms extended between the bars. The blood flowed, in periodic surges from both wrists and down onto the steel floor of the tier. With each heart pump, a new jet of gory red was ejaculated.

"Please, please, please," the boy screamed. "I'm going to die."

The entire jail was now caught up in the scene. Most were yelling insults at random: "Die, you prick, shut the fuck up. Hey, man, I'm going to kill you if you don't die, you motherfucker."

Gradually the other prisoners became uncommonly disciplined and began yelling and banging metal cups in near perfect time. This in-phase sound drowned out the kid's pleas.

As the victim realized what was going on, he began moaning and pleading, "Please don't, you guys, don't do this, don't let me die." Cans of Comet and toilet paper rolls, the only available projectiles, began to bounce off the kid's cell.

Leon could see that the arms were now down near the bottom of the cell. The boy was obviously on his knees. His pleas had dropped to low moans. A large pool of blood had amassed directly in front of the cell door.

Just then a guard appeared, grumbling at being torn away from his nightly bottle in such a manner. "You stupid asshole, get out of there." He unlocked the door and yanked the kid to his feet. "Damn fool." He began pushing the frightened kid, who was maintaining a precarious balance, down the tier.

They took the slashee to the hospital, stitched and bandaged him, and sent him to isolation for a day for the disturbance he had caused. When the kid returned to the jail he did not speak to anyone, but spent long periods gazing down at his bandages, as if he was unsure what had transpired.

I've got to get out of here, Leon thought. This is a mistake. This is not my life. I'll do whatever's necessary.

"I want to make a phone call." Leon grabbed the wrist of the deputy serving the excuse for breakfast.

"Tough shit. You had your call when you were booked."

"No, as a matter of fact I did not. And if I don't get a call now—when I finally do, my two lawyers, who have nothing to do but sit around spending my retainer, are going to sue this city, this county and, most importantly, you personally. I hope you make a hell of a salary, I need the money." He smiled through his broken teeth.

The officer appeared to consider a reply and then decided it wasn't worth the risk. Any risk. "All right Mr. Rockefeller, one call, that's it."

"Hi, hero." Lisa seemed more amused then put out by her unexpected trip.

"I've paid your bail and," she leaned forward and dropped her voice, "the screws here don't know who you really are so we've got to scram quick like."

"I'm sure this is really funny to you." Leon bit his tongue and began again. "Thanks for coming Lisa. I'll pay you back every cent of the bail and I really appreciate you showing up so fast. You didn't, ah…"

"Relax, Baby Face, I didn't tell anyone anything." Lisa took her receipt from the desk sergeant after blinding him with a smile. She turned back to Leon. "Let's go home, tiger," then she noticed his bruised and battered face for the first time.

"Oh, my God! What happened to you?" Her hand flew to her mouth. "You look like shit."

"Fell down the stairs." Leon muttered. "Let's go."

He grabbed his thin pile of possessions from the uniformed sergeant. "Thanks," he hissed between his broken teeth.

"Take a piece of advice pal?"

Leon seemed to consider the question for a long moment. "Why not?"

The man bared his teeth like Bogart in Casablanca, "Leave town…"

"Right on." Leon replied. "You don't have to ask twice."

The blast of takeoff acceleration forced Leon back into his airplane seat. "I can't tell you how much I appreciate you doing this for me. You're really a friend."

"Uh-huh. You want the bad news, friend? I think you lost your job some days ago. Your boss has sorta stopped calling and I don't think he was real happy." She took a long pull at her rum and Diet Coke.

"Not totally unexpected. Shit, I was pretty fed up at the agency anyway. I think it was part of the problem…"

"Speaking of problems, Leon, you have a minor one with dope, don't you?"

"Nope." He shook his head quite honestly. "Not anymore. Believe me, the desire has most suddenly wilted."

Lisa looked at him as she killed the drink. "Okay. I believe you. Suppose I told you I know an A.D. job open at one of the biggest shows in town?"

"Assistant director on a live show—oh, God wouldn't that be a dream? Thanks for the thought, honey, but nobody would hire me for a real show."

"Why not, you direct real people in those stupid ads don't you? What's the difference?"

"The difference is that directing, along with acting, for a camera is a whole different ball game than performing live in front of an audience. The camera works miracles—people don't really have to act, a good cameraman can still pull the shots; you can fix almost anything in editing. Real actors have to *overact*—big movements so the cheap seats can still see them.

"Don't get me wrong, I'd kill for a live show but nobody would hire me to direct anything, except maybe a grade school PTA show. Ad agency credits don't stretch that far in the real world."

"Kill for it, huh?" Lisa seemed to be thinking that statement over. "Honey, oh waitress!" She raised her hand while watching Leon grimace. The stew reluctantly responded.

"Two more, honey, and why don't you make them doubles? Kill for it, huh? What else would you do?"

"Don't fuck with me Lisa. It's been a long day. What are you trying to say?"

Lisa didn't respond.

"Okay, who do you want dead?"

Lisa laughed. "No, not that... Let's just say that, suppose, just suppose, I had some pull with a certain producer who just fired his A.D. and I could tell him that I knew the perfect man for the job.

"What would you do for me?" She seemed to be teasing, but Leon could tell there was substance under the light tone.

"Anything. Money? A job? My fraternity pin? You name it, Lisa, it's yours."

"Great." She looked at Leon sideways. "Head. That's what I want. Head. You'll give me lots and lots of head. Think your tongue can hold out for a couple of hours?

"It's no joke, you know. I've had guys freeze up on me with tongue cramps. Nothing in the world worse than that. Just on the verge of coming and some clown breaks down on you like an old horse. Can't get it moving again, just lays there and moans. It can be very distracting.

"You should be an expert at that particular act, Leon. I mean that's sort of what you guys do anyway isn't it? You can just shut your eyes and pretend that you have an ugly cock in your mouth and hairy balls hanging against your chin instead of my beautiful clit."

She sipped her new drink. "I'm not trying to be rude, Leon, but I figure you're probably really good at it—and, God knows, I love it—so it should be a fair trade, okay?

"And you're so damn cute. I guess every woman figures she's irresistible, you would be my proof. A crossover hit, every woman's fantasy. We can just work out some sort of informal deal for a number of hours. Or a number of comes, but of course that would be unfair because I could lie—not that I would, of course, but the potential is there, see? So let's just set up a preliminary schedule."

She sucked in some more booze, then leaned over and kissed Leon on impulse. "I've always dreamed of doing something like this—it's like we're both real stars. Rich and famous, can do whatever we want and we decided to do a real show business deal—no money involved, just a trading of faith—no, make that of soul."

Lisa moved her hands along an invisible headline. "Famous Director Claims 'Owes It All To Best Friend.' "

"Or maybe, 'Best Actress Says 'He Inspired Me!' " and God only knows it would do that. We could hint at the truth, but, needless to say, we could never actually tell it—but that would add to our mystery.

"I could suggest, in an offhand manner, that you had a boyfriend and I considered it completely disgusting. Think of the ink we'd get Leon. But," she leaned back and shut her eyes, "that's not the point.

"The point is that we made a solemn pact and helped each other in our hour of need—you in jail and me so horny I can't see straight. A handshake sealed in heaven.

"This might open a whole series of new doors for you—no pun intended. Have you ever actually made it with a woman? Not that that's really necessary, it's just that it would be nice to see a little excitement on your part during this operation. I am okay-looking you know—a lot of guys would give their right... well, a lot of guys would like to be in your place."

Lisa took Leon's hand and gently rubbed it on her right nipple. Leon grimaced in spite of himself.

"You motherfucker! Damn you, Leon!" The passengers occupying several rows on each side of them looked over. Leon scrunched down in his seat but didn't say a word.

Lisa took several deep breaths, holding each one for the count of five and then repeated the sequence.

"It's a good deal, it's just that…"

She held up her hand to silence him. "Never mind Leon. I saw that tremor go through you. Don't try to pretend. I really make you sick, don't I? Is it just redheads or women in general? Did you like your mother? Ever think a gorgeous pussy might be nicer than some guy's—"

She took in a final breath, "Hey, I'm sorry. I guess I really put you on the spot, didn't I?" She slapped her honey-baked-peanuts wrapper onto the floor. "The thought of going down on me makes you puke, doesn't it? How rude. How very, very rude."

"I'm sorry, Lisa, you really surprised me. I am so glad that you came out to get me and I swear I'd do anything, anything, to pay you back but, it's just that…" His voice faded off to silence. "I guess this means you won't mention me to your friend?"

"No, you asshole, I already mentioned you to my friend and the job is yours. You start Monday. This just means," she held her wrist up at an angle, "that we're going to have to be best friends, not lovers.

"But you're still an asshole," she added.

"I really owe—"

"Yeah, yeah, bear that in mind when you become rich and famous— or straight. Okay?" She turned away and shut her eyes to prevent further conversation.

"I guess there are some friends you can fuck and some you can't." She was mumbling, half in her sleep. "My luck I'd draw the kind that is sickened by the very thought…"

Leon didn't say anything.

Leon started his new job with more than a bit of trepidation. Not only was he an unknown factor in an ongoing show, but his face had decided to puff up and turn seventeen shades of purple in order to illustrate the healing process.

Leon could hear the ill-concealed whispers along with an occasional giggle whenever he turned his back on the cast. Still and all, the uncertainty of the situation probably helped rather than hurt—everyone was a little too unsure of the proceedings to be outright disobedient.

It was just too strange to take for granted.

On the set Leon felt like he was swimming upstream day in and day out—nobody wanted to seem too anxious to obey him lest he prove only to be a flash in the pan. He had not come up the ranks like most A.D.s and no one seemed to know anything about his background.

In spite of the problems, he flat out loved the job. How great it was to be a part of something alive, something in motion rather than directing a static commercial for deodorant soap that could be reshot eighty-seven times until the correct take was solidly in the can. This was live theater and the air was becoming more and more charged as the first performance drew closer.

Leon was also becoming more and more charged; he had no idea if he was doing a good job or if he was a total flop. Things seemed to be coming off on schedule and he felt it seemed to be hot—a good solid show. But his opinion was no doubt colored by his closeness. What would the rest of the town think of it? More to the point, what would the customers think of it?

In all probability it was not the best show ever written; anybody could pick out various bits that were drawn from here or drawn from there—usually Broadway—but the entire production seemed to work and that was all that counted in the end.

The job had consumed him with a fire he hadn't known before. It was not unusual for Leon to be on the set at least an hour before anyone else and to be the last one to strike for the night. It was not a chore—he had fallen in love with theater in general and this show in particular. This was what life was supposed to be like.

Work was a passion that bleached out life's other stains.

Leon had also fallen in love with the director.

John was great. He had control of not only the actors but the crew and the various hangers-on as well. Leon watched him smile and nod at suggestions from the writer's brother-in-law, or some such shit, who wore a director's eyepiece around his neck on a heavy gold chain and was constantly trying to impress some new broad clinging to his side. John never flinched.

He used the same "I understand" smile when he had to tell an actress that she wasn't holding up for the cheap seats or when he had to fire a dancer who was too stoned to work. The amazing thing was that everybody believed in the smile, believed in John. He seemed to really care about whatever he was talking about, and his patience ran to the surreal.

Everyone seemed to respect John no matter what he was doing. The entire cast ran more smoothly than most families and John never once had to raise his voice.

Fucking amazing. The man seemed to embody the second coming of Christ in an Arnold Schwarzenegger body.

More to the point John was extremely pleasant to Leon, going out of his way to teach him pointers and seemed quite surprised by both Leon's zeal as well as his work. "It's nice to work with someone who's not burned out on this business or is constantly trying to undercut me and show the producers he could do a better job. I appreciate it."

Leon felt himself glowing like a school kid.

It was a type of magic the way the individual components wove together to make a tapestry of a show appear. Day by day things clicked into place, turning chaos into order. It was as though an invisible hand reached in and grabbed various individual scenes and twisted them into shape. The whole was emerging in spite of the fragmented appearance of the single acts.

It was a thrill. I'm proud to be a part of this number, Leon thought to himself, as he directed the second unit dancers through a complicated change-over. I can't believe they pay me for this. It sure beats writing sophomoric radio copy for a hemorrhoid pain reliever. Life certainly could be full of changes…

Leon sat in the corner and sipped his Perrier—designer water, Lisa called it—watching the colors swirl about the packed hall. It was just after their first full dress rehearsal and two days before the show opened. The eve of their only day off and everybody was making the most of it at this "wrap" party.

The entire cast and crew was in attendance plus the usual lot of rollers and hangers-on. Leon watched Lisa dance with John. It produced a strange feeling which he finally admitted was jealousy.

He knew he shouldn't go green over a woman—that was John's choice, mother nature had solidified it. In fact, his ire really shouldn't even be directed at Lisa. John had shown up with a gorgeous, young, and, in Leon's opinion, brain dead actress from the show. He was probably only dancing with Lisa out of friendship.

Still, that's what made life interesting—the ability to dream. He looked at his fancy water and debated the damage one drink would do. Hell, he'd have a beer...

A light beer...

"Quite a guy, huh?" Lisa sat down next to Leon, grabbing a glass of champagne from a waiter's tray and downing it in one swallow. "Why do you suppose God does that, Leon? Is it something I've done personally or is it repayment for Eve's screwing around?

"How long do you figure we've got to suffer until the score is even? Bad enough I lose a week every month to cramps, not to mention the blood gushing from my body. Do you suppose I really deserve this extra punishment?"

Leon looked at her not understanding one word of the conversation. Then he glanced at his light beer and thought, "I've done it—one sip of Colorado Kool Aid and I'm loaded. Talk about coming around the entire circle..."

Lisa looked at him strangely. "My God, you really don't know, do you?" She broke out in peals of laughter, causing a number of people to look in their direction. "If I hadn't seen it with my own eyes I wouldn't believe it."

She pointed at the glowing woman John had brought and visibly grimaced. "She's a beard, Leon. You know the expression?" She laughed again, but this time to herself.

"His date's a beard—you know, a screen." She ruffled her hands about her face. "I can't believe I'm really going to do this. Talk about condoning the competition. It seems unbelievable that I'm losing not one but two hunks in one fell swoop...

"You still don't get it?" She watched Leon in wonderment as the news settled in.

"You mean he's... John's gay? And I couldn't tell? No way... Not possible. You're just fucking with my head, aren't you, Lisa?" But still he looked out over the swaying crowds and focused in on John.

Can't be. Not possible that I could work closely with someone and not pick that out. Especially someone I have the hots for. Nope.

"Never con a con man," he said, shaking his head. "Why didn't you pick a more believable lie? Tell me he's a Mormon with four wives, or that he used to be a tennis playing female physician until the operation...

"He's not a homosexual." He faced Lisa dead on and downed the rest of his beer. "I should know. I can spot them a mile away."

"Well, you're about three miles off on this one, killer. I should know. I used to be able to spot them a mile away." She reached up and grabbed another glass of bubbly. "Another skill gone by the wayside. We all get older. You want to bet who's on the mark here? Oh, that's right, you're not into sexual betting with females are you? More's the pity..."

"Still, for the sake of my reputation." She broke quickly away and slid through the crowd until she had John cornered and was whispering in his ear.

Lisa grabbed his hand and pulled him towards Leon's corner. It was like a nightmare in real time. Leon could see his job and his new life going up in smoke, prompted by Lisa's idea of a joke. What could he do to save it? Pretend he didn't know her? That was out of the question...

Pretend she was completely loaded and he didn't know what was going on? Slim, but better than nothing.

He prepared his story in the fleeting seconds while Lisa dragged John towards him. Gotta appear sincere...

"Now tell Leon the truth." Lisa bent John's arm behind his back in a half Nelson.

John shrugged his shoulders as if he had no idea what was going on. His eyes sought out Leon's.

Don't mind me, Lord, I'll just die here quietly. "Never saw her before," Leon said lamely.

"Good to see you Leon." John patted him fraternally on the back. "It's a fine party and you know, it's a pretty damn fine show. We did good. It feels nice to be able to let my hair down and relax for a few minutes."

This was followed by a moment or two of silence. Leon tried to just let the party soak in but he couldn't help but feel self-conscious.

"Oh, oh," Lisa said as an exceptionally hot-looking young guy walked by flashing the three of them a smile. "You'll have to excuse me, my kind of man just walked into my life." She grabbed another glass of wine and rushed into the crowd.

They both watched her go.

"Know something?" John commented. "Mine too..."

John and Leon became an immediate item—and neither cared particularly who else knew about it. Leon felt that his life was on a continuous upward spiral since his soul-cleaning trip to Redding. He liked his job, he liked his relationship, he liked not having to pick up strangers, he even liked living with Lisa—not that they saw much of each other, what with show schedules, but it all came out okay.

In fact there was only one thing that bothered him...

Leon found himself on the floor drinking a beer, scarfing sweet and sour pork from a cardboard container that said "thank you" on the side, and having a heart to heart with Lisa.

"I hear you got an offer to A.D. with Apcar." Lisa squeezed out in between bites.

Leon shrugged.

"I see. Translation reads as follows, 'Yes, I got an offer. No I'm not taking it. I want to stay with John.' "

"It's not like that." Leon reflected for a moment over a bit of rice. "Well, it is like that, but the logic is that I'd just get lost in a big outfit. If I stick where I am I know I'm number two...

"Actually I'm a lot more than just second in command. I get to do pretty much whatever I want and I've learned more in the last year than I have over the other twenty-three put together. Cram course.

"I'll be directing a major show in one year. Want to bet on it?"

"Nope. I gotta feeling that's a pretty safe bet from your side. Now you do remember our deal right? You direct and I get the lead..."

"Lisa, I don't think there's a show worthy of your talents."

She reached over and pinched his cheek in a strong grip between thumb and forefinger. "Then you'll fix it so it is. That's what separates the great directors from the merely good.

"So," she let go of his cheek. "If everything is coming up roses why do you look like death warmed over?

"Oh, no, don't tell me, let me guess. Because our third musketeer isn't here, is he? And furthermore, if I was forced to press my guess I'd have to say he's probably out slumming with some of his biker friends. How am I doing so far?"

"I don't know what the attraction is, Lisa. For a while everything's great and then he gets a wild hair up his ass. Has a few drinks and becomes a different person. He really does.

"It's not like when you or I get loaded: A door opens in John that wasn't there ten minutes ago and he really becomes somebody else. I don't recognize him. His mother wouldn't recognize him."

"Well, he's big time—a lot of stress goes with the territory—maybe it just builds up in John until something has to blow and then he cuts loose for a while and then he's okay again."

"But one day it won't be okay. You've seen him when he gets that way. He immediately wants to do something dangerous. And lately, lately…" Leon faltered.

"Rough trade." Lisa filled in the space after she licked the cardboard clean of red sauce.

"Yeah. That's a good term for it. I really love the man you know, and I want to stand by him and help any way I can, but I can't be around those assholes with their leather outfits, studs, motorcycles and attitudes. Besides that they scarf down any pills they can get their hands on along with God knows what else. Beer and codeine for breakfast, a little Demerol for lunch and then the serious fun kicks in around suppertime.

"You know I really don't have any urge to do smack again, but it doesn't help my self-control to hang around with people who ooze drugs. Besides, there's nothing in the world so boring as being the only straight person in a room full of totally loaded people. Or loaded assholes for that matter."

"Are the flipouts coming more often?"

"Yeah and that ain't all—he's starting to be high at other times. Oh, not so anybody else would notice, but it's pretty obvious to me. It takes him longer to get normal afterwards. I'm covering for him pretty well but sooner or later…

"If I told anyone but you they would think I was crazy, or trying to stab him in the back because he's so fucking normal—suits, ties, sharp young director who went through all the right schools. Who'd figure there's a Dr. Jekyll buried in there somewhere.

"I don't even think he remembers most of the time he does it. It's as if a day or two just vanishes from his life. I get a call from some weird place and he's all apologetic, doesn't remember exactly what happened. In my heart I want to believe him—every time—but it just goes on and on and I don't think it's going to end on a high note."

"How about a shrink?"

"He won't go because he doesn't remember how bad it was, and then next time he does it all over again because he doesn't remember he doesn't remember.

"I really wanted to settle down with him—don't laugh, I know the odds aren't good. Bad enough we're both in the business, then to be gay on top of it. Do you think I'm just dreaming, I mean to be in love and just be with one person?"

"Even animals don't mate for life." Lisa was eyeing the last pot sticker. "I don't want to make jokes, but it's true."

"Swans," Leon said.

"Huh?" She was no longer eyeing the dumpling, she was chewing it.

"Swans do. Even if one dies the other never takes another mate. I think it's the same with mountain lions."

"You're a strange man, Leon, but I guess I still love you." She shrugged. And swallowed.

Three nights later, well after midnight, Leon was roused by a loud and persistent knocking on the door. At first he tried in vain simply to wish it away. Finally he decided John had forgotten his keys again and got up to let him in.

It was John, in a manner of speaking. He was being supported by two of his new biker friends. He was not conscious.

"What the hell's the matter?" Leon was still rubbing the sleep from his eyes.

The larger of the two behemoths spoke up. "Uh, your friend here, he's sick. Better get him to a doctor, okay?" At which point they put John down onto the doorstep like some abandoned orphan in the funny papers and merged into the night.

Lisa was behind Leon by this time. "Help me get him up. We've got to walk him around."

"What's the matter?" She was straining under the load.

"OD'ed, I guess. Come on." After some walking, Lisa commented, "I think we'd better call a doctor. This isn't doing much good."

Leon was holding one of John's wrists in his hands. "No need, he's finally found his ultimate rush."

"Huh?"

Leon turned to face her. "He's dead." Lisa collapsed onto the floor.

LISA

Carol was trying to keep her mind on the book she was reading but there was so bloody much to absorb and it could hardly be called exciting reading. Each time she thought she had grasped a section more ideas seemed to leap out of the pages. It was a lot like going back to college and majoring in gambling—plus she was trying to earn her keep by coming up with some ideas for Nick. Ideas that hadn't been done in the fifty-year history of Las Vegas.

About fourteen hours a day, she figured. And worth every second of it…

The door to the office opened and she jumped involuntarily—it was rare that anyone got by the outer protective layers of receptionists and secretaries without at least one formal announcement.

"Enjoying your reading?" It was Taylor and he wore the small smile he seemed to be always armed with, as if he was enjoying a private joke on life in general.

He indicated the thick red volume of *Casino Management* with a tilt of his head as he sat in one of the leather chairs.

"Well, it's certainly not *Valley of the Dolls,*" she said. Damn, I wish he didn't affect me that way, she thought. Everything I say comes out sounding inane…

"Ah, but what is? On the other hand, you seem to be making considerable headway. Tell me, Carol, what conclusions have you drawn from studying the glitter world?"

She set the 542-page book on her desk. "It all comes down to angles and percentages. Chance really never becomes a factor. Chance never has a chance."

He nodded his head in agreement, "Or at the most to a very limited degree. Sort of an oxymoron-controlled chance. But you're right, in fact, you're right about a number of things. And I'm wrong…

"About you making it here." He started and Carol realized just how piercing a set of eyes could be.

"About your first report…"

"Mr. Salerio found it satisfactory?" She felt herself biting down on her lip. A lot of thought and a lot of work had gone into that document, yet it seemed like such a small output for six weeks of work. Where had the time gone?

"Satisfactory? A good choice of terms—he found it so 'satisfactory' he's decided to implement the part about using experts to attract and please our foreign guests. In fact, it's now my job to hire a number of consultants and draw up program guidelines. Immediately."

"Sorry," Carol smiled as she said it. I'm not in the least…"

"I bet," he laughed lightly.

Then, for the second time in a matter of minutes, the door burst open with an unannounced visitor.

"Oh, God, you've got to help, Carol. You're my only chance." Lisa put her elbows on the edge of Carol's desk, buried her face in her hands, and burst into tears.

"Lisa, what's wrong?" Carol rose to her feet and reached out for her friend.

Lisa put her hands on the flat surface and raised her head slowly. "Fired. Just because of…" Fresh sobs broke through and she stuttered something about suicide and re-buried her face.

Fresh tears broke from the edges of her hand and ran down her face in a small stream.

Taylor rose from her chair, "Listen, I'll just let you two talk…"

Lisa turned as if suddenly aware of another presence in the room. "Taylor!" She brightened for a split second. "Please stay, please, maybe you can help."

Taylor looked at Carol, "She seems to be a little upset."

She offered, "Maybe you should stay." She half hoped he would leave and ease her embarrassment, but Taylor sat back down in his chair. The half smile had reappeared.

"That queen came in… and years went right down the slats… Nobody gives a fuck about what I had to—And for no reason…"

Carol was aware that the door had not shut completely and that bodies from the outer office seemed to be drawn to the wailing.

"Lisa, calm down and explain what happened. We can't understand you if you don't get hold of yourself."

"I am explaining," Lisa wailed. "Everything." She quieted down a bit and peered out from between her fingers to see if Taylor was still in the room. "You could fix it," she sniffed, "they'd have to listen to you."

"Lisa," Carol said. "We can't ask…"

"No, Carol, *you* can't ask. I have to. I don't have your degrees or your smarts… I don't have a fall back. *This* is my life. This is my shot and I'm not going to lose it because of some… some bent-wristed cocksucker."

"Lisa!" Carol lifted her hand to her mouth but Taylor just smiled.

"I'm just telling the truth! This bitch walks onto the set, our set, and just takes one look, and it was like *Star Wars*—these lasers shot out of the creature's eyes and I was just meat.

"Red meat. Hamburger."

"But what actually happened, Lisa?"

She rung her hands together, "Please Carol, I've got to tell it in order to get it all straight."

"Why did he can you, Lisa?" Taylor cut into the interchange.

"That's the worst part! It's not my dancing…even that, that *thing* had to admit I can dance." She broke into tears again.

"Short. I'm going to kill myself."

"What?"

"SHORT! She said I was too short! It's not my fault that I'm not six foot seven like some of those monsters. What can I do about that? I spend my life in fucking dance lessons and then get shafted because the rest of those androids' parents screwed the Los Angeles Lakers…"

"That must be a little hard to take, but its all part—"

"No. NO. It's not part of anything. I'm good, I've got talent, people watch me, even in the line. Why should I lose my one shot at opening for a super star because I'm not some male whore's idea of the golden girl?"

"He's not Wayne Newton, Lisa." Carol couldn't tell if Taylor was kidding with her or not.

"Oh, no, Johnny Star is better. Much better for me… Every time he appears half of Hollywood flies out with him. There will be more producers and directors in that audience that there would be if we billed the second coming of Jesus."

Taylor shrugged. "There's some truth in that, but how many people do you figure got their start because some drunken producer saw them in the line at—"

"I wasn't *in the line*, I was the lead, and I don't care how many other people made it that way. It was my shot. And now it's gone." She was sobbing intermittently.

"Lisa, I know it's too bad but I don't know what I—" Carol started.

"You could let me in to talk to Mr. Salerio," Lisa said, brightening. "I know if I could just explain directly to him… He would put it right…"

A rather disheartening scenario was unfolding in Carol's mind's eye that included a pleading Lisa, much running eye liner, and Carol's job ending before it really began.

"Lisa, I can't, I mean that's not the way to go here. We've got to figure out an angle, a percentage." She felt, rather than saw, Taylor smile from across the room.

"Come on! Carol, you're my best friend. If I can't ask you for one little favor that can make the difference whether I live or die, who can I go to? What can I do? If you can't help, I'll go to a fucking lawyer! Let them explain their idea of a master race in court."

The proverbial rock and the hard place, Carol thought. If I do, it'll be my last act at The DollHouse. If I don't, I'm not even being a friend.

Suddenly she was conscious of Taylor's watchful stare. She felt her face coloring and silence was becoming uncomfortable. Well, it simply came down to where her values really lay. What was important here? An obvious violation of the trust placed in her by Mr. Salerio or the simple slashing of her friend's wrists from a safe distance?

Hand me the razor, Carol thought, and let's get the bloodletting over with.

And then a blot came from heaven. "I'll make you a deal," Taylor said. "You go home and relax for the rest of the afternoon and I'll go down and check the situation out. But you've got to go home and not bother anybody until I call you."

"You'd do that? For me?" Lisa seemed genuinely surprised at the suggestion.

"Only if you keep your side of the bargain. Don't call Carol, don't call your lawyers, just relax and I'll call you."

"In an hour," Lisa pushed. "You'll call in an hour."

"Make it two," he sighed.

"Okay. You win." Lisa smiled, wiped her eyes, further smearing her makeup, and left.

"Don't leave town," Taylor told Carol, and then he too walked out the door.

Carol tried to go back to her reading but her eyes kept straying to the wall clock where the second hand seemed to be moving way too slowly...

Taylor knocked discreetly and then let himself into the office. He sat down slowly. "Basically," he said, "your friend has a very good handle on the situation."

"You mean she got fired from her job because she's not six feet tall, in spite of the fact that she is very good at what she does?"

"Life isn't always fair, and this really isn't life. And the contract we signed with the Star organization gives them complete creative control; the final cut, as they say in Hollywood."

"Unfortunately, his director has every right in the world to adjust the cast as he sees fit. For whatever reason.

"Lisa really doesn't have any legal recourse, although, of course, she could go to an attorney and cause some minor waves. In the end she would probably be overruled. Nevada courts rarely rule against major casinos and, as they also say in Hollywood, she would probably never work in this town again."

Carol shook her head, "Well, I appreciate your efforts. I guess it's my turn to be the bearer of ill tidings. I'll call and see if I can smooth the waters any." She picked up her phone and punched in the first digits of the number.

"It's too bad Lisa can't do anything else..." Carol hesitated as Taylor spoke very deliberately.

"Like what?"

"Well, oddly enough there was a rather ugly incident earlier this morning involving one of Johnny's three backup singers. Suffice to say she was released on an O.R. bond with the stipulation that she return to Los Angeles on the next flight.

"The union is sending over several possible replacements as we speak."

Carol took her hand away from the dial. "Lisa sings like a skinny Linda Ronstadt on a good day. Lisa sings like a female Bruce Springsteen."

Taylor laughed. "We're only talking about 'shabooms' and 'la la la's' here, not creating another Elvis Presley. Is she a quick study?"

"Would I lie to you?" Carol asked.

Taylor looked directly into your eyes, "I don't know, would you?"

"You're about to make a friend for life," Carol resumed her dialing.

"There is one small condition." Taylor said flatly.

"You know I'd really like to finish dialing here... What condition?"

"That unfortunate incident I referred to earlier in this conversation... It also involved Mr. Star and a quantity of controlled substance. In fact, only due to the intervention of our legal staff, and possibly through a personal favor or two, was he not also subject to the legal ramifications of the state of Nevada."

"So?"

"So, I'm already fielding nasty questions from the press and I don't want any further problems with Mr. Star. To summarize, I want Lisa to keep an eye on the situation and keep me apprised of anything I should know."

"I want to be certain I understand what's going on." Carol was still holding the receiver, "these services are in return for her getting the position."

"In return for my strong recommendation that she get the position. She better be able to carry a tune."

"Rat?" Lisa shouted. "You want me to be a snitch?"

Carol glanced up to make sure the door was closed for this performance. "Lisa, Taylor just got you a shot at backing up one of the top stars in this country. I would think you'd be a little more thankful."

"Well, actually it is pretty hip... and I guess getting tight with Johnny would be part of my duties, right?"

"As tight as you want," Taylor said, "as long as you keep him out of trouble and let me know what's going on. You understand that?"

"Sure, sure," Lisa said with a distant look on her face, "I can handle that." She got up, "I've got to get home and practice. Shit! I hope Leon's around, and I don't even know if the Kurzweil's programmed, or if I—"

"Just be back here at nine A.M. tomorrow, right?"

"Uh-huh," Lisa drifted out.

Carol watched the door shut with a feeling of impending doom that she could not entirely place.

"That was really nice of you. I think." She looked at Taylor and spoke impulsively. "Did you really do that for Lisa?"

"I'd like to think it was a no loss situation. She won, I won, hopefully Johnny won, and most importantly, maybe you won."

Carol sighed, "I hope you're right. I just have this premonition. Do you remember what Khrushchev said when Nixon was elected president?"

Taylor shook his head.

"He said it was like sending a goat to guard the cabbage."

Lisa felt alive, on, buzzing at the morning call. Everybody seemed to be a bit in awe of her Phoenix-like reappearance in the place of the now disgraced backup vocalist.

She felt an undercurrent of dissension and emotion running throughout the cast. No one here thinks I can sing, she realized, and felt a black hole open in front of her.

Can I really?

In one quick moment she felt a layer of confidence disappear. My God, can I even stay on key? Maybe if I just mouth the words... But as soon as that thought appeared she realized the futility of the situation.

Everybody here is waiting to see how I do. It feels like glass is breaking under my feet.

A strange silence fell over the entire cast as Lisa took her place in front of the microphone. She smiled sweetly at the other two members of the trio. They looked through her.

So that's how it is...

Thank you, ladies, I hope you both choke on a chicken bone. And she felt her body tighten up as if she had grabbed an electric wire. They're all waiting for me to fall on my ass...

And suddenly she realized she was daydreaming. The music director was waving his hand for the band to stop.

"Excuse me, dear." He was pointing his forefinger at Lisa. "You want to join us here while we rehearse, or are you busy elsewhere?"

"Sorry," she stumbled. "I was, ah..."

"We don't really want the *Cosmopolitan* version, okay? Just follow the cues."

"Right." I'm dying here. Someone in the back of the line giggled and the tallest of her fellow backup singers laughed out loud.

The music began again and once again Lisa wallowed, attempting to follow the complicated melody and once again she was off a full beat. The director put his hands over his eyes and grimaced. He looked up towards the ceiling, "Why me?" The other two trio members elbowed each other and bit their lips in an obvious effort to keep from laughing.

It's not my fault your asshole friend got tossed out, Lisa thought. Give *me* a break.

She looked up at one of the gloating singers, and then, strictly on impulse, kicked her pointed toe into the women's instep. The victim gasped and leaned over to grab her pained foot.

Lisa turned so that her body blocked the director's view. She reached inside and slipped her hand under the sequined costume. The taller woman jerked to a caricature of attention as Lisa tightened down on her nipple.

"Listen, Twiggy," she hissed, "one more crack out of you and we'll reverse your sex change operation right here. Get my drift bitch?" She bore down harder, concentrating on her grip and was rewarded with a sharp intake of breath from her opponent.

Lisa released her hold and pivoted towards the director. "Sorry, my friend here just explained it to me. I'll get it this time, no problem."

He smiled and Lisa felt the glow come back.

And it will be...

The rest of the rehearsal was on... Tight. Lisa knew she had filled in and pulled it off to everyone's surprise. She felt she was not only on key, she caught every cue, and her voice seemed to be at least inoffensive.

By the end of the session even the big bitch she had tormented gave her a thumbs up and a small smile. Life was okay...

Lisa wiped the sweat from her forehead and started off the stage, caught up in the general milieu. I just want to go home and crash, maybe a Scotch, maybe a double Scotch and soda, and then the latest copy of *People* and...

"Pretty slick." A voice cut in on her mental picture. "You've got quite a set of pipes for a dancer."

Lisa turned to see the one and only Johnny Star smiling and falling in step with her. She was irritated by the sudden attention.

"Oh? I didn't think you noticed what the peons were doing. But thank you." She turned away.

He grabbed her elbow. "You'd be surprised at the things I notice. I noticed your dancing and I noticed when you left and I noticed when you put the move on Marie's boob."

"Actually that may have been the highlight of the show. If I could figure out how to incorporate that into the act, we'd leave it. I've never seen her back off on anybody, or, for that matter, sing so well."

"Maybe she just needed a little incentive."

"Yeah, maybe you're right." Without breaking stride he smiled at a buxom woman in a three-foot hat who put her hand on his shoulder.

"You were wonderful, Mr. Star."

"Thank you, dear." He gracefully slid the hand off and turned back to Lisa. The other woman shrugged good naturedly and drifted off.

"What do you say you and I do up the town tonight?"

"What do you say you and Miss 'oh, you're so great Mr. Star' do up the town tonight? You probably wouldn't even have to pop for dinner. You could just head straight to her lovely garden apartment."

"Whooh. You've really got an attitude on you." He touched her and jerked his hand back as if burned.

Lisa gave him her best drop dead look.

"Okay, okay, the fact is I could have any broad in this show if I snapped my fingers." He did just that to add emphasis to the statement.

"Wanna bet?" Lisa turned and walked away… Her heart beating…

Out of the corner of her eyes she noticed two burly men starting from the wings towards her and Johnny.

"Ah, your personalized dating service, I presume? Is this how you meet most of the people you associate with?"

Johnny waved them back. "There are a lot of nuts in this business. Everybody has a bodyguard or two, it's just business and I don't want to go home with a groupie tonight. Professional or otherwise…"

"Why not? You're not going home with me, I flat out guarantee it."

"Maybe I'd prefer to go out with someone like you than go home with someone like that. Just to have a good time. No pressure, I promise. Nothing but a good time."

"Listen, Mr. Star…"

"My friends call me Johnny."

"Like I was saying, Mr. Star," she watched him grimace. "Okay, Johnny, I'd destroy a lobster tail with you but I'm just too beat. It's been a really long day…"

"That's true. It has been a long day," he stepped over to a prop room and opened the door. "Come here a minute."

When she hesitated, he impatiently waved her inward. He shut the door behind them. "I can fix that, for both of us."

He took a small brightly colored metal cylinder from his pocket, turned a knob on the side, tipped the unit over and handed it to Lisa.

"The silver bullet at your service. Do a hit."

Lisa took the small tube and looked at it for a long second. Why not? she thought. I'm supposed to keep an eye on him. She held it up to her nose and inhaled deeply.

The chemical stung her nostrils and produced an immediate rush of crystal joy.

"Do another," he said, "one for each slot." Johnny then duplicated the procedure and opened the door for Lisa.

"All better?" he asked.

"A step in the right direction, that's for sure, but I'm not at all hungry anymore."

He laughed, "We'll eat later, let's go do it right!"

The hot, dry desert air hit Lisa full in the face as they ran out into the night barely missing stumbling over the Sahara's doorman. Johnny took both her hands and swung her around and then collapsed on his rear end, dragging Lisa down on top of him.

The doorman smiled and helped them back to their feet. He gave no indication of anything out of the ordinary as he brushed off the back of Johnny's coat.

"And you call yourself a dancer. Look at what you just did. No coordination whatsoever. I'd be ashamed if I were you."

"You're the one who should be ashamed. I'm half your size and you just threw me on the ground without a thread of mercy."

"Mercy, mercy me," Johnny sang. "Come on, beautiful, let's go out and find something exciting. I'm tired of lame lounge acts. Bring on the bullfights."

When the valet brought the car around Johnny started to climb in the driver's side but Lisa put a restraining arm out. "Uh-uh, I'll drive. You've had three times as much to drink as I have."

He started to protest but she cut him short, "Don't be a macho asshole, okay? I like you and I don't want to have to call your mother and introduce myself, 'Well, hi Mrs. Star, you don't know me, but your son is dead...' Know what I mean?"

Johnny slid across the seat and then reached over to kiss her cheek as she sat behind the wheel. "Wow, that's pretty cool. Most people wouldn't give a shit if I got in trouble, they just want to get whatever they can out of me."

"Thanks," he was quiet for a minute as Lisa headed the BMW out of the parking lot. "This kraut mobile was the only thing we could rent in this town. When you come to L.A. I'll take you for a real ride on Mullholland in my vette. Roooom! Roooom! Screech!" He added sound effects to Lisa's entrance on the street.

"God, I'm having a ball with you, let's do a bump." He took the bullet out of his pocket and held it up to his nose.

"Be careful, will you." Lisa looked in the mirror. "I know you're a headliner and all, but that shit's still illegal and it would make some patrolman's day to bust you."

"Yes, mother." He placed the unit at waist level and began smacking it against the dashboard. "The little savage is plugged up anyway."

He unscrewed the cap and peered inside. "Still loaded but it won't fire." He poured a small amount out onto the back of his hand where it quickly fell onto the floor with the motion of the car.

"Shit!" He peered down at the darkened floor. "Pull over, Lisa, right here by the curb."

Lisa watched him out of the corner of her eye as she steered to the side of the street. "Hey, don't do anything stupid. We can wait a few minutes. Okay?"

"Naw, don't worry, ain't nobody gonna notice anything. This is Las-fucking-Vegas. People screw in the streets here, the only crime is not having money, and only then if you get caught."

Lisa looked unconvinced. He reached over and hit her in the arm muscle. "Come on, I listened to you about the driving thing. Believe me, it'll be no problem. We'll just do a quick line on the glove compartment and then we can split."

He unsnapped the glove compartment door and spilled a pile of powder onto it. "Ah ha! Here's the problem, the patient has clots." He got out a small pen knife and began chopping.

"This is weird." Lisa flicked her gaze back and forth between the rear and the side mirrors. "Shit, here come some people."

A laughing couple materialized by the passenger door and then strolled onward arm in arm. Johnny nonchalantly covered the coke with his hand and smiled at the couple.

"Ah, they didn't even look at us. What did I tell you? Relax, go with the flow here. Roll up a dollar bill and lean over."

Lisa took a final look in the mirrors and then did as she was instructed. Johnny ran his hand through her hair as she bent over the lid.

"That's what I like to see in a date," he cracked. "The top of her head."

Lisa snorted outward through the makeshift straw scattering one of the lines all over the plastic door.

"A joke. A little joke. A bad little joke." He pleaded, "Don't spill anymore. I'll never say it again."

Lisa turned her head sideways to glare up at him. "I'm sorry, it slipped out..."

"Actually, that's pretty funny. But, Johnny, I wouldn't count your chickens, know what I mean?"

He nodded and began scraping the coke back into some sort of line. Shiny pieces clung to the black plastic of the glove compartment. "One quick intake of breath and we'll be on our way."

He stretched his neck until the dollar bill touched the middle of the next line of coke. "Shit," he mumbled and twisted his head sideways, pushed it further into the glove compartment and twisted it back straight.

Partially straight.

"...hit " he mumbled.

"What? Hurry up, let's go." Lisa was looking around the street.

"Stuck." Johnny twisted his body towards the steering wheel, put his hands under his chin and pushed. "Ouch!...fuck...it..."

"Quit screwing around, let's go."

"Uck!!" He yelled. "Hym stuck..."

"Not funny," Lisa hissed and yanked backwards on his shoulder.

He screamed.

"My God, you're stuck! Your head is stuck in the glove compartment. I don't believe this. This is happening to someone else. I'm parked on the strip with a man whose head is stuck in the glove compartment of a BMW."

"Come on." He twisted again and bit his tongue. "Ohhh, fuck... This hurts. Ow, my ose is aught. Elp!"

He tried to force himself loose one more time and blood began to drip from one nostril. "Oh noooo..." He snorted loudly to clear the blood and a fine red spray flew onto the car seat. "Hesus..."

Suddenly the situation was too much for Lisa. She burst into laughter and then covered her mouth, still laughing through her hand. "I'm sorry," she slapped Johnny on the shoulder, "I'm really sorry but this... this is pretty outrageous.

"You should see yourself. Oh God, if I had a camera right now I'd own the *National Enquirer*.

"And you. I'd own you forever. You'd be cleaning my apartment until you were eighty-five. Oh my God, this is really funny. I think this is the best date I've ever been on.

"How about you? You having a good time?" She slapped him again. "... itch..."

"What was that?" she leaned her head close to his mouth. "That had better not have been a naughty word. If you call me names I'll take out my mad dollar and call a taxi... I'll go home..."

"No, no, no..."

"Ah, that's better. Now I want to hear you laugh. Right now, or I won't help you."

"Ha ha..."

"No, no it's got to be a real laugh." She waited expectantly. Have I pushed it too far?

Suddenly Johnny began shaking all over. "Pretty funny." He snorted, "Please get me out."

"Okay. Okay. Hold still." She leaned over him and slid her left hand under his chin and grabbed the top of the compartment.

"Hold on, I'm going to pry it open." She took a deep breath.

And jumped when a loud knocking came at the glass. Lisa blinked directly into the beam of a powerful flashlight.

"Roll this window down, lady, and keep your hands in plain sight. Do it now."

Lisa peered out trying to see the face behind the light. The beam dipped down to highlight Johnny. He groaned.

"Roll it down now or I'll break it."

Lisa hit the switch and the window whined down.

"Open your door carefully and step out of the car. Both of you. Keep your hands in view at all times."

"I'm afraid we can't do that."

One of the cops' hands fell to his side, touching his holster. "I'm not going to ask you twice, ma'am." He looked down, "What's in the glove compartment?"

"Officer, my friend's head is in the glove compartment. He'd love to take your advice. But he can't. His-head-is-stuck-in-the-glove-compartment."

"Why?" The cop looked back at Johnny. "Why was his head in the glove compartment before it got stuck?"

Inspiration. God, I don't ask for much, just give me a little boost here. Help me... "It's sort of a long story. He lost... See, he had this, this thing... And it fell into the glove compartment." This isn't working, oh, my God, this is working badly...

The cop unclipped a walkie talkie and pointed the antenna at Lisa like a weapon. "I'm going to call for backup now and I don't want either of you to move a muscle. You understand what I'm saying?"

"Wait," Lisa said, "give me one second to talk to you, okay? If you press that button we're both going to regret it... One, little second..."

He looked uncertain.

Johnny groaned.

"Okay, you can step over here for a few seconds but this better not be one of those 'Do you know who this is' chats because I don't give a fuck who this is. You still want to talk with me.?"

Lisa bit her lip and nodded.

"Okay, Mr. Star, I want you to turn your head as soon as I pull these apart. On three..."

Johnny rubbed his nose and reached out his hand. "Pleased to meet you officer Connors... Boy am I pleased... Ohhh, sniff."

The cop reached over and picked up the rolled up dollar bill and dropped it into the gutter. "You should have the rental car people clean up that glove compartment. It's a shame what people will leave in these cars."

He wiped a trace of crystals off the surface and shut the glove compartment door.

"Right away, officer. Right away..."

They both watched the cop's back as he walked away. "I owe you. Babe, do I owe you one. I'm on probation in California from a rather tawdry little episode and the judge would like nothing better than to wipe my nose in something like this.

"No pun intended. What did that cost us?"

"Four front row seats for opening night and a long hard look at my boobs."

"Could've been worse, could've been worse," he sighed. "You're a doll, Lisa, you really took control there... I was sort of at loose ends, but, man, you handled it like a pro.

"You're not just a knockout, you've got brains."

Lisa looked over at him and smiled. "Bingo, that's the best thing you could have said." She slid the car into gear. 'Let's go see if my roommates are home."

Lisa shook her head and thought, I wish this rehearsal was over. I'm going to sleep for a month. Marie, the woman she had terrorized a few days earlier, gave her a gentle shove to remind her of a cue.

She smiled her thanks and began singing. It's amazing the way people warm up to you when they realize you're sleeping with the star of the show...

She felt something on her leg and glanced down. A man in a DollHouse blazer was tapping her ankle gently. "Phone," he yelled up to her, "over there!"

Lisa jumped off the stage and fixed the messenger with an evil stare. "This better be important." Johnny waved at her discreetly as she left the stage.

"Yeah?" She yelled into the phone in order to be heard over the production.

"So?" A voice said.

"Who the fuck is this? I'm busy."

"It's Taylor, Lisa. How's it going?"

Suddenly she was on guard. What could he have heard? She knew the power of the DollHouse reached far and wide.

"It's going just fine. Just fine."

"I've been waiting for a report from you. Just a friendly phone call. Reach out and touch someone. Tell me how Johnny is doing, how the show is coming along. Why haven't I heard from you?"

"Because everything's going great, that's why. There was nothing to tell you."

"Uh-huh. And Johnny. He staying out of trouble?"

"Trouble? Johnny?"

"Don't gimme shit, Lisa. How's it going?"

"The man is an angel. We haven't had a single problem. Don't worry, Taylor. Go home and read a good spy novel, get involved in somebody else's plots for a while. I'll let you know anything you need to know."

"Okay, Lisa, I just wanted to thank you for taking your duties so seriously. You and the Star are quite the item around town. I guess you'd know if there was a problem."

"Right. And I'd tell you."

"Don't forget where your loyalties lie. Stars come and stars go."

"'Bye, Taylor." Lisa hung up the phone.

Prick. She thought. You prick.

Carol took in the entire scene in one glance. Half-filled glasses glowed with different hues of booze, glass water pipes lay haphazardly strewn about the landscape, the penthouse interior had been transformed into a glass menagerie.

The stereo was blasting so loudly she felt disoriented by the wall of sound. Someone pressed a glass of champagne into her hand and shut the door behind her. The swirl of pulsating colors seemed to suck her inward like a melodious whirlpool.

A few people acknowledged her presence, but most seemed too preoccupied with their own activities to notice much of anything else. A dozen or so members of John Star's band were scattered about the landscape smoking joints or sipping drinks, or both, but the Star didn't seem to be in evidence.

Carol experienced a sudden desire to turn and flee the pandemonium, but a management appearance was mandatory. She swallowed half the glass of bubbly and wrinkled her nose at the taste. Damn, I know that's Dom Perignon but it still tastes like grapefruit juice to me. She swallowed the remainder and looked around for a place to put her empty glass.

"Hey, Princess, over here." Lisa waved her hand in a "join us" gesture. "I don't believe it, the ice queen is actually here. Want a hit?" She held a glass plate up to Carol's face. The gold logo of the Doll House was partially visible through a thin white frost-like layer of crystals. The remainder of the plate was covered with a strangely beautiful growth of inch-long snow trees.

Each individual crystal formation grew straight upwards for a half an inch or so and then branched off into tiny white shoots, ending in a microscopic cluster of snow leaves.

Carol drew back as the plate was shoved into her face. "Sweets for the sweet. Have some ice Carol." She realized Lisa was staring blankly; her eyes seemed to be blackholes devoid of color. She was not blinking.

Lisa seemed transformed into some sort of China doll; her expression remained frozen in place as she withdrew the plate. She picked up a single-edged razor blade and scraped it across the glass plate heaping the white crystals into a bulldozed pile.

"Don't drop the diamonds, Lisa." A hand adorned with a ring on every finger appeared out of nowhere and steadied the edge of the plate.

Sparkling gold filled Carol's vision. How can anyone lift their hand with so much extra weight?

"Star," the owner said, "like the ring?" And he lifted a huge, black, starred opal into Carol's face. "Why don't you introduce your cousin to me, Lisa. I think she's lost her voice."

Lisa lifted a blade's worth of softly crushed white velvet and dumped it into the glass bowl of a small water pipe. "Johnny Star, meet the ice queen. And vice-versa."

She held the small pipe up to eye level and gazed at the compact crystalline mass, "And keep your hands off the goods, he's mine." She placed the stem of the pipe in her mouth and then raised a miniature butane torch until the outer pinpoint of the blue white flame kissed the bowl.

Immediately the contents began to melt down to a clear liquid and then vaporized into a cloud of white smoke. Lisa inhaled to the depths of her soul, making the pipe water bubble and dance for a solid ten seconds. She shut her eyes, leaned back and shuddered as a spasm of pure pleasure passed through her being.

"Oh, really," Carol felt herself saying, "in that case you must be married." She put out her hand and shook the offering just in time to see Lisa choke and reluctantly spit out a cloud of white smoke.

The man laughed loudly. "I can see where you get your nickname from, sweetheart. Real style." He reached over and took the glass pipe from Lisa's hand. "And you, dear, are shaking like the proverbial leaf. Easy does it now."

Johnny Star set the waterpipe down and scraped the remainder of the white frost into the bowl, watching as it melted down onto the steel screen that lay in the bottom. "So pretty," he said softly.

In spite of her revulsion, Carol felt mesmerized by the detailed process. "That's crack, isn't it?" She watched as Mr. Star picked up the bare plate and scrutinized the now empty surface.

"Crack? Crack? What peasants you take us for. No, my innocent friend, crack is for misguided ghetto children to spend their ill gotten gains on. No one with any class fools with baking soda. This," he gestured towards the pipe, "is a far better thing we do. Free base. Pure and perfect. Base."

"Base?" Carol repeated blankly.

"Why don't you lose the conversation, Johnny, and do us up another hit or two." Lisa was now holding her hand horizontally in front of her and staring at it intently – it was shaking badly. "Steady as a rock," she said.

"Okay, princess, watch Mr. Wizard now and maybe you can learn a trick or two, if you'll excuse the expression." He reached in the pocket of his designer jeans and withdrew a small glass vial. A quick shake and a small pile of cream white powder spilled out onto the tip of his finger.

"Flake, live and direct from downtown La Paz, the real stuff, Peruvian marching powder." He lifted his finger to one nostril and inhaled. "Buzzzz, now the lesson begins, first a touch of flour," and he dumped a pile of the cocaine into a small jar. "And then we add the water, and now the oil. Or in this case, the petroleum ether. Shake until dissolved, and voila!" He held the closed jar of clear liquid up to Carol's face. "We have ignition. Now for the final secret ingredient and the recipe is complete."

"Go for it, Julia!" someone yelled from amid the general chaos. Johnny waved a hand in recognition and opened yet another bottle of clear liquid. He angled an eye dropper to the surface and drew some of the chemical carefully up.

Suddenly waves of odor from the dropper assailed Carol and she jerked back as if she had been slapped. "Oh, yes, I forgot to tell you," Johnny said as he squeezed the rubber bulb carefully, "don't inhale, it's ammonium hydroxide." He looked up at Carol. "Smarts, doesn't it?"

Carol nodded and wiped the tears from her eyes. In the jar clouds of milk seemed to explode downward as each drop struck the surface. Several people jostled Carol as they crowded around to watch the demonstration. Someone turned the stereo down and Carol sensed the woman next to her suck in her breath and hold it.

"You see," Johnny shook the jar violently. "Pay attention, princess, this is the big scene here, the chemical acts as a catalyst separating the pure cocaine from the base of hydrochloride. As sort of a side benefit any and all cuts are also dropped out along the way. Ahhh, here we go, right on schedule."

Inside the all-important jar the contents divided up into two neat layers – one clear and one cloudy. "You see," he continued his lecture in a louder voice to include the ever-growing crowd, "the pure cocaine is now held in this top layer, which I carefully, oh so carefully, draw off with the aforementioned dropper…"

"Oh Jesus, hurry it up." Lisa turned to face Carol and took a large swig from a bottle of Stolya. "He never could resist an audience – any audience."

"Patience, sweetheart, all good things in life require patience." He turned several of his rings around so the large cut stones did not interfere with the operation.

"Light getting in your eyes?" Carol inquired sweetly. Johnny grinned but did not look up. Drops of liquid fell out of the dropper onto the surface of the glass plate. Carol watched as each drop turned suddenly opaque and then seemed to freeze instantly. As if ordered by some unseen force, tiny crystal branches sprung out from each drop and shot upward. Carol felt the world around her stop in anticipation; the tension in the room was almost sexual.

"Poetry, sheer fucking poetry." Johnny lifted the plate to his mouth and blew softly to speed up the metamorphosis. "Come to papa now…"

"Use the fucking hair dryer. Let's get this show on the road." Lisa took another mouthful of booze and picked up the torch and a lighter. "Come on, Carol, you must carry one with you – a hair dryer, I mean, or does the natural windblown look just come naturally for you?" She lit the torch, "I guess that's a double natural, huh? Well, if anybody would know the rules it'd be you, wouldn't it, princess? How would they say that at Vassar?"

Lisa made a grab towards the plate and Johnny pulled it quickly out of range. "Remember what I said about patience and virtue…"

Lisa grinned wolfishly and shoved the hissing torch at Johnny's face. He leapt backwards and his eyes widened with the heat of the near miss. "Scrape me off a hit, Star, or I'll fry your fucking ass, starting at the wrong end."

"You know, I think she would, too." But he picked up the razor and began scraping a swath down the middle of the virgin-white forest.

The noise of the metal against the glass snapped Carol back into the present. She set her now-empty glass down and walked into the hall. "Don't let the door hit you in the ass," she turned to face the crowded room, "the line forms behind me, and don't shove."

Carol was dreaming. She was living with a man and knew she was madly in love, the only problem was that she couldn't see his face… And then she was sitting upright in her own satin sheets and daylight was streaming in the window. And there was someone knocking on the bedroom door.

It was so real, so there—then it was gone.

"Can I come in?" Without waiting for an answer, a very sheepish-looking Lisa opened the door and sat on the edge of the bed. She blew out a breath and several dank strands of hair lifted off her face only to fall back down a second later.

"Shit," she sighed and manually tucked the offensive hair behind her left ear. "It's going to be one of those days, I can feel it." She turned her head towards the window and grimaced. "Shut those things, please," she groaned as Carol reached up and drew the drapes. "Why does God do this to me?"

"Somehow I don't think the fault is all God's." Carol took in the bloodshot eyes and the sweat-stained night shirt. "You look terrible, Lisa."

"Yeah, rub it in why don't you? How do you think it looks from this side? I haven't even shut my eyes in the last forty-eight hours. That stupid party is still going on and then Johnny wanted to —" She looked up sharply at Carol, "Well that's not really important. Jesus, my throat is so sore I can hardly talk. I wish I had kept a line or two to get straight with but that son of a bitch split just after —

"Ah, what I'm trying to do here is—" She stopped and took a deep breath. "If I could only get some sleep. Look," she grabbed Carol's hand and put it on her own chest.

"My God," Carol grabbed her hand back involuntarily. "Your heart is beating a mile a minute."

"Tell me something I don't already know. Listen, honey, I came here because, frankly, I don't remember too much about last night and, ah, a few people sort of inferred I, ah, sort of possibly insulted you a bit. You know?"

"Uh-huh."

"Ah, fuck it, I'm sorry. When I get too much demon rum in me, I get really bitchy." Lisa shook her head, "I don't know why I take it out on people close to me. I really love you, you know that? I really do…"

"Oh?"

"Oh, please, don't kid around. You know what I mean, you're like, ah, ah…"

"If the next words out of your mouth are 'older sister' you can find yourself another roommate."

"God, I'm sorry. I must have put away a fifth and a half of vodka last night. I don't even have any idea what I said to you. I barely know what I did." She looked away with a start. "Scratch that, I do remember some of what I did." Lisa stuck her tongue out and grabbed it with her hand.

"Yeech." She scraped an unseen substance from her tongue. "I do remember some of what I did."

"Lisa, can I ask you a personal question?"

"Carol, honey, you could ask me to… well, you could ask me damn near anything and I'd do it for you."

"Why do you drink so much if you lose control? Especially if you don't enjoy it?"

"Why do I drink that much? I drink like that to take the edge off the coke. I drink like that to be able to talk. I drink like that to be able to stop talking. I drink like that to be able to stop thinking. I drink like that to be able to sleep. I drink like that to be able to drink like that." She let out another long sigh. "You've got no idea what I'm saying, do you?"

"I'm not sure. If you have to take the edge off the coke, why do it?"

"Oh Carol – you've never had a real rush, have you? Have you ever had an orgasm, Carol? Have you ever let loose?"

Carol nodded silently. I wonder if I'm really living, she thought.

"Yeah, well, be that as it may, you've never really had a real rush, have you? I mean, your life is probably really nice and all, but have you ever really had a rush? Had a rush just go on and on. Rush on."

Carol shrugged her shoulders noncommittally.

"Well, you see you've had to have had a rush to know a rush. Understand? Well, never mind. The point is, oh shit, what is the point? Oh, yeah, coke is a rush, a rush with a capital 'R.' Maybe it's the ultimate rush, who knows? Although some say death is supposed to have that honor. It makes life work, at least for a while."

"But it's not good for you and, besides, it's addictive. Think of what you're doing to yourself, Lisa."

"Just say 'no,' huh? You've been watching too much television, honey. Coke isn't really addictive, it just makes you want more. I can handle it, believe me, I've been through stuff that makes coke look like ice cream.

"Maybe it's addictive to some people but not me. I can give it up anytime I want. And I should know, I've been doing it for ten years."

Lisa fell back on the bed, her red hair fanned out framing her face like a Vargas painting. She laughed. "That's pretty funny, isn't it? I hate dealing with reality, you know that? Sometimes I just want to stay as far away as possible."

"Maybe you should just check in with life occasionally," Carol said.

"Oh shit, I don't know, maybe you're right. Carol I'm crashing bad, I've got to get some sleep."

Immediately Lisa's eyes shut and her breathing slowed. Carol got up softly, grabbed her clothes and opened the door to leave.

"Princess…"

She looked back at the prone form on the bed.

Lisa's eyes snapped open. "You want to know the real reason I get so fucked up? 'Cause I need a reason. You know what I mean? Sometimes I just need to chase a reason. Any reason." Her eyes shut and she began snoring loudly.

Carol shut the door quietly.

Leon shut the door behind him and tripped over Lisa's prone body sprawled across the living room rug like a rag doll. She was still in full costume and makeup. Her arms were outspread and the dancing spangles made Leon think of a disco turned upside down.

She's dead. He lifted his other foot to avoid stepping directly on her arm and reached to the wall in order to steady himself. She's finally done it.

"Go ahead, kick me again. Why not? Everybody else does," a muffled voice filtered up from the floor. Lisa still had not moved.

"New act, honey?" Leon walked around the body. "If you don't mind some constructive criticism, it lacks action. On the other hand, the sense of drama is quite strong."

"Go away, Leon, and let me die in peace."

"What's the matter, Lisa, two shows a day, rehearsals, partying with Johnny and an occasional meal, not leaving any special time for Lisa?"

"That's pretty much the picture, you're so fucking perceptive." There was still no movement from the floor.

"Hey, I've got an idea, maybe you should get some sleep. Three out of four doctors say that a night or two of sleep every two weeks not only prolongs life but makes it more fun at the same time."

"Can't sleep. Gotta get up in a few minutes and meet Johnny. Maybe a cold shower and a quick hit of base."

"You're going to die from that shit. Really. I tell you this as a friend."

"Maybe, maybe," she mumbled, stopping only to spit out a few carpet fibers. "But right now that and faith are the only two things pulling me through."

"Faith? You've gone Buddhist on me?"

"Faith in me, Leon." She turned her head to the side so her voice rang clear. "I've really got faith in my talents. You should've been there—I fuckin' wowed 'em."

"I know. I was there."

Lisa suddenly sat up, energy beginning to flow into her eyes. "You were? Tonight, I mean?"

"Fifth row, seat 2-B. Best view in the house."

She shook her head and smiled. "So tell me, no fucking around, how was I?"

"The show was so-so. Weak here, good there..." He let the silence build.

"Why do you do this to me, Leon? I'm sorry I'm a woman. Okay? Tell me the truth."

"You were outstanding. I had to come tonight. I was getting tired of the rumors and the local columnists claiming the next Janis Joplin was about to be discovered right here in Vegas...

"I have to tell you, Lisa, you were dynamite. If I were Johnny Star I'd fire you."

This brightened her noticeably. "You're not just being nice to be... well, I don't know what for... Tell me you mean it." She stood up.

"Lisa, you have a voice to kill for. You move well and you carry that stupid show. Why do you think it's sold out day after day? The novelty has worn off. Star's voice was never great and now it's ripped by inhaling this and that. You're the real star. Don't think the director doesn't know it. Don't think your good buddy Johnny doesn't know it.

"He may be madly in love with you, house in the suburbs, four kids, all that shit... I don't know. But I do know that he's very glad you're there. With you the show works. Without you... Who knows?"

"Yes! Yes!" Lisa jumped into the air and spiked an invisible football. "This is what I need to hear. I love you Leon," she kissed him.

"The show ends tomorrow night but I feel like I'm going out in a blaze of glory. Do you know, do you know that when I left the show tonight there was this, this crowd of the usual jerks around the door and I started to push through them and someone yelled, 'Look, it's her,' then they started pushing autograph books and pens in my face.

"Do you understand? Because I didn't at first. I thought they had mistaken me for someone else. I started to sign the first one 'Madonna,' then someone else pushed their way in and said, 'Oh, Miss Steel'— Lisa pantomimed ecstasy— 'I've always wanted to sing like you. Please sign mine first.'

"I was surrounded—but I was alone. It was like I was living on a step ladder. A plane above everyone else. I could see them, but it was like I wasn't part of them anymore.

"Everybody was smiling. They were smiling, I was smiling. 'Please, Lisa, sign mine. Look here, would you take this good luck charm, I love you Lisa.' What a fucking rush. They really think I'm somebody.

"I had people following me out to the car—trying to touch me. Me, for God's sake. I thought maybe Elvis had come back and was living in my clothes.

"Do you know what that's like? All my life I've been on a bus, a fucking Greyhound bus, going who knows where. Now I'm starting to arrive. I know I am. Everybody is all smiles when they talk to me, I get the best seats, nobody wants my money.

"Kee-rist, Leon, I used to want to be able to tip like I was somebody. Now that I'm starting to actually be somebody, nobody wants my money! They want my autograph instead. If I had known it was this easy, I never would have spent all those years trying to make a decent salary. I would have just worked on my signature...

"Oh, I know I'm not Elizabeth Taylor here or anything, but this is a small town and I'm starting to be somebody. It was great..."

"You probably should get used to it. I think you are going to be a real big somebody."

"I'm really glad you feel that way, Leon, 'cause I need your help."

Warning bells were going off in Leon's head.

"The show ends tomorrow and Johnny wants me to come back to California with him," she stated flatly.

"Congratulations. That would probably be the—"

Lisa cut him off. "I want to work here."

"No sweat, Lisa. I can get you a part, I can get you a good part in a couple of weeks. We're just starting to choreograph—"

"No, no, ain't going back to the chorus, Leon. Ain't going back to a walk on, a smile and two lines. I want my own show. I want the lead in something juicy. You can get it for me."

"I can get you a part. I owe you. Besides that you're good. You really are." Leon was pacing the room. "The problem is that you are just not a headline, Lisa. You don't have the drawing power of a name. Even a lame actress with a couple of films would outdraw you." He held up his hand. "Problem number two is that I'm not that hot of a commodity either.

"Oh sure, I've got some say, but I don't have the final cut, honey. I'm a cog, a replaceable part in a giant wheel. I'll stick up for you, I'll tell them that it's you and me or it's neither of us if you want me to. But I guarantee we'll both be pounding the pavement tomorrow if I do.

"I do owe you and you are really good, but it ain't what you know, it's who—"

"Yeah, I suppose so. What happens now? One more night and then I'm history, huh?" She slouched back to the floor like a wilting flower.

"No. I've got a better idea." Leon smiled. "A much better idea."

"Yeah, well if it's anything that keeps me from disappearing back into a sea of bare tits, I'll kiss you. Or cook you something"—she leaned against the base of the couch and closed her eyes—"Whatever turns you on."

"If I remember correctly your new pal, Mr. Star, has a much heralded special coming up on cable TV. HBO, I believe—the best comics around, cameos from Jesus, maybe God himself. Sure to be a winner, gather some of those nameless award statues media people seemed so enthused with giving each other…"

"So what? Could we cut to the chase here. Maybe I can still get a quick nap in before my presence is required."

"Well, I was just thinking that if you somehow—I don't know how of course—were to get a song on a major television show and got some attention from it, how much more marketable you would be..."

"How I could probably talk certain people into building a show around you. Hot new talent, catch a rising star—that sort of thing."

"My God." Lisa leapt to her feet with a surprising energy. "What if I got more than one song?" She was thinking our loud. "What if I was to steal the show from a certain, ah, aging male singer. What then?

"I'll tell you what then." She clapped her hands together. "I would be on the fucking golden road. I'd be cruising. I think you've cinched our friendship forever, Leon."

"Can you convince him?"

"Honey, I own that man—he just doesn't know it yet. I may not be any competition in the name department, but I can get on that show and I can walk away with it. I know I can.

"Yes, I think I'll go to California with Johnny and see what —"

"No," Leon said.

"What do you mean, 'no'?"

"Let him go back by himself. Give him a going away night to remember. If you're as good as you think you are, he'll be begging you to leave all your new admirers here and come out to Hollywood within a week. He'll be offering terms..."

"Whew!" She shook her head. "There are times I'm really glad you weren't born a woman. That's devious. Where do you come up with these ideas?"

"I'm a very inspirational person. I used to train guide dogs for the morally blind."

"That's really cute. I owe you the dinner of your life. Do you like Stouffers? Or do you prefer Lean Cuisine?"

"Either, I'm starving."

She hugged him. "Me too, but tonight I've got other plans. I've got to grab a shower and at least do a line. I can't look wasted tonight. I've got to make some lasting memories...

"Have you got any vitamins? I'm feeling in need..." Her voice trailed away as she shut the bedroom door behind her.

* * *

"Have some popcorn, and try to relax a little bit, okay?" Carol scooted an aluminum bowl full of fluffy white kernels across the table top.

"How can I relax? I feel like I'm having a baby here. This is how Dr. Frankenstein must have felt before the lightning storm came through for him. 'Here I give you life...'"

"I think you're giving yourself too big of a pat on the back. Lisa really is good. Don't forget she's been in show business since she was sixteen. She landed this shot all by herself."

"I know, but I've already pulled a lot of favors to put together a showcase for her. If this show doesn't come off, I'm the one who's going to look like an idiot."

"Don't worry about it. I have a feeling it will flow like magic."

"I hope you're right." They both concentrated on the television screen where Johnny Star was busy introducing "The hottest thing since sex. Lisa Steel!"

Both watched in rapt silence as Lisa literally tore through a punched-up version of "House of the Rising Sun," then backed Johnny on a standard love song, and then he *reintroduced* her to sing with one of the hottest rock groups in the country.

She was fantastic. The sets, the lighting, everything all seemed created only to highlight her talents. Even her costume—a simple black evening dress that clung to her body like a new paint job—did nothing but make the other women in the show appear overdressed.

That night Lisa *was* style.

Neither Carol nor Leon was prepared for the sheer impact of her performance. Neither spoke during the entire show. At one point Carol glanced over to see if Leon's mouth was hanging open as widely as her was.

It was.

At the end of the show, Lisa took three bows as the audience pelted her with single red roses. Hundreds of them fell onto the stage at her feet.

"Why didn't they just call it the Lisa Steel Show and save the expense of all those extras?"

"She must have set up that rose thing. Either that or some fans actually did follow her out from here. That's going to be her trademark."

"Was she as good as I think she was?" Carol felt a shiver pass down her spine.

"Better." Leon said softly. "She was unbelievable. There's not a single act like her anywhere. If we owned twenty percent of Lisa, we'd both be filthy rich in about two hundred days. Other people are going to realize that, and they may not be as much in line with her general welfare as we are…"

The phone rang. "I wonder who that could be?"

"Hello," Carol said as she picked it up. "Well I'm surprised you still talk to the common folk." She motioned for Leon to pick up the extension. "Show? Yes, I think we managed to catch the tail end of it, didn't we, Leon?"

He could hear the resulting burst of noise from Carol's handset. "Hi, star."

"It worked. Didn't it Leon? I mean be honest. It came off didn't it? I was good?"

"I hope you didn't hurt them," he said.

"Who?"

"The producer's children. I presume you're going to live up to your part of the bargain and return them unharmed…"

"Don't be a jerkoff, Leon, just answer me."

"Lisa, you knocked their eyes out. And their ears. Wait until the reviews hit the stands. You're going to have offers from everybody and their brother. You still want to come back here?"

"Yes, yes, I want to more than ever now. Don't do anything foolish like rent my room."

"Somehow I think you're going to be able to afford a place of your own."

"NO! I need you guys around for support." She switched subjects in mid-sentence and dropped her voice to a whisper. "You know what the best part of all this may be? I, uh, met Bret Henley the lead singer from the Hawks.

"Did you see us sing together? He wants me to do 'House of the Rising Sun' on their new album! Me! With the Hawks! Can you believe that? It's like a dream. I still can't believe I'm awake.

"Know what else? Singing's not the only thing we do well together."

Carol gasped, "What about Johnny?"

"Oh, God, that's another story. He's just... so old, you know?"

"Lisa, he got you this break, didn't he? Don't you feel any sense of gratitude?"

"Yeah, yeah, but I earned it. I've been nursemaiding him for the last month. It's not just that he's old, he's loaded all the time. Don't get me wrong. Not that I think a little happy-happy is wrong now and again, but shit, the man is never straight. Reality isn't in his vocabulary. He's too loaded to get it up and he's too spaced to notice that I am involved with someone else. He's an okay guy but he's played his part in the scheme of things."

Leon pantomimed eating with his fingers, "Ain't it great to be on top of the protein chain."

Carol reached out and kicked him.

"Huh?"

"It's just that I'm happy for you. So if I get you a show, can you be here in two weeks for rehearsals?"

"Yes, great. I'm going to record this week and that will give me a couple of days to unwind."

"You're sure you want to come back out here?" Carol asked. "It sounds like you have got a lot going on right there just to pack up and leave."

"I need to make a clean split with Johnny and I need a week or two to get Bret hooked on Lisa and then I'll be there. Let him miss me. It's a trick I learned from an old friend."

Carol looked at Leon. He shrugged in response.

"I gotta run. Some people are having a party at Capitol Records. Put it together, Leon, I'll talk to you in a couple of days. Love and kisses." She hung up.

"She's going to be a success story, isn't she?" Carol wondered out loud. "Some people are putting on a party..."

"She deserves it. Our girl has a lot of talent packed into that beautiful body. I'm just not sure it's going to be so good for her. Lisa does have a tendency to become a bit manipulative, not to mention a trifle obsessive when she wants something badly enough."

"The mark of a true star," Carol said.

"Maybe, maybe... but I'll bet she isn't quite so chummy with us common folks when the ball really gets rolling."

"This isn't all bad for you, is it?" She regretted it as soon as she said it.

"No, no, you're absolutely right about that, Carol. If I can put together a winner, I'll always be associated with the making of a star. It sure won't hurt my chances of landing other shows or other stars. I really don't like the idea of riding into town on Lisa's coattails, but there is some truth to that statement.

"Know what else she has besides the obvious? Sometimes the way she cuts right to the heart of things is refreshing. It seems everything is filmed in black and white for her. Not much gray ground to puzzle over.

"Remember what she said about 'hooked on Lisa'? That's going to be both the title and the essence of the show I'm putting together. It's so basic it can't help but work."

"Refresh me," Carol said.

"'Hooked on Lisa.' I can see it in lights. It's going to be great. We'll use a single red rose as a backdrop. Hooked on Lisa. Man, they will be by the time I get done with her."

"I suspect you're right. Do you suppose this is what it was like when someone first said to Frank Sinatra, 'Kid, have you ever thought about singing for your supper?' "

"I think this is more the way it was when someone said to Jesus, 'Have you ever thought about taking this act on the road?' "

The phone never stopped ringing. It was as if a neon sign had been tacked to the front of the house, "Lisa is in—call 555-2178." Long lost friends, new friends, would-be producers trying to hustle Lisa into one elusive deal or another, reporters, show directors, people she would talk to, people she would not.

"Lisa!" Carol picked the phone up for the third time in twenty minutes. She punched the "hold" button, knowing full well the scene that was to come. "Pick up the phone, it's Johnny."

"Tell him I'm not home," the disembodied voice floated down the hall.

"This is his third call today, Lisa, you've got to talk to him."

"All right, all right." Carol listened on the extension just long enough to hear Lisa answer with a very flat "Hello" before she gently hung up.

A few minutes later the phone rang again. Can't be, Carol thought, waiting for Lisa to pick it up. It kept ringing.

"Lisa! Please pick it up, this time it's Bret."

She came running into the room with her index finger pressed to her lips. "No, no, you've got to tell *him* I'm not in. Say I'm rehearsing or something."

Carol bit her lip, shook her finger at Lisa and lied.

"Why did I do that? I thought you two were a hot item?"

"Oh, we are, believe me." Lisa whirled around splaying the hem of her skirt outward in a swath of color. "Four hundred dollars. Can you believe that? Me, little Lisa from Hamtramck buying a four-hundred-dollar dress. An everyday dress, not even a gotta-get-the-job dress. Four hundred big ones and I don't feel a second's guilt."

Carol looked at the dress and winced. They saw you coming Lisa, she thought. "The question is why don't you want to talk to Bret on the phone?"

"Because we are a hot item. Bret just doesn't realize how hot. He knows rehearsals don't start until tomorrow, let him stew for a little while. Make him wonder what I'm doing tonight.

"Then when I do finally talk to him, I'll just say he must have misunderstood—or maybe Carol thought I was rehearsing..."

"Thanks a bunch. He's certainly going to have a great opinion of me, isn't he?"

"Oh, he'll know I'm lying, that's the idea..."

The door opened and Leon entered the room. He looked at Carol, who was still touching the phone as if willing it to not ring. "Morning, ladies. Carol," he nodded towards her, "I'm here to take over my shift as the other half of Lisa's answering service. Do you want to hand the phone over? I prefer to hold it in my lap so I don't have so far to reach."

Carol looked at him solemnly and passed the instrument over with great dignity.

"Very funny. When I signed up for this place I didn't realize I'd have Robin Williams and Rosanne Barr as roommates."

"We were just discussing Lisa's new four-hundred-dollar dress."

"Slick all right." Leon glanced over at Carol who was giving him a "don't you dare" look. "I'll bet that makes them sit up and take notice at the old tractor pull on Saturday night... Do you suppose she could afford an agent now?"

"I have an agent." Lisa was fingering the gold embroidery on her blouse.

"Then maybe you could swing a personal manager."

"Come on, Leon, that's silly—I'm not that big. Not yet."

"Okay, you win. I'll settle for an answering service. How about it, star? Can we go back to some semblance of normalcy around here?"

"I'm sorry—this really is a mess for you guys, isn't it? I'll get an answering service this afternoon, I promise. No more office in the home routine. Things will be just like they were before. How does that sound?"

"Fair," Leon said. "Eminently fair."

"Great, then it's all settled. I gotta run, but I'll be back in time for…" She froze in her tracks. "Right. There's a television crew coming in to film here about five o'clock…"

"Film? Here?" Carol was struggling with this concept.

"It's just one of those stupid local talk shows. Boring bimbos and crime, or some such shit. But it's all publicity, right, Leon? Gotta fill those seats, not to mention my career."

"A crew. In here?" Visions of trampling herds of buffalo breezed through Carol's head.

"Look, I've got a great idea! You two can be in it! Sort of background stuff about how an upcoming performer lives. That would be great. All right!" She left.

"Just couldn't bring herself to say the word 'star' could she? That memorable moment was brought to us by C and L records."

"Tell me again why you and I are letting ourselves be dragged through this," Carol said. "It's so I can say I knew her when, isn't that right?"

"Oh no, it's much more than that. Stick with me, Carol. I can probably even get you an autograph."

Leon shut the door of the apartment as quietly as possible. He grimaced at the noise of the door clicking shut. Let them both be asleep, he thought, I don't want to explain why I'm coming in at this time of the morning.

He glanced down at his ripped shit. Jesus, why do I feel like I'm living with my mother?

Two mothers?

I'm grown—

"Leon?" a voice stage-whispered into the living room. "Is that you?"

"Yeah, go back to sleep, Lisa…"

"Oh, God, come in. Please. Come to my room. Please," she was still whispering.

"Honey, I'm tired and pretty burned out. I've got to get some rest before morning— well, before afternoon anyway. I'll talk to you later. I promise."

He tiptoed towards his room.

"COME IN HERE NOW!!" she screamed, still attempting to whisper. "Please, it's really important."

"Come on, Lisa," he squinted in the dimly illuminated room. "Turn some light on in here. I can't even see you. Put the shades up, it's getting light out." He reached over and grabbed the bottom of the window shade.

Lisa's hand grabbed his and held fast. "No, don't," she said quickly. "No light… Sit down. Here." She scraped a pile of dirty clothes from the couch onto the floor.

He peered at her as his eyes got used to the lack of light.

"You look terrible. Are you sick? God, I haven't seen you in days. When's the last time you were out of this room. And why does it smell like a whorehouse in here?

"Oh, oh." His glance fell on the desktop. He picked up one of the miniature propane torches scattered amidst the rubble.

"New hobby?" He inquired flatly. "Model trains perhaps. Or have you been watching daytime TV again? Maybe you've enrolled in one of those study courses in electronics. Or welding? Trying to better your life through the auspices of home correspondence?"

"Okay, okay, so I've been baseing a little bit lately. I've got some shit happening, you know? So I apologize. That's not the problem."

"Oh, no, how long since you've had a night's sleep?" He touched her face. "I can see those nasty little wrinkles forming as we speak. And I'm not talking about laugh lines. How long Lisa?"

"So I've been on a run for a couple of days, so what? I'm okay, I don't do this very often. I need to get through this period. I need this. That's not the problem."

"Okay, I'll bite, Lisa, what exactly is the problem?" He picked up a water pipe and turned it over in his hands.

"Be careful with that," Lisa snapped and grabbed it back from him. "Hey, I'm sorry, but I'm really upset."

"You mean you're really wired."

"No, no, I'm sick. Something terrible has happened. Really bad."

"What?"

"Oh God," she buried her face in her hands. "I'm not sure what it is, but it's bad."

"Lisa you're not making sense. What has happened?"

"This!" She rolled up the sleeve of her bathrobe and stuck her arm out at Leon. "Look at it," she wailed.

Leon took it as if it might explode at any second. Automatically he searched for needle tracks.

"God, what do you think it is?"

He looked up into her face carefully, "Honey, I don't see anything at all."

Lisa impatiently blew a lock of dirty hair off her face. "This, God damn it!" She rubbed her free hand over her arm and particles of some undefined substance fell off onto the floor.

"The heartbreak of psoriasis?" Leon watched, fascinated. "Is that what this is all about?"

"It's not funny!"

"Okay, I'm sorry for the crack, but I don't know what to say."

"It just started a day or two ago. I've got some terrible disease. It's all over my body. It's coming out every pore. I just know it's some sort of major VD. Maybe it's herpes."

Leon involuntarily dropped her arm and moved back half a step. "I don't think herpes shows up on your arms."

"You don't understand. It's all over me. Everywhere." She buried her face once more. "I just know I got it from that asshole, Johnny. He'd screw anything in a skirt and some things that never were."

She looked up at Leon, "No offense."

"None taken," he replied dryly.

She thrust her arm back into his face. "Crabs. Have you ever had crabs? They're all over me. Is this what crabs look like?"

"I'm sorry to disappoint you, but there's a whole list of afflictions I've never had and crabs leads the list. But I know they're lice and I think you only get them in selected hairy areas."

"What am I going to do?" she began crying loudly. "Maybe it's leprosy. Is that still around? I bet it is. It's coming from every pore. Can you get leprosy from fucking? Fucking some asshole... Oh, they itch." She began scratching her shoulders.

"Does he have any symptoms?" Leon was watching her from a safe distance. What am I doing here? a part of him was asking silently.

"How the fuck would I know? You think I can talk to him when I'm... I'm... dying? You think I could tell him?"

"You didn't get it from him, did you, Lisa?"

"How do I know," she wailed. "He never calls, and I'm not a fucking nun, you know... I like to get laid occasionally too. You think you men are the only—I'm sorry..."

"Lisa, if you make one more reference to my sexual preferences, I'm going to leave."

"*No*, no, please stay. I'm sorry, Leon, I'm really scared. And you're my only friend in the whole world I can talk to like this.

"What am I going to do? I'm dying. Maybe it's herpes and leprosy. Oh, God." She picked up the water pipe and began scraping bits of dried cocaine from an overturned petri dish.

"You could start by not doing any more dope for a few minutes. Let your body catch up. Face physical reality."

"I need a hit, Leon. I'm really under stress here. You've got to help me."

Leon watched critically as she packed the hollow glass bowl. "Let's call Dr. Rosen."

"Nooo..." She lit the torch and melted the chemicals. "I can't have this get around. There's always some bitchy dancer in his office getting her Valium script or waiting for a D and C. Besides, he gossips all the time. It's been so long since he took the Hippocratic oath he's forgotten what's involved. I need someone else. Now."

"What do you want me to do?"

"Oh, come on, Leon, you must have a friend. Or, or maybe someone your friends go to?"

"You mean someone discreet?" he asked sarcastically.

"Yes," she sobbed and sucked in the cocaine vapors. "Exactly."

"Get your act together, Lisa." Leon nudged her as her head tipped towards her chest. "This is a respectable doctor's office."

"Shhh..." She looked at the only other occupant of the waiting room who was lost in a copy of *People*.

"What's taking him so long? I'm dying here." She scratched her arms carefully watching the other woman to see if there was any reaction.

"Her. And we've only been here ten minutes. You're lucky you got an appointment at all."

"Her? Oh, God, no. You've got me some bull dike who's probably not even a real doctor. Where did she graduate from, University of the Philippines?"

Lisa shut her eyes and scratched her arm madly. She watched the long red blood lines come to the surface. "It's itching like crazy. It hurts. I know it's herpes."

The other patient looked up, startled. Leon shrugged to indicate events were beyond his control.

Lisa began madly scratching each arm with the other.

"Oh, God, thank you doctor, thank you, I feel so much better… I mean…" Leon looked up from his copy of *Time* to see Lisa backing into the reception area.

"And you've got to follow my instructions. Do you understand?" A muffled voice followed after Lisa.

"Oh yes, I… I'm so relieved…"

"Don't be," the voice said and the door shut.

Lisa turned to face Leon, clutching a white prescription slip in front of her. "Let's get our of here." Some of her former chutzpah seemed to have returned.

In the car Lisa once again broke into a crying jag. Leon gently took the piece of paper from her hand and read it. "Lisa, this is just a script for Halcyon, a sleeping pill. Couldn't the doctor figure out what's going on?"

"Oh, yeah," she sniffed and then burst into deeper tears. "She knew. It's pretty rare." She rolled a sleeve above her elbow and scratched a patch of skin.

Debris dislodged onto the car seat. "You want to snort it?"

"What are you talking about?"

"COCAINE! It's fucking cocaine! My pores are exuding cocaine! *Look*." She held her finger tip up to his face. Several small light colored granules rubbed off.

"Do you understand? My pores are sweating cocaine. My body is passing cocaine. Oh, God… Oh, God. I'm not just sick, I'm crazy.

"How could I do this to myself? I'm a walking drug factory. I'm worth more money then some South American countries. It's almost funny."

Suddenly the tears broke through the dam again. "But it's not! Dear God, Leon, its not even humorous…"

"What did the doctor say?"

"She was pretty cool. She said she'd seen it once before or it would have fooled her too. If I stop basing it should clear up."

"How much have you done?"

"Since when? I mean, you know, you get some and you do some and you give some to friends and then you lose some…"

"Lose some? How do you lose something that costs about one hundred dollars a teaspoon? How much did you lose?"

"I don't know, I had some people over, you know, and I distinctly remember putting an ounce on the night stand, in reserve, you know, and the next day…"

"An ounce? $2,000 worth of cocaine. You lost it?"

"It comes and it goes. What's the difference? I'm never going to do another hit as long as I live. I swear it. As soon as we get home, I'm going to toss everything."

"Sure."

"No. I mean it. I've got to stop. This really shakes me up. Coke coming from my pores. Ehh…" She shuddered visibly but Leon noticed that she didn't sound as frightened as she did a few minutes ago.

Sleep, Leon thought, just let me sleep for a few years. I'll be okay. He hesitated and then back stepped to open the hall closet. He slid his coat from his shoulders and carefully hung it up. Oh, yes, wonderful, dear sleep.

The front door opened behind him.

Shit…

"Leon?"

He turned to face the voice. "Hi, Carol, how are you doing these days?"

"Okay," she said, "probably better than you, as a matter of fact…"

Leon followed her gaze to his shirt front. He hit his forehead with the heel of his hand. "I forgot, I forgot all about it and nobody said a thing…

"Princess, you ever have a day where you knew when you got out of bed God was telling you to sit tight? And sure enough as the day wore on you discovered he was absolutely correct?" He fingered the tear in his shirt.

"Just one little hair-raising episode after another. Sort of like a John Carpenter film, just when you thought it was safe to go back to the water…"

"I wish you wouldn't call me that, you know… Want to talk about it?"

"No, I want to sleep about it, but I just happen to know someone you'd better talk to…"

"Oh, no, what's the third musketeer done now? Another broken heart? I haven't seen Bret lately. In fact, come to think of it, I haven't seen much of Lisa lately either."

"There's a reason for that. And I don't think I'm up to explaining it, but if you would just go upstairs and present yourself to our mutual friend you might find a rather interesting story. Not the usual soap opera, I might add, no long lost boyfriends, no broken hearts, nobody dying of cancer." He laughed, "Not even a good solid case of VD."

"Leon, what are you talking about?"

He took her softly by her shoulders, "You wouldn't believe me if I told you. Suffice to say that she really needs your help. I shit you not. Really bad news."

"Why me?"

"Why you? Because in this whole world Lisa Steel respects only one soul. She has little use for the entire human race with one glaring exception—Carol.

"She thinks you are just about the smartest thing since Einstein fell into a black hole. You know it? She really respects you."

"Oh come on, she's called me—"

"Carol, Lisa is really in need of a friend and some hard and fast advice and you're the only person she'll take it from. Believe me. Go up and see her."

"Okay," Carol said, resigned to the fact. "But you come too."

"No, no, I've gone far beyond the call of duty today, and I need to go to bed. Good luck." He shut the bedroom door behind him.

Carol peeked in the partially opened door. "Lisa? Are you okay?"

"Come in, only I don't want any cracks or lectures. Okay?" The room was now brightly illuminated. Lisa was busily gathering up an armload of paraphernalia from the top of the night stand.

"I don't know what you're talking about."

"Come on, come on, I'm sure good old Leon told you the entire disgusting story from A to Z." She looked up.

"All he said was that you could use a friend."

Lisa walked over to the back window and opened it. "Feel that air. Great, huh?"

"Lisa, can I ask what you're doing?"

"No. As far as you're concerned this is a spectator sport." She threw the water pipe out of the third floor window and listened for the sound of exploding glass.

She smiled at the expected echo and then flung the remainder of her armload out in the same trajectory.

"Gone," she said. "Just like in a fairy tale, it's all gone and everybody lived happily ever after."

"Some junkie is going to have a great night going through the garbage."

Lisa laughed. "Christmas on Third Street. Raining dope. I've had dreams like that.

"Ah, well, fuck it, life goes on. I feel so free, that's the last time I'm ever going to base." She opened the bottle of petroleum ether and dumped the contents out of the window.

"Fly little birdies. Be free. I feel so much better now. I don't think I'll ever do coke again. I was so scared, but I know I'll never base again, no matter what."

"Lisa, I don't mean to be a pessimist, but you've done this before."

"Not like this. This is different." She turned the gold handle and water flowed into the sink. She began to carefully wash the petri dishes and other glass implements.

As soon as each was scrubbed clean she placed it on the white porcelain counter top and then methodically smashed it into bits of crystal. "It's not really the coke you know. I can control that, but once you get into basing it's a whole different attitude.

"It comes on so quickly and then the rush fades and you want to duplicate that feeling. That's what it's all about… You're always trying to catch up, do it again. Get that first push back again." She searched the tiles for any fragile remnants that might have escaped her blitzkrieg.

A small glass mixing bottle was lodged under a washcloth. Lisa moved it to the center of the counter top and hit it with a heavy glass ashtray. Fragments exploded from the point of impact and she used the rag to gather them all together.

The only thing remaining on the naked surface was a large folded bundle of shiny paper. Lisa unwrapped the coated paper exposing a moderate-size pile of glistening crystal. She shook her head and then moved the pile towards the running water in the sink.

She hesitated in mid-flight. "You know, it wouldn't be so bad just to snort a little bit every once in a while. Just occasionally, you know."

"Lisa, if you're really going to stop, do it, don't kid around."

"Hey, you don't know what I'm talking about. It's the not the same thing at all. A little snort now and then never hurt anyone. Besides, it's self-limiting. Your nose gets too sore to keep it up for too long."

She set the pile down on the corner of the sink and looked at it thoughtfully. "Still, I really should stop all together..."

Aimlessly she carved her initials out from the pile with a gold American Express card that had been sitting by her toothbrush.

"Oh, yeah, some of my fondest memories are American Express coke. Don't leave home without it." She swirled the tail of the "S" artistically.

"I'll compromise." She flicked her wrist and deftly flicked half of the pile into the sink where it quickly vanished in the swirling waters. She jumped a little at the sight.

"Oh! It went so quickly... You know how rich I'd be if I had all the drugs flushed down the sewer system in this country in a given week? Oh, well," she bent over and snorted the "L" up into her nostril using the bottom half of a plastic ball point pen as a straw.

Carol watched as the jolt hit. Lisa suddenly looked awake and several years worth of wrinkles seemed to vanish as she shook her head from side to side.

"Oh, yes. Sometimes I think Grace was right."

"Grace who?"

She drummed the pen against the tile, "Slick, Gracie Slick. 'Only lines too short lines that you want to snort,'" she sang. She nodded over and sucked up the last initial.

"Okay, okay, before you start with the lecture. I'll knock it off." She held up the medicine bottle they had picked up on the return trip from the doctor's office. "I know I need to sleep. I'll quit."

Carol watched as Lisa popped a blue pill, thought it over and took a second dose. "Well, at least I did the right thing, no more basing. And I'll lighten up on everything else.

"I feel better already." But she rubbed the skin on the back of her hand absently and peered into cold darkness of the sink drain where the water had disappeared.

Carol was sitting at her desk watching columns of figures blur and merge into each other when the phone rang. She picked it up automatically, "Davis."

"Hi, Davis. Stevens here."

"Hi, honey." Carol rubbed her eyes with the back of her hand. "What's up?"

"Dinner. I thought maybe I could con you into some Hanoi soup and then a movie afterwards. One of those film things they show in theaters with no chorus girls, no bands. I know it's not what you've come to expect from life but it might be fun."

The mention of her favorite Vietnamese dish caused Carol to lick her lips. The smell of lemon grass seemed to be in the room with her. She looked at the clock, surprised to find it was after six already.

"I'd love to, but… I can't, not tonight anyway."

"Oh, oh, I feel a Lisa about to enter this conversation, don't I?"

"It's just that I promised her I'd come to the show tonight."

"Uh-huh, that makes, what, three times in the past two weeks? What's different about tonight? I admit she's good but it is the same show you've already seen. Twice."

"I know but I did promise. She even called a little while ago to make sure I hadn't 'forgotten.' She's really up about tonight for some reason. She even hinted at some sort of surprise."

"Really? Hearing that would sure thrill Leon to death. I can't picture him okaying any changes in the most successful show in town. Improv isn't exactly Leon's forte. If it ain't on the page, it ain't on the stage."

"The main thing is that I did promise… Why don't you come too? Maybe we could catch a quick bite beforehand."

"No, no, I got plenty of work I can catch up on. I'd rather have you all to myself. How about tomorrow?"

Carol hung up the phone with a grimace. She could tell Taylor was a bit miffed about the turndown, but she had promised Lisa… Besides, she would make it up to him tomorrow…

Leon was, as the expression goes, having a cow. Something was in the air—the show had started off okay but then a vague sense of uneasiness had settled backstage as surely as a ground fog.

It wasn't that anything concrete was wrong—the show was working—but, *but* something was not kosher. And that something was Lisa...

She hadn't missed a cue or a mark—in fact, she seemed more on than usual. And that worried Leon. It was not like Lisa to give one hundred ten percent—she was a knockout at one hundred percent—but tonight she wasn't just acting—she was directing.

And that was Leon's job.

Little things. Things no one in the audience would ever notice. Adding a few bars to a number that was working better tonight than other nights. Controlling the band with her motions, talking to the other performers ON STAGE! During the act...

Leon had a sinking suspicion that one of his worst nightmares was going to come to pass tonight. Maybe she was loaded—too many drugs, too little time. Going to pull a Janis Joplin right here on stage, and somehow, some way, they're going to blame me.

Like a virus gone mad, Leon's tenseness wordlessly infected the other members of the crew. Backstage was becoming a show all of it's own...

"God damn it, be careful," Leon hissed to an A.D. who tripped over an electrical cord that wasn't taped down well enough. That's it, he thought, even as he did it, yell at the help. That will solve everything.

"Sorry, I don't know..."

Suddenly the band stopped in mid-number. Or tried to stop, at any rate. Leon could hear each individual instrument wind down in midnote. The effect was not unlike that of a huge record player that had had someone brutally yank the power cord from the wall socket.

It wasn't pleasant.

Afraid of what he would see, he looked on stage. Lisa was standing in the spotlight waving both arms towards the floor. "Quiet everybody. Hold on a minute. Everybody wait a second."

So much for the old tradition that the show must go on, he thought, as the other actors looked from Lisa to where Leon was standing in the wings, to receive some guidance.

"Ladies and gentlemen," Lisa's voice boomed out of the monitors like a maddened carnival barker. "Have I got a deal for you. I've got a surprise for everybody. In fact, it's kind of a surprise for everyone here, I mean in the show, too."

"What the fuck is she doing?" The A.D. muttered to himself.

"Got me." Leon felt powerless to do anything but watch the spectacle unfold.

"The only problem is that I need a few minutes to prepare." An audible groan swept through the audience. "Okay, if you feel that way about it, I'll buy you all a drink while you're waiting. A round on me, please," she cupped her hands and yelled towards the service area.

The crowd began stamping and clapping caught up in the spirit of the thing.

"A round for the house? Do you suppose she left a credit card with the bartender? What the hell is going on?

Lisa cued the drummer who responded with a roll. "Now if we can just lower the stage lights for a few minutes." No one moved a muscle. It looked like a game of statues, with everyone frozen both on stage and in the crew area.

"Leon!" Lisa yelled, pointing her finger in his general direction. "Turn down the damn lights!" More shouts from the audience. Leon drew his fingers across his neck in a signal to the light people and the stage was plunged instantly into blackness.

Along with my career, he thought.

Leon heard someone, presumably Lisa, make her way across the stage. The figure's super-high heels made sharp noises that ricocheted from the nearby walls. Just as Leon's eyes started to adjust to the darkness, someone opened a stage door letting in a crack of artificial light. A number of figures seemed to be stumbling into the room from the night. He could sense that a number of them were carrying and/or pushing large objects.

He caught a bit of reflected light and recognized Lisa. Just as someone handed her a joint and she sucked in a huge hit of smoke, held it for a moment, exhaled slowly and then rudely sucked the smoke back into her lungs.

"Lisa!" Leon hissed. She reached out and pinched him on the shoulder. By exercising every ounce of control he processed he lowered his voice to a whisper. "What the fuck are you doing?"

"Trust me, Leon. Just trust me." She took another hit and giggled loudly. Leon was now conscious of an unknown number of people surrounding him like a sea of humanity. They seemed to be setting up some sort of equipment. He could see tiny red LEDs flashing on like miniature stars as power was introduced into the formula.

"You're gonna love it." Lisa twisted away from his grasp and handed the joint to someone he could not identify.

He heard Lisa blending in with the people on stage, organizing, cajoling. Then she began to shuffle people from the stage into the wings. A person of unknown gender fell against Leon, recovered, and handed him a joint in the way of apology.

"Sorry man. Have a hit."

"Oh, Jesus," Leon cold feel the entire situation floating away from him like a stick on the tide.

"Hey, sorree," the voice said as it sucked in some more smoke. The entire stage was beginning to reek of marijuana. Suddenly Leon could clearly see legions of cops rushing in, flashlights bouncing from the walls, to add a twist ending to the whole scene. He had to find some way to regain control of the situation immediately. Lisa was obviously crazy. In fact, he could probably strangle her and convince any jury in the land that it was the act of a sane man.

If he could only find her... He looked about wildly. Maybe I could start by strangling someone else—anybody. Just to show that I'm serious... He realized he was hyperventilating.

"Hey, hey," Lisa's voice boomed over the PA system. "You folks ready to party yet?" A rush of sound answered her. The audience was obviously enjoying the drama and expecting the moon. People began clapping and stamping their feet in a wave of coordinated noise.

Leon had a sinking feeling they would turn like cornered wolves when this cornball scheme fell through. Maybe he should be making his way towards the exit instead of worrying about the show...

"*Okay!* With my compliments, only for you... Hit the lights Leon."

Without thinking he reached out and tapped the gaffer to signal agreement. The stage was flooded with a too bright light and a screeching guitar chord rang out.

Leon rubbed his eyes and tried to focus on the now-crowded stage. He wasn't entirely sure but it looked like...

"We didn't come to talk—we came to play!" And the number one rock group in the world began to do just what they promised...

"Taylor?" He could hardly make out the words, the phone seemed to be jammed with noise, but it was definitely Carol's voice. "Can you hear me?"

"Is the show over already? It's still early." He found himself unnecessarily yelling into the phone.

"Not exactly. I think you had better get over here, right now."

"What's up? Is Lisa okay?"

"I can't explain this one—you've got to see it for yourself..."

Taylor couldn't believe his eyes. The Sahara was jammed with people. No, that wasn't right—it was overflowing onto the street. Massive lines of people stood in front pressing forward against a few overworked security guards, like someone was giving away free money... He wasn't sure he had seen anything quite like it before.

He milled around the edges of the cheering crowd when the casino manager came out and waved for silence. "Hey, listen to me!" he yelled over their heads. "We're moving tables out of the way and we'll get as many of you inside as we can. Please be patient."

The crowd roared its disapproval with the speed of the process. The man stepped down, glanced over and recognized Taylor. He grabbed a security guard and they formed a loose flying wedge, leading Taylor inside the packed casino.

"You guys ever heard of fire regulations over here?" Taylor asked his friend dryly.

"Fuck that shit. We gave up on that some time ago." The man took out a handkerchief and wiped his forehead. "Fucking A-mazing. Were you at Woodstock?" He looked Taylor over critically. "Stupid question, you're a fucking kid.

"Well I was, and it was just like this. We've torn the fence down and let the masses in free. It was either that or the national guard..."

"For what? What's going on?"

The other man looked at Taylor and burst out laughing. "You really don't know? Oh, my God—well, see, tonight's show took a bit of a different turn. The Hawks showed up to sit in with our hero Lisa Steel.

"It's all over town. Somebody leaked it to a couple of disc jockeys who put it out on the air, people started calling their friends—shit, somebody told me it was even broadcast on CB radio. It's been like this for half an hour. It's a great show—we decided to open the doors and let as many people in as possible.

"Like we had a choice." The man laughed. "Come on, my personal army and I will try and get you somewhere near the theater. You've got to see this for yourself."

"So I've been told." Taylor braced his shoulders and followed his friend's lead into the human press.

"You want to get down to it, Taylor?" Lisa pushed the assortment of raw seafood around on her platter with a fish fork, taking only a small pinch of caviar from the offerings. "Much as I enjoy your company, time is money and I've got a busy afternoon ahead of me."

"That stunt with the Hawks was a stroke of pure genius, Lisa. I have to admit it. It's pretty hard to shake this town but that certainly did it." He hesitated for effect, "I'm curious, was it your idea or Bret's?"

She shrugged and winked. "In the end the only thing that matters is who thinks it was their idea...

"I want you to come to the DollHouse and do a spectacular. Design your own package; you can have whoever you want on the show—writers, directors, we'll try for anybody you want."

"What an interesting idea," she commented in a neutral tone. "Anything I want, huh? You know it might be kind of fun to make some of the sons of bitches that I used to have to bow and scrape in front of take direction from me...

"Life shouldn't be just whatever comes along. Oh, I know most people say that at some time, but then they turn right around and let it paint them into impossible corners. I'm not going to do that, I'm going to reach out and twist the little fucker into the shape I want it in.

"God I feel like I've wasted so much time..." She hesitated, thinking.

"Lisa, you're what, twenty-two or twenty-three? Not exactly over the hill; you don't have to cram it all into six months, you know. It's a little early to be having a mid-life crisis. Take a little time off and then we can put on a show to end all shows. Special effects, lasers... Hell we can hire Spielberg to design it if you want...

"I, I started everything too early. If I had known then what I know now—well at least I do know it now.

"I've got all the important ingredients for the recipe of life. Money? Got some, more on the way. Fame? Starting to jell. I can close my hand and feel fire inside it pulsing like a small animal trying to escape. I don't care if I sleep, I don't care if I eat, I just need a little time and I'm going to make it big.

"One day I won't be able to eat in a public place, and you know what? I'll fucking love the feeling. I'll eat alone and relish it. It'll be like going back to a high school reunion in a new Ferrari—like when Nero retook Rome. Do you remember that?"

"That may have been a bit before my time," he said dryly.

Lisa leaned back in her chair and bit her lip. "What do you do for kicks Taylor? What's your idea of fun? Going up to your suite and watching the 49er's kick the shit out of some poor bastards on Sunday afternoon? Maybe on big days you have a couple shots of Cuervo 1800 and slam the Corvette around in the desert a risky ten or fifteen miles above the speed limit.

"Maybe you should grow up and get a life."

"I can't believe it." Taylor knew he was blowing whatever slim chance he had left at the deal, but he couldn't stop himself. "In a few short weeks you've gone from the chorus line to a rock star and now you're trying to crack the philosophy market. It's pretty tough, I'd keep singing…"

"You are still such a funny man, Taylor, I hope you find a woman dumb enough some day to appreciate it." She nibbled on one of the raw oysters and made a sour face. "For the prices you guys charge, you think you could fly over to Japan occasionally and pick up some real Kumamotos, wouldn't you?

"What was I saying? Right, the other ingredient in the magic recipe is career. Nice of you to ask, Taylor, but I just got my own album. Talked to the old agent just moments ago. The company is tossing in a little, you know, say two-hundred-thousand-dollar advance—but that will change soon—for the better…"

Taylor whistled. "A lot of money. What are you going to do with it?"

"First I'm going back to lovely Los Angeles. Then I'm going to buy a house."

"I'm sorry to be the one to break it to you but two hundred won't even buy a shack in the part of town you would live in. I don't even know if it would be a down payment."

"Not to sweat it, I've got a roommate and you'll never guess who it is."

"Bret?"

"Smarter than you look, Taylor. We've already got a deposit on this lovely little place up in the hills. My agent says there's no way we can lose on it—California dirt is changing to gold."

"Things really are happening fast aren't they? How much is this little love nest?"

"I don't know—a couple or three million, I guess. What's the difference? I'm putting up my advance—well, not really all of it. Got to keep enough for the bare essentials of life—a car, some dresses, that sort of thing—Bret will cover the rest.

"I think he's really in love with me—ain't life amazing? Who would have thought it could happen to little old me?"

"Are you in love with him?"

"Got me?" She shrugged. "What difference would it make? They come and they go—he's here. For now anyway."

"Some things never change, do they?"

"Don't give me that holier-than-thou crap, Taylor. I can remember you dipping your wick once or twice without the benefit of true love.

"Besides, this will do my career nothing but good. It's not like I'm tricking anyone into anything. Bret is enjoying the ride just fine, thank you. I think he likes strong women; maybe he had a mother fixation or some such bullshit. I'm just what the doctor ordered.

"You have no idea just how strong I can be when I want to, Taylor. No idea at all..."

"You always were built for distance, Lisa, not for speed."

Lisa leaned over the table, carefully setting her elbows on the tablecloth to avoid the myriad of seafood scattered about. "Fuck you, Taylor, I'm going to be a big star and you'll still be a restaurant manager. Think about that for a while."

"I guess this means no show, right?"

Lisa laughed and clapped her hands together. "I like that in you. Never say never... The thing is, I don't see any reason to be nice to people on the way up, 'cause I ain't coming back down."

"It must be nice to have that much confidence in the way things are going to turn out."

"I got enough confidence to last me forever, with some left over for the peasants."

"Ah, yes, but the question is, how much of that is real and how much is the result of artificial ingredients?"

Lisa blinked and stood up slowly. "Be a sweetheart and catch the lunch, would you, Taylor? It sucked."

She walked off.

HOLLYWOOD

LISA

Lisa glanced at the brightly lit "recording" sign in the hall of S and L Records, kicked the soundproofed wall and threw the door to the control room open. A surge of raw 110-decibel sound struck her with the force of a breaking wave.

"Hey!" The second engineer leapt to his feet and started across the room to intercept her. "You can't come in—" He stopped in his tracks as recognition set in. "Oh, uh, it's you, uh, Miss…" The man was stuttering.

"Erudite fucker, ain't he?" She indicated the flustered second with a tilt of her head and stormed towards the mixing board. "Turn that crap down. I can't hear myself think."

The first engineer slid a small plastic mixer down a notch and the noise level dropped to almost bearable. "Good to see ya, Lisa, what's up?"

"Skip the sweet talk, Jimmy, and hit the intercom." She reached across the massive board for a red button. The man grabbed her hand and held it poised over the controls.

"No, no, Lisa, please don't make trouble. This is the last track and he's finally on a roll. Give it a minute, okay?" He carefully moved her hand over to one of the upholstered side cushions where six rails of coke were carefully arranged into white S's, offsetting the black leather. "Do a line and relax for a minute. Be friends. Okay?"

Lisa looked from the engineer to the drugs. "Anybody ever tell you this shit is still illegal?" She picked up a hollow gold straw and bent over the offering.

"Cut me some slack." He glanced at one of the VU indicators and made a hairline adjustment in a control. "You and I both know how many records would get produced if it wasn't for a touch of Peruvian Marching Powder. You think maybe it's time for the big Captain and Tenille comeback? Maybe a Tony Orlando & Dawn reunion." He laughed to himself and completed another minor adjustment. "Although, to be frank, I always thought 'Tie a Yellow Ribbon' was really a loadie song, you know?"

Lisa straightened up, shut her eyes, snorted upward and shivered. "You're such a jerk, you know that, Jimmy? You're lucky the Job Corps taught you a usable skill or you'd still be selling sets of encyclopedias at Woolworth's."

Jimmy laughed, held up both hands and wiggled provocatively. "Magic fingers, trained in many arts. I'd be happy to give you a little demonstration. At your convenience, of course…"

"You can take the boy out of the encyclopedia sales racket but you can't take the…" She bent over quickly and scarfed up another line in one sharp intake of air.

"Tell me, Lisa, what do your close friends call you, Eureka or Hoover?"

"Funny man, you want a piece of advice?" She didn't wait for an answer. "Don't give up your day job."

The second engineer laughed. "Steve, how about making yourself useful, you know, maybe go and get some more tape, or clean the floors or something. Okay?" The other man shook his head and left the room. "Flunkies," Jimmy said, "that's all they send us anymore, flunkies."

"Yeah, I don't know what's the matter with kids today. Hand me that Heinekin, will you, babe?" Lisa pointed to an open bottle balanced on the far side of the board.

"Anything for you," he stepped to his left and reached for the green bottle. Lisa quickly slid over and slammed the intercom button down with the heel of her hand.

"Break time, boys. Union rules." She yelled into the microphone.

On the other side of the thick double-glass windows Bret jumped as if an electric shock passed through his body as Lisa's amplified voice cut through his headphones. He instinctively grabbed the neck of his guitar, causing a tortured note to echo throughout the control room.

Jimmy stopped in mid-step, turned and smiled resignedly at Lisa. "I don't believe I went for the sucker play. And after you accepted the bribe in good faith..."

Lisa reached down deliberately, wiped a wet fingertip through the middle of one of the remaining lines and rubbed it on her gums. "I guess there's a moral in this little story somewhere, isn't there?" Lisa smiled and the music stopped.

"Hi, honey." Bret's voice came through the studio monitors and bounced around the control room. Lisa waved her arms in an impatient "get in here" gesture. Bret smiled and unhurriedly unstrapped his twenty-four carat gold-plated Fender Telecaster and opened the studio door. He walked over and kissed Lisa deeply.

"What are you doing here, lover?"

"I'm in the music business too, remember? I work here. But now I want to go home. Our home. And you're going to come with me. Right now." She smiled sweetly and started to lead him by the arm.

"Oh, come on, you're a cute couple and all that but we really need to finish laying this track," the engineer implored Lisa. "The tour starts in three weeks and we've got to have this turkey ready to fly..."

"Oh, you're so clever, Jimmy, you can fix it," Lisa pointed to a digital recorder. "All these pretty blinking lights. Maybe you can just splice something together, make it sound hip, spiffy, right on, together... You can do that, can't you, Jimmy, you must have a razor blade in here somewhere. Just take this old piece of tape."

Lisa reached into the recorder and lifted the two-inch-wide tape away from the recording head.

"Don't fuck with the master tape, Lisa. Please," he added as an afterthought.

"Just take the old Swiss army knife and cut it right about here." She began splitting the plastic tape with her fingernail.

"Jesus!" The engineer jumped towards her and grabbed the partially cut tape away out of her hand. He turned to face her. He was shaking.

"Do you know how much fucking money this fucking room costs? Do you know how fucking much money I cost? Do you...?

Lisa held up a hand to stop him. "Not exactly, but I know how much you're worth and it's not relevant." She shrugged and breathed out a long sigh. "I'm sorry, Jimmy, I didn't come here to fuck up your day."

He appeared partly mollified. "Well, you're doing a pretty good job of it anyway…"

"Jimmy, Bret and I are getting married in exactly forty-eight hours and I want a little quiet time alone with him between now and then. No roadies, no groupies, no engineers…"

The door opened and the second engineer came back into the studio. Lisa looked directly at him, "And no flunkies. Just two little days and then you can have Mr. Music back all to yourself. Okay?

"Come on, honey, let's go home and throw everybody out, kind of a reverse party." Bret walked through the door she was holding open. "Oh, and Steve, every once in a while you've got to remind Jimmy here that it's only rock and roll. Okay?"

She left with Bret in tow.

The second looked over at Jimmy. "What did I do?"

"Fuck off." Jimmy bent over and scraped together the pile of coke that Lisa had left behind. "You got any more on you? It's going to be a long day…"

Lisa could sense Bret starting to have second thoughts as they reached the parking lot. "Honey, maybe I should just go back and finish the track. I could meet you at home."

Lisa's eyes flashed as she fought to control herself. "Bret, we're getting married in two days. You have an album to finish and then it's off to Europe where you'll be surrounded by adoring fans and adoring groupies with big tits and little minds and I've got a miserable shoot coming up and we don't even have time for a honeymoon. I want two days. Think of it as a pre-honeymoon. Two days with nothing to think about." She took both his hands and spun him around like an ice skater.

"I want to just stay high for two days. Fucked up and fucked. Get my drift? You and I, we can pretend we're on the Riviera. Oh shit, we can pretend we're anywhere in the whole world. All the places I want to go, we'll go in the next two days.

"Okay? Seriously, we'll stay high from this second now until after the ceremony. Promise me, promise me, we won't see this side of straight again for two whole days." She took a thin rolled joint from her sequined jacket pocket and lit a match.

Bret took the glowing joint from her, inhaled, exhaled slowly and then sucked the cloud of smoke back into his lungs. "I'll make you a deal." He walked past a green XKE and slid onto a gleaming chrome Harley Sportster.

"Oh, hell, you're on that stupid machine. How come when you've got a Vette and a Porsche you have to ride a donor cycle? Let's take my car." She threw him a set of keys. "You can drive." He caught the keys in one hand and tossed them back at her in a high arc. He tapped the rear of the bike's seat with the butt end of the joint and continued as if he hadn't heard the interruption.

"The deal is, we'll do what you want if I can get married on my cycle."

"Are you out of your mind?" Lisa screamed and the lot security guard glanced up from the book he was reading. She waved at him wearily as visions of reporters filled her world.

Lisa bit into her lower lip to keep from screaming again. "Bret, this is sort of a big occasion in my life. I've never been married before and I'd like to see it get off to a good start. Let's not make it a circus. I'm not saying you have to rent a tuxedo or anything drastic, but we're not getting married in the hot tub, in the ocean or on the motorcycle."

Bret threw his leg over the seat, rose up on his toes, and kicked down on the starter. The machine immediately roared into angry life. He twisted the throttle without releasing the brake and the bike raised up on its rear wheel like a maddened horse.

"You know," he shouted over the roar of the angry engine, "next to you this chopper is the most important thing in my life. In fact," he took the jay back and did another hit, "riding you and riding the beast are the only things worth a shit in my life. They can take the rest away, everything else is just a possession. But you and the bike have soul."

He leaned forward putting his body weight over the front wheel until it slowly eased itself towards the asphalt.

He squeezed in the clutch and revved the throttle. "I love you both and I want to start it off with the two things I love there. Don't be jealous, please, I... I'm serious about this, I've thought it over."

"But, the reporters, the photographers... My mother," Lisa sensed she was losing headway.

Bret patted the rear of the leather seat. "Come on, just say yes and we'll go home and fall in love all over again, I promise."

Lisa smiled, "So you're telling me that you love me and this, this thing, the same, huh?"

"Don't think of it that way... You're the only two women in my life. Ever again. Ever."

"Okay," she shook her head resignedly, her smile frozen in place. "I guess I can live with that." She lifted one leg over the frame of the chopper, forcing the split of her skirt upward to her panty line, the seam on the leather rubbing a bright red irritation mark on her tanned thigh. Over the cliff, she thought. One more day and bye-bye. A picture of the high cliffs off the Pacific coast highway flashed into her mind's eye.

"Cross your heart?" Bret turned in the seat to watch her, suspicious of his easy win.

"Yup," Lisa made an invisible X over her chest.

"I'm in love with the two most beautiful creatures in the whole world," Bret yelled as the bike fishtailed and left behind a patch of Goodyear all the way out the asphalt driveway onto La Brea.

I hope you can swim, you bitch, Lisa thought, holding tightly to Bret's waist...

"Be it ever so humble, there's no place like Malibu." Bret punched the code into the keyboard and watched the wrought-iron gate roll slowly back across the driveway.

Lisa got off the bike, rubbing her kidneys. "Put my competition in the garage, please, I'm going to walk from here." She started up the gentle grade of the estate. "Oh, and I wasn't kidding about it being just you and me... If any hangers-on are sleazing about, get rid of them."

"Okay." He re-revved the engine listening to the throaty roar. "I don't want her to get dirty before the big ceremony." He wiped an unseen speck of dirt from the gleaming gas tank. "Maybe I should get her detailed, whatya think? A little gold pinstriping maybe..." He framed the machine between both hands and tilted them from side to side as if taking a photograph.

A personal flotation device, maybe... Lisa smiled at the thought. Coast guard approved...

Bret leaned the bike up against a fifty-gallon steel drum. The meeting of metal gave off a loud "clunk." "I can't believe I've got a fifty-gallon drum of petroleum ether sitting in my garage. I mean, shit, what it if leaked and we got a single spark. *Boom!* We'd be beach front property in the state of Nevada."

"What do you want to do, keep four hundred quart bottles? That wouldn't attract any notice down at the old head shop. 'Well-known rock stars buy eight-hundred pints of pet ether… Reason unknown…' Besides, we entertain a lot. Think of it as a nineties wine cellar. Vintage ether, from a small Monterey ether… squashed from grapes grown only on the side of a hill, exposed only to the indirect rays of the afternoon sun…"

"I guess…" Bret sounded doubtful. Suddenly there was a small "click."

Lisa was the first to react. She spun on her heel and faced the garage door. A man stood with an expensive looking camera pinned to his face.

"Just one more," he said, followed by another click.

"What the fuck do you think you're doing?" She lowered her voice like a snake's hiss. "This is private property, you asshole. Just what the fuck do you think you're doing?" She advanced a step towards the photographer, clenching her fists.

"My job Lisa." He snapped another photo, the whir of the motor drive filling the still air. "Just doing my job. You two are hot, today's news, wedding bells ringing in two days and the whole world wants to know what the blissful prenuptial couple is like in real life."

Click.

There was a strained silence as the man slowly lowered the camera to his breast. "Let's be honest here, kids. I get paid for this just like you two get paid for being 'in the news.' You think you'd sell a single record if it wasn't for people like me? Don't make me laugh. What we got here is a symbiotic relationship. You scratch my private parts, I scratch yours."

He depressed the shutter without lifting the camera. "The public's proverbial right to know is at stake here… We can make this wedding the hottest thing since Romeo and Juliet."

"I'm so sorry," Lisa smiled without unclenching her fists. "But the wedding's going to be a small, intimate affair and none of the press are invited. But hey, if we change our minds yours would be the first name on the list."

"Uh-huh." He turned to the side and snapped off a shot of the bike and the garage wall. "Tell me kids, speaking of the public's right to know, just exactly what is in that barrel over there? Pool cleaner?"

"Barrel?" Lisa said. "What barrel?"

The man involuntarily aimed towards the offending canister with his camera. He realized his mistake in the same second that he completed it.

Lisa shifted her weight to her right foot and swung her left hand from below her hip in a perfect arc, catching the camera and throwing it against the wall and knocking the photographer onto the floor. "Thank God mom made me keep up the karate classes," she grinned. "I never thought they'd come in handy."

"Four thousand dollars," the man muttered without moving. "I've got over four thousand dollars in that camera."

"Oh yeah, how much you got invested in your fucking face?" Lisa lifted her leg up, tucking her heel back against the underside of her thigh, aiming her toe at the man's nose. "I can do that up just as easily asshole."

Bret stepped between the combatants. "I think you'd better go, man. I think you'd better go now."

"I'll call the fucking cops. Assault. See how you lovebirds like to get hitched in handcuffs. See how you like to explain some of your toys here," he sputtered.

"Great," Lisa laughed, "bring 'em on! Figure you'll get about two years for burglary, maybe I'll be moved by your impassioned pleas and drop the trespassing and battery charges. You'll love the joint. And God knows they love asshole reporters. Maybe you'll meet some of our fans inside. Think you'll ever enjoy sleeping on your stomach again?"

The man picked himself up slowly and reached down for the parts of his camera. Lisa brought her foot down on the Nikon with a resounding crunch. "Leave it. Go now or I'll not only take up your offer about calling the pigs, I'll kick the shit out of you first. Think of the exposure you'll get with that reputation, faggot…"

The man looked at Bret and shook his head. "I'm sorry, man. I'm sorry for you. This is just a day in my life, but it's your future. Scary, man, real scary." He walked slowly down the driveway.

"Goddam registered jackals," Lisa said. "They're worse than lawyers. Maybe we should do some sort of revolutionary fund raiser to help hang all the attorneys, writers, and photographers. Inquiring minds want to know, my ass…" She pulled the overhead door down into its track.

* * *

Lisa stretched out cat-like onto the oversized couch and lit a joint. "The pause that refreshes." She held her breath and passed the glowing stick to Bret. Lisa leaned her head forward and let her long red hair cascade forward over the end pillows.

"God this feels s-o-o-o good. Get the water pipe will you, hon? And maybe a few beers from the fridge while you're up and about."

"You want some Stoly? I've got a bottle in the freezer." Bret's voice came in from the kitchen.

"No, no." Lisa was filling the bottom of the glass pipe with Perrier. "That hard stuff will kill you, you shouldn't get started. It's fine for a while and then you want something stronger and then something stronger. There's not telling where that road can take you." She filled the tiny bowl full of fluffy crystal trees and packed them together like a snowball.

"You think things will be a lot different after we're married? I mean…" She stopped to study the glass apparatus closely. "I know I'm pretty casual about some things some times, but, ah, I really wouldn't want us to get off on the wrong foot. You understand what I'm saying?"

He looked over at her. "No, actually I don't have the faintest idea." Bret spread his hands in an 'I'm sorry' gesture.

Lisa picked up the large propane torch and cracked the valve open a hair. The compressed gas hissed out like an angry rattlesnake. She snapped the flint wheel on her lighter and the stream of invisible gas flashed into an iridescent blue streak. "Simply put, fuck around and I'll kill you." She brought the tip of the pipe to her lips and watched the compound vaporize under the blue hot tip of the torch.

Lisa shut her eyes holding the drug smoke in her lungs. She could feel the beginning of the rush hit somewhere back of her eyeballs. She felt Bret unpeel her fingers from around the pipe and remove it gently from her grasp.

Bret dropped a small pile of crystals into the bowl and watched as the leftover heat melted them instantly into liquid. "Wouldn't," he said and lifted the pipe to his mouth.

The inside of her eyelids were exploding into purple tracers and her heart had begun to pound inside her chest like a captive animal. Shivers ran down her spine and she shuddered. "What?" His voice had suddenly been moved to a distant point and it was made out of shiny metal. It flowed in and bounced around her brain like quicksilver.

"Get married," Bret said and inhaled deeply.

"Oh, God, this must be Peruvian." She forced her eyes open and winced from the light. "'Cause it's so strong I've already lost touch with reality completely. You wouldn't what?"

"Get married," he choked out without opening his mouth.

Lisa suddenly stood up and began pacing. "Oh, God, this is good, this is good." She took the pipe back and began shoveling base into it. "What do you mean you wouldn't get married?"

"If I was going to fuck around. I wouldn't. I mean..." Bret's eyes were closed and for a split second Lisa thought she could actually see his heart beating under his T-shirt.

"I like your logic, but could you speed it up a little bit?"

"Sure," he said, "if you could hurry up with that a little bit." The pinwheels were starting to explode inside his eyelids.

Lisa was still pacing back and forth. "Let's do another hit. Come on." She reached down and rummaged about the table top.

"I don't know, it's only been fifteen minutes and we said we'd wait an hour. I'm pretty wired." Bret walked jerkily over to the front of the stereo and stared at the flickering LEDs.

Lisa picked up the half-filled bottle of beer and drained it in one swallow. "Not me, I can hardly feel it. Shit, get the vodka out of the freezer will you, and please stop fucking with the music, it's so low I can hardly hear it now."

Bret walked over to the window and cracked the curtain back a hair. He peered out around the empty yard.

"Paranoia raises it's ugly head. Jesus, who would be out there? We own two fucking acres surrounded by high tech fences... Take a hit of alcohol, it'll calm you down."

"I don't know... that reporter got in, didn't he?" Bret let the curtain slip back into place. "Maybe you're right, I'll just do one drink, that'll help. You go ahead with the base. I don't want another hit just now. I'll wait... Just for a minute or two."

Lisa scraped some more crystals from the rapidly decreasing pile into the now-warm water pipe. "No way, I want you to keep up with me. Don't be a wuss, you're only young once." She inhaled heavily and leaned back against a large metal tank with a groan.

"So fine, so very fine." Lisa banged her head against the tank. "Shit that's a great idea, I wonder what nitrogen oxide and base is like? Great idea." She reached up and took down the face mask that was attached to the green tank with a thin rubber hose.

"I don't know," Bret said dubiously. "I don't think I can get any higher. I'm sort of speeding." He clenched and unclenched his fists and took a shot of vodka. "I don't know if getting any higher is such a great idea."

Lisa poised with the mask halfway to her face. "No, that's not the point. It's like my life, you know? I may not be getting any higher but, by God, I'm going to come down slow." She fit the mask over her nose and turned the valve. White light began to flow through her veins as the ice-edged gas spread in her lungs. A tingling flow of sensation swept up her body and she shuddered visibly. "Oh, my God," she muttered as her body pounded in step with her pulse, both racing at a thousand miles an hour. "Rush on, you fucker, rush on!" she yelled and swooned against the NO$_2$ tank. Her words were pouring out in an unbroken stream. "That's right, that's what life is supposed to be about. God what a rush! It's like everything is coming at once. My pores are coming!"

She glanced over at Bret. "Sometimes I don't think you understand that concept. The rush concept… Life should always be like this. Fuck that, let's get higher. This is what I live for… It's like writing the ultimate song, reaching the ultimate note, it's like pure fucking power flowing through your veins and you can do anything… That's amazing. You have to do some of that. Here, I'll fix you a hit and then you can do the nitrous right afterwards. You're going to love it, it's just the thing for you… scatter your paranoia like leaves before a hurricane."

Bret exhaled and shook his head in mute acceptance. "You think there's always some place higher to get to? What if this is it? What if there really is no place any higher than this? What then?"

"Oh, no, there's always someplace higher. You can always add to what you've got. Just do something else, you know, do some more, rush fucking on. Rush on. It's like having sex forever. Death is probably the ultimate rush… The ultimate orgasm… Heaven or hell, who cares… Just so it's a rush all the way."

He did the coke, exhaled and took the mask from Lisa's hand. Without thinking about it he sucked in deeply on the NO$_2$. The walls seemed to glow and then grow far away as a series of shudders ripped through his soul.

The next thing Bret knew Lisa was helping him off the floor. He was shaking with fear and pleasure as he leaned on her shoulder. "Wow, I think maybe I passed out for a second, that's…" His voice trailed off.

Lisa helped him sit on the couch. "Pretty good, isn't it? Listen, you just sit here for a second. I'm going to go in the other room and surprise you." She leaned over and kissed him. "I want to get fucked..." She whispered, "Maybe we can figure out how to do a hit just as we're coming. My God, can you picture that? God what a rush that would be..." She shut her eyes.

"Ah, honey I'd like to screw, but I'm pretty ripped, you know. I'm not sure if I can."

"Don't worry about that, I'll help. You'll see. I'll surprise you, just wait here." She left for the bedroom.

Bret shut his eyes on the couch and shook.

"Open your eyes." Lisa ran her fingers lightly over Bret's face. "Surprise..."

The first thing Bret saw was the face painted like a mask. Lisa had applied makeup in an exaggerated fashion: red lips pouting and blue eye shadow curling up into her hair. She had a ribbon bow pulling her hair back into a pony tail and was wearing only a sheer silk teddy. White elbow-length gloves covered her hands and a black garter peeked out on her left thigh. Petite white shoes adorned her feet. She ran her hands under her breasts, pushing them up, and then slid her hands down to her legs. She lifted the teddy and began stroking herself slowly and sensually.

"I can't tell if you're a cheerleader or a whore," he said.

"Either." She ran her tongue over her lips, wetting them. "I can be whatever you want me to be. I can do anything you want me to." She reached over and put his hand where her's had just been.

"I can be a little girl or I can be your slave. Maybe I'm in a slave market and you're coming to look us over to buy one of us... but I'm still young and I'm frightened and I think you'll be good to me but I'm not sure yet and then you reach over and sort of pinch me. And then I'm afraid because I think maybe you're going to be cruel and make me do things I've never done, but that I've thought about, and it scares me. It scares me very much but at the same time in a strange way I really want it...

"Come on, let's go in the other room," she led him out of the living room, then stopped and reached towards the table with her free hand. "First let's do one more hit and then you can do whatever it is that you really want to do to me..."

She picked up the water pipe and continued towards the bedroom.

"Did you ever play suicide ice cream?"

"Wh... What... do... you... mean?" Bret watched every word pour carefully from his mouth. "I'm not sure, ah..." He tried again, "Not... sure..."

"When you were a kid." She reached over and lifted the nearly empty vodka bottle and shook it from side to side. "You're losing the power of speech. I think maybe you're getting drunk. Have another hit of coke."

"I... don't..."

"Trust me, you need it. The yin and the yang." She tipped her hand horizontally and moved it back and forth. "The balance beam is tipping, tipping, tipping. Think of it as concrete... If you don't do up an additional hit the leak will grow and the dam holding back the alcohol will burst..." She demonstrated this concept with her hands. "And suddenly you'll be really drunk.

"Maybe even really sick. Once the dam goes..." Her hands finished the sentence. She picked up the still-warm water pipe. "I know what a drag making a decision can be under the present circumstances. Wait here." She got up and began walking into the living room. "I'm going to get the nitrous and maybe some ether and then we can play... "

"Play," Bret repeated dubiously.

"Now." Lisa smoothed the pile of free base with her index finger, carelessly spilling the overflow into space. She watched as the loose crystals floated randomly on the room's air currents.

"See, when we used to play suicide ice cream, Bonnie, that was my best friend's name, Bonnie... well anyway she and I used to head on down to the old thirty-one flavors and then we'd take turns ordering the grossest combinations we could come up with."

She hesitated to look at Bret. "Are you following this?"

"Suicide," he said. "Ice cream." He swallowed and squinted his eyes, forcing them to focus.

"Okay, so the idea was to come up with something the other person couldn't handle. Then you won." She watched as he shut his eyes and rubbed them. "Maybe you had to be there, but it was really fun... You know, the challenge of eating bubble gum and peanut butter and artichoke... well, I'm not positive about the artichoke actually, but it was fun. See the point?"

"Ah, well, I guess the point was that it was fun…"

"Right!" Lisa clapped her hands together. "We'll take it just one step further. The same rules, but we'll use drugs instead of ice cream. Whoever's turn it is gets to make up the combination for the other person to take, and, to make it an even better game, that person can make the other person do whatever they want." She winked and slowly licked her lips with the tip of her tongue.

"You go first."

He looked over at Lisa, suddenly wanting her beyond belief. "Okay, you do a hit of pot."

Pouting, Lisa picked up a fat roach and lit it. "No, it's got to be a combination, at least two things." She sucked the jay and held her breath.

"Do a hit of coke with it."

"A line or a base hit?"

"Just do a line, okay? You get sexier on coke."

Lisa giggled and picked up the hollow gold straw. She shook some powder onto the back of a *Radio and Records*. "Now tell me what you want me to do."

"I don't know… Maybe you could, maybe take off your clothes…"

"Don't be shy." She smiled and threw the thin nightie over her head. "I know what you want me to do." She bent over and began trying to pull Bret's belt open. Impatience racked her and she grabbed the loose end with both hands, yanking it backwards.

"Easy!" he shouted. "Be gentle. Be nice."

"Fuck that attitude." She ripped the button from the front of his pants and pulled them down over his thighs.

"God, I do love your cock." She began licking the tip and then running her tongue up and down the entire shaft. "But do you know what I love most of all?"

"Oh God, don't stop…"

"I love to feel you getting hard in my mouth. You have no idea what that feels like." She took almost the entire length of him inside and then slid her head slowly up and down. "Do you? Mummm…" She sucked in and then began licking his cock still buried in her mouth.

"Oh, please don't stop." Bret looked down as Lisa broke the connection with a sucking sound and then licked her lips.

"MMM-mmm. Now it's your turn."

"No, no, let's just keep going…"

Lisa laughed. "That's the game, lover. It would be cheating if we broke the rules. Where would the world be without rules?"

He groaned in response.

"Okay, we'll compromise." She reached over and began stroking his semi-rigid member in her fist. "I'll play with you, but you've got to do a hit of base then of ether. Or I'll stop."

"Okay… Okay… Just don't stop." He bent over carefully so as not to dislodge her hand while he picked up the water pipe.

"It's almost clogged up, I don't know if I can do any more in this one."

"Well, then scrape the residue off and we'll do that. It's more concentrated. Even better…"

Bret began loosening the yellow-brown melted coke with a dentist's pick. Large chunks fell onto the magazine cover. He scraped them into a pile.

"Hurry up," Lisa commanded. "Or I'll put a time limit on this…"

Bret watched as Lisa's face popped in and out of focus, as if she was moving in and out of his range of vision. Her image remained in place a split second after each movement, so there were actually a number of Lisas all facing him and seemingly yelling something.

But he couldn't hear what.

"… Okay?" A voice exploded through the crowd. "Are… you… okay?…" Lisa was speaking very deliberately.

"Holy shit. What happened?"

"You did the ether right after you did the base and then you sat down and sort of shuddered for a minute. What did it feel like?"

"An incredible rush." He listened to the metallic echo of his own voice. "Pretty amazing, I don't think I've ever felt like this. Maybe I should write some songs or something…"

"Forget it." Lisa picked his hand up and placed it on her bare breast. "It's my turn, remember? You've got to do what I want now. And you can start by getting yourself hard."

Bret looked down to his now-shrunken cock. "Myself? In front of you?"

"Do it," she whispered huskily, "do it now… I want to watch."

Bret reached down and began rubbing himself with one hand. Lisa began to move his other hand back and forth on her breast, forcing his fingers to pinch her erect nipple.

"Can't you speed that up a little bit?" Lisa cupped her free hand around Bret's balls. "You're not doing your part in this game..."

"Christ, honey, I want you, believe me... Coming on coke is so good, you know? But I'm really loaded and it's hard to get hard... Besides, my body, uh, tends to think everything is over when we stop to inhale... Maybe if I gave it a few minutes to recover..."

"Bad idea." Lisa reached down and stripped her panties off in one motion. "I'm too horny to wait. Use your hands." She lay down and spread her legs, running her fingers up her thighs like a character from the Arabian Nights.

Bret reach down and felt the heat burn his hand. Lisa groaned and shoved her hips upward into his palm. "Oh yes, harder, do it harder." She put her hand on top of Bret's and began to choreograph the movement. "Rub your finger in little circles right there. Just on my clit. Ohhh, yes, yes..." She increased the speed of both hands. "Like that, like that... God I'm coming, I'm coming, I'm coming..." Her body stiffened and she arched her back away from the bed. "Oh yes, now stick your fingers inside of me. Oh, God, yes, like that, I'm still coming, everywhere you touch me it's like I'm coming from a hundred little places all at once..." Once again she increased the pressure of her guiding hand.

"Okay, it's your turn. You can stop for a second." Lisa lifted his hand tentatively away from her body. "But only for a second."

"I want you to do a hit of base and then one of nitrous and then ether. You can skip the pot for now."

"Can't," Bret mumbled. "Too wired, it's like my mind just keeps skipping around. I'm kind of freaking, you know."

"Stop staring at the fucking door, okay? We're all alone here, try to relax, no one is coming in."

"I know that, but ah, it's just that I'm sort of wired..."

"Jesus, give me a break." Lisa shut her eyes in annoyance. "Okay," she brightened, "in that case we'll change the recipe. You can do a couple of shots of vodka." She poured the clear liquid in a water glass and then sprinkled some pepper on the surface. "But you've got to do up some more coke. I want you to get hard and fuck me. Okay?"

"Can I just do a line?"

"Sure, take your medicine first." She handed the glass of booze across the bed. "I'll just do a fast hit of base while you shake some duff loose." She reached for the water pipe.

✿ ✿ ✿

"Use two fingers. Put them both in at once." Lisa was lying on her stomach. Two pillows were bunched under her pelvis thrusting her hips into the air. Her red hair splayed over two other pillows and she held her hands as far in front of her as they would go. Her wrists were clamped tightly together as if she was bound by invisible handcuffs.

Bret kneeled between her legs sliding the first two fingers of his left hand into Lisa while massaging his flaccid prick with his right. His hand made a sucking noise as he slowly slid it out of the quicksand of Lisa's pussy. "Oh yes," she sobbed, "put them back in and reach down with the tips... there's a, a special spot you can rub and I'll just keep on coming and coming..."

Bret put three fingers tightly together and forced them back inside, the heat raging and burning his very skin.

"Tell me what you're doing. Please," she begged, "tell me what you're doing..." She wiggled her body searching for his fingers.

"Fucking you," he said, pausing to wipe dripping sweat from his forehead with his other hand. "My hand is part of me too." Slowly he slide all five fingers into her, amazed at the ease of the movement.

"Tell me. Tell me..." She wiggled down on his hand like a speared fish. "What it is you are doing to me. Talk to me, please..."

Bret leaned directly over her head, so close he could feel her breath reflected from the satin pillow case. "I'm making a fist. Inside of you." And he slowly rolled his fingers into the palm of his hand and tensed his grip.

Lisa felt her body stretch to an unbelievable limit and then her smooth muscles reversed themselves, contracting around the foreign object inside of her very soul. She screamed softly as her body molded itself into a new being.

"I'll never stop coming, never... So good, ohhh, so very, very good..." Bret watched as individual shudders flowed up Lisa's naked spine.

Bret studied the motion of Lisa's enraptured body with awe. He felt disjointed... On a different plane... Above her and inside her at the same time. He swallowed a half glass of vodka in one gulp and gasped as his eyes teared. He started to fall to the side and caught himself with his free hand, spilling a few drops of liquor onto the bed sheet.

"Oh no," Lisa moaned. "Don't stop, keep going." She wiggled her ass upward wantonly. "You'll lose the game if you stop now." She panted.

"Who says?"

"I do, I'm in char—" Lisa yelped in mid-sentence as a strong slap landed on her bare ass. "Uh-huh," she squirmed from side to side as a bright red handprint appeared on her pink flesh as if drawn by magic.

"What are..." The fist curled and uncurled inside her. "Again, do it again."

Bret wasn't sure which hand she was referring to; he slapped her again, feeling her ass squeeze tight around the offending hand. He held it in place and began stroking her, feeling the roughness of her skin where her cheeks separated.

"Oh," Lisa squealed and jumped involuntarily as Bret inserted his fingertip into her anus. "Slowly, go slowly, let me relax the muscles..." She spread her legs to their maximum.

Bret pushed slightly and felt his finger slip in to the first knuckle as her body gripped it tightly from all sides. Slowly he began working the finger back and forth in opposite time to his other hand. He could feel both hands almost touching each other through the thin membrane of muscle.

"Can't believe it..." He wasn't sure who said it, but someone did. "Incredible..."

"I can't believe I always want to get fucked up the ass when I'm on coke. Ohhh..." She forced her body up and down in order to speed the rhythm. "Your finger sure fits in there well, doesn't it? Why don't you just go ahead and slip your cock in instead. Okay? Do it now..."

Bret looked down to see a semi-hard-on at best. He withdrew his finger and grabbed himself with his hand, trying to force his body to respond. His cock stopped at the tiny opening and bent double. He tried again.

"What's the hang up here?" Lisa propped herself up on her elbows and looked back over her shoulder. "Oh shit." She reached down and grabbed his wrist, sliding his hand from her body. "Honey, I really want to get fucked. Now."

"I know, I know... It's just that I'm pretty loaded. I feel kinda dizzy, the room is sliding around a bit."

"Maybe you're just not man enough." She looked into his face. "I'm sorry, babe, I shouldn't have said that, I'm just really horny. Try and get hard will you?"

"I've been trying for about an hour... I'm getting really sore."

"Okay, okay, I'll make a deal with you. My turn for suicide ice cream... You do what I say and then if it doesn't work I'll let you make it up to me some other way." She stuck her tongue out and smiled...

"Oh, man, I'm really pretty fucked up. I don't think I should do anything else. I might start puking."

"It's my game. Don't be such a wimp, either get it hard or get it on." She passed the glass pipe over and lit the propane lighter. "I'll even hold the torch for you, but the deal is you've go to do one of everything... First the base and then a shot and then..."

"No more. No more..." Bret was mumbling. Did I say that out loud? His synapses were starting to mix their inputs; sound was becoming vision and vision was become touch and touch... From an incredible distance he heard Lisa's voice. "Just the ether, that's all, just do a quick sniff and we'll go back to playing. I think it's starting to work, you look like you're getting hard. This is the last round, I promise. If you can do this you'll win. Well, maybe not win, but you won't have to play anymore. Come on."

He felt the cold bottle being shoved into his hands and the rough smell of the ether jumped into his nose... And then everything started to glow with a bright white fire.

I've never seen anything like this before he thought as the multiple rush grabbed his being and twisted him sideways.

"Be careful," Lisa lunged at the bottle as the rag came out of the neck and it slipped to the bed. "You're spilling that shit all over the sheets. You jerk, pay attention here. This is life, we can't change the channels..." She stopped abruptly.

Bret slid slowly down to the bed. He looked up at nothing and smiled like he was seeing something that was not in the room.

"Oh, God, no!" Lisa's eyes widened; she slapped Bret hard across the face.

He did not respond.

"No, no," she slapped him again and again.

"No, NO! You can't do this to me. Oh, God, make him wake up." She grabbed both of his shoulders and shook him roughly.

His head flopped back and forth like an old rag doll, the strange smile still on his face.

"Oh, God, don't do this to me. NONONONO!" She screamed into the night.

* * *

Carol walked over to the white leather couch, started to sit down and then, like a sleepwalker, collapsed into the cushions, her limbs flying loose like a Raggedy Ann doll. When she opened her eyes the first image they focused on was a thin powder of dust evenly layered across the surface of the chrome-and-glass table exactly at her eye level.

Christ, how did I ever let Leon talk me into graveyard furniture — bones and glass. And why can't I find a maid that actually wants to clean instead of daydreaming about becoming the lead in an ice show?

I miss my nice plain eighteenth-century New England living room. Sometimes I think I miss my nice plain eighteenth-century New England. How did I get here anyway? Am I really any happier than I was?... Only if...

Oh, God. Carol shut her eyes. If I go to sleep now, could it be just like in one of those fairy tales — I'll sleep forever.

It seemed just a moment later the phone on the table next to her head rang with an explosive force. Carol's entire body hurt for a moment and then jumped as her muscles uncoiled and the noise dragged her to unwilling consciousness.

Damn! She fumbled for the receiver and swore again when the coil cord wrapped itself around her arm and the instrument fell from her fingertips onto the thick pile of the carpet.

Carol held her hand out, fingers brushing the hard plastic skin of the telephone. She blinked and focused on her hand.

It was shaking.

"Miss Davis? This is Marie at the switchboard?" Why does this girl have to make everything a question, Carol thought. "Are you there?"

"Yeah," Carol said, "semi-here anyway."

"Uh," the other woman said, "are you all right?"

Please, no more questions, I feel like I'm on a game show. "I'm fine, but I did leave specific instructions that I wasn't to be bothered." God, what a bitch I sound like...

"Oh, yes, I know that, but this one sounded really important. You know what I mean?"

A sense of dread began to quicken Carol's pulse. Had something happened to Taylor? No, the phone call would be from Nick or at least someone on high; there would be no meaningless interchange with a switchboard operator, maybe...

"Hello, Miss Davis?" A brusque, efficient voice suddenly replaced the operator's. Without waiting for any response it continued, "My name is Ms. Billings and I'm with United Airlines."

Carol was fully awake and beginning to find the situation absurd. "Some special award on my frequent flyer card? I've finally logged enough miles to qualify for your free wakeup call program?"

"I'm calling you from the employees' lounge at McCarran airport. We have a Miss Steel here and, uh, she's not in very good shape."

Suddenly Carol felt her heart kick into overdrive. "There? Lisa is there? What's she doing?"

"Doing? Frankly not much at the moment. At least she's conscious, that's a step in the right direction."

"Uh-oh," Carol was starting to get the picture. "Is she okay? If she's sick why isn't she at the hospital?"

"She asked me to call you... Personally." The unseen woman dropped her voice to a loud whisper and at the same time seemed to lose some of her composure. "She, she threatened legal action if we called anyone else. She can be pretty persuasive when she wants to be."

Carol tried to imagine Lisa being persuasive. It was not a pretty sight. A sudden sympathy for the woman on the other end of the line began to develop.

"What happened? I mean exactly."

"Miss Steel passed out on the plane. The pilot was going to make an emergency landing to get her to a hospital, but there was this doctor on board and he examined her, and, well, he seemed to think that it wasn't that serious. Miss Steel had quite a bit to drink on the plane and we knew who she was, of course, and we all were anxious not to overreact if she wasn't in any danger..."

It was obvious that the speaker was not second guessing this decision. "Listen, you did exactly the right thing, if we can possibly keep this between us..."

"I'm afraid it's already gotten a bit past that stage. You see, your friend woke up right as the doctor was examining her and she was, uh, as you can probably picture, sort of, well, I guess startled would be the right term, and she became rather, ah, verbal and we had to kind of restrain her. So she wouldn't hurt herself, or anyone else. You understand?..."

Carol was doing exactly that. You poor, poor woman, she thought. "What did the doctor say?"

"Well, he thought she had just overdone things a bit. Actually he's a vet."

Carol felt the thin web of the plot drifting further out of reach. "Pardon me? Who's a vet?"

"The doctor was — is, rather — a veterinarian. He was the only medical person on board. Or at least the only one who would come forward... It's not the most popular request in the world: 'Is there a doctor on board' "

"Oh, Jesus." Carol laughed in spite of herself. "A veterinarian. If Lisa only knew. My God!"

"I think he identified himself. I'm sure he was only trying to be helpful, to convince her to get medical attention. If you don't want to deal with this situation we can call—"

"No, no," Carol said quickly, "I'll be right down. She's, well, Lisa's a friend, I guess, and I'll take responsibility." She paused, trying to grasp the entire scenario.

"I really appreciate your calling me, you did exactly the right thing. I, that is, both of us, appreciate your kindness. Are you sure Lisa knew he was a veterinarian?" she asked as an afterthought.

"Yes, once you've heard the phrase 'Fucking horse doctor' yelled repeatedly in a small area it kind of sticks with you. You know?"

"Oh, God! I'll leave now. I'll be right there."

"One more thing..." The trained voice said. "The doctor said he was pretty sure she was really, really loaded. I mean she isn't just drunk. Do you understand?"

Carol shook her head silently and slowly returned the phone to its cradle.

I understand. I understand.

Lisa leaned quietly on Carol's shoulder as they followed a flying wedge of airport security guards elbowing a path through the mob of tightly pressed reporters and gawkers.

Lisa turned her head to the side as a flash exploded directly into her face. One side of her sunglasses slipped down the side of her cheek exposing an angry red welt.

"Hey, Lisa!" A reporter yelled, "Tell us what happened up there."

"Is it true you decked a stewardess?"

"No comment." Lisa tucked her chin to her chest and shut her eyes, letting Carol lead her across the tile floor.

"Are you here to work?"

"Is it true the captain was going to land the plane because of you?"

"What kind of attack did you have?" The questions were now coming one on top of the other.

Lisa bit down on her lip in an attempt to keep some vestige of control. "No comment, no comment." She struck her hand out like she was tearing down invisible spider webs. "I don't want to talk to you bloodsuckers right now."

Her voice was so hoarse Carol didn't think her thoughts had carried through the general din of the crowded airport. She stepped the pace up in an attempt to get Lisa outdoors and into the car before she had a chance to repeat her statement.

Carol breathed easier as they broke from the building. Just a few feet to the curb and the limo... The press people were fighting each other trying to get through the door.

The race was almost over when a too-white light switched on, trapping both women in it's glow. A field reporter from a local television stuck a microphone directly in Lisa's face.

"Did you really bury Bret with a motorcycle?"

Lisa froze in her tracks and peered at the woman. She was clearly taken aback by the question.

"Yes," she said quietly, "that's true..."

"Could you speak up a bit, please." The woman waited expectantly. Lisa was silent.

"Why did you do that? Was that a stunt just to publicize your new album?"

"No. It wasn't." Lisa stopped again, seemed to think about things, and started in again.

"It was what he wanted. You see," Lisa seemed almost patient with the obviously raw reporter, "he, he loved that bike. It was something special. He was something special. They seemed to go together."

The woman plunged on, not appreciating the rare interview she was getting.

"We're here at McCarran Airport interviewing Lisa Steel. Tell us, Lisa, in your own words, exactly how the tragic death of Bret Henley occurred."

Carol could feel Lisa stiffen her body. "Don't you read the papers? He had a stroke."

"Is there any truth to the rumors that his body was full of illegal drugs?"

Here it comes, Carol thought. She tried to push Lisa towards the waiting vehicle, but she held solid. "Does your mother know what you do for a living?" Lisa asked, but her heart wasn't in it. "Retroactive birth control. People like you are the perfect argument for it."

She flipped the bird to the camera and then let Carol drag her off to the car.

"I need to go home with you, Carol." Lisa burst into tears, "I think maybe you're the only real friend I've got left in the whole world. I think I've killed all the rest off. One way or another. Bang. Bang. Just like in the movies.

"I can't take any more reporters or assholes for a while. Just for a little while. I need to get away and get some rest. I really need some sleep."

"John, call the desk, have them get a suite ready, put it in my name. Don't mention Lisa."

The driver picked up a cellular phone and hit the auto dial button.

"No, wait!" Lisa implored. "I can't go there. The jackals will find me. You've got to take me to your place. Please, Carol, just for a few days."

"Lisa, we'll put you on the security floor, nobody will get in to bother you."

"No, you don't know what those people are like, they could get in a bank vault if they thought there was a story or some rotting meat inside.

"Besides, I really need to be with someone normal for a little while."

"Well ..." Carol could feel herself starting to feel sorry for Lisa. It never fails...

"Just for a little while, just a few days. I won't be any trouble. I promise. No trouble."

Carol tapped the driver on his arm and indicated that he should put the phone back in it's cradle.

Lisa yawned and plopped herself down on the couch where Carol had been asleep only an hour before. "Your place is gorgeous, you've come up in the world since I left. I never seem to stay in one house long enough to have anybody decorate it so it's a part of me.

"I know you did this yourself, Carol. I don't know where you get the time or energy. Sometimes I really envy you."

"You envy me?" Carol laughed lightly. "I'm not sure I believe that, Lisa. I think you do pretty much what you want. I think you're pretty much who you want to be."

"No, that's not true. You don't know what's it like sometimes... The pressure is so tough—and everyone you meet is always after something. If they don't want your money, then you can bet your ass they want a piece of your soul and that's even more expensive in the long run.

"Johnny Star was right all along. Everybody in the business has got a handful of gimme and a mouthful of much obliged. I always thought he was exaggerating, you know, just being a whiner.

"God, he could whine when he wanted to," Lisa sighed heavily. "Get me a drink, will you, honey?"

"Lisa, you've had enough for one day." And probably enough for one lifetime, Carol thought.

"Tomorrow, Carol, I promise we'll sit down and have it out. I know I'm fucking up. I admit it. I won't argue, but please not today. I can't quit cold turkey and I'll never get to sleep if I don't have a couple of pops."

She opened her flight bag and spilled the contents out onto the leather couch. Several airline one-shot drink bottles lay mixed in with the rubble.

"Never mind, we'll do this BYOB." She cracked open a mini-Scotch and drank it down in one gulp. "I had to steal these... Fucking cheap airline... and after all the free publicity I got them today. Some people have no sense of gratitude at all.

"Where was I? Oh yeah, good old Johnny. Maybe I should have stuck with him. He was an asshole, but he was a predictable asshole. He was my asshole."

She paused in reflection, "Do you know what happened to him?"

"Rumors," Carol answered. "I've heard vague rumors of a comeback but I haven't really seen anything concrete."

"When I first met him I thought he was TWTBT—Too Weird To Be True—but then I realized he was just To Wired To Be True...

"He'll never come back. He went needle happy. That's the heaviest Jones there is. He started shooting coke and then downers and once when we locked ourselves in the house to straighten out, I caught him shooting coffee.

"Coffee... Kool Aid... fuck... Anything for the needle rush. He'll never give it up. He'll never come back.

"After Johnny my life was a big pit. It's sort of blurry, like watching MTV in fast forward. I'm not even sure how much of it really happened or how much was just part of some private script…

"And then I met Bret. Jesus!" She burst into tears again. "I really fell for him. I mean, I was really in love. And we were going to be married, and then…" She unscrewed another bottle of Scotch and chugged it down.

"Did you really bury his motorcycle with him?" Carol couldn't keep herself from asking.

"Yeah, Bret had a thing about that piece of junk. But he had class, he had style. God, you should have seen his relatives at the funeral when I demanded the bike go down with him.

"But I did it… . He went out with style." She grabbed Carol by the hand, "When I die I want to be buried in my Ferrari. With the top down. Like that rich broad in Texas… I want to take it with me. I'm not kidding. I'll write it down and you can take it to some fancy lawyer and get it legalized. Okay, Carol? Promise me?"

"Sure, Lisa, if you go first, I promise it."

"Oh, I dare say I'll go first. Live fast, die young and leave a good-looking corpse. Fuck 'em all anyway.

"God, I wish he hadn't died, Carol, I'd give anything." Her voice was beginning to slur and she was getting really dizzy. "I guess I'd better get some sleep." She bent over and started stuffing her possessions back into her bag.

The last item was a worn Bible. She caught Carol staring at it. "Yeah, I know, weird, isn't it? But when I grew up, God was always the sixth member of the household. Sometimes I like to read the book again, like, you know, it can't hurt." She shrugged. "At the very least it's full of good bloody stories, people getting crucified, people getting zapped into pillars of salt… Sort of like Hollywood on a slow news day.

"Besides, Carol," she was stumbling over her words badly now, "only God can really love you—all the rest are liars or just trying to get in your pants…"

Carol put Lisa to bed in the guest room and then took a quick shower before putting on her new clinging dress. By the time she arrived at the restaurant, Taylor was already seated and eyeing the cold bottle of Dom Perignon.

He stood up as she arrived and kissed her on the cheek. "You look beautiful tonight—more than ever." He popped the cork on the expensive wine and poured them each a glass.

They touched rims and the leaded glasses gave off a pure tone as they met.

"To you," Taylor said.

"To us," Carol replied.

Taylor sipped the champagne and watched Carol. "You know, I think you're actually developing a taste for the stuff. At least my influence has had some results."

Carol laughed, "You knew I didn't like it? I tried so hard to look like I was enjoying it every time. I mean, I sort of do now, but at first it was a bit of a struggle. How could you tell?"

"Carol, I know just about everything that goes on in this town. It's what I do."

"Oh." Carol played with her oysters, her mind elsewhere.

"Speaking of things that go on in this town, how's your new room-mate doing?"

"My, but you do keep up. You having my house watched, Taylor?"

He laughed, "Nothing so dramatic. She was on the news, and I know the way Lisa's mind works. I also know that besides being beautiful you're the original soft touch."

"She was in pretty bad shape. She needed a place to stay for a few days."

"Carol, it may surprise you to realize this, but there actually are several hotels in this town. I'll bet we could've found a room that would even approach Lisa's high standards of excellence."

"She's a friend, Taylor."

"Lisa has never had a friend in her entire life. She was born without a certain chromosome. A genetic defect, she's unable to care for anyone in the whole world except for Lisa Lewalski-sorry, I mean, Steel. She's just playing with the concept of friendship in order to guilt trip you into keeping her."

"You're wrong about her and about this situation. You really don't know everything in the whole world." She felt the color come into her cheeks.

Taylor didn't respond.

"I'm sorry, Taylor, she really is a friend and she needs help and I couldn't refuse. She won't interfere with us, I promise. Just for a few days…"

"I agree she does need help—the kind of help only a professional can give. From what I hear she's still doing drugs like there's no tomorrow. That stunt on the plane was really the capper. That's going to be all over town by morning.

"Do you think she'll change her spots now that you're taking control? Why should she?" Taylor moved the plate of oysters to the side and leaned close to Carol.

"If you really are her friend, you'd better get her into a treatment program immediately. She's killing herself, and what's worse, you're helping kill her… Unless you can get her into a heavy duty addict program."

"I don't know…" Carol frowned at the thought. "That's not going to be easy. If I talk to her, if I can reach her… maybe I can keep her straight."

"Don't kid yourself, Carol. People like Lisa never straighten out on their own and they never listen to people who think they're being a friend. If you don't want the responsibility of fixing the situation, I'll do it. I really don't care if she hates me.

"Lisa is a user—people, drugs, money, it's all the same to her. I admit she's a talented bitch, but I figure that's just one of God's little jokes on life—a touch of irony, just to keep the universe interesting."

"Okay, this conversation is over." Carol started to stand up.

"You win, I'm wrong. Let's not let her mess up the evening. I won't mention the subject again."

Carol looked at him doubtfully, "Promise?"

"Eat your last oyster, it's about to die of loneliness."

Taylor pulled the car to the front of Carol's building, parked, and then opened her door. They kissed deeply and Carol pushed her lower lip up over her upper into a caricature of a sad face.

"Oh, oh, here it comes. You know, Carol, if I told anyone you were even capable of making a face like that… They'd think I was lying through my teeth."

He raised his hands. "Don't say it, I'm not coming upstairs tonight, am I? Oh, that's right, you've got a roommate now—one who's not going to interfere with our relationship, right?"

"Please, I… it's just the first night, and I think…"

"She knows you were married before, Carol. I don't think she's a virgin either. It's okay to have your boyfriend up."

Carol kissed him on the cheek. "Next time, I promise."

Carol noticed the Bible laying askew on the coffee table as she turned off the lights and closed the door to her room.

Bright. White. Pain. Lisa put her arm over her eyes and groaned.

"Come on, Lisa, wake up, it's after nine already."

Lisa opened her eyes and blinked at Carol. "Shit," her voice cracked. "I'm really here, aren't I?"

Carol handed a glass of fresh orange juice. "Drink this, you'll feel better."

Lisa sipped the thick liquid. "Get me an aspirin. A bunch of aspirin. My head is coming apart at the seams."

"Right here, and I've got breakfast ready."

"I can't face food. I don't know if I can face life. Leave me alone."

"Lisa, you've got to get up, we've got to talk. It can't wait. Take a shower if you want, but then come into the other room."

"Okay," Lisa mumbled from underneath the covers. "I'll shower."

Lisa locked the door, turned on the shower, and then spread two long rails of cocaine on the peach-colored tile. She inhaled them and then rubbed the residue on her gums, which immediately turned numb.

Lisa floated into the dining room and kissed Carol. Her hair was bunched under a towel and she looked human once again.

"You certainly look better."

"Nothing like a hot shower for curing a hangover," Lisa smiled.

"Thank you, honey, for what you did yesterday. I was pretty wasted, but I guess you know that. I really appreciate you letting me crash here for a few days."

"That shower did you a world of good... Lisa, you were really messed up yesterday. You passed out on the plane. You could have, well, done something serious..."

"No, no, it's just that everything is sort of ganging up on me, all at once. I just need some time to get my act together. I need to shed a while."

"Shed?"

"It's an old music term—you know, go out to the woodshed and just work. In my case, I think I could shed my skin, too."

"You can stay here on one condition. I want you to... to enter a program." Quickly Carol added, "Just to help you. You've got to lay off the booze and the drugs, Lisa, it really is killing you."

"Oh-oh, I smell Taylor behind this speech."

Carol looked startled.

"I woke up when you came home last night. You guys looked pretty serious out there on the step. He didn't want to come in with me here? And now he wants to send me off to the house of straight jackets? Pretty convenient."

"No, it wasn't his idea," Carol lied. "We both care about you. He wants to see you well."

"Oh, yeah, I bet he speaks real highly of me right?"

"Don't change the subject, Lisa. That's the deal—you have got to get help or you can't stay here."

"Cut me some slack, Carol... Have you ever been to an AA meeting? No, well, I have—'Hi, I'm Lisa and I'm an alcoholic...' In chorus now—'Helllloo, Lisa, we all just want to help you...'

"And then they start telling these stories. Oh, God, they're so fucking dull it's what hell must be like. Hundreds of petty, dull, boring, little people rambling on about their dull, petty, little lives and you're tied to a chair." She grabbed her neck and pantomimed a strangling.

"And then they want you to go every day for, I forget, maybe a hundred fucking years, or maybe it's two hundred. Even murderers get cut loose in seven. I couldn't take that... People like that are the reason I use drugs in the first place! I would never get any work done if I had to go somewhere for a big chunk of my day every single day of my life. Twelve steps of crap!...

"They just try to substitute one addiction for another. I don't need that shit, I can't take it."

"I've got to be tough on this. I can't watch you hurting herself."

"Okay, we'll compromise. I'll stop doing any hard stuff and go to a shrink."

"Well, I'll pick the doctor."

"You mean Taylor will pick the shrink... I don't care, it's just so good to be here, I'll do it."

Lisa sat in front of the cluttered table for several long minutes after Carol left for work. I'll just take a bump and then I'll clear the table... She spread two more lines of powder on one of the plates and snorted it.

Immediately a feeling of guilt swept over her. I can't do this to Carol, I really should stop. She picked up the bundle of powder and walked over to the sink.

Oh, Jesus, this is so stupid!... It's not like I couldn't stop if I wanted to... And here I go again throwing away a few hundred dollars... If I could just get it out of sight for a few days, clear out... Then I could have it around if I really needed it to get some work done...

She snapped her fingers out loud and walked into the study. Lisa wrapped the coke in a manila envelope, stared at it for a few minutes, tore the envelope open, dumped out two more lines, re-wrapped it, and placed it in another envelope and addressed it to herself.

I get one line now and one line when I get back from the mailbox and then that's all. Right. She scarfed up one of the lines, looked dubiously at the other, and then ran out the door.

It was mid-afternoon by the time Lisa started getting anxious. God, I wish I hadn't mailed all that. If I'd just saved a little, this wouldn't be too bad...

By four o'clock she was pacing back and forth. Her stomach was cramping and she was ravenously hungry. She drank down her last two mini-Scotches and then started rummaging through Carol's cupboards.

Sherry! I can't believe it, doesn't this woman ever have guests? Finally she came across some gin and poured herself a large glass over ice.

When the gin was gone she began pacing again. This sucks, I really need a hit. I'm going to have to do something. She changed from her bathrobe and walked out the door.

Four hours later Lisa stood in front of the red and blue mailbox and stared at it. I can't break the fucker, it's metal, and besides there are probably laws against that.

Still, there has to be a way to get in there... She pulled the lid down and the collection hours glared up at her.

Shit! They picked the fucker up at noon. I've got to get a cab and get to the post office. She walked over to the curb and waved down a passing taxi.

"Post office," she said.

"Which one?" This was a new, and ugly thought.

"There's more than one?"

"Yup. You going to mail something?"

Stupid. This is really stupid, if someone recognizes me... "Forget the post office, take me to a liquor store."

"I don't want to eat dinner, I don't want to come out of my room, I don't want to see another living soul. Go away and let me die in peace."

Carol opened the door and peered in. She sucked in her breath in spite of herself.

"That's it, make me feel better, Carol." Lisa ran her fingers through her hair, which had mysteriously gotten greasy already. Her eyes were bloodshot and her hands were shaking.

"What's the matter?"

"I'm fucking giving up fucking drugs, like I promised you, remember? Cute huh? Make a good 'just say no' ad." She threw herself down on the bed. "I can't remember feeling this bad in my whole life. I've got to get some sleep before I go crazy. I've still got some Halcion in my bag. Maybe that'll knock me out."

She swallowed two blue pills and choked them down with Glenlivet, spitting the amber liquid out of the corners of her mouth.

"Do you suppose that's why they give them with water in the hospital?"

"Be nice to me, Carol, I'm this far from death." She framed a half-inch gap with her thumb and forefinger. "I'll be on your conscience forever. You'll be sorry you were mean to me..."

"Okay, Lisa, have it your way. You sleep, I'll get you up for break-fast."

"A late breakfast," she replied picking up the Glenlivet.

Twice that she could remember Lisa woke up in the darkness sweating from every pore in her body. Her ears were ringing and her heart pounded as if awakened from a violent nightmare. She jumped and something small and quick seemed to run from the corner of her bed into the darkness of the room.

Shit, I know there's nothing in the room... there can't be anything there. But she peered into the blackness anyway, as if expecting a rat to materialize in the corner. Maybe I need a night light...

Each time she awoke she lay awake in the blackness for a few minutes, fearing that she would never go back to sleep. Each time she reached over to the night stand and fumbled with the plastic pill bottle until it freed up a sleeping pill. Each time she held the pill under her tongue to speed the effects of the sleep-inducing chemical and each time she fell back into a troubled slumber.

When Carol went to Lisa's door she could hear the sound of running water coming from the bathroom. She knocked gently.

"Are you okay?"

"No, I'm not okay, I'm hugging the porcelain pony." This was followed by the sounds of vomiting.

"Go away, Carol, let me be sick by myself. I'll call you if I need help."

Carol let herself out the door and walked silently to her car.

By ten o'clock Lisa had eaten some toast and drunk a large orange juice with only a touch of vodka. I think I'm going to live, although it would sure be nice to wake up with just a small line.

Oh, my God! The mail. What time does it get here? She tried to recall what the postal schedule was in Las Vegas. Maybe it had already been delivered. She threw on a sweatshirt and a pair of Carol's slippers and rushed out to the mail box. It was empty. Damn, damn, damn. She looked down the street but there was no sign of a postal vehicle. She went back inside and turned the television set on. Stupid game shows, who watches this crap anyway? Maybe one more vodka would help ease the tension...

"Are you sure this is all? I mean I was expecting a letter. From a friend, see I know they mailed it and it should be here."

The mailman looked carefully at Lisa and wondered where he had seen her before. Well, this was Las Vegas, anything was possible. Rather than confront the wild-looking woman in the bathrobe he made a concerted effort to search through the remaining pile of undelivered mail.

"I'm sorry, that's all there is... Maybe it will come tomorrow."

"Shit!" Lisa threw the letters at the empty mail box. "I don't want it tomorrow, I want it now!"

"I'm sorry." The man backed away, keeping a wary eye on Lisa, who was now stamping her foot on a book of coupons. "Maybe tomorrow."

"Can I be of service?" The man leaned over the counter.

"Are you in charge?"

The man nodded. "I'm the postmaster. What seems to be the problem?"

"I was expecting a letter... And it didn't come..." It sounded so lame, as if she was whining about a note from a boyfriend. "It's real important," she added.

"The mail has already been delivered today. When do you think it was mailed?"

"Yesterday. Yesterday morning, but right here in Vegas. Wouldn't I get it today?"

"Maybe it didn't get mailed on time—that's what usually happens. Someone just makes a mistake about when they mailed it. If it was deposited after pickup..."

"No, no, I know it was mailed on time. I saw"—she realized she was digging a hole—"it being... A friend of mine... He mailed it, ah, to me at the office."

"Why didn't you just take it with you?"

"Thought, I, ah, would be out of town. I was supposed to catch a plane last night. For Hollywood, California, but I didn't go, and so we mailed the scripts and I need them back today. I got a whole crew standing by and we can't shoot until we get the scripts. The scripts in the mail." She was improvising rapidly as the story began unfolding almost of its own will.

The man spread his hands wide in front of him. "I'm sorry, you'll just have to wait until tomorrow. I'm sure they'll be there tomorrow."

"But I need them today!" Lisa could tell she was starting to yell but she was unable to prevent it.

"Did you send them express, registered, or even certified? Something with a number that we could trace?"

"Well, no, but I can tell you exactly where they were mailed from."

"I'm sorry lady, but we got several hundred thousand letters lying around, I just can't personally look through every one."

"I'll look for it! You don't have to. I could find it, I know just what it looks like. I could probably find it real quickly." She smiled to reassure the postmaster of her investigative abilities.

"I can't do that. I'm afraid you'll just have to go home and wait until tomorrow. The police don't even trace missing people until they've been gone twenty-four hours." He smiled to show it was a little joke they could both share.

Lisa slammed her fist on the counter so hard that a little pile of first class stickers fell onto the floor. "I NEED IT TODAY. I need it today."

The man backed up from the counter and waved off two approaching clerks. "Listen, Lisa, I recognize you, and other people here probably do too. I like your stuff, in fact, I'm a fan. I think you're really hot stuff. There are two ways this can end up; one is you go and find some replacement for the scripts and we all live happily ever after. Two is much more unpleasant and involves security guards, large crowds of unruly people and reporters. I'm trying to protect you here but..."

Lisa stared at the man as the truth of his words began to seep in. She looked around and noticed that other people were indeed following the conversation intently. Close, she realized, this was close. "So you're a fan, huh?"

The man nodded and blushed a bit in the process.

"Thank you, fan." And she leaned over and kissed the man full on the mouth. "Better than an autograph, huh?"

The blush developed into a full fledged red-on as he stammered something in response. The entire lobby broke into spontaneous applause. Lisa curtsied and left, the noise bouncing from the marble floors as she walked out.

"Just cruise up and down the strip," Lisa told the hack, "I want to feel this town in my bones again."

"Sure lady, it's your money." The incredible mixture of neon sunshine flickered into the interior of the cab, giving it an unearthly glow.

Maybe the post jerk was right. It ain't like I've got a corner on the market — or like I don't know anybody in this town. Maybe I should get a substitute script. "The Eagle. Stop at the Eagle." The cabby pulled to the front curb. "Wait for me, I'll just be a few minutes." She opened the door and got out.

"Honey, don't stiff me, okay? I got a wife and three hungry kids. I don't want to have to come looking for you."

"Yeah." Lisa walked off without glancing back.

Lisa could feel the heartbeat of the casino pulsating through her being. She stopped and shut her eyes in order to let the sounds wash over her. God, it's been a long time. She edged over to a craps table. If I put on my sunglasses will it make me stand out more? I really don't want anyone to make me, I must look like shit. A few people glanced up momentarily as she joined the crowd but they quickly looked back to the table where a three-hundred-pound black man with a shaved head and gold nugget rings on all five fingers shook the dice and tossed them against the back felt wall of the table.

"Come home! Come home!" He yelled as a hard eight appeared. "*Yes!*" And he lifted the twenty-year-old blond dancer clinging to his arm and kissed her on the mouth. "That mouth of yours is pure gold. I keep kissing you, I can't lose."

Lisa grinned to herself. Oh yeah, I'd almost forgotten what it was like. Ain't nobody gonna ask for an autograph in this town... I'm fucking normal here. I fit right in... She caught the eye of the pit boss and tilted her head towards a closed blackjack table. The man walked over and joined her.

"Hey, Lisa, I heard you were back in town. I'm surprised at the honor, you've gone a long way from the chorus. Congratulations."

"Thanks, Eddie. God, it feels good to be somewhere where people still act alive. I miss this town."

"Hollyweird not all it's cracked up to be?"

"Nothing in life is, Eddie, nothing is... I need a favor..."

The pit boss smiled, "And here I thought you just came by to pay your respects, pass the time of day. Turns out you need a favor. Exactly what kind of favor you got in mind? Need a credit line? Want me to recommend a good restaurant?"

"A little blow Eddie, that's all."

"We talking keys here? Ounces? What?"

"An eight ball would handle the situation. For me and a friend. You know..."

"Oh, yeah, I know. I'm off in two hours, I'll meet you—"

"*No!* Now, it's gotta be right now! I got an important engagement and a meter running."

"Really want it, huh?"

Lisa bit her lip silently.

"Okay, I got a room upstairs, we'll do it there." He waved a dealer over to take his place. The other man winked as they left.

Eddie tossed an envelope on the bed. Lisa picked it up and tucked it in her purse. The weight felt so good in her hand. She took out two hundred dollar bills and tossed them on the bedspread.

"Don't go yet, you got to wait a minute or it'll look suspicious. Besides you haven't even looked at the goodies."

Lisa laughed, "I trust you." Another thought hit her. "Your buddies think you're getting a piece of ass, right?"

He shrugged noncommittally. "Do a line, it'll improve your mood."

She chopped a small pile, then picked up one of the bills still on the bed and rolled it. Afterwards she handed the bill to Eddie.

"Why not? You're only young once." He snorted the remaining line.

"That's good Eddie." Crystal bells were ringing in the distance. "Real good." She handed him a second bill but he waved it away.

"What's the matter, you don't want my money?"

"I thought maybe we could work out a deal."

She eyed him sharply, her face drawing tight.

"Just like old times," he said.

Lisa picked up the smooth folded paper and carefully threw it at his chest. It bounced from Eddie onto the rug. "You're slicker than snot on a doorknob, you know that, Eddie? But your memory's failing you, I was never a coke whore. And I'm not now…"

"Suit yourself, but that's the deal. Just a little head."

"So you can say you've fucked the most famous mouth in rock and roll, huh? Well, fuck you." But part of her was already missing the coke. She could feel it next to her foot, burning, burning, hot…

"So what's ten minutes of your time worth? It's flake, Lisa, pure flake."

She could tell it was good—no, it was great coke. "I've had better," she said casually. "Why don't you just stay here and jack off and then you can tell everyone we made it?"

He laughed. "Oh, I plan on at least doing that. Me and the coke—we'll just have our own little party."

"God, you're an incredible asshole, Eddie." She looked down at the coke. "But you're not the only asshole in this town. I'll do my shopping elsewhere. Someplace where I can afford the price." Lisa turned her back and took a step towards the door. *I hope I look better than I feel.* She reached for the door handle.

"Okay, okay, gimme the two bills. Can't blame a guy for asking." He handed her the coke. "You thought about it for a minute, though, didn't you?"

"You'll never know, Eddie, you'll never know…"

❖❖❖

"Hi, honey," Carol could tell by the blank look that Taylor had no recollection of their date. "Why are you still working?"

"Because I've got a show cancellation, a major overbooking and… We had a date, didn't we?"

"Damn it all, Taylor,"

"Hey, hey, I'm sorry, it's no problem, I'll get ready."

"No, the problem is that your priorities are screwed up. You take me for granted. We date, you forget, it's okay, good old Carol, she's always there on short notice."

"Honey, what's bothering you? This isn't like you."

Carol sighed and lifted a wisp of hair from her forehead. "What's wrong with me is that life just goes on. What kind of relationship do we have here? I mean is this going anyplace or is it going to stay 'good old Carol' for ever? I'd like to talk about our future, I mean in sort of exact terms. I was hoping we could do it over a nice dinner somewhere but since you managed to forget that I'm willing to talk right now." She smiled sweetly.

"I admit I haven't thought about that too much lately, but it's just that I've been working double time. Oh, by the way, Lisa's shrink called today and he thinks she's really doing well, maybe it's time—"

"No! Don't change the subject. Taylor, I want to talk about us. Not Lisa, not the DollHouse."

"Hey, she's your friend."

"Stop it! I want you to go home alone tonight and think about our future. Take your time, Taylor, take a week, take two. We won't talk about it until then, but after that I want some commitment."

"Commitment?"

"I know it's one of those words you have to search your memory for, honey, but I want you to do that." She turned to leave. "I love you Taylor and I want to see some visible sign of your plans for me in exactly two weeks. No, no"—she held up a finger—"we won't even allude to this little problem for two weeks, but then I want some small, physical sign of commitment."

"What sort—"

"Something that means something, Taylor. Something that means I'm not just wasting my time here, you figure it out."

"Or?" Taylor said. "What happens if I decide that I like things the way they are?"

"Then, my love, I'm going to reevaluate my situation. Think about it Taylor."

Carol left.

Carol slammed the door of the apartment without thinking. I won't give in this time, she told herself. This relationship is just too one-sided. That's a laugh in itself, I can't even get him to say the word—relationship. If I give in on this...

How can I expect him to share my dreams if I can't get him to listen?

Sometimes Taylor could be so unfeeling, so perversely self-contained, so damned macho. I know he loves me but there's still a shell deep inside. I just can't break through. A place where his real feelings live. How can I trust him if I'm never really sure I get all the way inside him?

How can I love him so much if there's a part of him I don't even know?

"Lisa? Are you still up? I'm sorry I slammed the door." She knocked lightly on Lisa's door and started to walk away. When there was no reply, she turned back suddenly and pushed the door open a crack.

Lisa was sprawled out on the bed, snoring loudly. She was still dressed in a warmup suit, although it was unzipped and half off her shoulder as if she had fallen asleep before she could finish undressing herself.

Carol watched her for a moment. She must be off coke, she seems to sleep about twelve hours a day. Carol looked around the room; there were no booze bottles in sight, nor did she see any half-filled bottles of sleeping pills in evidence.

Conspicuous by their very absence, she thought, and little warning bells began to go off somewhere in her head.

Oh, that's silly, I'm being too hard on her. She's working hard and she's tired. And that's all there is to it.

Probably.

On impulse she reached over and shook the inert form. "Wake up, Lisa, I need to talk to you."

There was no response from the prone form on the bed. Carol shook harder. Lisa's head rolled onto her breasts but she continued to snore, oblivious to Carol's best efforts.

Carol sucked in her breath. This is for your own good... I think... She slapped Lisa lightly across the face.

"Uhmmm," Lisa moaned, but did not open her eyes.

"Lisa, wake up! Wake up now."

After another moan Lisa's eyes blinked open, although she didn't seem to be focusing on anything in particular.

"I don't wanna go to school." The eyes shut tightly once again and the snoring resumed full force.

Well, at least I know she's asleep, not dead, Carol thought. I'll talk to her in the morning, and suddenly she was very envious of Lisa's deep sleep.

It's going to be a long night...

Carol arose late after hitting the sleep alarm three separate times to beg a bit of rest from the alarm clock. I don't think I slept until the alarm went off. What a miserable night.

She walked into the kitchen to find a wideawake Lisa poking a fork at a burned pop-up waffle. The toaster was still smoking and blackened bits of crust were strewn in a direct line from the appliance to Lisa's plate.

"Good morning. Breakfast is ready." She flipped a brittle, black layer of waffle onto Carol's plate. "Might want to consider some syrup, these disgusting little bastards are pretty dismal without it."

Carol nodded in silent agreement.

"I know, I know. I'm not Mrs. Middle America in the kitchen, am I? Well, who cares, I can afford a maid to fix my prefab breakfast. In fact, that's a great idea, we could get a cook here!

"I mean not to live here or anything, she could just come in and fix the meals, like the cleaning woman." She could sense a lack of enthusiasm on Carol's part.

"We've got to talk about the living arrangements, among other things..." Carol left the rest of the thought unspoken.

"Carol, it's so great living here, doing this. It feels like the old days— the *good* old days. I know you don't want a roomie forever, but I'm just getting my shit"—she glanced at Carol and grimaced—"uh, my act together, and I owe it all to you.

"I feel like I've been born again. Oh, not in the church or anything, but where it really counts, in my life. I'm feeling better than I have in years, and I've got a surprise for you." She reached over and squeezed Carol's hand.

"My witch doctor says I should start to work again. He thinks it would be 'beneficial' for me."

"You think you're ready for that? I mean"—Carol's words were racing out before her thoughts could catch up—"it's not that I don't think it would be a good idea, but plunging right in, going back to California…"

"The land of drugs and money you mean? You think I'd succumb to the evils of temptation again, right?"

"I just think you might not have as many friends there as you do here."

"You don't know how right you are."

Somewhere in the back of her mind Carol clearly heard the snap of steel jaws shutting tightly… "I am?"

"Yes! That's why I'm going to start here. Right here," she thumped the table with the heel of her hand, "in lost wages, Nevada."

"You are?" Carol felt serrated edges digging into her ankle.

"I've decided to do two weeks. Exclusively. At the DollHouse."

"Does anybody else know about this decision?"

"Well, not exactly. I mean I could have my agent call Nick, I suppose, but…"

"You thought I'd ask Taylor." She could feel herself starting to chew on her own leg, anything to escape the trap.

"Please, please, please." Both hands were now on Carol's arm. "It would be so good to work there, where I know people, with you."

"And Taylor," Carol added.

"I know we sometimes don't get along, but he knows I'm gold. Lisa Steel doesn't do live shows. Everybody knows that. Some people think I can't really even sing—that it's all fixed in the recording studio.

"I'd knock 'em dead, they wouldn't know what hit 'em."

"Lisa, it's not your drawing power I'm worried about. Are you sure you're strong enough?" Carol saw her face fall. "I mean it's still pretty soon…"

"Translated, 'Is she off drugs?' "

Carol shrugged her shoulders.

"Look at me. I'm not even boozing any more. Have you seen any bottles lately? Smell good old Black Label on my breath? I don't want to leave yet, I need your support… If I can get one good show in, it would change everything.

"I'm clean, Carol! What do you want me to do to prove it?" She picked the telephone off it's cradle and thrust it toward Carol.

"Here. Call my shrink. Ask him. Ask if I'm ready. Ask him what would help the situation. Ask him if I'm fucking clean!"

"Okay, okay, I believe you."

"My agent called the other day and they've put together a live album of Bret's and my performance and they want a good release trigger. This show would get my cute face on the front page of every paper in the country. Think of the publicity for the DollHouse—'Comeback of the Century.'"

"I don't know what Taylor would say," Carol responded, but she did, she knew exactly what he'd say. What would any casino say?

The same thing.

"Well, let me sweeten the pot a little bit. I tell you what else I'm going to offer and then you'll *want* to ask Taylor…"

No, I won't, but probably will…

Thank you, God, Lisa thought, and uncrossed her fingers from behind her back. And I'm sorry for lying.

But then, again, it was just a little lie…

"What is that?" Taylor watched as Carol placed a huge Caesar salad on his cluttered desk and swept away piles of paper to make room for a carefully folded napkin and silverware setting.

"Food," Carol said.

Taylor poked at the salad with his index finger. "Are you sure? I don't recognize it, what kind of pouch did it come in? Stouffers? Budget Gourmet? Safeway Special? I don't seem to be able to place it. You know my motto, 'If it doesn't come in plastic, it ain't edible.'"

Carol leaned over and kissed him on the forehead. "Poor baby, you really have been working too hard, haven't you?"

"For the greater good of mankind," Taylor said as he ate a piece of blue cheese. "Uhmm, great. Homemade, isn't it?"

Carol nodded.

"You're going to make somebody a great wife." He felt, rather than saw, Carol wince, and put the fork down. "I'm sorry, bad subject, bad joke. It's been a bad day.

"I'll make it up to you. Tell me why Madame Nhu is sitting in the outer office and we'll cut to the chase with no pain."

"Who?" Carol was genuinely puzzled.

"That's it, make me feel better, bring your age into the conversation. She was known as the Dragon Lady a number of years ago." He shook his head and ate another bite of salad.

"You're referring to Lisa?"

"I saw her before you shut the door. What did I do to bring on a royal visit? It's not enough that my headliners cancel with three weeks' notice, I've got to…

"Tell me, Carol, why are you here?"

She looked over and smiled briefly. "Maybe to make your day. I've got a surprise for you…"

Taylor listened intently while straining to keep his face neutral. My God, he thought, in my lap, it just jumped in my lap. "I don't know…" he said.

"Okay, in that case there's a sweetener. She'll play with the whales."

This caught Taylor by surprise. "You're kidding? The great Lisa Steel will mingle with the riffraff?"

"Only the cream of the riffraff," Carol said.

"Do you know what a draw that would be?" Taylor was running the possibilities over in his mind. "If we could guarantee a semi-private dinner with her, a few drinks and some photos for the boys back home…

"Hell, you know, Carol, there are only so many seats in the theater, but if we could line them all with preemies… Figure a minimum bet of twenty grand each—no, hell with that, let's milk it, figure fifty grand each, against…" He folded his fingers and shut his eyes.

"How sure are you? About that bi—About Lisa. Is she clean? Can she handle it? Will she listen to direction for a change?"

"I think she's okay. She says she's clean."

"Think? She says? Lisa would tell you the sky's black if it suited her purpose. She would tell you—well, the point is I can't risk another screw up and she's sort of a screw up waiting to happen."

He chewed another bit of the food. "What do you think? In your heart do you know it's right?"

"I couldn't guarantee anything. But from all indications…"

"No, no, that doesn't make the nut. If I put my neck on the line with Nick and the shareholders, somebody's got to guarantee Lisa one-hundred percent. We can't do this one halfway, it's got to be put together right and pushed through right. If she decides to take a powder in the middle of this, I can't just call the union and order up a replacement...

"Okay," he sighed, "bring her in and let me take a look."

Taylor extended his hand, "It's good to see you again, Lisa." He looked at her closely and was surprised to see a glowing, vibrant woman standing there. She was smiling a little girl smile and Taylor felt himself being sucked into the image.

"Did Carol tell you about my idea?" she asked anxiously.

"Yes, and I will admit that your doing a show would solve a number of my problems, but I think it would just create a whole slew of new ones and I can't deal with anything else going wrong right now, so I'm afraid..."

"Wait." She held up a hand. "I know I've been a major fuckup in the past and I'm sorry, but things haven't exactly been going my way for a while either.

"It's not like I'm asking for a big favor. You know I'd bring in every high roller in the country. Spend a few bucks for a decent show and I promise I'll sing my heart out. I'll cut 'em off at the knees, we could make the whole town stand up and take note."

Taylor could feel his objections crumbling. "Two weeks isn't enough to justify a major outlay. I'd want at least a month, two shows a night... if I were to go along with it."

"I need a break, Taylor. I'm trying to get on with the rest of my life. I promise I'll do whatever you say. I won't even have a single drink for the whole month and I'll be friendly, clean, courteous, helpful, uh, kind, uh..." She looked down at the floor and shut her eyes. "Please?"

"Ease up, Lisa, this ain't a parole hearing, it's just that I'd have to have some guarantees, we'd have to work it out to everyone's satisfaction."

"Yes! You mean yes, don't you?" She kissed him, "You won't regret this I promise. *Yes!*" She made as if spiking a football and then danced out to the outer office.

"Las Vegas, Lisa Steel is back in town!"

Both Carol and Taylor stared at the door as it shut behind her.

"Too easy," Taylor said. "That was altogether too easy. I feel like a mouse that just invited the cat to dinner."

Carol didn't answer.

＊　＊　＊

Taylor passed the show's assistant director in the hall. He was going in the wrong direction and didn't look at Taylor as they passed.

"David, early wrap today?"

The man stopped and turned towards Taylor. "For me. I was fired."

"Leon fired you? Why?"

"No, Leon wasn't there."

"Did I fire you? I don't remember doing that, and since we're your bosses..." Taylor let the conversation hang in the air.

The A.D. simply stood mute.

"God damn it!" Realization crept across Taylor's features. "I knew it was too easy. Where is she?"

The man shrugged. "In her dressing room."

"Go have lunch, David. You're not fired."

"Frankly, Taylor, I think I'd rather go get a job washing cars or maybe become a monk somewhere. You know, one of those places where women can't come in or they behead them?" But he headed for the cafeteria.

"Don't you believe in knocking, Taylor?" Lisa didn't even turn around to see who it was.

"It's my door Lisa, I don't have to knock."

"I believe it has my name on it."

"You know, Lisa, I didn't come here to discuss the furnishings."

"He's a prick, Taylor, always on my case. I canned him."

"Two problems with that Lisa—it's his job to be on your case, and you can't fire anybody. You're not the boss."

"I can refuse to work with him. What happens then?"

"Then I get Leon to get on your case. Leon can fire anyone he wants, except me. I can fire Leon. Try to remember that."

Lisa turned to face him with an odd smile on her face. "Oh, really? Could you fire me, Taylor? What would Nick say if I got canned right here in the middle of the hottest show in Las Vegas?"

"Nick would back me up."

"Uh-huh... Sure he would. And all those sold-out tickets, all those big spenders coming to spend a little time with little old me, how would they feel?" Lisa smiled and took out a compact. She opened the case and began spreading the powder inside over the hinged mirror, arranging it in small lines.

"I can't believe you are doing that in front of me, Lisa." He sighed.

"Well, you see, Taylor sweetheart, I'm knocking out two shows a day, we're getting the best reviews in town, you've got requests for my time from the richest down home boys in A-Fucking America, and I am supposed to remain cheery and bright twenty-four fucking hours a day?"

She snorted one line. "I just thought you should understand the situation here—I'm doing a good job and if I need a little bump now and then, that's my business, nobody else's."

Taylor put his hand out. "Give it to me, Lisa."

Lisa looked at the last line, "Well, sure Taylor, if you say so. After all, you are the boss." She held the case out to him. "But I gotta level with you and say I think I feel a little tired today. Too tired to do the second show.

"Be a good boss and go get my stand-in, will you Taylor? Maybe I'll feel better tomorrow. Maybe not."

Taylor looked at the compact, looked at Lisa, turned around and quietly walked out.

"Oh, and Taylor, keep that asshole David away from the set. Okay?" Lisa yelled at the closed door.

Carol parked her car in the underground stall and slammed the door behind her. Damn sports car, why did I let Taylor talk me into a convertible? She ran her hand through her hair, where it caught in some tangles and held fast.

Damn it all! It just messes up my hair and covers my face with grease. I'd be better off in a nice family Ford.

With air-conditioning.

She kicked halfheartedly at the Toyota's bumper and her heel bounced off the chrome and shattered one lens of the tail light. Carol stared at it stupidly.

I did that? Why did I do that? She bent over and picked up a few slivers of red glass. I'm sorry car, she patted it, it's not your fault, it's just, it's just that I never see my boyfriend anymore and I don't want to go inside my own house and find my roommate and friend passed out.

Again.

Slowly she walked up the stairs. Maybe she's just working too hard. I know the show is a killer, maybe she's just sleeping. God knows I haven't found a single bottle.

A wave of guilt washed over Carol as she recalled going through Lisa's drawers the day before in an effort to find and catalog incriminating evidence. The fact that the search was unsuccessful only made her efforts seem more tawdry. What's wrong with this picture?

She opened the door loudly and called out for Lisa. As usual there was no sound from the seemingly deserted apartment. She knocked on the bedroom door and then quickly pushed it open.

Lisa lay on the bed, still in full makeup. Her lowcut gown reflected the light from the door in a thousand blue shimmers and it bounced off the white walls like a cheap disco.

I hate to do this, but I'm going to… She shook Lisa several times in succession, but there was no response. She put her ear by Lisa's lips and listened. Lisa was breathing, but the effort sounded harsh and the air seemed to catch in her throat.

Maybe she's got asthma. Maybe she's dying. Maybe I'm going crazy. Carol sat down on the bed and looked at Lisa. Maybe I need a couple of shots of booze, maybe it's me who's going crazy. How ironic that would be: Lisa's fine and I'm having a breakdown worrying about her.

On the other hand, she's getting strange again. Impossible to wake up, cheery at breakfast and then bitchy about everything from then on. And then she's dead to the world for ten hours.

She lives in her room, I can't remember seeing her eat a real meal, and she looks terrible. The eyes are almost as blotchy as when she got back to town. It's like watching someone on a ride at the fair.

If I'm really her friend… well, what would I do? Get her in trouble, mess up the show?

I wouldn't let her die, I know that. She walked into the living room and picked up the phone. Who am I going to call for help? Taylor has been living on the edge, he's under a lot of pressure and this might not be the best thing for him or for Lisa… What if I'm wrong and she's fine? Taylor would never understand.

A doctor? What do I say? What if it get's around that I had to call a doctor for her again. Oh shit, there has to be somebody who can handle this better than I can.

She sat down in frustration, and then, like a lightening bolt, it came to her.

"Hello?" The voice on the other end of the wire cracked in mid-greeting. "I certainly hope this is important, or that God strikes you dead for this…"

"Leon? It's important."

There was a moment of silence while Leon thought it over. "My God, it's the only woman in the world that I would straighten out for… How are you, Carol?"

"I'm fine Leon but I've got a problem."

"Right," he said, sounding more awake with each passing moment. "How is Lisa anyway?"

"Does everybody in this town know about my private life?"

"No, honey, but everybody knows Lisa. Why else would you call me at three A.M.? Either another earthquake has destroyed San Francisco or Lisa's in trouble. Which could it be?"

"Okay, you win. Can you come over? Please."

"Not for anybody else in the world, Carol. I'll see you in a few minutes."

"I don't know what it is." Carol detailed her fears to an interested Leon. "Actually I feel kind of stupid calling you now. I guess I overreacted, you could probably go home and…"

Leon got up and walked into the bedroom. He watched Lisa sleep for a few moments and then reached out and slapped her sharply across the face. Carol gasped involuntarily and brought her hand to her mouth.

Leon slapped her again. There was no reaction from Lisa. He picked up a small hand mirror and held it under her nose. He watched as the condensation slowly formed on the reflective surface, then he wet his finger, wiped it across the mirror, and licked it.

"Oh, no," Carol exclaimed, "coke?"

He shrugged his shoulders noncommittally. "I don't know what the problem is, but there is something wrong."

"Should we call an ambulance?"

"Well, let me think a second, she doesn't appear to be in any danger." His gaze fell on the Bible resting next to Lisa's head. "What the hell is this doing—"

"It's hers. I don't know, some days I think she's going nuts and other days I think I am. She reads it, I've seen her, and it's moved around the room every day. She even talks about going to some sort of Bible study class. I don't know if she really goes or not, but she talks about it."

"That would surprise me. Yes, that would really surprise me. Make me rethink my life. Lisa turning to God? A miracle that would rival the Red Sea."

"She can quote it," Carol added. "I've heard her. It seems to be important."

Leon picked the Bible up and it fell open. "And there came one of the seven angels which had the seven vials, and talked with me, saying unto thee the judgment of the great whore that sitteth upon many waters."

"Why that particular verse?" Carol asked.

Leon looked at her, tipped the Bible vertical. A small glassine bag full of white powder fell out and bounced off the nightstand.

"Oh, my God." Carol felt her legs give out, forcing her to sit on the bed. "Cocaine, again."

Leon opened the tiny ziplock bag and tasted the powder with his fingertip. He turned to face Carol, "Don't worry, it's not coke."

"It's not?" She felt the world begin to edge back into focus. "Then why is it in that bag? Hidden in the Bible? I don't understand."

"It's smack." He watched the lack of reaction on Carol's part. "You know, heroin…"

Carol fainted.

The first thing Lisa saw filtering in and out of her consciousness was Leon sitting in the chair by the window. The light coming through the cracks in the curtains surrounded him with an unearthly glow and Lisa was sure she was still dreaming. She shut her eyes and willed herself back into full sleep.

"Morning, rosebud." Leon jerked the curtains open. "It's a beautiful day outside. A beautiful afternoon, actually."

"Is that really you, Leon?" She opened one eye and blinked against the intruding light. "It's great to see you and what the fuck are you doing here?"

"Just a friendly visit, Lisa." He lifted a bottle of light beer to his mouth and drank a long swallow. "Thought we'd talk over old times."

"Uh-huh." She was now sitting up in bed. "I see you're still drinking faggot beer, I assume there's been no change in the rest of your habits? Where's Carol?" She looked around the rest of the room as her eyes adjusted to the light.

"She's resting, I gave her a Valium. She had a bit of a shock earlier this morning."

"And she took it? Carol took a pill? A downer? You're shitting me, it must have hit her like a ton of bricks. I wish I could relive my first Valium—talk about a cheap date…

"It must have been quite a shock to drive the princess to drugs. Who died?" A shadow of suspicion crossed her face. "And how did you get elected to break the news to me?"

"Nobody's dead, yet. And believe me I didn't take this little chore on voluntarily. Carol thinks you might have a problem."

"Oh, shit, she's back on the 'poor Lisa' kick, isn't she? Leon, I can tell you honestly that I don't even drink socially. I ain't got the time. Get her off my back, will you. Friend to friend, have her cut me some slack."

"I don't think she's particularly concerned about the drinking. I think it's the horse that's really bugging her." Leon picked up the small plastic envelope, tore it open and flipped the contents out with jerk of his wrist.

White powder burst from the bag like a cloud of flour.

Lisa threw the covers from the lower half of her body and started to leap from the bed. She looked over at the Bible and quickly glanced to the closet.

"No, the rest of the stash is still safe. I figured you'd just replace it anyway. What are you using for the upside? Crystal? Black Beauties? Tell me, love."

Lisa laughed viscously. "No, no, just a little bit of pharmaceutical coke. You know what it's like, Leon? Persian smack and Merck coke? A fuckin' roller coaster from God." She laughed again and moved her hands over an invisible track.

Leon raised his eyebrows. "Real flake? Must be pretty hard to come by. Maybe I should have raided your stash after all."

"Don't concern yourself, honey. I've got a buddy who's got the keys to the narcotic safe at Our Lady of the Many Mercy's. A plastic surgeon, no less. It's not only pure, it's free."

"Come a long way from the dentists, haven't you?"

Lisa slapped the flat of her hand into the sheet. "Listen, you cocksucker, what gives you the right to come in here and search my room like some asshole narc?" Her voice was growing louder. "Who the fuck do you think you are? Besides being a poor excuse for a man, you're a professional mealy worm. Know that, Leon?

"Vegas is as far as you'll ever get, and from what I hear you're already on the backslide. I wouldn't come see—"

"Lisa!" Carol stood in the doorway with her hand over her mouth. "It's true, isn't it? How could you do this to yourself? How could you do this to me? I actually believed you..."

"Yeah, sure, until you hired Dan Tana here to search the premises." Lisa lowered her voice and dropped her eyes from Carol's gaze. "I'm not like you guys. I'm doing a major show here, every day I'm putting my ass on the line. I haven't got any free time, if I'm not on stage I'm supposed to be some kind of coy hooker with any number of big spenders your boyfriend has pimped me for, and I'm doing OKAY.

"Do you have any idea what it's like to spend your entire social life with dentists in snake boots? They all have reddened nostrils and a thin white line on their studio tanned necks where the gold chains used to hang before their current girlfriend convinced them that isn't hip anymore.

"Jesus Christ, what do you people want? My album is number eight with a fucking bullet, I've got three film offers, I'm packing the damn casino three layers deep every night with whales, SO I USE A LITTLE HELP TO GET ME THROUGH THE DAY. SO WHAT?"

"They all told me you needed help when... when you got here." Carol was talking in a loud whisper. " 'For her own good,' they said. But I stuck up for you, Lisa, I let you con me and use me and I got you your show and I was a friend for you. I really believed you..." She shook her head and rubbed her hand over her eyes.

"You got me the show? Carol, wake the fuck up, this isn't some nursery rhyme. I got whatever I got. Me, my talents, my skill, my body, my act. I EARNED EVERY FUCKING SECOND OF IT! And if I want to get just a little bit of enjoyment out of this mess, just this much fun off the top of what everyone else is making from my skills, I guess I fucking well deserve it."

"No," Carol said, as if speaking to herself. "That's not how the script goes this time. We're going to get you help in spite of yourself. You're going in a serious help program, Lisa, right away... Or else—"

"Or else what, Carol? What's the ultimate threat?"

"I'll call Taylor and get you canceled, get you blackballed."

Lisa got out of bed, "You still don't' get the picture do you? It's still some kind of good versus evil battle with you, isn't it?

"Carol, the world just isn't made that way." She picked up a cordless phone and threw it across the room. "Don't break your fingers on the buttons, but do it in the other room. I want a little privacy."

Leon hesitated at the door, listening to Carol speak softly into the phone in the living room. "Don't hurt her, don't do it. She's just about the last person on earth who loves you. Don't mess with her head. Leave the world an okay place for Carol."

"Why?" Lisa said, pulling her blouse off and heading for the bathroom. "Why should she be any different?"

Taylor was feeling good. The day was running tight, right. Some days you got up and the very first thing that happened signaled the mood for the rest of the day.

Some days you tripped over the covers, the toast was burned, the clock was early, and you were late. On those days, Taylor firmly believed, God was trying to tell you something: Go back to bed, take it easy, contemplate life, don't operate heavy machinery… Do what you will, the day is going to be a disaster. Predestination. Fate, karma, kismet, call it whatever… Every phone call will be bad news, every knock on the door a telegram, every parking place a loading zone with a cop waiting to happen. Days when the dark curtain of doom hangs over every action, every thought, precluding luck, precursing darkness.

And then, on occasion, bright crisp days came along. Mornings when you wake up feeling good, feeling like you managed to pack ten hours of delta sleep into the six available… Mornings that shouted, "Anything you do today's going to cruise, going to be cool, be okay." Do no wrong. Sin no more, the light's shining through on *you*. Days when your timing was exquisite, you were in sync with life and the universe was flowing in your veins.

Rhythm, that was the secret of life. Timing. Sliding in and out without burning your fingers, keeping loose. Feeling good.

Today was one of those days.

Oh, yes, Taylor thought, watching Jenny hit a soft 17 and catch the four of diamonds, laughing at something as she scooped in a stack of one-hundred-dollar chips, treating the suckers to a dazzling smile. Making them happy to lose, eager to play, to lose…

It's going to be a great day. I haven't felt this good since I was counting cards. I've got the edge. He rubbed his hands together and walked down the pit between the blackjack tables. Maybe I should start playing again...

No, never push your luck, Steven's first rule to live by. He watched a number of conservatively-dressed Japanese leave the elevator and walk toward the tables.

He knew the stats by heart: The average amount each of these particular Japanese bet each day was a little over $142,000. They were losing an average 12 percent per day, a bit ahead of the odds. Twenty-seven of them were staying at the DollHouse for five days.

Even with full comp on the security floor the total take... well, suffice to say, it was one of the better coups of the year. He smiled and bowed to the leader of the group. Bowed correctly, as an equal, as he had been taught to do by the "consultants" Carol had hired from a local Japanese restaurant.

In fact, this group was just one of the payoffs of Carol's suggestions about catering to each particular group of whales with style. More elan than they could expect anywhere else. And it was paying off in spades— not only were they getting, and keeping, the preemies, the DollHouse was fast getting an international reputation as a first-class act.

An act where you were treated right, treated with respect. Good, fast, fresh Sushi every morning for the Japs, Bangers for the Brits, the Shinbumi flown in every day and placed at their doorstep, lessons in international etiquette for the staff.

But it was worth it. Paying off in spades. That woman took to the job like a fish takes to water. And not only was she beautiful in a way that stood out in this flower bed, she doesn't know it.

Carol may have been the only truly gorgeous woman he had ever known that wasn't always looking for a way to use her looks. Grab some guy by the cock and drag him around for life.

And, God, was she smart. In a quiet sort of way, things happened when Carol was around.

True, she was a little naïve in bed, but that was part of her charm. At least with her you didn't have to wonder who taught her every move in the books, or, for that matter, who she'd been with before she came to see you. It was kind of refreshing to be with someone who hadn't been around the block too many times. Someone who still thought a blow job was kinky sex...

And besides, she liked to learn.

Oh, oh, I'm getting soft. She's just a broad, be careful. Easy boy, back. Down.

Still, she was quite a broad. Taylor felt himself drifting with the flow of the endless action in the casino. The sounds blended into a soft mishmash of people having fun.

Maybe this is how life is supposed to be. One of the pit bosses caught his eye and unobtrusively waved to a bank of slot machines that bordered one of the fancy coffee shops on the edge of the floor.

As Taylor watched, a man reached down and picked up a small, blond-haired boy of maybe four years old. He guided the kid's hand to the arm of the machine and helped him pull it down.

As Taylor walked toward them, three oranges spun into line and twenty quarters poured into the metal tray. The child squealed with delight.

"Excuse me, my friend," Taylor dropped to a squatting position. "These quarters yours?"

The child looked from his helper and back to Taylor. He nodded solemnly.

"Well, you can keep them then." Taylor stuffed the quarters into the boy's overall pocket. "But you can't play any more and we've got to find your mother. I'll give you a lift." He picked the boy up and headed towards the coffee shop.

"Why?" The boy crossed his arms and demanded in a strong voice. "Why can't I play more?"

"Because you have to be a certain age to play in casinos," Taylor explained patiently as they entered the restaurant.

"I'm twenty-one! I'm twenty-one!" his charge wailed as the entire restaurant broke into spontaneous applause.

"Sorry," Taylor said as he deposited the boy in a booth with a pair of red-faced women, "but he didn't have any ID on him and there's some question as to whether he's old enough to be playing."

"Oh, my God, I'm sorry, I just turned my back for a second." She shook her finger at the child. "I won," he said and began piling quarters onto the table.

"No trouble." Taylor patted the boy on the shoulder and the kid grinned back at him. "Save that money until you're old enough to play and then I'll expect you back."

The kid nodded.

Cute kid. Cute kid. I wonder if I'll ever have the time, I wonder if I'll ever know what it's like... Wow, something's in the air today, what's wrong with me? One good morning and I'm ready to be Ward Cleaver.

But the feeling wouldn't go away.

Taylor glanced at his watch and realized with a start that it was almost time for his meeting with The Man. The morning had evaporated before he was aware of it.

As the elevator silently whisked him straight up, Taylor felt a tremor of anxiety. Only twice before in his years at the DollHouse had he been summoned to unexpected meetings with Nick. Neither time had pleasant memories attached to it.

Well, what could be wrong this time? Everything had been flowing like a river lately, and today, yes, there was still something special in the air. Nothing would go wrong today. He smiled into the mirrored walls as the private elevator glided to a halt. He looked good.

"So?" Nick watched Taylor seat himself in front of his huge desk.

"So?" Taylor turned his hands face upward. "So, what?"

"Tomorrow. Tomorrow I've got a meeting with the board of directors. You probably already know this."

Taylor nodded carefully.

"So what do I tell them?"

"Well," Taylor walked around the question as if it was a land mine. "You could tell them that things are going well," he ventured cautiously.

"Actually, I could tell things are going great. The DollHouse is booked solid with spenders, we've got the cream trying to get a show on our stage to follow Lisa, the percentages are holding strong, and I can't find a major problem, even when I look hard.

"Maybe I'll tell them things are going smoothly because you've got more time to spend on your job, 'cause you don't find the need to hustle every broad in town anymore."

"Could," Taylor said through closed lips.

"She's quite a lady. If I were twenty years younger, you wouldn't be in the picture." Nick's eyes sparkled. "Sometimes I think I've spent too much of my life in this room... If I could do it over, well, maybe I'd have a woman like Carol and maybe I'd have a son like you."

He's dying, he's got cancer, something bad's happened.

As if he could read Taylor's thoughts, Nick waved his hand. "No, no, nothing like that. It's just that every once in a while it all catches up with you. Just wait, you'll see what I mean." He snapped his fingers, "Okay, enough of the sentimentality. How's Lisa holding up?"

"Dancing the world away. You know Lisa." He sensed this wasn't the answer Nick was looking for. "She's okay, getting bitchier as her ego catches up, but the show is dynamite. I have trouble believing it's really her, larger than life."

"Yeah, I know. Her record company called today, they want to do a live album here: Lisa in the DollHouse."

"Not bad," Taylor nodded in appreciation. "We'd get some press off that."

"Better than that, they want to salt the show with cameos from guest stars, back her with the Los Angeles Sound Machine. They'll record a few tracks every night over a week or so and then put the record together. Figure we'd get some interest in people wanting to be part of the audience for a night or two? People with money."

Taylor whistled, "But she's scheduled to close the end of the week."

"Schedules can be changed. I want her for another month. Can you hold her together for thirty days?"

Taylor didn't even miss a beat. "Yes, I can."

"Somehow I knew I could count on you. I've counted on you a lot lately and you've come through. I appreciate that more then you know, Taylor." Nick stood up and Taylor sensed the talk was concluded.

I know I'm missing something here, I'll catch it later, Taylor thought, as turned to leave.

"By the way, I'm putting you in as executive vice-president at the board meeting. Number two in the DollHouse."

Taylor felt the news wash over him like a tumbling wave.

God is trying to tell me something, Taylor thought as the private elevator plunged him silently downward. Too many signs, too much good stuff... Something is out of sync with the universe. Something is about to go wrong, very wrong. Has to.

As the doors slid open with a metallic hiss, Taylor's expectations were fulfilled. Cliff, the shift manager, stood at attention directly in front of the metal cage. Obviously he had been waiting for some time.

"Just a minor problem," he said, wiping one hand with the other.

"Our old friend Mr. Jackson is on a losing streak tonight, a big one—and he wants to prolong it beyond its natural life span. Way beyond."

"Cut him off—but do it nicely." The other man nodded, "Wait a minute, I'll do it myself, maybe it'll make the blow a little easier. Bring him in, Cliff—and smile. Okay?"

"Don't say anything, okay? Just listen." The gambler man held up both of his hands in a "hold on" gesture. "You're going to cut me off at the knees, I can see it in your face. Right?"

Taylor opened his mouth to respond.

"No, no, don't say anything. How long have I been coming here? Six, eight years? How much you figure I've spent here? Don't answer that."

He shut his eyes for a second and then opened them, hands still outstretched. "Have I ever, *ever* welshed on a debt? No, no, have I *ever* been late on a debt? You know I'm good for it…"

Taylor shrugged and bit his lip.

"You can talk, you can talk."

"You're a valuable customer and I don't want to lose you, but let's face facts. You're almost eight grand over your limit now. And to top it, you're losing steadily. Some days things just don't go your way. Take it as it comes, don't push a losing proposition."

"Not today, Taylor, please not today. It's been a bad day, I know my luck's about to change, I can feel it. I need a lift, just loosen the DollHouse purse strings for a minute, you won't regret it and it would really help me."

"Well, tell you what, let's put together a compromise. I'll set you up in a suite and get you some very pleasant company. On the cuff. In fact, I'll get you a couple of very pleasant companies. Close friends of mine, dinner, drinks, whatever you want. No obligation, no salesman will call. Just stop gambling for a while. I'll even give you a fresh line in the morning. Just back off for a few hours."

"You don't understand, it's not the money. I've got more money than I know what to do with. I've got to break the bastard's back, it's like falling off a horse…

"Yeah, I know I probably sound like I'm loaded, but I swear to you I'm as straight as the day I was born. Taylor, this has been the flat-out unluckiest day in my life. You know how that goes? Some days just don't work."

Taylor nodded in sympathy.

The other man dug into his pocket, fumbled around with a wad of contents and then casually tossed a huge diamond ring onto the desk. It bounced twice and came to rest, scattering a hundred small rainbows onto the office walls.

"Twenty years I've been fighting off gold diggers who figured getting me to a justice of the peace would be the last bit of strenuous work they would ever have to do—and then I finally find true love.

"Took me about a month to finally realize I really wanted to do it. The bitch laughed at me... 'Marriage? Do you think I want to be a housewife? Whatever gave you that impression?'

"I spent twenty two thousand bucks on that little fucker this morning and if you don't up my line I'm going across the street and pawn it. And come right back here and play it out.

"I've got to get it back. My luck is going to change today. I ain't going to go down this way. I'm not getting drunk, I'm not trying to beat up a shitkicker bar, and I don't want to see another broad for a few days, but I can't quit a loser.

"Do you understand? Some things you just gotta do, get back up on the fucking horse. I want my luck back."

He watched Taylor for any sign of reconsideration.

"Ah, forget it. I'll pawn the little bastard. What do you figure they'll give me for it? A thousand? Fifteen hundred? Nobody likes a loser in this town. Fuck 'em all anyway." He scooped the ring up in his fist and turned towards the door.

"Ten thousand."

"What?" He turned to face Taylor. "You're going to gimme a line?"

"The ring," Taylor said. "Ten thousand cash."

The other man looked into his fist and back at Taylor, "Are you serious? The DollHouse is going into the pawn business?"

"Nope. Not the DollHouse. I'll give you ten grand cash. Myself."

"You got it!" He tossed the ring into the air and watched Taylor make a one-handed catch.

"Like you said, there are some things you just have to do." Taylor reached into the desk drawer. "You mind a check?"

"Hell, no, just make it out to the DollHouse. It ain't going far...

"Thanks, Taylor. I owe you one." He walked out the door, hesitated and turned back towards the office. "I hope the bad luck doesn't go with the ring."

"It won't," Taylor said and turned the stone over so the little rainbows spun around the room. "It won't."

Taylor stood and stared at the closed door for an uncertain amount of time. It was as though an unseen hand had taken over control of his life and was moving it forward in little steps. Faster and faster the pieces were clicking into place.

I can't believe this is really happening; no, I can't believe I'm doing this. It's not like it's really me... On the other hand it seems silly to fight it. An immovable force...

If only Rod Serling were still alive to see this.

Suddenly his pager vibrated under his jacket and jerked Taylor back into present. Touchy, I'm getting touchy.

"Taylor here," he said to the switchboard operator. "You paged me."

"Yes sir, it's Miss Davis and she says it's really important."

Amazing, bloody amazing. Couldn't stop the reaction if I wanted to... It's taken on an existence of its own.

"Hi, honey, I was just thinking about you." *You wouldn't believe it,* he thought, you really wouldn't believe it.

"We need to talk, Taylor. I'm sorry to bother you, but we really have to talk."

"I agree, Carol. The sooner the better."

"What? You do? You do?... Ah, well, okay. It might be better if you could come over here, I can't exactly leave at the moment."

"On my way," Taylor said, setting the gold-leafed house phone back into it's cradle with a touch of uneasiness.

Across town and on the other end of the phone line Carol did the same thing... That was just too easy, she thought. Too easy...

"Hi, good-looking." Taylor leaned over to kiss Carol as she opened the door and found her lips tense. "What's the matter?"

She started to speak. "Wait, don't tell me anything, I've got something for you." He reached inside his pocket and pulled out a small brightly wrapped box, casually tossing it to Carol. "I thought you might like some chocolate, it's Godiva, your favorite."

Carol glanced down, started to undo the wrapping paper, shook her head and pulled Taylor inside by his jacket cuff. "It will have to wait. This is really important."

"Well, I think that is, too," Taylor said carefully.

"It's not the same thing. I'm going crazy and I need your help! It's, it's Lisa."

"Oh, Christ, I'm really a bit tired of hearing about Lisa. Lisa this, Lisa that. Lisa is just Lisa. You know that. You were her first 'real friend,' remember? You've stuck by her through thick and thin. I've always been the heavy in this scene, why do you need my help now?"

Taylor felt himself getting more and more irritated as Carol threw the unopened box onto the bookshelf in the living room.

"Because now it's serious. Really serious. We've got to put Lisa in a hospital."

"She's hurt?" Taylor saw the show sinking under a wave of white gowns. "What happened, what did she do?"

"Oh, she's still okay physically. But she's back on drugs. I mean heavy drugs. It's not a hobby anymore, and it's up to us to get her professional help. She needs to be committed."

"Lisa has a constitution of iron, Carol. Chipping here and there doesn't hurt her—in fact, if anything it seems to improve her temperament. Smooths out some of the rough edges, lets her mix with us common folk."

Carol put her hand on Taylor's shoulder. "But we're her friends, we're her only friends in the whole world, it's our duty to help her."

"First place, I'm not her friend. I'm responsible for her showing up twice a day and doing a dynamite show. I'm responsible for her convincing high rollers to lay out their hard-earned cash and I'm responsible that she doesn't get arrested and put the DollHouse in a bad light, but I'll be damned if I'm her friend.

"And secondly, Lisa has never had a friend in her life. Believe me she doesn't consider you a friend—just room and board and someone to pick up the pieces when she goes too far. This really isn't your problem, let me take care of it. I'll have a talk with her."

"*No! No!*" Carol stomped her foot in frustration. "I'm sorry but no more talking, she needs to go away somewhere for real treatment. I mean this, Taylor. You have to help me, or..."

"Or what?" Lisa said with a yawn from the doorway. "Discussing me behind my back, kids? Really rude... But go on anyway, just pretend I'm not here." She began picking at her fingernails distractedly.

"Carol thinks you need to check into a funny farm for a while. Get your act straightened out. What do you say?"

"Oh, you know Carol," she looked at Taylor and winked playfully.

"She's always exaggerating things a bit. On the other hand, I could use a few weeks of paid vacation sitting by the pool and telling some shrink how screwed up my father was. Who knows, might do me some good.

"And surely you won't mind me checking out of the show a couple of weeks early, would you, Taylor? And, oh shit, the album, well you can always explain that to the people, can't you, Taylor? After all, I do seem pretty strung out, don't I?

"Why don't you both just make the arrangements and let me know. I'll go pack my bags." She smiled ever so sweetly and went back into the bedroom.

"She doesn't seem too bad to me."

"She's bluffing, you know that, Taylor. Two days without dope and she'll be climbing the walls."

"I don't think so, Carol. I think you're misreading the situation, and it's my opinion that counts in this particular decision."

"I don't understand, you're talking like this is business, some sort of buying and selling deal. This is *not* business, this is Lisa's life—and, and our responsibility as human beings and friends."

"It's a nice speech, honey, but the point is that business is just exactly what we are talking about. It's my business to squeeze Lisa like an orange if it's necessary to get orange juice out of her. It's what I do; she's got layers of agents and managers and attorneys who are all there to protect her from villains like me, but it's my place in the scheme of things to see that she works if she can."

"And she can."

"That's all bull and you know it. Her agents and other 'protectors' are out to get their fifteen percent—no work, no income. They don't care if she burns herself out in a few good years—hell, she might not make it that long anyway. They just want their share of the goodies. It's you and I who have to make the real decisions."

"Me and you? Who the hell died and appointed you God here? Wake up, Carol, Lisa's an adult—white and over twenty-one, she can do what she wants to, and right now our needs happen to coincide. You're not her mother. You never were.

"Buy a dog, or have a kid of your own or become a big sister—something else to focus your motherly instincts on. Let Lisa be Lisa."

"I can't believe you're saying this. I guess there are some things I don't really know about you." Carol was biting her lip, trying to stop the tears that were welling up in her eyes.

"I guess that's true." Taylor's eyes flickered to the unopened package lying on the bookshelf. "And there are apparently some things we don't even know about each other..."

Lisa came back out holding a small overnight case. Choosing to ignore the tension in the air, she cheerily asked, "So what's the verdict? Do I get a break or what?"

"Get your stuff and report to the DollHouse. Tell Sherry I said to give you a suite."

"A suite, my ass, you mean *the* suite. I'm headlining now, Taylor, don't forget it."

He jerked his head towards the door. "There's a car out front, take it."

"I'll send for my things," she told Carol sweetly, and walked out the door.

"Taylor, you've got to choose, put her in a hospital or..."

He held up his hand and smiled. "Okay, if that's the way you want it, I'll choose. Take care, Carol." He kissed her lightly on the cheek, turned, and walked out the door.

Taylor shut the door behind him carefully, stepped into the hallway and punched the white plaster wallboard. Amazingly all four of his knuckles embedded themselves into the material, leaving deep dents.

He looked from the wall to his hands, watching as his scraped knuckles began to seep blood.

"Not a good day, huh?" Leon stepped into view from down the hall.

"It's taken a rather sudden downturn." Taylor put his big knuckle into his mouth and sucked on it.

"Mine's running neck and neck with yours. You'll have to excuse me for not beating up some very hard and inanimate object but I need my hands for my work. Want a beer?"

"No, I want something to drink. Come on, Leon, I'll buy, and you can tell me all the advantages of being gay, I'm thinking of switching. I don't want to look at a woman again as long as I live."

"Don't even joke about it." Leon shook his head, "You think you've got problems now..."

As they walked out Taylor punched the back of the door with his other hand, the rough surface sheared the top of his knuckle as cleanly as if it had been a knife. He watched the blood well up. "Shit."

"And you didn't even dent this one." Leon rubbed his hands over the door before closing it. "Look at the good side, you're out of hands."

Taylor waved impatiently at the bartender as Leon looked around the small casino and winced at the brassy lounge act playing loudly enough to just compete with the obnoxious ringing of multiple electric bells every time a small jackpot was coaxed from one of the slot machines.

"Why are we here, Taylor?" Leon asked as the bartender drifted over. "Two beers."

"And I'll have a triple Scotch." The man looked at Leon, who shrugged.

"We're here because I want to get a little loaded and this is as far away as we can get from the DollHouse and Carol and still be in Vegas."

"And still be in a casino," Leon added.

"I want to be in a casino. I want to look objectively at my world. The environment I've chosen to spend my life in. Not the DollHouse, someplace where I can really see what's going on." Taylor took a tall glass from the bartender and swallowed a third of it in one gulp.

He made a face and gagged. "Great stuff." He tossed a fifty-dollar bill on the bar. "Keep 'em coming, just tell me when that gets low."

"Yes sir." The man pocketed the bill and eased away. "He ain't going to ring it. If I ran this place I'd fire his ass." Taylor swallowed another third of his drink.

"God, I'd forgotten just how interesting downtown Las Vegas really is," Leon was looking around the ill-lit interior. "I'd also forgotten they make biker casinos. Maybe we can buy a couple of automatic weapons while we're here, you know, do something constructive with our time."

"The music never changes, does it, Leon?" Taylor was watching an obnoxious group of craps players. "Squealing like fucking stuck pigs over their measly two-dollar win." He slammed his empty glass on the bar surface and motioned to the bartender to fill it.

"It's just amazing to watch professional people come into a place like this and make complete fools out of themselves. It's like going on the Newlywed game, you know? Making a complete ass out of yourself in front of anyone who wants to watch for a fucking dishwasher or some shit."

He took another drink, this time managing to drain almost half the glass. "I really loved her, you know that, Leon? I really did."

"They're like streetcars Taylor, every five minutes, especially in this town."

"But not like Carol, not every five minutes."

"No." Leon took a long pull on his beer. "That's true."

"You know what I think is wrong with them? I mean collectively, as a species?"

"Uh-uh," Leon responded.

"I used to think it was hormones. Some strange hormone that God gave to women to punish them for their feelings of superiority. Every time they approach happiness the hormone kicks in and makes sure they do something to totally fuck up the situation. I used to dream of winning a science fair by isolating the little bastard. Developing an antidote, letting women become normal, join the human race.

"A sure Nobel. I'd be famous. Every man in the world would send me birthday cards, gifts at Christmas. People could live in harmony. A medical breakthrough." He stopped talking and swigged his drink.

"So what happened?"

"During the course of my investigation I discovered there is no hormone. It's deeper than that. Genetic malfunction. It's the XX chromosome. That little extra leg contains a built-in fuck-it-up code.

"It's sort of like a rare cancer. The malicious cells lie dormant until too much happiness starts to register on the imprint and then they begin to multiply at an unbelievable rate. They attack the central nervous system first and then the bitch syndrome kicks in.

"PMS, the piss and moan syndrome, is just God's little monthly reminder that the genetic code is altered beyond repair. It's also a periodic warning to men that things are rarely what they seem to be."

Leon tipped his bottle up and thought it over. "Christ, you might be right. Although I really couldn't be considered an authority on the subject."

"I want another Scotch," Taylor put his hand out and stopped Leon's as he moved to take another swallow of beer. "You too this time, nobody likes a lone drunk in this town."

"You know, Taylor, I never thought I'd see you drink again." Leon tasted the bar Scotch and shook his head. Then he took a drink.

"You know, Leon, I never thought I'd see myself drinking, well, drinks again." Taylor looked back at the noisy craps crowd. The most noticeable player was wearing cheap leather cowboy boots and speaking with a definite Texas drawl. Several of his giggling partners responded with a New York accent.

"The only race known to man lower than Texans are New Yorkers," Taylor said rather loudly.

Leon finished his drink and shook the empty at the bartender. "Taylor, let's go back to talking about Carol, I really don't want to get in a fight here. At least give a minute to see if one of these nice gentlemen here at the bar has a gun he'd like to sell."

The bartender surveyed them both as he brought the new round and decided they were loaded. "Your tab is up gentlemen."

Leon spit part of his drink out in laughter.

Taylor shook his head sadly and tossed another fifty onto the bar. "You've got to stop drinking that twenty-year-old stuff, Leon, we're going through the rent here." Taylor kept his hand on the bill until the man reached for it.

"Your boss might like you to ring this one up, just to break the rhythm." The man scowled and Taylor smiled.

"Are you happy, Leon?"

"You mean right this minute or in general? This is life, Taylor, you're not supposed to be happy, you're just supposed to get through it with a minimum of bruises."

"Do you really believe that? I don't know anymore. Look at this place, look at what we do for a living. Think mankind is better off with either of us around? Oh shit, look at this joker." Taylor indicated a man of about twenty-five approaching the only semi-high stakes blackjack table in the house.

The man was wearing a ripped, red T-shirt that said "Toledo" on the front. His jeans were scuffed, one gym shoe was untied, and he obviously hadn't shaved in several days.

"My God, nobody wears a shirt advertising Ohio. Especially Toledo. I can't believe he stumbled in the door. Look at him. Want to bet he can't come up with the twenty-five dollars for a bet? Not even once. Christ almighty, I love it. Toledo…"

The man was fumbling around in his pocket as if looking for his money. Then he began patting his pockets down trying to find something to bet. Several people at the table began to titter.

"This is too good, I'm going to spot him a bet. Maybe my luck will change." Taylor left the stool and headed for the table just as the man pulled out a fist-sized roll of hundred dollar bills and began laying stacks of one thousand dollars each on the hands in front of him.

Taylor watched for a moment then returned to his stool where he killed the drink in front of him. "I don't fucking believe it, I didn't even call that right. I'm losing my touch. I've been in this town too long. Time for a change."

"He's not exactly typecast for the part, Taylor."

"Yeah but it's not your job to know that and it is mine. Nobody would have the balls to wear a Toledo T-shirt unless they were loaded. Nobody. I should know. It's what I do. It's what I do best."

"Or at least for a living." Leon added.

"God, look at these people." Taylor waved his arm in a semi-circle towards the floor. "What's wrong with this picture? It's like looking in a mirror that's been reversed—everything's a little out of phase.

"Money really is the great leveler, isn't it? Everything evens up if you've got money. Talent, smarts, they don't count at all. Isn't that right, Leon? If you've got money you don't have to have talent, intelligence, or even style. It all comes with the territory. You've joined a very elite club, no matter if the price of your membership came from family, hard work or selling drugs; you've arrived. Tell me I'm wrong."

He didn't wait for an answer. "You know that young lady three seats down from you is starting to look better and better for some strange reason I can't put my finger on."

"Three-drink women." Leon said. "Three drinks and the women around here start to look good. Or in your case, seventeen drinks."

"The more I see the more I realize Andy Warhol was right—everybody should be famous for fifteen minutes. Get a chance to tell their story. That's what it comes down to with most people anyway. And we give them that opportunity—as long as the money lasts.

"Lisa's right too. Even the DollHouse is full of dentists with snake boots, red nostrils, and a white line around their necks because their new girlfriend convinced them it's not hip to wear that gold chain anymore. What are we doing here?"

"Getting drunk. Go easy on yourself, Taylor, you could be working for a living. Standing behind the counter at a McDonalds in Sparks watching those fries burn brown."

"Who knows, maybe I'd be better off." He took another swallow. "God, I can't believe it. I was really going to marry her. Quit. Settle down. No more fucking around."

"Do you realize you're not talking in complete sentences any more?"

"Leon, when I was young I once memorized the phrase 'Are you eighteen' in twenty-three languages. Including Swahili. Although, 'Donde Es Bimbo' always seemed to work best in tropical climates. Marriage. Me. One woman, the rest of your life. I was going to try. I really was. What happens to us?"

"We get drunk and life goes on, Taylor. Let me call us a cab, it's time to go sleep it off."

Before Taylor could answer several showgirls spilled out of the backstage door and washed past them in a wave of colored spangles. Two of them stopped directly in front of Leon.

"Hi there, sweetheart." One leaned forward to kiss Leon on the cheek. "Slumming this evening? Seeing how the other two-thirds live? Looking for some new talent? Need a replacement? Just say the word..."

"Who's your cute friend?" The other asked, turning towards Taylor.

"Don't bother," her friend laughed, "that's Mr. DollHouse and he's *'spoken for.'*" She laughed again.

"Well, let's cut our losses then." She turned back towards Taylor. "You are cute, always remember I was the one who liked you even before I knew who you were." They started to walk off.

"I'm not." Taylor said.

The two women stopped, their costumes making flickering shadows on the surface of the bar. "Not what?" the first asked.

"Spoken for. And I am hungry. Either of you?"

"Spoken for or hungry?"

"What's the difference?" Taylor opened his hands in front of his shoulders.

They looked at each other like a gift from heaven had fallen to earth, landing exactly between them. "Neither and both." The first one said looking back at Taylor. "So it's up to you, make a choice."

"Oh, no," Taylor got up from the bar on unsteady feet. "I've made too many choices of late. That's the problem. I'll take you both. Dinner anywhere you want, then whatever you want. Anything. You name it."

They looked at each other. "Sure you're sober enough to handle us both?"

"Honey, if you like to ride, I'm a rodeo. Let's do it." He took hold of one hand from each woman.

"Taylor, do you really think this is a good idea? Burning your bridges and all that?" Leon asked, knowing it was a useless question.

"Like someone once told me, my friend, every five minutes, just like a bus. There's a new one every five minutes. You okay?"

"Having the time of my life," Leon said and ordered another drink.

The bartender watched Taylor leave, supported between two beautiful showgirls, one arm around each. "Looks like your friend is going to do all right for himself tonight."

"You don't know how wrong you are," Leon said. "How very, very wrong."

Water. I need water, was Taylor's first thought of the new day. His second was to wonder whose hand was wrapped so gently around his cock. In spite of massive head pain he felt himself becoming aroused.

"Well, well, welcome back to the land of the living." A voice whispered in his left ear, and the hand began moving up and down, teasing him into erection.

"Hi," Taylor said. Then he realized there were more people in the bed than he had originally thought. "I'm having a little trouble, here, re—"

"Oh, God, not another man who's going to claim he got drunk and can't remember a thing." The second woman said, "How do they think they can get away with that lame excuse time and time again?" She got out of bed and shook her finger at Taylor. "Don't lie to me, now."

Taylor looked at extended legs and the curly blond mound staring him down at eye level. He was becoming harder and harder. The other woman giggled.

"You do remember it, don't you?"

"Some. I remember some things," Taylor said, reliving a most pleasant experience.

"Do you remember telling us your theory of female genetics?"

"Oh, no." Taylor put his hand to his forehead. "Tell me I didn't."

"Whoever she was, she sure cut you to the quick." The woman standing said, "Mean."

"I'm not sure what…"

"Whoever took the knife to you. She did a good job. I mean you were enjoying yourself last night, but you weren't. Know what I mean? And that's kind of insulting."

"Well, I wasn't trying to be…" Suddenly Taylor saw red glimmers of light bounce from the ceiling. Showgirls. He was with two show horses.

"Did I, ah, promise you anything? I mean for…"

He felt the hand around his member squeeze tight and jerk him to attention. "Listen, you asshole. You may be Mr. Show Business, but you've got to learn a basic lesson. It ain't all for sale. Not every woman in the world is a whore. Just because you've had a bad go around doesn't mean…"

The second woman sat down on the bed and Taylor felt the hand relax. He looked over with thankfulness.

"You're here simply because we enjoyed your company. You were loaded but you were funny—entertaining. It was a three-way decision. Nobody did anything they didn't want to, and nobody expects anything else. Do you understand that, Taylor? Be careful how you answer."

The hand had started moving again and he felt his hangover being replaced with a very pleasant sense of desire.

"Yes. I understand perfectly."

The first woman giggled again. "You ever been with two women before? I mean before last night? You were pretty creative for a virgin."

"Well," he said, swallowing.

"Oh, shit, the male ego comes into play." The woman held up her hand. "Don't perjure yourself. Just shut up." She slid her head down and replaced the hand on his organ with her mouth, carefully sucking him in.

"The point is—if you ever want to do it again—I mean we enjoyed your company. If life is getting you down," she cupped his face in her hands and he felt himself swelling as she plunged her tongue deeply into his mouth.

"You know who to call."

"Cocksuckers!" Taylor sat in a corner watching Lisa hold court, the events of the morning still lying sweetly on his mind. It was nice to know somebody, somewhere still thought he was okay, just for himself.

"Men are all cocksuckers at heart." Lisa jumped up and screamed at her director. "How can you even think about taking that song out of the act? That's the best number in the whole fucking show! Don't tell me you don't see that!"

The man sighed resignedly. "It's the last number. You're tired by then, it'll give you a break. You can pace yourself better, you won't have to save energy for it—it's lame anyway."

"Lame! You wouldn't know lame if it bent your wrist. That particular song is going to be number one with a bullet next month and you're going to be looking for work. You've just got the hots for the little opening act. The bitch can't carry a tune but I bet she can carry you.

"To think I had faith in you at one time. William, you're just another macho asshole!"

The man blew the air out of his cheeks. "Make up your mind Lisa. I can't be a fag and have the hots for a woman at the same time. At least get your insults together."

"Cocksuckers! Don't feel bad, William, it isn't just you. It's your fucking race. All men are born fucked up. You're problem is that you're propagating the stereotype." She put her hand in front of her mouth. "God, I'm sorry. I didn't mean to use a word with three syllables and leave you out in the cold."

The man's cheeks visibly reddened and at least one person in the entourage laughed out loud. "I think I've about had it with you and with this job."

"No! No! Don't quit, I want the pleasure of firing your ass. Another blow for womankind. Another cocksucker falls for the cause."

"I don't work for you Lisa. I work for the DollHouse and, as a matter of fact, you work for me." The man explained after regaining his patience. "You can't fire me. It's my job to do what's right for the show and I say the song goes."

Taylor saw the next step coming. "Taylor! Help me!"

He walked over and put his arm around Lisa. "Let's talk it over. Everyone else take a few minutes, okay?" The room cleared and Lisa visibly relaxed.

"Do you see anything unusual about giving a public speech downgrading all men and then asking me for help in the same breath?"

"You're not like other men."

"That's the second time today I've been told that and the morning is still young..."

"What?"

"The point is that you know he's right. You can finish bigger on the song before that and it will be less of a strain. Nobody will notice the change and you'll feel better. But you know all this, so what's the problem?"

"I don't like him." Lisa began to pout. "I don't like directors as a matter of course. Fucking know-it-alls. It'd be nice to actually have someone worry about me for a change."

"William worries about you, Lisa. I worry about you."

She looked at Taylor sharply. "You worry about the DollHouse. You don't even know I exist except as an act."

"Don't change the subject. I've had a bad couple of days sticking up for you. And speaking of bad things—drugs. How bad is it this time? Hobby or habit?"

"Oh, come on, I'm hardly even using anything. I just have to sleep and I have trouble crashing in the daytime. I can stop anytime."

"Don't lie to me—"

"*I'm not!*" Lisa stamped her foot. "I'm just really beat." She flopped onto the couch. "And we start taping for the album in two days."

"Okay, tell you what. I'll cancel tomorrow's show. That gives you two days off in a row."

Lisa clapped her hands together like an excited child.

"But, the deal is—I want you to see our doctor, get something legit to sleep if you need it, no drugs, no parties. You work out both days, take a massage, eat right. I'll set it all up."

This sequence of events took Lisa by surprise. "You're kidding me? You got it!"

Taylor nodded. "I'll take the heat for the decision, but you stick to your end of the deal. Your word?"

Lisa jumped up and kissed him on the cheek. "Sealed with a kiss."

Taylor sat in the front row and held his breath. No matter how many times he saw it happen, it still took him by surprise. It was magic. Lisa had the audience in the palm of her hand. There was no other word for it.

She paused in mid-beat, shut her eyes, and the spot lights collapsed inward, highlighting only her. She looked like a frightened deer caught in a headlight. She held her hand up for the band to hold the silence for a few extra seconds.

For a split second you could quite literally hear a pin drop—then the audience went crazy. A giant scream tore from the throats of three hundred people and Taylor felt the hair on his neck stand up with the electricity in the air.

Then he realized he was screaming with the rest of the crowd.

Lisa opened her eyes, smiled coyly and asked softly, "Now?"

"*Now!!!*" The crowd thundered back at her. She spun around and finished the song perfectly. The curtain fell as several hundred roses pelted the stage. The crowd was on its feet screaming for an encore. Taylor saw the two sound engineers slap each other on the back.

It was going to be a hell of a live album.

Lisa sat upright on the giant bed and kicked her feet. "Yes! Yes!" The adrenaline was still rushing through her veins. It had been one hell of a day. It felt so right when it all came together like that.

She looked at her watch. Four fucking A.M. already and even though she had left the party early to get up here and get some sleep, it would be hours before the buzz from the show would cease. She picked up the phone to call room service.

Just a bottle of Glenlivet. Lisa punched the button and then slammed the phone down as soon as the front desk answered. Okay, okay, I said no booze, and I do feel better. She lay back down and stared up at the mirror.

I really don't want to see dawn here. She got up, paced over to the table and lit a cigarette. It tasted like shit. She ground it out and dumped her purse out onto the table. Carefully she opened a gold compact and spilled white powder onto the shiny table top.

Just a little bit—not to get high, just to relax. Drift off, sleep… Lisa rolled up a hundred dollar bill and leaned over the pile.

And stopped dead. An image of Taylor in the front row appeared before her. I don't believe this, I feel like I'm on parole here. It's my life… She leaned back over, waited a second, and then blew outward, scattering the powder like dust in a sandstorm.

Jesus, I'm turning into a wimp. She slammed a pill bottle out of her purse and took out a small blue pill, put it under tongue, and waited for it to dissolve. Then she took out two more, added them to the partial pill in her mouth, and leaned back on the pillow.

Twenty minutes, you little fuckers, you've got twenty minutes until

I hit the horse. Tomorrow, I'll make Taylor deal with me tomorrow. That was her last thought of the night.

"Take me out to dinner," Lisa commanded into the telephone.

"Is this a date or an order?"

"Come on, Taylor, you owe me. You owe me."

"How did you figure that one?"

"Eleven days, I haven't had a drink or a hit of anything illegal for eleven days. Just like I promised you. Now it's my day off and I want a nice dinner and a bottle of the best champagne in the world. Do you happen to know what that is?"

"No, but I've got friends in this town, I can find out. Tell you what, I'll send a bottle to your suite."

"No! Not unless you bring it. I want to be taken out to dinner. I want to dress up like a lady and have a gentleman caller take me out on the town."

"I'm tired, Lisa."

"You're depressing me. I think I'll go see what I can scrape up in the way of powdered entertainment."

"Okay. I know when I'm beaten. Pick you up in an hour."

Lisa carefully sat the phone back in its holder and smiled to herself. Don't laugh Taylor, you just might get luckier tonight than you think...

"To you," Lisa said, lifting both champagne glasses together and handing one to Taylor. "How does it feel to have the hottest act in Las Vegas totally taken with you?"

He took the glass and sipped from it. "You're being too nice, Lisa. Don't queer your act."

She immediately frowned. "You should know better than that. I haven't felt this good in... well, in my life. I love what I'm doing—I love what you've done to me."

"This is all leading up to something, isn't it?" Taylor sipped from his glass. Dom Perignon '81. It just might be the best champagne in the world.

Lisa looked genuinely hurt. "Don't do this to me. I feel like it's me against them—do you know what that's like? If I slip up, there's a photographer for the *New York Post*; if I'm tired and forget a line, there's *People* magazine with a pen in hand.

"These last few days—it's been like somebody really cared about me. I've done this for you."

"Thank you." Taylor held the glass up between them.

"And now I need your help."

"Surprise," Taylor said.

"My agent called. I've just been offered the lead in a film. It's about a rich singer who peaks out and fakes her own death and then goes to live in Europe. Always planning a comeback but just grows older."

"Taylor it's MGM and it's a biggie. They want me." She leaned over the table. "It's pretty overwhelming, but the show closes here in two days and this could just be my ticket."

Taylor felt a sudden sense of interest. "You're kidding me? Congratulations, Lisa. A couple of months ago I would have doubted—well, frankly I don't think you could've handled it. But after seeing you do the show—hey, that's great!" He lifted the glass and saluted her. "To you. Someday I'll tell people I knew you when..."

"No, no, I don't want congratulations, I want help." She pushed his hand back down to the table and held on to it. "I'm in over my head, I don't know if I can act for shit. I don't know if the script is any good, I don't know if the deal is any good and they want an answer."

"Lisa, you have an agent, an attorney, and a business manager. Use them. They're on you're side," Taylor said carefully.

"No, they're not," she replied flatly. "They all own a percentage of me—or rather, what I can bring in. No output, no input. Lisa doesn't work, Lisa doesn't take every script, we don't get paid.

"Agents are like marlin—they're hard to land and then they go bad fast. Lots of power lunches until you sign on the dotted line and then you'll never get them on the phone again."

"You're being paranoid. Besides, I've seen you act in a number of unique situations and you do just fine..."

Lisa gripped his hand tightly. "Taylor, I need to ask you something. Please promise me you'll consider it before you laugh or say no." She shut her eyes and suddenly Taylor saw her as a little girl, helpless and alone.

He shook his head to clear it, then poured another glass of bubbly. "Lisa, I don't know what this is..."

"Just promise me you'll consider it. Is that too much to ask?" She put her index finger to his lips. "Shhh, don't talk—just listen. Please?"

"Right." He nodded.

"I want you to come to California with me." She stopped to watch his reaction. "Shhh, remember? Consider."

She began counting things off on her fingers: "You would be my personal manager—or whatever title you want. I'll do whatever you say—anything. You go between me and all those people I can't deal with. I'll give you twice what I pay anybody else, and I'll do whatever you say, and you can make whatever deal you think is right.

"You hire and you fire. Then I can concentrate on what I do best. It would work, I know it would."

"Lisa, that's a really, uh, interesting idea, but I would be out of my league in Hollywood. A lamb among wolves. It wouldn't be in either of our best interests."

"No, you're wrong. Look at what you do here. Look at the characters you deal with, the egos you handle. Hollywood is minor league compared with this." She spread her hands wide.

"You'd knock their socks off. You can still use the registered hyenas as much as you need to, but you'd be in control of everything."

She leaned over the table until her face was only two inches from his. He could feel the body heat reflecting from her in a sensual wave. "It's a three picture contract. I'll put you in charge of everything—the films, the albums, promo's, side shit, everything.

"Do you have any idea what that would be worth? Figure you'd make one and half, two million *next year!*" She punctuated the last two words with her fingers.

Then she whispered. "Next year... Do you know what kind of money that is?"

He shook his head and swallowed some more wine.

"That's fuck money. That's the kind of money where you can tell the world to go fuck itself. If you don't like somebody you tell them to go fuck themselves. If you like a house or a car you don't ask how much it is, you just say, Fuck it, I'll take it, and write a check." She pounded the table three times.

"I know you do okay here, but have you ever wondered what it would be like to write a check for anything you want? 'What a lovely Ferrari, how much was it?'" she pantomimed. "I have no idea. I just wrote a check for it." Fuck it, who cares? What a nice suit, what a pleasant house, your swimming pool? I'm impressed. Don't be—it's just money. Fuck it, *it's just money.*

"Here money is your identity because everybody uses it and nobody has enough. I can take both of us out of that stratum.

"Think about that, Taylor. We'd be a team. TaLisa Productions." She rolled the words off her tongue. "Lisor Productions? What ever you want.

"What do you call a relationship when the total adds up to more than its parts?"

"Synergistic," Taylor said. He was picturing things in spite of himself. Changes.

"Right. That's what we'd be—but I'd call it something more. I'd call it magic." She waved her fingers to the waiter, who came to attention at once.

"My friend and I would like some cognac—in fact, bring us a bottle of the best you can lay your hands on."

"Certainly, Miss Steel."

"Oh, and you know what? We don't care how much it costs." She smiled, and the man smiled back, uncertain what was happening but trying hard to please.

The waiter left.

"Fuck it." Lisa smiled at Taylor. "It's only money."

Taylor swirled the golden liquid around in the snifter. He was surprised to see that most of the bottle had mysteriously disappeared. "This was fun."

"It's not over yet, Taylor." Lisa shook her head and looked up at the ceiling. "I know sometimes I seem really hard, but you know I'm not. I need someone to help me get through the bullshit. Somebody that I can depend on...

"Promise me you'll think about it."

"I already promised." Taylor was surprised at his own reaction. "I just can't see myself leaving here—and Hollywood?" He took another swallow. "That's nice stuff..."

"Still think she'll come around, don't you?"

"What?" Taylor could feel the buzz coming on. I seem to be doing this a lot lately, he thought.

"Carol. You still think she'll realize she made a mistake." She took a long drink. "Won't happen. She's a real lady, but she's screwed up— too much Vassar, not enough Vegas." She squeezed Taylor's hand impulsively.

"Man, she was a fool to give you up, but you'd be a bigger fool to sit around like a lap dog waiting for her highness to cave in. Ain't gonna happen. If she was really in love with you, would you be here with me? Think about that, too."

"I owe Nick. I owe the DollHouse..."

"Bullshit. You ever hear of a man named Lincoln? How many years do you plan on working for the plantation before you're freed? They pay you a salary, you do your best for them. There's no debt of honor involved. It really is that simple.

"Life is what happens while you sit around and wait for something better. What are you going to tell your grandkids you did in the war? You were a clerk? Life went by? You watched?"

"I get the idea, Lisa, don't oversell it."

She kissed Taylor spontaneously. "Good, you will think about it? In the meantime I want to dance until I drop. Take me out, gentleman caller. Let's party..."

"Are we having fun yet?" Lisa swung Taylor around and kicked her leg over her head in time to the music.

"I wish you wouldn't do that, it makes me feel old."

"Don't worry, Taylor, you couldn't do that even when you were a kid." Lisa laughed and spun him again. "We are having fun, aren't we? It's nice to have friends..."

Lisa pressed against him and Taylor felt himself dancing with a beautiful woman, not a friend. Watch it boy, keep your wits about you...

She appeared so self-confident when she was dancing, never seeming to notice the ever-present space the other people on the dance floor automatically allowed her—nor the continuous elbowing and whispering as people realized who she was...

Yet when she talked about needing someone to run interference for her, the image was that of a mere girl—which, of course, is what she really was—rather than that of a rich, sexy, self-assured woman, which is what the world thought she was.

Things are rarely what they seem to be...

What a major life change it would be to actually go to Hollywood and have the decision-making power on a major film and a major record and live performances and God knows what all.

It was a beguiling fantasy, but that's all it was. Lisa was Lisa; a different animal by anyone's standards. Maybe she was cut out for la la land and maybe she wasn't, but either way, it wasn't his problem.

Not my job, man, he thought, as Lisa stood on her tip toes and kissed his ear lobe. "Getting tired old man?"

"That's not fair. Besides being about eighteen years old, you're a professional."

"Oh, to be eighteen again. I can't even remember that far back. Besides, women age faster than men. Let's get a nightcap. I really feel good."

Taylor turned his wrist over to look at his watch. Lisa grabbed his arm and prevented it from moving. "Don't do that, don't even think about looking at that stupid watch and telling me it's getting late."

"Yeah, but it is."

"Not when you work nights, sweetheart, and besides, I'm really enjoying myself and so are you. I can tell. Please, please, please..."

"One more drink, but that's all."

Lisa laughed at her victory and led him toward the door. "Let's do it at the DollHouse—nobody will bother us there—or we could just have it delivered to my suite." She rubbed her fingertips lightly over his thigh.

"Maybe it would do you some good to get a new perspective on things."

"Lisa, I know you don't have much of a social life with your schedule, but if you just snapped your fingers, you could have any man in this place. You don't need me. Besides, it would probably fuck up our friendship."

"You just think I'm horny, don't you? Sometimes you have an amazing lack of self-esteem, not to mention perception. I've always liked you Taylor. I like you a lot, but we just never had a chance... well, you know, you were always hanging around Carol."

Lisa noted Taylor's grimace and hurried on: "I never wanted to put the make on a friend's man, but, believe me, I've thought about compromising my high ideals several times lately. And now there's no reason I can't let you know how much I appreciate you.

"Have you ever been with a woman who's spent the last year in prison? With no visiting privileges?"

"Not to my knowledge..." Taylor was trying to follow the change in subjects.

"Tonight's the night." She kissed Taylor full on the mouth, and he could feel the juices surging in spite of his attempt to control them.

"Come on, Taylor, let's go, your suite or mine…" She brushed her lips over his cheek and teased the surface of his flesh with her tongue. "You ticklish? I bet you are."

"This is not a good idea, Lisa." But he didn't pull away.

"You're right—it's a *great* idea. I need you. Look, I've given up all my bad habits. I need to substitute at least one good one. One fun one…

"I know you don't want to say no—and I won't appreciate it if you do."

Taylor could feel her eyes burning into him. Thin ice. She's not going to take rejection well—and then again, why am I rejecting her? Am I really that pussy whipped?

No, that's not it, he answered his own question. I know where this path leads—death and destruction, bodies on the trail. One of them probably mine.

"Okay, I'll level with you. I think you are just about the nicest-looking woman I've ever seen and I suspect we would be more than fair in the sack together and I'd sure like to get in your pants."

"So. The town's full of taxis. My treat." She took his hand and began rubbing his fingers.

"But if there is any real chance of our working together, I mean if we went to California, I couldn't be your lover. I'd have enough trouble getting respect as it is. If everybody thought I had the job because I was a stud, and only because I was a stud, well, they'd walk all over me.

"I couldn't represent your best interests if everybody in town was smirking behind my back. It just wouldn't work."

Lisa put her hand to her mouth, "My God, you're serious." She threw her arms around him and hugged him tightly.

"I knew it. I knew you'd do it! This is so great. You're right, you're right about everything. You take control, boss, I'll do whatever you want.

"Oh yes," she spun in a tight circle. "Things are looking up. Ha-ha!" She was squealing to the delight of the nearby tables. Then her voice dropped to a husky whisper, "Whatever you say…"

"I say I'm just considering it, Lisa. Don't get carried away. I also say you should go to bed—alone. Tomorrow's a working day."

"You win. I love it, I love it." She kissed him and skipped like a child.

"Tomorrow, we'll talk about it tomorrow." And she was gone.

Now what in the fuck possessed me to do that? Short term solution. I've got to tell her tomorrow that I can't give up my life here and go with her.

Can't just pack up and start over. He sipped his drink.

Can I?

He leaned back and shut his eyes. It was so difficult to sit at a small table with a big hard on. That was one thing about Lisa nobody could deny; when she put her mind to being every man's dream, it worked so very well...

So now what? Go jerk off in the shower? Dig out the old address book? Jesus, it was probably completely out of date by now. Carol had probably fixed that too.

A sudden thought crossed his mind and be began patting his pockets. He reached in his back pocket and withdrew a small slip of paper. On it was a phone number—and a one-line message: "You know who to call—Sherry and Kristin."

Reach out and touch someone.

Or two...

Taylor started the morning with his second hangover in a week. Something is not working here, he thought. Maybe I need a second opinion. Could I really take a break, go to Hollywood? The concept seemed as alien as going into space.

Taylor looked at the clock. Five A.M. and I feel like the day should already be over. Hell with it, I'm going to work. He dressed and went to the DollHouse.

"Hi Taylor," the floor manager greeted him, "a bit early for you isn't is? Looking for Nick?"

"Nick?" Taylor stopped in his tracks. "Nick's here? At this time of day? Where?"

The manager suddenly realized he was talking too much. "Ah, no, I think he's in back."

Taylor strode past the cashier's cage and into the rear of the casino. The thick steel door to the counting room was closed and a large guard Taylor did not recognize stood in front of it like a statue.

"Is Nick inside?"

The guard shrugged.

"Okay." Taylor walked to the door and started to punch in the electronic combination. The guard grabbed his hand. "Uh-uh. Nobody goes in."

Taylor carefully removed the man's hand. "My name is Taylor Stevens, perhaps you didn't know that. I'm the exec VP here. I need to talk to Nick." He reached for the lock again.

"I don't care if you're Alice In Wonderland, touch that lock again and I'll break your arm." He put his hand on his gun. "I ain't kidding, pal."

Taylor was uncertain of exactly what was happening. "You work for me." That sounded lame even as he said it.

"I don't work for you, pal. Now leave."

"Let him in." Neither Taylor nor the guard had heard the door open. Taylor gave the guard a last look and walked past the casino's head accountant, who shut the door behind him.

"Would you mind explaining what the hell is going on here? Who is that ape and why are you here at..." Taylor let his voice trail off as he saw Nick seated at the desk surrounded by piles of bills and an electronic counting machine.

"If I hadn't seen it with my own eyes..." Taylor shook his head.

"You had to find out sometime." Nick was watching him closely.

"Skimming. Nick Salerio. Fuck me. Mr. Honest stealing the house money."

"That's not exactly what we're doing."

"Oh, an early morning collection for homeless orphans. Is that it?"

"No, we're skimming—you got that part right. It's just not for me. You get it now?"

"Oh, shit, you're connected." Taylor bent over and supported himself with both hands on the table top. "How could I not know that?"

"It's just a cost of doing business, Taylor, just like paying the electric bill, it's just overhead. Cost of doing business."

"Now you're going to give me that speech about how everyone does it, aren't you? I can't believe it, this has been some week."

Nick shrugged. "Grow up, Taylor. It's no big thing."

"Think a federal court would agree with that assessment, Nick? Seems to me they might consider it stealing. Not to mention the little problem of tax avoidance."

"Well let's not tell them then, what do you say?" Nick smiled, "This will all seem natural in a day or two, just take a day off and think about it. Now what did you want to see me for?"

"Not a damn thing you could help me with." Taylor turned and walked out. Nick and the silent accountant looked at each other.

Leon called the next day. He was cautiously optimistic about the entire scene. "You have to remember, Taylor has an exaggerated sense of honor. He works for Nick—no, more than that, he gave his word to Nick that Lisa would finish the gig. You really put him on the spot Carol. What else could he have done?

"You can't make him choose between his job and you—it's not the same thing. He does what he does, don't try and change him—or if you really have to, proceed gradually. Ease into it. Don't force the issue."

"But Leon, the issue *needed* forcing. Lisa is back to her old habits. It's not just a moral thing, she's killing herself and the DollHouse is footing the bill. It's disgusting, it may even be illegal. I can't condone that!"

"Nobody's asking you to condone anything, Carol. Just back off a little and let Lisa be Lisa. She'll be gone in a couple of days and life will return to normal and this will just be a little, meaningless, closed chapter in the great scheme of things."

"Oh, God, you're probably right, Leon, I'm just not as easygoing as you are. I let things get to me too much. I lie awake because I can't get Lisa out of my mind—or Taylor."

"Oiled feathers, Carol, that's the secret. Let it roll off you like water from a duck's back. It's just today, tomorrow will be different. Don't think about Lisa, she's an anomaly in the universe. A black hole. She's unable to really care for people, much less love anyone. She views us as chess pieces—no, that's not right, just as checkers, to be pushed around a board.

"That's all any of us mean to her. Give her a little rope and she'll hang herself higher than Clint Eastwood. Believe me, let Taylor miss you for a day or two while he deals with Lisa-the-python and he'll forget all about yesterday. I promise."

"I know you're right, but I miss him already… I mean just to know he's there if I want to talk…"

"Carol, promise me when he calls tonight you'll be cool—not cold, just cool. Don't see him right away, make some transparent excuse. See him tomorrow, he'll be quite tired of Lisa; more important, he'll be missing you.

"Make him come to you, Carol. Just between us girls, it's time to draw the line. You are one in million, make sure he's knows it."

"Okay," Carol sighed. "I promise."

The only problem with the scenario was that Taylor didn't call that night. He's probably sulking, Carol thought. I guess this is what most people have to deal with all the time. Except for a minor tiff or two, this was really their first fight. Maybe it wasn't all that bad compared to a lot of relationships...

She looked at the phone and bit her lip. She couldn't give in. Leon was absolutely right, if she called now it would set the precedent for any and all future disagreements. As a compromise she would call him tomorrow at the office and suggest they get together for dinner—just to talk.

That would establish the parameters.

She spent a restless night only to put the call in at ten A.M. Taylor wasn't in. On an impulse she called Nick; he wasn't in either. She finally got through to Nick's secretary and was immediately sorry for the connection.

"I haven't seen Mr. Stevens since yesterday and Mr. Salerio left this morning for Atlantic City. I can leave a message for him, if you'd like."

Bitch. Don't be so damn smug about it. You're still a bloody secretary and I'm... Don't be that way, she's just doing her job. "No, that's okay, I'd forgotten about the trip. I'll catch him later. Thank you, Paula." She slammed the phone down.

It was the worst Thanksgiving Carol could remember. It didn't even have the decency even to be cold outside. Just the usual Vegas sunny monotony. Nobody else in town seemed to know what day it was. There was just the constant stream of middle-aged tourists looking for what they considered "action."

She didn't have to go to work, but that made things even worse. The apartment was bleak and empty. In a rare burst of parental feeling she tried calling her mother, but there was no answer there either. The phone seemed to be mocking her. She sipped some obnoxious brand of "flavored" water and picked at a tasteless salad from the local Safeway salad bar.

The stupid shows on television did nothing but depress her. Even the local radio disc jockeys seemed unbearably tacky. This was a day to celebrate life and she was sad and alone. Even Leon was with somebody he cared about, but she was dead in the water. In Las Vegas...

Thanks for nothing...

She spent the next two days at home clearing up back-logged work and taking a few calls. There was no word from Taylor. Finally Carol could stand it no more. She tracked Nick down in Atlantic City.

"Nick, where is Taylor?" She asked as calmly as she could.

"Actually, I thought he was with you. He took some time off. I just assumed..."

"I haven't heard from him in four days. I, I was getting a little worried..."

The concern was evident in Nick's tone. "You two have a fight?"

"Not exactly. It's a long story, but it wasn't anything major. Just a little misunderstanding." It sounded lame even as she said it. "But I can't seem to find him. He's not at home or at the DollHouse."

"Relax, Carol, I'm sure he just took a couple of days off for the holidays. It's Lisa's last night, she probably knows where he is, call her."

"Thanks Nick, but I really can't do that. I'll talk to you when you get back."

"I get in tomorrow morning, Carol. I'll track him down and call you."

She put the phone back with a strange premonition that things wouldn't be the same when he did...

Carol woke with a start, unsure what had jolted her into consciousness. It was almost eleven o'clock but she still felt as if a truck and run over her. Maybe if I went to sleep before 4 A.M. it would seem more like I actually slept...

She checked with both her machine and the switchboard—no messages. Damn! Could Taylor really be this childish? The fight was over and gone. Maybe something had happened to him...

She walked over to the bedroom phone to dial Nick. As she reached for it the small box of candy Taylor had brought her the other night fell from the table where she had set it down. How nice of him to remember special things that she liked—even if it was a little gift, it was an effort most men would not have gone to.

Carol unwrapped the package with one hand and dialed the phone with the other. "This is Miss Davis, is Nick back yet?" The switchboard put her through.

It was difficult to get the wrapping loose with only one hand so she shook the tiny box back and forth. The secretary answered. "Hello,

Paula, this is Carol. Is he in?" Then she gasped loudly as one of the biggest diamond rings she had ever seen dropped onto the carpet at her feet.

Everything snapped into place with a bang. No wonder he was so upset, he came over to ask, and then she—oh, no...

"Is everything all right Miss Davis?" Paula asked, momentarily losing her built-in attitude. "Are you okay, should I do anything?"

"No." Carol picked the ring up amazed by the way it sparkled in her fingers. "No, no, ah, I'm fine Paula, just a tack in the carpet. I stepped on it. Surprised me. I'm fine now. Is Nick in?"

"No, actually I think he's on his way to your house." She sounded confused.

"Right. Thank you." There was no good reason for Nick to be coming to her. She held the ring to her forehead where it burned like dry ice and did something she hadn't done since she was a child.

Carol cried.

Nick noticed the tear tracks and averted his eyes. "Hi, good-looking, you got a minute for your boss?"

Carol silently showed him in.

"There's no easy way to say this Carol. Taylor's left the DollHouse. He's left Las Vegas. I'm not sure of all of his reasons, but he's gone, at least for a while."

"What happened?" Carol held her breath.

"He wanted some time off—just a break—so I gave him a leave of absence," Nick fibbed. "He'll be back."

"Where did he go, Nick? Tell me the truth, please." But she already knew.

"He went to Los Angeles." There was no other way to say it.

"He went with Lisa." It wasn't a question. "I can't believe that, but I know it's true. Damn it, Nick, he didn't even call me. He just left. Just like that. Just like that. Lisa snaps her fingers and he obeyed. He obeyed."

"Don't put more on it then it deserves. He went to work with Lisa— it's a pretty big opportunity. He didn't 'leave' with Lisa, he took a job offer. It just happens to concern Lisa."

"Everything in this town 'concerns' Lisa! Everything in the world 'concerns' Lisa! I cannot, I do not, I *will* not believe that." She stamped her foot. "What Taylor and I have doesn't concern Lisa.

"I love him Nick. I really, really do—and I didn't even get a chance to tell him. What do I do now?" She swayed and then leaned her weight on his shoulders. "Tell me what I do now."

"You show up at work tomorrow morning, young lady, and do your job." He held her at arm's length. "You go on with your life. We both know Taylor well enough to know he'll call in a day or two and break the news to you.

"When he does, you congratulate him and tell him you miss him. Act like the lady you are. He'll be tired of Hollywood and tired of our dear friend Lisa in about eight days. Don't make it hard for him to admit his error and backtrack.

"No man in his right mind could stay away from you for long, Carol—and so far no man in any frame of mind has been able to endure Lisa for any length of time. Time is really on your side."

The letter arrived in the next day's mail.

Carol,
I want to thank you for forcing me to take a long hard look at my life. I didn't particularly like what I found there but I'm glad I found it. I keep thinking I have some vague talent, something that makes me different from the people that stream into the DollHouse day after day, but when I really get down to facts it just sort of blurs together.
I think it was John Lennon who said that "Life is what happens while you're sitting around waiting for something to happen." That's exactly what I feel like...
If I don't take a chance now I'm just going to get older. Not happier.
I may not be going to write the next King Lear *or invent penicillin II but I can do something that nobody else can—I have to believe that. The longer I sit here and do nothing except be another business man the less chance I have of ever really being somebody.*
Does that make sense? It seems to at the moment.
Maybe I am running away from things, but after our talk the other day I finally realized I'm not capable of being the man you want—and I don't blame you. You are one of a kind, Carol, you really are. As the old saying goes, You'll make somebody a great...
Well, at any rate, I just may fade into the Hollywood wood-work. Maybe I'll finally get that elusive McDonald's manager-

ship—standing around watching those fries turn golden—but in the meantime I've got to give it my best shot. I've really got to try.

I see myself becoming more and more scattered—Taylor, this needs to be taken care of, Taylor handle that. I guess it comes down to putting my energy into a single project that actually has a chance of breaking through to the other side.

And to think I once told you I never gambled...

I need to take a chance. Oddly enough, I guess I need to roll the dice one time before I get too old to play the game.

Wish me at least inspiration, if not luck. I love you dearly, I'm sorry we're not cut out to be together—but we're not. I wish you happiness.

Thank you for a fantastic year.

Taylor

❉ ❉ ❉

Part of me refuses to believe that it could possibly be Christmas Eve again. Already. Where has it gone? Two years slipped away like quicksilver. Carol sipped carefully at a glass of chilled Chardonnay. "Where has it gone?" she asked out loud. "Where does it go?"

There was no answer.

She hadn't even gotten a single call—well, at least not from anyone who mattered. What was wrong with everyone? This had all the markings of the worst Christmas in history. She held the state of Nevada personally responsible.

The house was not only empty, it was cold and dead. Even with two sawdust logs burning in the fireplace it was chilled by the presence of whispering ghosts. Nick was back east, Lisa was in Beverly Hills—and, let's face it, probably with Taylor... God only knew where Leon was, or who he was celebrating with... She hadn't seen him since he had gotten the dream offer and moved to Monte Carlo to produce shows in the real ritzy casinos. Mixing with the high and mighty and no time for old friends.

What had she been doing with her nights since everyone moved away?

Nothing, was the answer. A wave of self-pity washed over her. The ice queen—maybe Lisa had been right.

Sure she had dated—well, at least she had gone out with a number of men—but for the life of her she couldn't conjure up even a single face no matter how hard she tried. All that would come was a very clear image of Taylor lying in bed next to her, stroking her breasts gently...

"I love your body, Carol, it's so, so efficient."

"Flat you mean." She knew she was blushing from the neck down. This was not the kind of conversation she was used to having at this particular junction in time. Let's be honest, she still wasn't used to having the lights on—much less discussing her body as if it was some sort of commodity to be rated.

"I know I'm flat..."

"No, you're sleek—svelte, like a wild cheetah, nothing wasted. Grace in motion."

"Flat." She repeated.

Taylor began running his tongue around her nipples in concentric circles growing ever smaller. Carol felt her nipples snap to attention. An overall tingling was replacing her blush. Inch by inch.

"Why," he said, replacing his mouth with his fingers, "does every woman in America think that every man wants a cow for a mate?"

She started to list reasons, *"Playboy, Penthouse, National Geographic..."* She inhaled a gasp as new sensations began to overwhelm her.

"Haven't you ever heard the expression, 'more than a mouthful is a waste'?" And he proceeded to demonstrate the theory.

"That feels wonderful."

"You ain't felt nothing yet." He began drawing little tongue circles on her stomach. Leaving a glistening saliva trail pointing downward. "You know what I'm going to do now?"

Carol's breath caught in her throat. "Yes," she croaked.

"What? I couldn't hear you. What did you say?" He stopped licking and looked directly into her eyes. "Say it again."

"Yes, I said yes."

"Yes? Yes what?" He pushed himself up on his elbows. "I'm not sure I understand. Yes what?"

"Oh, God, don't tease." Carol squirmed from side to side. "Don't do this. Don't stop."

"Well then tell me what I'm going to do. Better yet, tell me what you want me to do. You have to tell me or I won't do it."

"I can't." Her body was on fire where he had touched her. "I just can't."

"Sure you can, honey," he raked the tips of his fingers down her side, watching it convulse in time with his tracing. "You're not in Connecticut any more. Your mother can't hear us."

"Don't tease me, please."

"Tease? Me? No, no, I'm dead serious. I just need some simple instruction or I'll have to stop. I really don't know what you want." He pulled away once again.

Carol felt her body arching upward towards Taylor's mouth in spite of herself. "I want..." she said.

"Tell me Carol. You can say it. Don't be shy."

"Go down on me—oh God, I want you to go down on me."

Taylor held her face softly in both hands. "My pleasure," he said and slid his tongue into her belly button oh so carefully.

The doorbell chimed rudely, interrupting her thoughts, and like an over-stretched rubber band Carol snapped back to the present. Who the hell could that be? Not only was she not expecting anyone, she'd really rather go back to her memories than be forced to talk to anyone.

It rang again with an impatient shrill. "Hold your horses, I'm coming." She yanked the door open only to see a most unexpected face.

"Got some hot buttered rum for a cold pilgrim?"

"Leon!" Carol threw her arms around him and squeezed as hard as she could. "What a great surprise! My God, it's good to see you." She spun him around and held him at arm's length. "Are you okay? What are you doing here?"

He shrugged. "Maybe I could come inside for a moment and explain?"

"Come in, come in." She hugged him again. "It's so good to actually see you."

"Well, it's like magic seeing you again, Carol—especially today, tonight. I really just need to be with a friend. My best friend... Could I have that rum? In fact make it a double."

They spent the next couple of hours just catching up on the gossip—who was doing what to whom and where they were doing it... "So, enough small talk, how are you handling Lisa and Taylor?"

"Haven't lost your cutting edge, have you, Leon?" He didn't reply. "Better, I'm taking them better. I guess you can get used to anything in life if you have to."

Leon watched her face closely. "Never lie to your friends, Carol. I can read you too well for bullshit. Neither of them ever really appreciated what they had in you." He looked away and coughed several times. "Damn it all! Excuse me, I seem to have a bitch of a cold coming on." He sneezed three times in quick succession, then leaned back and closed his eyes.

"You sure you're okay?"

"Never better." He gulped down a slug of hot steaming rum.

"I thought you'd be spending the holidays with the Duke. I mean the last I heard…"

"Yeah, we were a pretty hot item all right. I guess that's still pretty much true, he seems to be pretty committed… Well, most of the time anyway. I really should be happier, I know. The shows have been working, I've got a rich, good-looking international playboy who seems to be madly in love with me—if you don't count the screaming, throwing-the-crystal fight we had a few hours ago…" He coughed again and again.

"Do you want some water?"

He shook his head.

"What did you fight about?"

"Ah, you might want to put your drink on the table for a second, just in case…" He pointed to the coffee table.

Silently she complied. "Bad huh?"

"He, ah, sort of came in at a bad time, see, I thought he was out of town and I was otherwise occupied and really didn't hear…" His voice was trailing off.

"You? Screwing around? I don't believe it—that's not like you at all."

Leon sucked in his lower lip. "There's more."

"More?"

"The thing that seemed to bother him the most," he coughed again. "I mean I think he could've handled the whole scene if I have been with another man."

Carol looked bewildered. "What?"

"Think about it, I don't do animals, you know…"

"A *woman?* Leon! You were with a woman?" Her eyes widened in shock.

He looked sheepish in reply.

"Just once?"

"Not exactly…"

"You've got a girlfriend? I don't believe it. She must be some woman."

"I'm still sort of in shock myself, to be honest with you. Oh boy, I'm beat. Can I tell you the rest of the story in the morning?"

She leaned over and kissed him on the cheek. "I won't sleep a wink. I'll go make sure your bed has sheets. You remember where everything is, I presume."

He nodded.

Carol stopped in mid-step, turned around and studied Leon for a second. "Just one question, am I going to be safe in this house alone with you tonight?"

"Pretty funny Carol." He coughed again.

There was a knock on Leon's door and then Carol entered with a steaming breakfast tray. "I thought you might like breakfast in bed." She put the tray across his prone form. "You really look pale, how are you feeling?"

"Pale. I feel pale. I haven't had a sniffle in four years and now I feel like I'm in a Clint Eastwood movie, 'Do you feel lucky, punk?' " He sneezed. "Nature is on a payback binge."

"Maybe you should go to a doctor?"

"What for? So he can prescribe Contact tablets for fifty bucks? I'll just ride it out. Hell, it's Christmas, I think I'll just stay sloshed for a day or two until it wears itself out. In fact, maybe a little vodka mixed in with the orange juice might work even better than silly pills. What do you think?"

"I think it's Christmas." Carol left and then returned with two water-glass-size screwdrivers and a game of Trivial pursuit. "We'll make a day out of it…"

It was two drinks and two games later when Leon broached the subject. "You're really doing well."

"What do you mean?"

"It's been over two hours and you haven't asked me about it, even though you're dying for the gruesome details…"

"Sort of," Carol admitted. "And don't think it's easy sitting here and not asking."

"You win. Where shall I start? You want to know about her?"

"Yes, but, ah, first I'd like to know about it." She sipped her drink tentatively.

"It?..."

"You know, what the differences are..."

"I see. You mean did I have to shut my eyes and imagine a cock and two hairy balls in order to get it up? No, actually it didn't require much conscious effort. Women are quite soft and kind of pleasant."

"You act like it was your first time."

"In a big way, it was..."

"Come on, Leon, you must have, I mean when you were a kid, in school, ah, with one of the dancers. Everybody's at least..." She paused, at a loss for words. "No, huh?"

He shook his head. "I was born with bent hormones. Sounds like a country and western song, doesn't it? When I was a kid my mother used to read romance novels—real soft core porn, lot's of stroking, the women in them always gushing and making liquid-like noises during sex.

"I guess I expected the actual act to be—well, I guess wetter would be the correct term. She's great Carol, you'll really like her—smart, gorgeous. Her touch excites me, do you know what that's like? Yes, I suppose you do. I know I sound like a teenager, but it's so new to me..."

"It's great. Don't stop, tell me all about her. You could start with her name."

"Anne. Like Anne Boleyn. Real classy lady.

"I wonder if I'll be a tits or an ass man? There's a whole new world out there to consider now. Decisions to make. I've never before even considered the fact that someone could get pregnant. New universes to conquer. Do you realize what a fascinating invention that little hook on the back of your bra is? Amazing concept..." He was racked with a brittle cough that wouldn't quit.

Carol watched him, choking with the effort. "You're getting worse. I'm calling the doctor."

"No, no." The effort brought on a new coughing spell. "It's Christmas, there won't be any doctors."

"I'll grab whoever's on call at the DollHouse."

"Please, please, not some retired obstetrician. Some of my best friends have gone out that way. It lacks any sense of style. Compromise." His voice was just above a whisper. "Let's compromise. Tomorrow—if I'm not better tomorrow I'll go without complaint."

She debated the situation only momentarily before choosing the path of least resistance. "Leon, if you're getting pneumonia and you die on me right after—if you die now, I'll kill you."

"No pneumonia, promise. I really want you to meet Anne and funerals are such a negative way to introduce people…" He tried to swallow another gulp of juice and coughed it up, only to put his head back on the pillow weakly.

"Sorry."

True love doesn't agree with everyone, Carol thought. Take, for instance, Leon. He looks terrible…

"No! No!" Leon leaned over and grabbed for his shirt, which had now fallen on the shiny floor. Carol deftly kicked it away with her foot. "Three points," she mumbled as the offending garment fell out of reach.

"I'm not staying in a hospital! That's it—we're done. Worked out well for all concerned. Fade to black, cue the voice over, roll the credits… This broadcast is property of the National Football League, all rights reserved… We're outta here…"

Carol stuck her leg out.

"Hey, up to you, I'll leave without my shirt if you want me to—do wonders for my reputation, strolling half naked with the Virgin of Vegas. Oh God, yes, think of the women I'd be able to get on that rep alone…" He was rattling on a double speed.

"Take a deep breath and tell me what the matter is, Leon. Relax, the good doctor just wants to run some tests to make sure that you're okay. You haven't had a physical for a long time."

"Since high school gym class, you mean, and that didn't turn out so fucking well, I can tell you. Damn right I haven't! Why do you suppose that is? Because going in for a few tests is like taking your car to the mechanic and saying, "Find something wrong, I dare you.

"Think they'll find something? Hey, I guess they just might. Normal? The specimen doesn't appear quite normal. No way. I'm doing just fine, thank you very much." He began coughing.

"Sure sounds that way. Don't be such a wussy, Leon. Would it make you feel better if I stayed too, held your hand through the rough parts?"

"Don't waste your breath. You can't guilt trip me into anything stupid. Sticks and stones, in one ear and out the other. Curiosity killed the cat." He covered his ears with his hands.

Carol grabbed both wrists and moved his arms to his side. "Feeling a little weak, Leon? Letting a woman push you around? Bad way to begin a relationship. Soon other men will be pointing at you and mouthing the word, 'whipped.' A new expression you'll have to get used to.

"Stay–in–the–damn–hospital–for–one–night"—She hesitated for a second—"or I'll, I'll call Anne and tell her we've been married for years and you lied about being gay and that she's just another broad who fell for your tired line."

"You would, wouldn't you?" He coughed again and physically surrendered to the inevitable. "One night only and then you've got to treat me to the best dinner in this stupid town."

She nodded.

"Then apologize, in a public place, at noon, for calling me..."

"Don't push your luck Leon."

He nodded quickly. "Carol, I really didn't mean to call to you the Virgin of Vegas, it just came out. Forgive me?"

"That's okay. I'm not any more." She turned and left the examining room.

Leon watched with a detached interest as two white-suited nurses and a bored doctor manhandled a comatose patient into the bed next to him. One of the nurses turned to him with a pat smile of apology.

"I'm sorry, but we're short of rooms. We need to force a roommate on you for a little while."

Leon raised himself on his elbows and tried to see into the mass of bandages and clear tubes dripping unknown substances into the mysterious form. He couldn't even see a face.

"Don't worry, he won't be any bother." The same nurse apologized. "Actually I'd be surprised if he even regained consciousness."

"What's the matter?"

"Cancer. We just took most of his stomach out. Poor guy." Just as she said this, the figure tensed and strained against its restraining bonds as if fighting her declaration.

Quickly the woman reached up and cracked open a glass stopcock allowing a clear drip to trickle down to the patient. Immediately the man relaxed, his body sagging as a wave of calmness crested over him.

The nurse patted him as the chemical took effect. She ran her fingers over the tubes checking on the various feeds that were sustaining what life was left.

"Pretty powerful stuff, there," Leon commented.

She shook her head in agreement. "He's pretty far gone. At least we can ease the pain. That's about all..." She was interrupted in mid-thought by a loud bell.

"Code. Room six! Stat! Let's go!" someone yelled. "God, what a night." The woman dropped the tubes and ran from the room.

Leon reached over and picked up a folded piece of paper from the floor where it had fallen from the drug cart.

"FENTANYL—Citrate Injection USP. A narcotic analgesic." No shit, Leon thought, looking back up at the other patient who now seemed to be resting comfortably. He continued to read the drug literature.

"Fentanyl Citrate injection in a dose of 100 mcg is approximately equivalent in analgesic activity to 10 mg of morphine." What do you know, one of my all time favs, good old tears of the poppy. Maybe those really were the salad days. Maybe I was cut out to be a junkie, just nod my life away in a pleasant "analgesic" fog. Never have to worry about the little things in life that can bring you down so easily.

Like dying of AIDS...

"What do you think, my friend?" he asked the other patient rhetorically. "You're going to die. In fact, if I understand your nurse correctly you're pretty much already dead. What did you think about when the anesthesiologist clamped the mask over your face?

"Did you realize you would probably never see anybody you loved again? Did you realize the inside of that mask was probably the last view you'd ever have of this world?

"I wonder what went through the doctor's mind when he cut you open? Rough night with the wife? Late for the afternoon golf game? This nurse is a real fox, how do I get in her pants?

"Well at least you're resting comfortably now. That's more than I can say. Fucking AIDS, I don't believe it. Three years, it's been three years since I fucked up and slept with a stranger. If I'd just gone back to the hospital for tests...

What? What fucking good would that have done? Would I have lived my life differently? Would I have found Anne earlier? Would I have shot a child molester, killed a crooked politician?

"AIDS." He buried his head in the pillow and pictured Anne. Please, God, don't let me have given it to her. Please, please. I know I'm going to die a miserable death, maybe I deserve it. Another homosexual bites the dust, but don't let her have it.

Get a hold on yourself you jerk. You knew the risks, you knew that asshole was screwing around. Shit, you were screwing around. Why did you think it would never catch up to you?

Anybody but me. That's the bottom line all right. And now I've got what, a year? Max? A year of dying inside. Taking stupid drugs, enduring pain and trying not to see the pity in everyone else's face when they force themselves to talk to me.

A miserable, lingering hell, followed by a miserable death. "No thank you," he said out loud and slid his feet onto the cold floor. Guiding his own IV drip so it wouldn't pop out from his arm, he stepped over to the drug cart the nurse had left in the room when she ran out for the code.

Carefully he picked up the small vials and scanned the labels. There were several bottles of Fentanyl. Must have been on sale, he thought. White Flower day at the old pharmaceutical company.

Leon slipped three of the small bottles into his gown pocket and got back into his bed just as the nurse came back into the room.

"I knew I left this somewhere." She placed her hand on the drug cart, started to look at the other patient's chart and did a double take back to the drug cart.

Oh, oh, Leon thought. About to be busted. But the woman only shrugged slightly, withdrew another small vial and proceeded to pierce the plastic top with an IV needle.

Leon watched her every move as she rigged the tube onto a nipple of the stopcock and cracked the valve to start the drip. I could do that. In fact, I bet I would make one hell of a nurse...

"You're good at that," Leon said.

She didn't even look over at him. "I should be, I've had lots of practice." She came over to Leon's side of the room stopped and stretched a pair of white plastic gloves over hands before placing a thermometer in his mouth.

"I guess I should get used to that, shouldn't I?" He formed his words carefully around the little glass tube.

"Pardon?"

"The gloves." He pointed with the thermometer.

"Yes," she replied quite seriously. "You're going to see quite a few in the near future." She withdrew the instrument and held it up to the light, tracing the little silver line of mercury with her forefinger.

"Not bad. How are you feeling?"

"Like a million dollars." Leon said. "How long will I have to stay here?"

"I don't know. The doctor wants to talk to you before I give you a pill to help you sleep. You can discuss your options with him."

"Options?" Leon chuckled dryly. "I've got options?"

"Of course. I know it seems pretty bad right now, but they've made a lot of progress in treating these kinds of things. New drugs, new methods."

"I think I saw that same movie. And there's always a chance that someone will develop a cure while I'm sitting around waiting. Isn't that how the script goes?"

"Well, it is possible. Anything's possible, but you have to have faith."

"Faith?" Leon said. "What do I need with faith? I've got options."

The nurse smiled. "At any rate, the doctor will be with you in about an hour. If you need anything else use your buzzer."

Leon watched her depart. Options? He thought, Babe, you don't know the options I've got right here in my pocket.

He remained motionless for several minutes after the nurse left. I hate hospitals. How do they expect anybody to recover in a place that's so fucking clean? It's unnatural. If they would just strew some dirty clothes over the chairs, maybe a couple of those nice little styrofoam boxes from McDonald's on the floor, with a bit of coagulating ketchup rubbed on the too shiny tile, people would feel more at home.

Like they had something to live for.

But maybe that's the idea. No false hopes in this ward.

God, I wish I had a bottle of Scotch. Well as long as we're wishing, I wish I had another chance. A new life.

He sighed out loud. "And a bottle of Scotch."

Leon withdrew the three vials and mentally calculated the amount of drug available. Just about enough to put the city of Detroit asleep for Lent, he decided.

That should do it all right. Without thinking he rubbed the inside of his elbow where a small black track remained from his days of shooting smack. *Sometimes I miss chasing the dragon. Maybe it's time I caught him.*

He took a pen from the table by the bed and looked around for a piece of paper. The only thing within sight was the Fentanyl product sheet. *What the hell. I guess that would be only appropriate.*

He wrote Carol's name at the top of the sheet and then scratched a few lines in the slim margin. Then he put the note on the night stand and hefted the pen in his right hand like a dagger and began to punch holes in the top of each of the drug vials.

When he had punctured each vial he poured the contents into a small plastic pill cup and swirled it around like it was a fine brandy. *I wonder if you dream on Fentanyl?*

I wonder if you dream when you're dead? I hope so. I'd miss dreaming a lot. He stood up and dumped the small container into the empty glass respectable and caressed the glass butterfly wing of the stopcock.

I think I'll probably miss life. I think I'll probably miss it a lot. He cracked the valve open and watched as the clear liquid began to run down the tube in slow motion. *Syrup, it moves like Karo syrup.*

How odd. How very very odd.

And he began to fall, arms out stretched, through clouds made of white cotton.

And he began to dream.

It seemed as if she had just drifted off when a persistent knocking brought Carol back to the land of the living. After wishing it away in vain for a few moments, she gave in to the inevitable, threw a robe around herself, and went to open the door.

It's got to be Leon. He's panicked and left the hospital. I can't blame him—what a shock! She steeled herself to be stern with him. *I've got to make him see that staying in the hospital is his only chance.*

Except it wasn't Leon. It was Nick.

Carol did a double take at the sight of her boss. One look at his face and she knew it was not going to be pleasant news.

"Hi, honey." He grimaced as he said it.

"What's wrong, Nick? Is...?" She faltered unable to think of exactly what new horror was about to be thrust upon her.

"We've got to go to the hospital. Grab a dress, Carol, I've got a driver waiting downstairs. We should go right now."

"It is Leon, isn't it?"

Nick nodded imperceptibly, "Yes."

"But I just saw him a little while ago, I mean he couldn't, nothing is that fast. He seemed fine." She tried to force her mind to work in a linear fashion, but it stubbornly refused.

"They called the DollHouse looking for you. There's been some sort of accident."

"I don't understand. An accident? In the hospital? What happened?"

"I don't know all the details." Nick looked away uncomfortably. "I called Doc Mayer, he's going to meet us there. If we can do anything…" He left the rest of the sentence unspoken.

Carol rushed into the small consultation room and saw two doctors talking in hushed tones. The DollHouse physician looked up as she came in. "Miss Davis, this is doctor Howard."

The other man nodded and touched Carol's arm. He struck Carol as the elderly and competent physician always featured in television shows. The one that's always elected to break the news to the relatives. It's funny the things you notice at the oddest times.

"Sit down for a minute, Carol." Doctor Williamson said.

She shut her eyes and remained standing. "Is he dead?"

"I'm afraid so."

She opened her eyes. "How? I just don't understand. How could he be dead? Even—even what he had, I mean it couldn't have progressed that fast."

"No, you're absolutely right. It didn't. It seems he somehow got an overdose of an anesthetic drug. He just went to sleep and never regained consciousness. We tried narcotic antagonists, but he was too far gone.

"For what's it's worth, there was no suffering. In fact, it was probably a pleasant way to die."

The words seemed to rattle around inside her brain. A pleasant way to die…

"We want a complete investigation into this matter." Nick spoke up for the first time. "I want to know how in hell a hospital can make a mistake like that. I personally want to know who fucked up."

The physicians looked at each other. "The thing of it is, we don't think that the patient actually received the lethal dose from a hospital employee."

It was all too much for Carol. "Would somebody please explain to me just what is going on?" She clenched her fist and shook it shook it. "In English, just explain to me what happened."

Wordlessly the doctor handed Carol a small piece of paper. She unfolded it and tried to concentrate on the tiny black print, but the words didn't seem to make any sense at all. Then she saw her name at the top of the page in Leon's handwriting.

She recognized the lines as soon as soon as she read them: "One pill makes you larger, one pill makes you small, but the ones your mother gives you don't do anything at all. Please don't let them hurt Anne. I think you are the only person I've ever really loved. Goodbye, Carol."

Carol let the words sink in for a minute. "Does anybody else know?"

The DollHouse doctor shook his head. "It was meant for you. Nobody else has seen it."

"I don't want anybody to know. Can we say that he died from something else? This is really important."

"We have to contact anyone Leon had sexual contact with—you can understand that. It's not just the law, it's a moral obligation. The hospital has to do that."

"Okay, I understand that—but can we not tell anybody else? If the newspapers get hold of this…"

"Then there is the matter of the death certificate."

"Doctor Mayer can sign that, can't he?" Nick said the words quietly but there was no mistaking the force behind his voice.

The hospital physician looked at Doctor Williamson, who licked his lips and nodded. "A stroke. He died of a stroke. I was there."

"Okay." The other man was obviously relieved. "It would be easier all the way around if that's the way it happened."

"Easier on you and easier on the hospital, you mean." Nick smiled.

"I can't deny that."

"Where did he get the drugs? I thought stuff like that was always locked up."

"I'm sorry, Miss Davis, but this is a hospital. We have drugs everywhere… From what I understand there was an emergency. The patient couldn't have had more than a few moments access."

"Apparently he had enough access," Nick commented.

"Nobody expected him to do anything like this. We aren't jailers. There's just not enough doctors and nurses in the world to watch everyone every minute. I'm sorry, I really am."

Carol considered the statement for a second. "Yes, I understand, that. Thank you doctor. For everything."

"We'll want the body. The DollHouse will be responsible for everything." Nick hugged Carol, and she was suddenly very glad he was there to take control. "We'll give him a funeral this town will never forget. Hell, we'll give him a wake. I think that would have appealed to Leon's sense of style."

Carol nodded.

"Do you need a sedative, Carol? Just something to get you through the night?"

She was tempted. "No, no thanks, doctor. I'll be okay." A big, wake. Yes, Leon would have like that.

But part of her was already ashamed for worrying if Lisa would come. And if Taylor would.

HOLLYWOOD

Taylor deliberately popped the clutch loose on the Ferrari, leaving a patch of Goodyear's best on the drive. The car skidded into a perfect half doughnut, whipping the back end around the street, forcing an oncoming vehicle to lock its brakes, jamming its front wheels over the curb.

The other driver honked his horn and pressed his fingers against the windshield in shock. Taylor flipped the bird in his general direction while gunning the red Ferrari sideways in a pirouette around the stalled vehicle.

Fucking Toyota owners have fallen for their advertising—probably go to a race school to learn to drive their "sports car." Taylor banged his fist off the dashboard. God damn it all! I'm really letting her get to me.

She's just another broad. He punched the stereo on with his forefinger and cranked the volume up until the car shook with pure sound.

What do you do when you're falling
You've got 30 degrees and you're stalling out
And it's 24 miles to the beacon
There's a crack in the sky and the warning's out.

For a moment Taylor thought he was having a nightmare. Lisa was yelling at him through the radio... That's it, I'm nuts, I'll just turn the car around and head back for Nevada. No one will even know I'm gone.

Five miles out
Just hold your heading true
Got to get your finest out
You're number one anticipating you.

He ran his hand over the face of the stereo. It *was* Lisa! KRZR, only the major rock station on the West coast, was flogging her latest release.

And damned if it didn't sound good. The emotion in her voice came through the air waves true. Taylor was suddenly in the cockpit of a helpless airplane. Trapped, afraid.

That woman can do no wrong.

Our hope's with you
Rider in the blue.

Her success is rolling over everyone in its path like some sort of rock slide. Not me, I'm still what I am. Just like Popeye. Once a sailor, always a sailor.

At least I think so...

He visualized his upcoming meeting with a group of studio heavies. Everybody in Hollywood thinks they're the original wolf in sheep's clothing. I know those clowns are sitting around figuring the fastest way to fuck me over.

He waved at the parking lot guard, ignoring the man's pullover gestures, depending on the flash of the car to see him through. It seemed to work. He slammed the door, collected himself, and headed for the front entrance.

Taylor checked in with a skeptical receptionist who had to check every name on her list at least three times before finding any record of his appointment.

Even then she looked Taylor up and down as if he might be some sort of terrorist sneaking into MGM in order to subvert the kingdom. She's been watching too many of her own movies, Taylor thought as she handed him a visitor's pass and silently motioned him toward him toward a bank of elevators.

"Thank you for your trust," he said clipping the pass to his suit pocket. "I'll try not to let you down." He turned and immediately slipped on the white marble of the atrium floor, catching himself just before balance fled. He refused to look back at the receptionist.

Winning through intimidation. These fuckers must have written the damn book. I wonder what's waiting in the elevator, a strip search by a security guard with cold fingers?

"Taylor! Hey, man, it is you. Far out." Taylor didn't see the face because he was still focused on the problem of snake boots meeting the slippery floor, but the voice was familiar.

"Its' me, Craig." The man grabbed Taylor by the shoulders. "I don't believe it, a friendly face in hell. Or have the pod people gotten to you too? Don't tell me you work for Consolidated Extortion now?"

Taylor mentally ran the face and the voice through a mental mug book, quickly placing the owner. Another one of Hollywood's "house husbands," Craig was a transplanted New York Jew. Taylor knew he was a semi-successful writer but overshadowed by his wife—one of the new "stars" that seemed to be everywhere these days. Although not close, they had mixed at a number of obligatory parties and Taylor had enjoyed his company.

"No, no, I'm still an outsider, chasing the elusive deal."

"Tell me about it." The other man wiped a line of invisible sweat from his forehead. "I just went through an unbelievable experience. I mean, I know this is Hollywood and God knows I'm no virgin, but sometimes..." His voice trailed off.

"Have you got ten minutes, let me buy you a beer and tell you a story."

"I'd really like to but I've got a meeting up there." Taylor pointed upward.

"Okay, for you the short version." He edged Taylor over to the side of the hallway. "I've got this treatment see, really nice, if I do say so myself. Lots of rewrites, clean, crisp but still schmaltzy. Real family hour, prime time stuff.

"Based on a true story that would bring tears to Joseph Wambaugh's eyes. Two cops, one shot while trying to rescue a kid, fights his way back in spite of a lost leg, partnership falling apart, alcohol, fights— then they get assigned to one of the major art crimes of the century... well, never mind all the details, the point is it was dynamite."

"They didn't like it?" Taylor was trying to move the recitation along.

"No, no, they loved it. I actually got to pitch it to three real vice- presidents, I mean besides the usual bullshit acquisitions VP. Three real producers and they ate it up.

"They asked me to leave the room for a few minutes so they could discuss details and when I came back in they were all smiling. Big smiles. It was really strange.

"And then it happened. One of the sharks looked me right in the eye and said they wanted to do it, just one little point. Could we make the main characters vampires instead of cops?

"'Could you still work with it?' one of them asked. 'Is that doable?'

"Vampires, they wanted to take this real story that I had researched, sweated out with my blood, my hands, a poignant tear-your-heart-out- of-your-chest story about the drama between these two...

Taylor laughed out loud.

"This is serious stuff. Don't laugh. I was at a crossroads, man. You don't know what it's like. I'm thirty-four years old with no feature sales. Do you know the average age of people that are pitching new movies these days?

"Let's just say they have to schedule most sessions after three o'clock to avoid problems with truant officers. What am I going to do with the rest of my life? Take treatment rewrites from twenty-five-year-old snot-nosed directors?

"On the other hand I had that sucker written to a T. The characters were developed, the plot was finely tuned. It was a racehorse. No fat, just muscle. Maybe the best thing I've ever written in my life. It cut a neat year from my life like a scalpel.

"I felt those guys staring at me and I knew right then that I wouldn't have an ounce of respect for myself if I took that offer. But at the same time I also knew two weeks from now there would be another writer in this town churning out a vampire script on my idea.

"My life, my existence came down to that single point on the plane. A crystal moment in time. I had to make a decision about who I really am."

"So what did you tell them?"

"Well, I thought," Craig put one hand out to each side, "respect, huge contract, respect, lot's of money, respect, a writing gig with a major studio." He was bending his body at the waist in increments as he spoke each line. The top half was now almost parallel with the floor.

"You did it, didn't you?" Taylor was half amused half amazed.

Craig straightened up. "Crossroads come and crossroads go. Meet the new writer of 'Vampires in Blue.'

"I never really knew I had it in me, that ultimate ability to sell out at a moment's notice if necessary. Well, my friend, there are seven million stories in this city, and that's just one of them, but you might want to bear it in mind. You might want to do a bit of soul searching before you climb the stairway to heaven." He pointed at the elevators.

"Or I might not," Taylor said.

"That too." He stepped back and saluted Taylor.

He felt the ice collect in the air as soon as he was shown into the conference room. It was reinforced by the fourteen-foot polished mahogany "conference" table and the already overbearing smiles on the faces of the shirts waiting for him.

In Nevada they'd be suits, here they're too hip for that—just shirts. Shirts trying for home field advantage. "Gentlemen," he nodded and sat down without waiting for an invitation.

"Mr. Stevens." One man nodded vaguely in his direction.

"Taylor." The VP at the end of the table corrected for him.

"We've got some good news for you."

"It's all on paper, we've got it all worked out." Several bound pages were tossed onto the table, although Taylor wasn't certain by whom. I wonder how long they've rehearsed this routine. He continued to watch in fascination as the conversation bounced from one participant to another without a hint of obvious planning, like a ping pong ball on LSD.

I wonder where the TelePrompter is hidden, he thought.

"Congratulations." He felt someone pat his shoulder as he reached for the contract and tried to cut through some of the jargon to get at the figures. As he suspected, they were hidden for a reason.

They sucked.

"Well, pretty good for a first time at bat wouldn't you say?"

"Three quarters of a mil for Lisa?" Taylor looked up from the papers, "You have to be kidding."

"Plus a hefty three percent. Very few actresses get anywhere near that. This picture's bound to clear a bundle. You'll be collecting for years. It's like owning a license to print money."

Taylor smiled indulgently, reached into his pocket and peeled off five hundred-dollar bills. "Here, I'll give these to the first person at this table who can tell me the last picture the point owners made any money from a cut of the net.

"Free and clear, five hundred bucks. Just give me a name."

"Taylor, Taylor, be reasonable. This is an untried script from a nobody. We don't have any big production values, no Russian subs, no helicopters exploding, no spaceships. It's a little story."

"Besides, the numbers don't matter."

"It's the *point* that's important here. Are you willing to work with us?"

"Can we set a deal in principle?"

They were back into their act without missing a beat. Taylor felt himself sinking into a dark pit with black oil-slick walls. Clinging by his finger nails.

Don't show it. Never let them see you sweat.

"Guys, I know what a rape deal looks like as well as you do. Let's be realistic, let me read you what we will settle for."—*five miles out just hold your heading true*—"First of all"—*Got to get your finest out, you're number one, anticipating you*—"Lisa's not an actress. She's a star. Don't forget that. We'll want two and a half up front." He heard muffled gasps, "but we'll settle for one and a half and three points of the gross. I don't want to hear the word 'net' again in the discussion."

"No possibility."

"Don't push it, Taylor. Go with us. Next picture, when you're both established you can hand us our heads, but right now we're all you got. Don't be a fool."

Taylor could hear the song running through his head as clearly as if it was on the stereo. *You're a prisoner of the dark sky, the propeller blades are still and the evil eye of the hurricane is coming in for the kill.*

"Unacceptable." He leaned back and shut his eyes. "Not in the ball park."

"Does Lisa know you're turning down her chance for a major breakthrough?"

Five miles out.

"That's an interesting point." The most senior member of the act was speaking. "Perhaps we should deal with her directly."

Taylor could feel the ground slipping away into a vague blackness. Lisa probably would deal directly with them to save this shot. No doubt about it. She would throw him to the dogs like so many table scraps.

Don't take that dive again, push through that band of rain.

"I represent Lisa and everything she does. Cut me loose and you'll never get a deal with her. Never." *Five miles out, just hold your heading true.*

"Okay, don't get upset here. We'll go another two hundred fifty K on Lisa but that's our final offer."

"This isn't Nevada, Taylor. These are the big leagues." Now two of the men were leaning forward. "Don't blow your shot over some silly differences in numbers."

He was being backed into a corner. God only knows what Lisa will do if I turn this deal down, but any two-bit agent could have done as well or better. Maybe I am out of my league here. Might as well go down in a ball of fire.

"No problem. Myerson over at NorthPoint pictures is interested too." He lied as casually as he could. "And now that her album has just gone platinum and she's up for a Grammy"—*just hold your heading true, got to get your finest out*—"I think our position is solid.

"You don't have an exclusive option on this package, do you?" He began to thumb through his papers as if to look this fact up for himself.

"Ah, well…" One of the VP's stammered, quickly looking up to see the reaction of a man at the end of the long table, only to be quickly overridden by one of the lawyers.

"That's irrelevant. We have what amounts to a letter of intent."

But Taylor was no longer listening. He had caught the tell… *Ah, well.* He was suddenly back in Vegas, playing blackjack for real money. He was broke and riding a tiger but he had *caught the tell.* He knew who was really in charge of the deal and where the power lay. And who was bluffing.

It was just like the old days, only the table wasn't covered in green silk and the stakes were bigger.

Much bigger.

Stammer away motherfucker, it's over now. The game is closed.

They were bluffing. Not only did they need this picture, they were afraid of his going to the competition. Desperate. The tell had been a fatal mistake.

It was all Taylor could do to keep from smiling. He needed to look serious here. "Fine. I can see I'm wasting your time. Thank you, gentlemen. Maybe next time."

He gathered up his papers, leaving their contract on the table as he stood up. "See you at the movies."

The current ran around the table like an electric shock as he turned to leave.

"Wait a minute. Maybe we were a bit hasty on some of the sections."

"No, I don't think so," Taylor interjected, breaking up the rhythm before the act could get started. "Sometimes the game is played in another park. My offer is not open to haggling. I don't mean to appear rude, but I have another meeting."

Now they were actually jumping up to block his exit.

"Okay, okay, okay. We'll spring for one and a half up front and two points."

"Three and we are talking straight gross—no cap reduction, no bullshit."

"Two and a half." The man's voice was cracking.

These people would never make it in a high stakes card game. Almost too easy. Time to let them save a little face.

"Well, shit, why argue? I can see you're locked in. Write it up before I leave the room." He sat back down and sighed. "Oh, yes, one last thing, I'm executive producer—not just in the credits—final cut goes with me"

"No way."

"Totally out of the question."

"Just not possible."

"Maybe an associate producer slot in the credits but it would be in name only…"

Taylor looked across the table to the man the tell had been aimed at. "Make it so." He said quietly.

"It's done." The man stared at Taylor with a flat metal glint.

Maybe you, Taylor thought. Maybe you could walk away from a table with your shirt, but not these faggots. No way.

As if he could read Taylor's mind, the man nodded in silent agreement.

Taylor watched the lawyers scramble to change the contract and the song continued to course through his blood. *Welcome's waiting, we're anticipating, you'll be celebrating, when you're down and braking...*

Five miles out.

Fuck the crossroads.

I won.

Taylor's briefcase felt like it was filled with twenty pounds of solid gold as he recrossed the slick atrium floor. He paused at the receptionist desk and waited for her to look up. Then he began to carefully unclip his visitor's pass from his suit pocket.

"How did it go?" She seemed really interested. "You okay?"

"Slick as polished glass. It went well." He flipped the badge onto her desk. "I won."

She giggled and then covered her mouth. "I would have bet on it, against the odds. Sometimes, you know, you just get a feeling..."

"Which one?" Taylor asked.

"Pardon?"

"Which film school did you go to—UCLA or USC?"

The girl's eyes widened appreciably. "Is it that obvious?"

Taylor held his hands out from his thighs.

"USC, for all the good it did me. A film degree is about as useful as a Ph.D. in history in this town."

"Tits on a steer as we used to say on the farm. As useful as tits on a steer."

The girl giggled again. "Yeah that about sums it up."

"So you figure one day God will wake up and strike every director in this town dead and they'll come downstairs and beg you to take over?"

"Actually, I'm counting on a return of the plague. But the rest of the scenario is pretty accurate: I've got some costumes, my dad's got a barn and you can sing. Let's put on a show."

"Seems like I've heard that somewhere before, but who knows, maybe you'll get lucky."

She put her hand out. "Lucky, that's my middle name, nice to meet you. Sharon is my first. Maybe you're going to need an A.D. on your project?"

"Maybe. You know anybody looking for a gig?"

"Mr. Stevens, I know more than you'd believe. I get off at five, why don't we talk it over."

"Not today, Lucky."

"I get off at five every day."

"I'll remember that." Taylor smiled and headed for the parking lot. Some days you were on a roll. On a fucking roll.

As Taylor drove the Ferrari out of the studio parking lot he noticed a quick wave and what seemed to be an out-of-place smile on the face of the guard who earlier had seemed anything but friendly. Could news have possibly traveled that fast? Doubtful, perhaps it's just policy. Always be nice to them when they leave, especially if they've been there more than fifteen minutes because they may now have power.

He drove down Sunset with no particular destination in mind. He glanced at his watch realizing he had another appointment set up at Fox studios to pitch a variation on the same film, but suddenly it all seemed rather redundant.

"Hell with it," he thought. "They're running scared and I've got something new and interesting. I'm going to do what I want here."

For a split second Taylor wondered if he was growing a skeleton on the outside. Perhaps I'm being changed by this environment, I feel like a character in Kafka's *Metamorphosis*. I was something and I'm becoming something else. And I'm not sure I like it all that much.

Yeah, but on the other hand, the hell with 'em, I won didn't I? I beat a whole swarm of those sleazy sons of bitches at their own game and that's all that really matters in the end.

Taylor looked at his watch. I feel like celebrating. He picked up the cellular phone, dialed the inside number at Fox and told some hyperventilating secretary he'd decided not to take the meeting.

"But..." He could hear the fear at this completely unexpected move in her voice. Taylor glanced down at his watch. "To hell with this. I feel like celebrating. I don't need any other meetings. I need to get some pleasure out of my life right now, and that's something that I may have forgotten how to do."

On impulse he turned into and parked at the local Safeway. Good Lord, imagine any other community grocery store in the States carrying fresh beluga caviar on ice and chilled Chrystall champagne. As he was paying for his purchases at the checkout, he knew what he wanted to do. He knew he wanted to drive back to surprise Lisa with the good news. Let her think that he wasn't earning his keep after she heard this one...

Taylor quietly opened the door to the bungalow balancing the opened champagne and the iced caviar with his free hand. He slipped down the hall, anticipating the meeting with Lisa. Looking forward to seeing her was a nice change; it had been some time since anything that would pass for pleasant had passed between them.

Lisa was not in the living room. Probably taking another "nap"— sleeping off breakfast of a little Courvoisier and a croissant or two... Well today she was going to be happy to be disturbed.

Lisa was in bed, but she wasn't asleep. Her red hair streamed out onto the white of the pillow case like a fan of seaweed. She was rubbing both of her own nipples intently while a naked woman— rather a naked girl—was busy licking between Lisa's legs.

Both women had their eyes tightly shut.

Taylor set the treats down on the coffee table. Both women opened their eyes.

Lisa giggled. "Hi honey. I'm sure you remember my friend here." The other woman started to lift her head but Lisa casually reached down and pressed her back into her pussy. "Don't stop, honey, it's just Taylor. He knows just good clean fun when he sees it."

The second woman looked at Taylor and grinned mischievously. She deliberately stuck her tongue out as far as it would go and inserted it, making Lisa gasp unexpectedly.

"Girl's got hidden talents, Taylor." Lisa reached over and slapped her on the butt, leaving a red hand print. "Great ass, too, why don't you join us? Neither one of us would mind as long as you stay out of the way.

"Or go make lunch or something if that doesn't appeal to you. We'll be done in a few minutes." Lisa groaned again. "Whatever turns you on. Like I always say, 'Eatin' ain't cheatin.'"

Taylor's joy of the last few hours evaporated in an instant. "You know, Lisa, the bars out here are full of good-looking women who'd love to find someone who gives half the attention to them that you get from me. Have you ever thought about that, baby?"

"Sure, Taylor, just be certain that when you're meeting these adorable ex-starlet waitresses that you explain to them that I own you. That your job is to step and fetch for me—that if I didn't give you a job, you'd be living in the streets. I mean to say if I wasn't supporting your ass—oh hell, what's the chic word for it these days—homeless, that's it. You'd be homeless.

"Now, Taylor, this is for your own good. I wouldn't want any of these lovely young things to get the wrong idea and pick you out for anything but your natural charms.

"You will do that for me, won't you, honey? Don't forget now we wouldn't want any of them thinking you're an up and coming producer who feels that whoever's good in bed is good on the screen. I mean that wouldn't really be proving anything you'd want to prove, now would it?"

Taylor looked at Lisa lying in bed with the other woman, who had now calmly reached over to the nightstand and lit a cigarette, apparently oblivious to her nakedness and a sudden image of Craig with his arms outstretched in a marble atrium appeared before him like a hologram. Taylor felt himself at a crossroads. There was Craig in front of him with both arms outstretched—"Respect—money, respect—job with a major studio"—the image was bending over with the weight of each added thought.

Crossroad, respect, money, Lisa...

In spite of himself, Taylor suddenly laughed out loud at the image and the decision it conjured up.

Then the phone rang.

Taylor reached over and picked up the wireless phone and felt a rush go down his spine as a voice from the past broke through. It was Nick.

Taylor's first thought was of Carol. What had happened? An accident? Was she okay, was she dead? Nick spoke in a flat tone: "A friend of yours died the other day, Taylor. I thought you might like to know."

"Who?"

"Leon."

"How?"

"What's the difference, Taylor. He's dead and that's really the bottom line in this case, ain't it? The funeral's tomorrow. Can you make it?"

"Where?"

Taylor listened intently to the answer, nodding his head several times in rhythm with unheard questions. Lisa's "friend" got up and strolled casually into the bathroom, her ass bouncing behind her.

Taylor could tell Lisa was watching him intently, sensing something that was out of order. He hung the phone up carefully and faced her. "That was Nick. Leon's dead. I'm going to Vegas."

He began throwing some clothes into an overnight bag. "Funeral's tomorrow. You wanta go?"

"Why?" Lisa picked up a cigarette and lit it carefully.

"I don't know, Lisa, I guess I didn't think before I asked that stupid question. I can't imagine why you'd want to go."

"Oh, don't cop an attitude, Taylor. You're just hot to see Carol again. Who knows? Maybe she's married with two kids, or fat, or something like that."

"Fuck off, Lisa," he replied with a notable lack of enthusiasm.

"Maybe you're right, but on the other hand, maybe it would be good publicity. Sure, I'll go. Call up the airlines, sweetheart, and book us both, okay?" She put the cigarette down in an ashtray and watched Taylor with the eyes of a hawk.

Taylor hesitated, started to say something, and then reached for the phone.

Carol sat quietly next to Nick in the penthouse office of the DollHouse, "Thank you, Nick. I'm not sure I could have talked to him right now."

"You're not going to be able to avoid Taylor at the funeral, Carol. Besides, if I know Lisa, she won't let him come unescorted. She's too smart for that."

"One day at a time. I'll just take it one day at a time, Nick."

The funeral crowd packed the chapel fully and spilled out onto the street like a wrap party after a major production. Carol recognized people from every major casino as well as some she knew were simply Leon's friends from one period in his life or another.

Carol tried her best to be stoic, but Anne, Leon's girlfriend, was leaning on her arm and crying in never-ending waves, and Carol herself was having a hard enough time blinking back the tears of her own to offer much support.

A rustle of sound swept over the room, even the minister delivering the eulogy looked up and stumbled as he momentarily lost his place in the speech.

A woman next to Carol turned to her neighbor and spoke softly, "My god, it is her. I thought Leon knew her but I never thought she'd show up here."

Carol refused to turn and look, but the rest of the speech seemed to drag on forever. As it ended, people milled about Carol, offering condolences and seeming to want to touch her even without words. For some reason Carol felt a stare at the back of her head. She turned around and there was Lisa looking at her. A split second passed and then Lisa threw her arms around Carol, she actually seemed to be weeping.

"How did he go, Carol, was it an accident? He was so fucking young."

Carol sensed flashbulbs going off and people pushing to crowd around them. "He, he, ah, a bubble in his brain. It was quick. Like a stroke."

"A stroke, huh? Probably caused by too many strokes."

"Lisa," Carol interrupted abruptly, "this is Anne." She indicated the other woman who was crying harder than ever and still clinging to her arm.

Lisa looked at her, obviously trying to place exactly who she was and what she was doing there.

"Anne was Leon's"—Carol stumbled in spite of herself—"girlfriend."

"Fiancée," Anne managed to get out between sobs.

Lisa blinked abruptly and looked from Carol to Anne without speaking. "His what?" she asked softly.

Carol shook her head in warning. Anne just sobbed.

"I don't get it. What's the punch line?" Lisa said.

"Not everything in life has a punch line, Lisa."

"Stroke, my ass. Probably died of shock. How long, I mean exactly how long—"

"Hi, Carol. How are you?"

Even as she welcomed the interruption, she dreaded the shock that was bound to follow when she turned around.

"Taylor!" She allowed herself to be kissed on the cheek. "It's good to see you."

She felt pulses racing through parts of her body that she hadn't known it was possible to have pulses in.

"Good to see you, Carol, it's really good to see you." Taylor seemed to be biting his lip as he stared into her eyes, or was she just imagining things, as she seemed to have done so many times in the past?

Suddenly Nick interrupted the proceedings to ask for everyone's attention. "We've got cars outside for any of you who want to come to the graveyard for the interment."

He hesitated a minute, and then began again, "But frankly, all of us who knew Leon don't think he would have wanted to be remembered this way, lowered into a hole with a bunch of friends weeping over shoveled dirt."

There was a shocked silence among the mourners.

"Leon got his start at the DollHouse. We gave him a big break"—Nick allowed himself a small smile—"and he repaid us in spades. Tonight the DollHouse is going to repay a fraction of that debt.

"We're going to have a wake. The fact is, we're going to have a party that's going to set this bloody town on its ear. That's what kind of wake we're going to have. Tonight the DollHouse is going to cancel its normal show and throw a party. A party just for Leon and a few of his close friends."

Carol overheard a whisper behind her from a showgirl, "God, I bet Susan Somers is going to love that."

"This is a private wake." He waited several seconds. Timing always was one of Nick's strong suits, Carol thought.

"This invite is limited to anyone who worked for Leon, knew Leon for what he was, or for anyone who loved Leon. The DollHouse and I, personally, expect to see all of you there. Don't disappoint me."

He squared his shoulders, turned away, and walked out like a Mafioso chieftain. The invite was obviously not a request. It was an order. Nick left the front of the room and walked over to Carol. He put his arms around her and squeezed her hard. "You look great, sweetheart. Even in black. If I was thirty years younger—"

"Nick," she said as she shook away a tear, "you used to say if you were twenty years younger."

"Time waits for no man, my love, although it appears to have violated that rule just for you. No, not for me." He looked over at Taylor who was standing a few steps behind, obviously within earshot, "And some people just don't have the God-given sense to see that."

He turned to walk away and then, as if remembering something, he turned back to Carol. "I'd appreciate it if you'd come up to the office for a few minutes after you get back from the graveyard, honey, as I need to double check some arrangements with you."

This time he did leave.

The actual interment had been much as Nick had described it. Carol found it dreary, weepy and agreed with Nick's assessment that it was hardly an affair benefiting Leon's sense of style. Later, she knocked politely on Nick's office door and then entered.

"Well, I see you did talk to them."

"Lisa's a bit hard to avoid, but when I looked into her eyes I'm not sure there's any particular Lisa I'm talking to." There was a poignant silence from Nick.

"And, yes, I did say hello to Taylor."

Nick nodded and shut his eyes, rubbing them for a few seconds and then coming back to reality. "I wasn't kidding about tonight, you know. I've brought the entire cast from Leon's latest extravaganza over on the Concorde to do a special tribute. All of Leon's big hits. I've got girls from every club in town and about half the population of Monaco, the best food, the best music, the best everything. You know why, Carol?"

"I have learned some lessons from you, Nick. Class counts, and when you have it, show it."

He looked at her shrewdly, "You have learned, Carol. You've learned a lot, but Leon had it too, and class owes class. It's one of my rules to live by."

Carol nodded and Nick seemed to drift again, deep in a private world. She gently waited. "Why did you ask me here, Nick? You didn't need any input from me for this affair. There don't seem to be any last minute details that you haven't thought of."

"Sometimes I wish you weren't so goddam smart, Carol. I asked you here to apologize and ask for your help."

"Apologize for what?"

"I'm dying, too, Carol."

Carol gasped and covered her mouth with her hand.

Nick held up his hand. "Oh, no, not physically. Nothing as dramatic as Leon. No heavy diseases. I'm dying of life and, to be real honest with you, the partners want me out before I become an embarrassment. Go with grace, if not with God."

He laughed and lifted his hands up in front of him and looked at them as if searching for calluses. "Carol, I've done something here that nobody else on this planet has ever done. It's like being the first man to put a footprint on the ice at the South Pole or find the headwaters of the Amazon against all the fucking odds.

"I put together a class act. A place where people came and didn't have to mix with the great unwashed, do whatever they wanted—within some limits, of course—and never have to worry about getting fucked over. There is no place else on earth like the DollHouse and let me tell you, it feels good, honey—it feels like I lived *for* something, and I really don't want to hang around here until I have a stroke or just get too old to enjoy life. I love this place, Carol. I broke ground and it was a hell of a lot of fun. I've got no regrets."

"So what's the apology?"

"I wanted you to take over everything, run the place like I wanted it to be run. You could do it, you really could. And no more Mrs. Housewife. You left that a long time ago, Carol. You have a real presence...

"The apology is that my partners could not, not in their wildest dreams, visualize a woman in charge of this place," he sighed. "You've got to understand," he dropped back into an Italian ghetto voice, "they're from the old country, Italy, New York, what's the difference? Women are born to take orders and make babies and that's about it. If you sat in on one of their council meetings, no one would even talk to you. They would all be thinking of ways to squeeze you out as soon as possible.

"So, I'm sorry. I wanted you to succeed me."

"Good God, Nick, I've got years of learning stuff you've forgotten. I'd blow it anyway."

Nick looked at her carefully. "Carol, I truly believe you could handle just about anything if you had to, but the point is, in this case, you simply can't... At least not directly."

"Not directly? I don't get it."

"Do me a favor. Front me some information, Carol. What do you feel for Taylor now?"

Carol was obviously taken aback. She started to say something, looked at Nick, and saw the intensity written on his face.

"I'm still in love with the son of a bitch. Nick, he excites me, I mean, mentally as much or more than physically. More than any man I've ever known. I'll probably always be in love with him."

"Even after good old Lisa?"

Carol thought about it for only a moment. "I'd take him back in a second and that's where it stands."

Nick nodded. "They're booked in town for a week and, take it from an old handicapper, Carol, from the look in Taylor's eyes I'd say he'd meet you any place, any time. I think Lisa's personality has finally bled him dry. I don't think he's going to take much more of her with or without you. He'll be at the party tonight, Carol. Talk to him."

"About what?"

"Maybe you can't take over the DollHouse, Carol, but Taylor could. You could be behind the scenes, keeping it like I wanted. In a way you'd really be running it.

"I know men, Carol. Pitch it right and he can't say no. Marry the bastard and raise a whole brood of beautiful kids. If I'm reading things right, he'll kick Lisa and Hollywood out of his life so fast it'll make your head spin."

"I can't ask him, Nick. His pride—and besides I hear he's doing really well in Hollywood. I don't think he's come back here for...well, for anything..."

"Maybe I hear things you don't, Carol. Maybe I've got an old boy network you never cultivated in Bryn Mawr."

"Vassar," she corrected him automatically, and then laughed. "How many years ago was it that we first said that line? Five?"

"Six, Nick, almost seven."

"Carol, I really wish you could..."

"Don't explain, Nick. I love you, you know."

"Never mind that," but she noticed he looked away, and she would have sworn there was a touch of a blush on his face.

"The point is, you've got more balls than any man who's ever worked for me, Carol. Let's put them to use. Do you want the deal? Do you want him back?"

"You know I do, but how are we going to do it?"

"Tonight, Carol, in the middle of the biggest blowout in the biggest little city in the world, I'm going to make my retirement announcement. I'm walking away. No strings attached."

Carol dropped her handbag onto the desk. "For God's sake why?"

"Have you forgotten there's more to life than running a casino, Carol? So many things I want to do. Did I ever tell you I love Africa? Imagine that. Of all the places on earth, I love Africa. I love the animals. I love the country. I could live in Lion's Camp right at the base of Kilamanjaro and be happy for a long time.

"I know it sounds like the *Reader's Digest* version of Hemingway, but in this case it's true. I want out."

"Taylor will never believe you. He'll figure you'll always be there, the invisible hand in the iron glove."

"No, no, that's not true. See, after a few drinks, my dear friend and compatriot, the most honest physician in the world and coincidentally the DollHouse's personal physician, Dr. Paul Mayer, a man who wouldn't fudge a codeine script if a junkie was dying in front of him, he's going to confide in Taylor off the cuff that I'm dying of cancer. If I don't slide an acceptable replacement into my slot, it's going to be a fucking war. In fact, there would be a good chance my dear cousin could conceivably land in this office. God forbid.

"I'm talking the kind of war that could tear the DollHouse apart—my house." He slammed his hand down on the desk so hard Carol jumped. *"This is my house."*

"Oh, God, Nick, no. You can't be dying." Carol stood up, "You can't be! Not Leon, not you, I can't handle it. I can't do it. Tell me it's not true. Oh, god, tell me it's not true."

"It's not true, Carol."

"What?" She looked at him unsure of what to exactly believe.

"Don't look so worried. Our distinguished Dr. Mayer is going to lie through his teeth. My old man died at ninety-three and I always swore to the son of a bitch that the one thing I would do for sure in my life was outlive him and I haven't seen anything that would make me change my mind on that score.

"I've got nothing worse than cancer of the surroundings. It's time to move on."

"Dr. Mayer would actually lie about something like that?"

"He owes me, Carol. He owes me."

Simple words, but they were spoken with a weight behind them that Carol could sense. Nick continued: "Taylor won't do it. Hollywood is still the greatest crap shoot in the world—unless there's a little more incentive added to the package."

"What incentive?"

"You."

"I tried that game months ago and, in case you don't remember, I came in a distant second."

"Not this time, Carol. I look in Taylor's eyes and I see the look that you see in a horse that everyone thinks has been broken to the halter, but he's just waiting to run off the track. Taylor's no longer in the race."

"What makes you so all-knowing, Nick?"

Nick looked at her. "I'm a man, Carol, so that's the deal. Are you in or are you out? I need an answer."

Carol looked at him and thought how her life had come down to this moment that could be determined by one syllable.

"In," she said without hesitation.

Nick nodded. "I never doubted it for a moment."

The wake was everything Nick had promised—and then some. He'd flown in the entire show company Leon had been directing in Europe, sent limos for virtually every local heavyweight that Leon had ever worked with in Las Vegas and even many minor show people who had never expected to be invited.

The casino customers who showed up expecting to see the advertised show were not only given a choice of their money back or a raincheck for a later performance, they were comped to a choice of a room and a dinner or a no-strings-attached hundred dollars in gaming chips to spend as they pleased.

No one complained.

When the enormous show hall had just about filled to capacity the house band stopped playing and the main spot zeroed in on Nick, standing alone on the stage. A hush traveled through the audience.

"Thank you for coming," he said. "The DollHouse owes you. More importantly," he deftly popped the cork from a bottle of Dom Perignon champagne and held it up to the light. The intense beam of the Klieg split the escaping foam into a beautiful indoor rainbow.

"We owe Leon. We owe Leon this evening. This is for him." Nick raised the bottle to his lips and drank deeply. " I think you'll find the food acceptable and the booze is non-stop. There is only one rule tonight—anybody who sheds a single tear will be forcibly removed from the premises.

"We are here to celebrate a passing, not mourn a death."

A huge cheer exploded from the seven or eight hundred assembled people who had never witnessed anything quite like this, even in Las Vegas.

"The old fucker always did have class, but this time he really has outdone himself," Lisa said to both Taylor and Carol, watching for their reactions as if awaiting a challenge. She grabbed a drink from a passing waiter and gulped it down. "Don't you think?"

"I don't know, Lisa. I would figure this would just be another typical evening in Hollywood."

Lisa laughed. "Haven't lost your touch, have you Princess? Still got the reverse Midas touch—everything turns to ice."

"You're right about one thing Lisa—Nick does have class. You know the funny thing about that? Took me twenty some years to realize you can't buy it. I think maybe God decides who gets it right as they are born, or maybe even as they are conceived."

Taylor jumped in. "Most don't." He looked right at Lisa and smiled but only with his mouth.

"I see some old friends over there, I think I'll go chat. I'm sure you and Carol can find some stories to swap about the star a few minutes without me to keep the small talk going?" She drifted off.

Carol looked at Taylor for at least five seconds before she could trust her voice not to crack. It seemed like minutes.

"Why do you take that, Taylor? What's changed you from the man who used to risk it all with a computer in his shoe? The man who was going to conquer the known world?

"Maybe you read too many of the old maps. The ones that used to say, 'Beyond here lie dragons.' "

"You really haven't changed, have you, Princess?"

"Don't call me that." She tried to sound authoritarian and failed.

He reached over and touched her cheek with his finger, tracing an invisible line. "No, it's okay, I'm the only one in the whole world who has the right to call you that. Because you really are a princess and only I know it.

"In some past life you were the kindly but smart daughter who took over the kingdom after the king died and ruled it wisely, setting your people free."

Carol turned away so not to have to look into those eyes. She had missed those eyes so much.

"I'm really sorry about Leon, you know. He was so unique. So Leon."

"You used to be unique too, Taylor. And I loved you for it. You know what did it initially? The first time you took me to dinner and everybody kowtowed to you and you didn't even notice. You didn't even care—but you walked with this stride that said, 'I'm me and I'm going to change the world.' I really loved that."

"Go ahead and say it, now you think I sit around the pool all day and make Lisa's drinks, don't you?"

Carol shrugged.

"Well, you're damn near right. I don't think I can ever really look at her again without feeling a mixture of hate and shame. Fun, huh? Still sound like the Taylor you once loved?"

He became suddenly pensive. "Have you ever thought about crossroads, Carol? To quote Mr. Clapton, 'I'm standing at the crossroads and I believe I'm sinking down.'"

She turned back to face him. "I've got something that belongs to you." She stuck her hand out. "Take it back, please."

And she dropped the diamond ring into Taylor's surprised hand.

"I apologize for acting the fool, I really didn't find it for days. I, I—" she could feel herself slipping. "I just didn't know and it must have seemed like I was really being a jerk. I'm sorry."

Taylor held the ring up to the light to catch the sparkle and then dropped it back into her hand. "I had almost forgotten about that. It wasn't just the ring, honey, it was a pivot point on which a whole chain of luck lived or died, turned, or froze forever. I'm still curious, what would you have said if you had found it in time?"

Carol bit her bottom lip so hard it began to bleed. "It was a crossroads." He wrapped her hand around the cold stone. "You keep it as a souvenir."

Carol looked at the stone and then at Taylor. "Keep what? The ring, or that proposal?" In spite of her efforts she felt a tear start to form at the corner of her left eye. *No!* Not now. Don't you dare betray me, body. Not now.

His hand wrapped tighter around hers. The ring had mysteriously gone from ice cold to blistering hot. "Are you kidding me? You would actually... I mean after what—"

"Could I talk to you a minute please, Taylor?" A hand grabbed his elbow and steered him away from Carol. "Alone?"

"Hey, Doc, how are you? Still treating slot machine elbow—take two aspirin and call me in the morning?" He grabbed the other man. "It's good to see you, have a drink, Doc, you're off duty." He waved at a passing waiter.

The other man shook his head, "I'm not going to tell you anything you want to hear."

"Were you with Leon? I mean did you see him?..."

"I don't want to talk about Leon, Taylor. There's something you need to know, although it'll sure as hell cost me my job if you tell anybody what I'm about to say. Job, shit, it will cost me my license."

Taylor caught the seriousness immediately, the edge sliding off his buzz. "Carol? Is something?..."

"No, it's Nick. Cancer of the liver."

"Does he know?"

"Yes."

"How long does he have?"

"Let me give you a piece of advice Taylor—one old friend to another. Make your peace with him now. Tonight. I think I will have that drink now." The doctor turned and walked off.

In a trance, Taylor drifted back over to Carol, "There's something I've got to do, Carol, but I need to see you later. I need to talk. Please."

That's the first time I've ever heard him say that word, she realized with a start. "I'll be here, Taylor." The ring was still in her hand eating through her flesh.

Taylor caught Nick's eyes across the swirling room. He simply stared as Taylor walked up to him.

"Your office or mine?" Taylor asked.

"Maybe you've forgotten something, Taylor, you don't have an office here anymore."

"I guess that makes it yours then, huh?" Taylor smiled.

Nick turned to begin walking, at the same time shrugging off the attempts of various people in the crowd to capture his attention.

Taylor sat uncomfortably in the chair he used to enjoy. It had somehow gotten very hard since he had returned. Never let them see you sweat.

"So, to what do I owe this visit from a huge Hollywood producer? Need a line of credit, Taylor? Just say the word. What's mine is yours." Taylor could sense a close scrutiny, underneath the patter. *He's looking for a tell, Taylor realized with a start.*

From me.

"Still skimming for the mob, Nick?" Taylor, even as he uttered those words knew he had just crossed the line.

Nick smiled. "Still kissing Lisa's ass, Taylor? I suppose the answer is yes to both. Some things never change. It's the way nature works."

Motherfucker, Taylor thought. "Well, there are degrees to the depth you have to insert your tongue, Nick, but once you start giving in to the guys in the suits you're totally owned."

"You wouldn't know the first thing about that, Taylor. Besides, I understand in California that any penetration, regardless of how slight, is regarded as sodomy under the law."

There was a long silence.

"It's a good thing you're doing for Leon." Taylor tried to break the tension.

Nick shrugged. "What are we doing here, Taylor? You've got your thing going, you don't need me. Why are we sitting here?" He began pouring two snifters of cognac.

"I want my job back." With some satisfaction Taylor noticed Nick's hand shake and spill some of the brown liquid.

"Why the hell would you want that? And more to the point, why would I want you back?"

"I just think I made a mistake and I could help, here, you know..."

Nick suddenly picked up one of the expensive snifters and threw it against the wall where it shattered into a thousand pieces. "He told you, didn't he?

"Goddam doctors and their kin everywhere. I most certainly do not want your pity and I don't need your help." He turned to face Taylor. "I've had a life, Taylor. I've done some shitty things. Maybe one or two people dead because of me, but it's never been boring and I ain't pissing and moaning my way out.

"I regret nothing. I paid a little bite to the unions, a minor skim to the guys that make things happen, but so did everybody else in the town, and I did some good.

"Not everybody can say that. I don't regret a second of my life. I've built things that will stand long after most people are dust. I don't think you will ever grasp that."

"You're wrong."

"Maybe. It's happened before once or twice.

"Tonight is not just Leon's wake—it's mine. I'm going to announce my retirement and then go live at Lake Mead lying in the sun like an alligator and drinking anything I want and fucking everything that moves. But I ain't going to tell anybody about this little problem. I would appreciate your doing the same."

Taylor nodded. Unable to speak for a moment. "So what happens to the DollHouse?"

"Fuck if I know. Let the boys put someone else in charge. I'm walking away."

"I don't believe you, Nick. You can't walk away from here and let some jerks take it over. You couldn't. You're bluffing."

"I ain't got a son, Taylor, I ain't got an old lady, and I ain't got anybody that hasn't crossed too many streets to trust with the job."

"Take me back, Nick," said Taylor. "I don't even want a piece, I just want to do it up right. Make it work like you have. You could do it."

"And what about the little hassles with the cash count? What would you do about that?"

"You can't believe the shit I've handled in Hollywood. I can live with the system."

"What about Lisa? Can you walk there too?"

Taylor laughed softly. "No, I can run there."

Nick watched him closely. "I'll think about it. Now get out of my office and leave an old man alone."

He sat without moving for several minutes until a discreet knock came at the door.

"Come in."

The doctor entered and sat down. "As I've just violated every oath I ever took about three, or was it four, times in the last hour, I'm curious how it came out."

Nick opened a desk drawer and tossed a thick Manila envelope on the desk between the two of them. The other man made no move to touch it. "I didn't do it for the money."

"Doc, I pay my debts. It went well. She believed you, he believed you, and I believe you. But I need one more favor, and I want you to owe me so there will be no hesitation in your mind when it comes due.

"You see, I really am going to move to Mead and party till I die. Literally. When that happens, Frank will set it up to look like I went out in a boating accident and you are going to sign the death certificate."

"Why not? I'm getting good at these charades."

"And never, never, are you to get drunk or lonely or whatever and tell anybody that I really did have cancer. If Carol ever finds out, Frank will break both your legs. Do you believe that?"

The doctor had no doubts.

Nick smiled. "No offense, of course. I appreciate your help, but you've given me a chance to actually make something right for one of the first times in my life. Don't mess it up. I guess maybe I wish I had kids to keep my soul alive and I guess I wish that they were like Carol and Taylor and..." he seemed to remember where he was.

"Take the money, Doc, buy a yacht, buy a plane, give it to starving kids in Ethiopia, but don't take a long vacation, because I'm going to need you one of these days pretty soon."

The doctor picked up the heavy paper container, turned, and left without another word.

Nick watched him go, secure in his planning. It was all going together like a carefully crafted jig saw puzzle.

It was too bad he wouldn't be around to see it all jell.

Taylor literally ran into a security guard he had known for years as he got into the elevator on the way back down to the main floor. "Do me a quick favor, Mark?"

"Name it, Taylor, I was sorry to see you go, always appreciated the way you treated us. Whose legs do you want broken?"

"I want to use a phone for a minute. Not a pay phone. Somewhere quiet."

The guard reached over and punched a button on the elevator control panel, causing the car to stop and the doors to open. He walked over to the first room and opened it with his master key.

"Help yourself, Taylor. Don't forget to lock the door on the way out."

"Get him. I don't care if he's sleeping with the entire cast of a Busby Berkeley film. Tell him it's me and get him on the damn phone." He waited a few minutes until the President of Wolf films came on the line.

"Sorry to bother you, buddy, but I've had a long, hard time trying to talk Lisa into our arrangement."

"Talk her into our *what!*" Taylor held the phone away from his ear. "We have a deal, man. I've committed money, crews, writers—don't try and hold me hostage for more bread you asshole, I'll have lawyers on your…" There was a pause and Taylor could sense the other man composing himself.

"It's not money, Doc, and I'm not trying to screw you out of anything."

"Sure, sure, who else have you signed with? Who have you rolled me onto my stomach for?"

"Listen to me, it isn't that. Lisa doesn't like the script, she doesn't like the co-stars, and she wants twice the money. Off the record, she said she wouldn't work for you, ah, well I believe the exact term was cocksuckers, no matter what the deal was."

Taylor could hear the sputtering on the other end of the phone. "I'll get you for this, I'll get both of you. Who does that cunt think she is?"

"I'm not getting through to you. I've quit her. I've quit that screwball business. This is a favor call. I quit the fucking business. I told her I gave you my word and I wouldn't go back on it. Cunt is a kind description of the lady. Sorry, but I'm history. I figure she's got some other source of money and wants to finance the whole thing herself. Let her dig her own grave, I'm out of it."

"You're leveling with me aren't you?" Taylor could hear the surprise in his voice.

"Yup."

"That cunt will regret this." The connection went dead in his hand.

Got that one right. Taylor carefully replaced the phone and locked the door behind him.

When he finally got back to the wake, Taylor spotted Lisa and Carol talking together. Lisa was obviously half plastered and Carol looked like she would rather be anywhere else in the world.

He joined them.

"I was just telling Carol what a great manager you are—how you just broke some records getting me the biggest advance in moviedom, and God knows what else." She raised her glass at Taylor in a mock salute.

"Oh, shit," He grabbed the back of his neck and looked up at the ceiling. "In all the excitement, I mean with Leon and—oh shit, I haven't told you."

Instantly Lisa was snake sober. "Haven't told me what?"

"They wouldn't go for the deal."

"What!" She tossed the contents of one of her champagne glasses into Taylor's face. He didn't even flinch. "So what the fuck did we settle for? No points? Some measly fucking advance I could have had the mail room boy at Morris swing for me? Is that the big deal you struck, Taylor?"

He carefully wiped the liquid from his eyes. "I just know in the morning my eyebrows are going to be sticky and I hate that." He looked up as if remembering Lisa was still there.

"Oh, no, nothing like that. They said you were a fat slut who had passed her prime and the best they could do would be a supporting role. Better than union rates, though. I did get you that."

Lisa looked as if someone had hit her with a hammer.

"Don't be too mad, hon, I stuck up for you. I told them as long as you kept the Spandex leotards on, the roll wouldn't show." He reached down casually and pinched a layer of fat on her waist.

Lisa tried to toss the other glass of bubbly at him but it was empty. Then she cocked her arm back to throw the glass instead of the contents.

Taylor reached up and grabbed her elbow, arresting the motion. "No! Bad idea, I'd hit back on that one."

"You're fired." She hissed.

"You've heard the saying Lisa, tomorrow I'll just be unemployed. You'll still be a fat bitch."

She turned and stomped from the hall, almost knocking over a woman standing directly behind her who was obviously eavesdropping on the conversation.

"Too many brain cells gone by the wayside," Taylor offered as an explanation. "Her coordination's shot." The woman nodded.

Taylor turned to Carol, "Can we go someplace peaceful and talk? Right now I need an aura of peace. Maybe your office?"

"I've gone down some stupid roads. Made some bad turns. But I'm back, Carol. I've no idea where I can get a job, or if, for that matter, but I'm home. And I don't think I'm leaving again.

"I'd like to see you. I know you've probably got a dozen boyfriends, but I'd still like to see you. Is that possible?"

Carol very carefully reached in her purse and withdrew the diamond and place it on the table between them. "If I keep this it means you are back with me, Taylor. It means neither one of us fucks around, no more showgirls. It means we're engaged. I don't care where you work, I don't care what you do. What you did out there with Lisa, that really took guts. That was the old Taylor."

Good God, Nick really did it. Does he really want to leave that badly, or was it all for me? Will I ever know?

"Take your ring and get out of my life." She let the silence build for a couple of seconds. "Or put it on my finger. And come home with me."

Silently he pressed the ring into her hand and wrapped her fingers around it, one by one.

"I'll get us a cab," Taylor said.

"Let's walk. I want to remember this night for a long time."

LAS VEGAS

Carol walked into the room and immediately noticed Taylor was buried in a copy of *Variety*. He was mumbling to himself and shaking his head. "I don't believe it—her own production company... She must have hocked the house."

"What's up?" Carol inquired.

"Lisa. She's actually formed a production company to finish that turkey. I know her partner, a real strange one. I never could figure out his trip. He lived down the street, drove a white Rolls, and every week, like clockwork, threw a party for the stars.

"I never figured out exactly what he did for a living but the parties always had stockpiles of really amazing coke. Kinda figured he was a wannabee, you know, 'Dealer to the Stars,' I sold Bob Dylan cocaine sort of thing.

"I can't believe he's financing half of an expensive film. He has to be in a cash business, how can he bury a chunk of operating capital like that?"

"Maybe he has family money or something."

Taylor went on like he hadn't heard her. "What a pair—business partners made in heaven. Well, it wouldn't be the first film financed by Colombia. No pun intended. What a mad house that town is..."

"And you miss it..."

He carefully laid the paper on the desk and looked at her. "No, no, I don't miss that part of it at all. Reading *Variety* is just a hobby, like when you—Jesus, you don't have a hobby do you?"

"Yes, I do. Right now it's reading *Variety*."

Taylor smiled. "The good news is that I firmly believe we are sitting in the middle of the next Hollywood. All the things the movie industry went there to California to get—sunshine, shooting weather, scenery—they're all here now. Hollywood is long gone, besides we've got access to everybody in the business, stars to techies.

"And I'll be sitting pretty when they come begging." He pursed his lips, " 'Taylor, we need a producer, Taylor we need a director, Taylor—someone with your contacts...' Well, you get the idea."

"Yes, I do, but I wouldn't hold my breath."

"No, life goes on." He picked *Variety* back up and shook his head. "Unbelievable..."

It was two weeks later to the day when the call came. Carol had just taken her shoes off and lain down to unwind from a long hot day when the phone rang. First she closed her eyes and willed Taylor to answer it, but it kept ringing.

No, I'm just going to let it go. But the noise was unrelenting. Finally she reached over and snatched the phone off the hook, only to hear Taylor's voice. Thank God, I can go back to... then a part of her recognized the other voice.

In spite of her better judgment, Carol gently lifted the handpiece back up to her ear, sliding her hand over the mouthpiece like they did in the movies. This is silly... but she kept listing.

"Hi, pal, how's life in the big city?" There was a forced cheerfulness in Lisa's voice.

"Not nearly as exciting as being a big shot producer, I suppose, but it goes on, that's the important thing."

"So you've heard, huh?"

"It's a small world Lisa." He sounded distant, but Carol swore she heard more than a casual interest in his comments. "How's it going in Hollyweird?"

"To be completely honest, not that good." Carol suppressed a gasp on the extension.

"I mean it's going to be great—the film is dynamite, almost wrapped—but it's so damn expensive. Do you know what the IATSE wants to man a goddam stage for a couple hours of overtime? You'd think they were going to war for what we pay them."

"Don't whine, Lisa, it's not becoming."

"It's not your money riding on this," she snapped.

"By choice."

"Oh shit, you're right. I'm sorry, honey, it's just that it's been so fucking hard these last couple of weeks—trying to direct, act and then deal with the money sharks in my spare time. You can't imagine."

Taylor did not reply.

"We're just about out of money, the word is out that I can't get a completion bond and the studios smell meat. It's like living through a shipwreck. I could sell it in a second but nobody will offer anything but the rape deal. I'd be lucky to clear expenses and some fat son of a bitch will make millions on my sweat."

"Uh-huh."

"Don't be that way, Taylor. I, uh, I really need your help." Before he could reply she plunged ahead. "If you would come back here, we could do a deal. I'll give you points, anything. You'll own a piece of the action."

"I have a job Lisa."

"Yeah, yeah, I know, you're a big shot now. This wouldn't have to be forever, just take a couple of months off, princess Carol can run things for a little while. Think of the money you'll make when this picture hits. Hell, you'd be doing it for Carol, too—I mean, I know you guys are doing okay but you could retire on this. This is the big one."

Once again there was a marked hesitation as Taylor remained silent.

Lisa started in again, her pace had picked up: "Or, you could both come out here and we'd form a production company—just the three of us."

Carol bit her lip to keep from entering the conversation. She felt the warm, salty taste of her own blood fill her mouth. Good lord, he can't really be considering it.

Can he?

"Lisa this is like one of those stories where the hero comes back, gets even with the bad woman and then kisses her off. I'd like to think I'm above that, but I'm not one hundred percent sure, so let's say goodbye before we both find out."

Taylor hung the phone up without waiting for a reply.

Carol, caught by surprise, hung her phone up as quickly as possible. Did he hear her hanging up? The distance was short, it was certainly possible. She hadn't really meant to spy, but once the conversation started there was no good time to unobtrusively get out of her situation.

Her thoughts were cut short as Taylor walked into the room. He seemed to look at the phone for a long moment. She could feel her face flushing—surely he could see it.

"What did Winston Churchill say, 'Gentlemen don't read other people's mail'?" He caught her eyes and she felt the warmth spreading.

"I've got an idea."

Oh shit, here it comes. How is he going to phrase it so I don't suspect Lisa is behind it? He wants to take a short vacation? Sure, then I'll get the phone call, "can't come back yet but…"

"…today. What do you say?"

Part of Carol's subconscious was desperately trying to replay the first portion of the exchange, but it seemed to be hanging just out of reach.

"Pardon me?"

Taylor punctuated his next words carefully. "I said let's get married. Today. Right now."

"Married?" Carol knew she was mumbling. "Us?"

"Somehow I thought that was the idea all along. Was I mistaken?"

Play for time, her mind shouted at her. Get your act together. "Yes?" Good answer. Sharp thinking. Keep him off balance.

Taylor laughed at her obvious flustering.

"Are you serious?"

"Never more so."

"But the arrangements, our friends, my parents, the dress, uh, I don't even have a dress…"

"I know the tackiest little chapel." Taylor ran his fingers down an invisible cascade. "They have a real waterfall, and I'm sure they rent dresses. I bet we could get in this very afternoon." His voice was as serious as his face.

"But," it was all happening a bit to fast—things were slipping away like ball bearings on ice. Suddenly something snapped, like a giant rubber band, and Carol was viewing the scene from another view point.

It was as if she had been picked up and held motionless above the room—there she was, making excuses, being protective, and Taylor's smile was starting to fade as quickly as it had appeared.

We've been here before, and I blew it…

Not again.

"Fine, let's go." She took his hand and felt it stiffen with suspense.

"I hope you weren't bluffing Taylor."

He looked down at the clasped hands. "You know why I never gamble?" he asked conversationally.

She shook her head.

"I can't bluff." He leaned over and kissed her full on the mouth.

It was seven hours later before Carol had a chance to literally stop and think. Taylor was resting with his eyes closed and his seat pushed back.

They were 32,000 feet above the desert and heading for Europe. Licensed, married in a corny but fun ceremony, and they were on their way to the continent for an unexpected honeymoon.

I wonder if the DollHouse can survive both of us gone for two weeks. She looked out of the tiny window and watched the United States slide effortlessly below them.

I wonder if Lisa's call precipitated this? Maybe so. She reached over and slid the plastic shade down. That would be the first thing she's ever done for me in her entire life.

I won. Carol shut her eyes and absorbed the hum of the jet engines.

I won everything that counts…

The first week flew by in a blur of London theaters, the Savoy hotel and four-star French restaurants. Carol was happier then she could ever remember being. Life was good…

They were inside the giant KDV department store on the Ku Dam being amazed by the selection of things Western. Carol was walking through the sportswear section gazing at the brightly colored shirts from Malibu, Huntington Beach, and Santa Cruz advertising various surfboard manufacturers.

"There's more California here than in California," she exclaimed leafing through the multi-colored rack. "Where do Germans surf?"

"Only in their minds," Taylor answered, drifting over to examine one of the many black leather motorcycle-type suits hanging like dead animals from a rack. He ran a silver zipper up and down, listening to the ripping sound. "Maybe I should pick up a couple of these while we're here. Think anyone would wonder about us if I starting showing up to work every day in leathers?"

"Why do so many people here wear these things? It's not like there is an abundance of motorcycles..."

"The Germans love a man in uniform," Taylor responded absently.

Carol grabbed his hand and pulled him towards the book department. "Don't be such a cynic, you're on your honeymoon.

"Look at all the books in English," she exclaimed. "I need something trashy to read in bed."

"I knew it. One week married and you're tired of me already."

Carol punched him in the arm. "You are getting old. I need something to read while you recover your energy in between rounds."

Taylor started to reply but his attention was drawn to a rack of newspapers. "Look at all the American papers." He picked up a day old copy of the *Times*. "I wonder if they have *Variety?*"

Carol gently pried his fingers from the newspaper. "No papers, no magazines, no business. No *Variety*. We're on a honeymoon, remember?"

"If you get a book..."

"It's not the same, newspapers make you think of—Oh, my God!" She slowly raised the paper back up to eye level, staring at the front page.

It was a photo of Lisa.

MOVIE QUEEN BUSTED!! The banner screamed. Carol began reading out loud: "Screen star and popular singer Lisa Steel was arrested today for allegedly attempting to sell eleven pounds of high grade cocaine to a federal drug enforcement agent.

"Sources in Los Angeles claim Miss Steel and her co-producer, Rick Severs, were arrested in the office of Tandem productions. Tandem is producing Miss Steel's latest film, 'SuperStar.'

"At her preliminary hearing Miss Steel refused to comment on the charges or rumors that production on the new film had been halted due to financial difficulties.

"Bail was set at $250,000."

"The John DeLorean school of higher finance." Taylor shook his head. "I wonder who fronted the coke? Somebody's probably very unhappy right about now."

"What about Lisa? Imagine what she is going through."

Taylor groaned. "Haven't you learned your lesson about her yet? Christ, she'll come through with flying colors. A little time in the joint might do her a world of good. Think of all the great songs that have been written in prison. Maybe she can do some crossover stuff, be the female Johnny Cash. Can a white girl sing the blues?"

"I can't believe you're taking this—I mean you were..." Carol paused as she ran out of words.

"Well, you see, we were, but we never really *were*—know what I mean?" He pressed his hands onto her shoulders and kissed her lightly.

"See? Besides she's not convicted yet, much less sentenced. Think of all the friends she can call on for help. I wonder how many calls are aging on your answering machine as we speak..."

"Eleven pounds—that's a lot isn't it? She's really in trouble." Carol tried to analyze her own feelings. Did she really care what happened to Lisa, six thousand miles away? It all seemed like a distant world, totally removed from where she was.

Fact be told, she felt a strange sense of satisfaction, but it was soon pushed out of the way by a sense of guilt.

"With her habits she can probably make a case for personal consumption. After all, what's a mere eleven pounds? Besides, there's always the uncertainty of a trial. Maybe her partner in crime will be a sport and take the fall."

"I don't know..." Carol was reading more of the article, "it sounds like they caught her red handed."

"They caught DeLorean red handed, how much time did he do? Come on let's jump in the old rental car and drive to Amsterdam. I spent some time there when I was in college and I loved it. We can rent a barge and sail endlessly down the canals."

Carol glanced down at the grainy photo. "Okay." She put the newspaper back in the rack and felt the weight of responsibility go with it. "That sounds like fun."

But Taylor was wrong. There were no messages from Lisa for either of them when they returned to the States.

Conspicuous by their absence...

It was almost two years to the day after Lisa disappeared that Carol saw a photo of her in the *Sun*. The image was grainy and the coarseness of the newsprint paper blurred the details somewhat, but it was undoubtedly Lisa.

She was lying on a bright white beach, apparently somewhere in Brazil, wearing only the bottom of her swimsuit, if you could call a piece of string a suit. She was looking over her shoulder directly into the camera and the look on her face vanquished any remaining doubts that it really was Lisa.

It was the look Lisa had always reserved for reporters and photographers, usually followed by some immediate act of violence.

The story was done in a "what ever happened to" style and recounted Lisa's meteoric rise to fame, then her fall, taking care to mention how the authorities had quickly discounted the suicide note found in her Ferrari parked by the side of the Pacific Ocean.

Looking back, Carol had to admit that even she had had trouble believing in the carefully staged note. Maybe if Lisa had actually pushed the car over some cliff into the water the scenario would have been a little more solid, but even though she had to leave it behind, Lisa obviously treasured the flashy vehicle a little too much to destroy it.

Still the trick had apparently bought her enough time to get out of the country, and now she was unquestionably living a life of comparable ease on a beach in Ipanema. For a while there had been wild sightings from fans and would-be reporters all over the world, but this photo was the first real proof that Lisa was still alive and well.

The edge of the photo showed half of an older man with his arm possessively encircling Lisa's bare waist. I wonder if she's found happiness, lying on a beach day after day? I wonder if she misses show business—and I wonder if it's better than working twelve hours a day and sleeping six?

And most of all I wonder if the bald guy is a dentist... Carol chuckled to herself, put the paper down, and looked into a wall mirror.

The years have tumbled by. At least it's rarely been dull, even if I'm not twenty-six anymore. God knows what I'd be doing today if I'd stayed married. Running the PTA in New Canaan? Planning bake sales and meeting the train every night with a forced smile?

My life has been like riding a cresting wave. I've been in the right place at the right time, it seems like the forces have just taken me along for the ride. How much of what I have is a result of my own skills?

At least I have Taylor, she thought, although a vague sense of unease had corrupted that concept lately. Maybe it was just the natural result of too much work and not enough play. He was thoroughly tied up in running the DollHouse's financial affairs as well as managing the promotion and marketing concepts, both of which had gotten more important in the last year or so and demanded even more responsibility for the day-to-day operations of the casino, as well as acting as an in-house producer for the shows. In fact, he seemed to be delegating more and more of the operations to various pit bosses and managers and concentrating his efforts on the entertainment end of things. It was if he was subconsciously drifting back toward the show business end of things.

Even though they worked in the same place, their respective duties kept Carol and Taylor at a distance during the day and both of them had long ago agreed that it would not be a healthy idea to bring their work home, so DollHouse issues were not mentioned outside of the Dollhouse.

But it seemed as if they gradually had less and less time to spend with each other—less time to *be* together. Maybe it was time to take a break in the routine. Take a vacation, bring Taylor's mind back to the issues at hand—namely, her...

She looked back into the mirror as she rubbed in some expensive skin conditioner absolutely guaranteed to take ten years of eye wrinkles and make them vanish into thin air. After that it was back in the hands of God...

Carol blinked involuntarily as the small brush drew close to her eyes and she was suddenly transported back to an earlier time.

She woke up lying in the DollHouse bed staring up at the mirrored ceiling, the sheets were tucked back over the end, her naked figure filling the reflective ceiling. I'm being attacked by a naked skydiver...

She blinked again and the present rushed back.

Makeup. I didn't know what the word meant then—100 B.L.— before lines. I still look good, but do I look great? She touched a small wrinkle. Footprints of time around my eyes. Who would have thought it?

Lisa's face appeared, unbidden, in the mirror. The last few years had been good, but had they been great? That was the question. It had been a long trip from Connecticut, had it been worth the price of admission? Could she honestly say she was any happier than Lisa— passing the days on a diamond cut beach, letting life slide by, the bills always paid by someone else?

Another wrinkle vanished under the careful strokes of the tiny black brush. If I had it to do all over again, would I? Have I missed out on the best parts of life? I run a major business, people seem to respect me, is it just the small frog syndrome or should it be totally satisfying? Should I feel a sense of profound accomplishment?

Because I don't...

I won. After all, isn't that what life comes down to? Isn't that what it's all about? I've gotten almost everything I wanted...

Another tiny line was dissipated by the chemicals.

Older, I definitely look older than that night in the suite. How did that happen? Had the time drifted away or had it been stolen by some sort of thief in the night? What had edged in to replace it?

Happiness?

Maybe. Life was full, but very predictable. Day after day the excitement line had flattened out. Was the original goal to be comfortable or was it to be excited? She wasn't certain anymore. Once it had seemed so clear, so tangible you could reach out and touch it.

Now?

Now it was like a vapor you could smell—you could sense, but couldn't quite see. Was happiness really the bottom line? Was satisfaction the ultimate goal? Did comfort equate with freedom? Point of fact, could she actually say she was happier than Lisa? At least Lisa had clung to the roller coaster for better or for worse.

Carol glanced at the clock on the counter. It was almost time to go to work. Her life was governed by one clock or another. Maybe it really was time to take a break, a vacation. Besides the usual business trips she hadn't really been anywhere since the honeymoon.

She reached over to the sink for her daily regimen of vitamins and scheduled pills. The loose tablets rattled in her hand like a pair of hot dice. She uncurled her fist and looked at the conglomeration with care.

Carol picked out an innocuous white tablet and twisted it around. What was it Nick used to say?—There are always options. Maybe it was time to force fate to mold to her wishes instead of the other way around.

One option would be to have children before the biological alarm rang for the final wakeup. Maybe that would be the way to the future, bring her and Taylor right back together... Besides it would be an adventure—a baby of her own.

Taylor would probably be resistant to the idea but she knew deep in his heart he would welcome a child. What man wouldn't?

She blinked again and another future unfolded in the mirror like a silent film: Taylor bending over a little girl in a white dress, trying to scold her and then picking her up and twirling her around and around...

He would spoil a kid rotten, no doubt about that.

To be fair, this step should be a mutual decision, but finding time to have a serious discussion with Taylor was becoming next to impossible these days. Business was off at every casino in town. A year of recession coupled with the bleed-off from Atlantic City and Laughlin were taking their toll. In spite of the DollHouse's status as a separate entity from the strip casinos, they were losing the bottom fifteen percent of their customers to the "normal" casinos.

She knew Taylor had even ordered a few slot machines for the main floor, to keep the light rollers happy. Nick must be turning over in his grave.

The strain of running the DollHouse was taking its toll on both Taylor and herself. They really should get away. Maybe a second honeymoon was the solution.

In fact, if she stopped taking the pill it really would be another honeymoon, especially if she conceived on the trip. Carol considered the proposition for a long moment then crushed the tiny pill between her thumb and forefinger until it was transformed into innocent white powder. Then she picked up the circular container to judge the number of pills remaining and tossed it into a drawer.

The way to do this was to just take the initiative, stop the pill, book a trip—then tell Taylor.

Leave no room for argument. She studied her image in the silvery glass.

"Mirror, mirror on the wall..." If it was a boy they would name it

Nicholas—"who's the fairest"—she stopped in mid sentence, studied her eyes closely and then added an extra layer of moisturizer.

Taylor was sipping a glass of designer water in the main DollHouse bar, mentally summing up the results of his daily rounds. Who was doing their job, who was slipping, who was nodding off from a big night or who was doing a little this and that to stay awake and together during the day?…

It was a time of day he particularly enjoyed, compiling a list of pros and cons, treating the entire casino as one being. Finding the dead flesh and massaging it back to life or cutting it out with surgical precision.

Gradually Taylor became aware of a grating voice behind him. At first he tried to ignore the tirade—just another happy spender—but then the conversation shifted tracks.

"Fixed, I tell you, the game was fixed. That dealer was as crooked as a whore's morals. She was working for the house, it's no wonder this place does so well. They can't lose."

A rational part of Taylor's mind thought to call security, but the part in charge decided to grab the stupid son of a bitch by the collar and personally escort him from the premises. He turned to put the plan into action and was greeted by applause from the offenders.

"Mine gott, I thought he'd never turn around." One of the men said in an affected German accent.

"Craig!" Taylor stopped short as he recognized his old friend from Hollywood. "What the hell are you doing here?" His gaze took in the small party of people flanking his friend, including one striking woman in a low cut gown he was certain he had seen before.

"Trying to get your attention."

"Don't tell me you've given up on the movies? Trying to make it as a gambler? At least you've come to the right place. We love high rollers from California."

"I'm shocked. Don't tell me you don't even read the trades anymore, Taylor. We're here to celebrate." He stopped, watching Taylor's face for a reaction. "I don't believe it, Hollywood must be completely out of your blood. Don't they carry *Variety* in Lost Wages?"

Taylor laughed, trying to steal a glance at the striking woman. "I'm a few weeks behind. What happened? Did you sell a script?"

"No, not exactly, just like in the movies. The proverbial axe fell—'off with their heads' "—he drew his finger across his throat. "To make a long story short—well, remember the last time I saw you?"

"Sure, in the lobby of the America building. You were pitching."

"Yes, well, I've come a ways since then. Come a ways from pitching. Guess who's now the head of production, American Films, Inc.?"

"You're kidding me." Taylor slapped the other man's shoulder. "I don't believe it, that's fantastic."

"If nothing else it's nice to be on the receiving end of the pitch for a change." Suddenly he remembered his companions. "Oh, and this is my assistant, Barton, and this is my friend, Nancy."

Taylor shook the man's hand and carefully took the woman's when she offered it. It was as pretty as the rest of her.

"Hello, Taylor, how's it going?"

"Uh, fine." She seemed to be about twenty-five, had the most complete tan Taylor could remember seeing on a human being, and one of the best figures. Her taffy colored hair swirled about her shoulders as she tilted her head back and laughed.

"I know we have met somewhere but..." The sense of familiarity was overpowering. "I apologize but I just can't remember exactly where."

She laughed again, like a little girl, genuinely pleased with the situation. "I don't blame you for forgetting, maybe we should just start all over again from here out. Is it a deal?" She stuck her hand out.

Taylor reached out to take it and then everything came back. He had a vivid picture of Nancy peeking out at him from between Lisa's legs. Naked. He stopped his hand in mid-flight.

"Why, I do believe you're blushing, Taylor. Something I said?"

Taylor felt his ears go red as the other two men watched the proceedings. "Uh, well..."

Nancy leaned over closing the distance between them and grabbing his hand. "Don't be afraid, I've mended my ways."

"You two know each other?" Craig seemed intrigued.

"Yes," Nancy said.

"No," Taylor said.

Then they both burst out laughing.

"Maybe we could work out some sort of compromise on the subject," Craig interjected.

"We were never formally introduced, but we had a mutual friend," Nancy covered the awkward moment. "It's good to finally meet you."

"Right." Taylor said, thinking back to Nancy standing naked next to the bed, daring him to say something. She seemed so much softer now.

She smiled, reading his expression, "It's good to see you again too."

Taylor laughed in spite of himself.

"If you gentlemen will excuse me for a few minutes I'm going to go take some of Taylor's money away from his friends out there." Nancy turned to leave, "I'll be back shortly, don't anyone disappear."

"Me too," the man introduced as Barton said. "I'm with you." They moved off silently.

"Pretty slick," Taylor said as he watched the retreat. "I can see you've been taking vice-president-of-a-major-studio lessons. I didn't even see the get-lost signal."

The other man moaned. "Taylor, Taylor, has Vegas done this to you? Where has your belief in the ultimate good of mankind gone? We're old friends."

"Uh-huh. I don't remember you doing a lot of gambling Craig, odd you'd come to Vegas to celebrate."

"I wanted to see a friend, share my good fortune. Have a night on the town. Let me buy you a drink." He waved at the hovering bartender. "Best drink in the house for my friend and me."

"The last time a good friend bought me a drink he wanted to borrow ten thousand dollars."

"So now you don't trust anybody?" Craig raised his glass, "La Chaime!" He sipped the viscous liquid. "This town is not so good for you, you think everyone is out to get something. Maybe you should come back to California."

Taylor smiled into his drink. "Maybe I am getting a little bit paranoid, it seems like you've got all you could possibly want." He nodded toward the floor where Nancy was about to roll the dice for her third straight pass.

"No, no, the term friend is not always a euphemism. My wife is at home resting, I've been blessed with twins since I last saw you, life is going good. I don't have to fuck around. She's a sharp girl and a damn fine actress."

"Where do you know each other from?"

"Acting. She was doing a bit part when I met her."

"I bet she was doing it well." Craig drained his drink and signaled for another round.

"As a matter of fact she was... Listen, I apologize for my suspicions, it is good to see you. Let me make a phone call to Carol, uh, my wife, we were going to have dinner. I'll get her down here and we'll make a party of it."

"If it's not too much trouble?"

"No trouble at all. Back in a second." Taylor walked out to the floor to use a house phone. Nancy held her hand up to him in a victory salute and then blew him a kiss as he passed.

The image of her staring back at him naked from Lisa's bed wouldn't leave him.

Carol and Nancy did not hit it off. Outwardly they were both smiling but Taylor could sense the tension as they traded light dinner conversation. Carol seemed coiled inside herself, as if she was going to spring at something. Nancy seemed to feed on the electricity. Animals circling a fresh kill.

"Lisa thought highly of you, Carol, your name came up often."

"Were you and Lisa close?" Carol asked, trying not to appear overly interested.

If I didn't know better, I'd think she's jealous, Taylor thought. Anybody but Carol, how could she possibly be jealous of a... a kid. Granted she's a very good-looking kid...

"You could say that," Nancy answered deadpan. At the same time she kicked Taylor's shins under the table.

"If you'll excuse me, I'm not feeling so hot. It was nice meeting you all and I'll see you again before you leave. Have a good stay."

Taylor caught up with Carol at the front desk. "I'm sorry, Carol, I didn't mean to screw up the evening. It's just that I haven't seen Craig since, well, you know. Are you feeling okay?"

No, I'm depressed, I'm tired, I'm getting old and to compound the problem you cancel our evening and drag me to dinner with some Hollywood sex kitten who's obviously dying to get into your pants in as little time as possible and you have the nerve to ask me if I'm okay... Carol felt like screaming.

"I'm fine." She smiled, feeling like her face might crack. "I'm just beat and I'm getting cramps. You go back to your friends, you have fun tonight. I'll see you at home."

"Are you sure?"

She squeezed his arm, "I'm okay, really I just want to go home and relax."

He turned to go. "Oh, Taylor? Don't have too much fun…"

He nodded, knowing something was up but not quite certain exactly what it was. "Okay."

Carol watched him leave. Imagine, all those stupid romance novels were right all along, men get better-looking and women get old. Maybe I'll find a dentist somewhere and buy my own beach and make the possession of a mirror a felony.

"Is your wife okay?" Taylor could detect nothing but concern in Nancy's voice.

"Long day," he replied, "but her last words were for us to have fun." He sat back down at the table.

"The least we can do is honor her wishes," Nancy leaned over and filled Taylor's glass from one of the bottles of Dom Perignon cooling off in silver ice buckets encompassing the table like a group of palace guards.

She playfully pinched Taylor's hand. "Right?"

Taylor was tempted to add the rest of Carol's instructions but, truth be told, he was enjoying Nancy's attention…

They were down to dessert sherry. Nancy and the silent Barton were back on the gaming floor and the band was taking a break. "So, Craig, you want to tell me why you're really here? Or should we just keep up appearances?"

"You win—I'll tell you." He took a long swallow. "I'm vice-president, legions of people doing the shuck and jive everywhere I go: 'Yes, massah, anything you want, massah.' I feel like Moses. It could get to a person."

"Life's tough everywhere," Taylor grinned.

"Yes, well, that's the up side, the down is that I inherited a huge debt that the stockholders don't know about yet, about six drastically-over-budget and rather thinly disguised copies of last year's Best Picture in one stage of production or another, and about two hundred and fifty sons of assorted bitches that had already spent the money they would have earned when they got my job and can't wait for me to fall on my ass.

"The final piece of news is that I've got just enough money in the budget to shoot a good, solid short."

"I was right, you are here to borrow money."

"Sure, buddy, a good solid fifty million would get us back on our feet. Can you spare that?"

"I'll have to ask Carol before I write a check."

"Taylor Stevens, pussy whipped, who would have believed it? No, actually I've got something better than money..."

"Heart?" Taylor asked.

"You're one funny guy Taylor. No, what I've got is twelve reels of an unreleased blockbuster that nobody thought would ever get made and it's ASF—Already Shot film—no production costs. Built-in publicity, top stars—and," he winked, "it's free."

Taylor thought for a moment, "My God, you've got 'SuperStar,' don't you?" He didn't wait for confirmation. "Do you own the rights? What about Lisa?".

"I have the negative. Possession really is nine tenth's of the law in this instance. Let her sue me from Brazil."

"But it's not done—"

"It's three-quarters done," Craig was now gesturing with his hands. "We just need a little script doctoring—elevate Nancy to the second lead, shoot around Lisa—and cut it. I figure we can bring in the hottest picture of the season for a couple of mil, and her legend just get's stronger and stronger. She'll be a bigger draw than ever."

"That's great!" Taylor was caught up in the idea.

"I hoped you would feel that way."

"Why?" Taylor was immediately suspicious.

"Because I want you to come back and produce it. Hell, you can direct it too if you want."

Taylor laughed, unsure if Craig was serious. "Why me? There must be about six thousand guys who would kill for a shot at that."

"The point is, you started it. I know you wrote part of the film and coached Lisa. Hell, you were living with her, screwing her, you know this story better than anyone. It would just take a couple of months and you could come home to beautiful Las Vegas as a home town hero."

"Is the footage any good?"

"Good? Better than that. You know Lisa was just playing herself, nobody could do it better. I just happen to have some highlight clips upstairs at this very moment."

Craig left the table and Taylor followed, his anticipation growing.

Taylor watched the electronic image die out on the television monitor. The film was raw footage—completely unedited—but it was impossible to miss the energy, the dynamics. The film would be a winner, Taylor could smell it.

"So what's the verdict?"

"It's good…" Taylor was trying to be noncommittal. "But I'm not convinced I'd add anything to the project."

"I am"—Craig watched Taylor closely—"and I'm willing to back it up. Points on the gross, final cut, hire and fire—whatever you want. Just say the word."

"I'd be a liar if I said it wasn't tempting, but I've got a life here."

"I'm not asking you to give it up, Taylor, just to come back for a few weeks. Two months at the outside, finish what you started. Didn't your mother ever teach you that? Think of it as a paid vacation. Or you could think of it as a paid vacation that will give you three points of the gross," Craig watched Taylor's reaction. "Plus of course, salary and expenses."

"Money isn't everything Craig. I do well here."

"Obviously. But I'm offering you a chance to sit at the biggest table in the world and run the game your way."

"Final cut?"

"Of course, it wouldn't be a game without that now, would it?"

"I need some time. I need to think."

"The shoot is scheduled to start in three weeks."

Taylor shook his head. "There's no way I could even get organized in three weeks, much less re-write a film. I don't even have any place to live."

"Yes you do. I've got a condo at Malibu, you can live there. We'll do the re-write together—at the beach."

"Malibu, huh? You really have come up in the world."

"It's actually the studio's—or it is until the next stockholder's meeting at least. It's all set up, Taylor, come out and let's do it right."

"Give me a night to think it over."

"It's all yours. I'm going to catch your show, I'll see you in the morning, buddy." Craig hugged him and left.

Taylor walked over and put the VCR into play. I've got to watch it one more time and see if it really is magic or if I'm just dreaming.

He was so engrossed in the video he didn't hear the door open and Nancy come into the room.

"Amazing, isn't she?"

Taylor jumped. "Bigger than life. Her only problem was that she knew it."

Nancy watched him for a minute. "I need to tell you something." He started to protest but she cut him off, "No, I really need to talk to you for just a moment. Okay?"

He nodded.

Carol tried to read a book but she was too keyed up to concentrate on the plot. I acted like a jerk and now I'm pouting. This is no way to start a pre-second honeymoon, besides I should be there to look after my interests.

I'll go back and put on my best face and smile and firmly take Taylor's hand and drag him home where he belongs. In a nice way, of course, so he'll be thinking it was his idea all along.

Carol couldn't find her quarry on the floor or in the restaurants. She was about to give it up when the floor manager told her Taylor and Craig had gone upstairs after Taylor had ordered a video tape player to be taken up to the room.

Carol was beginning to get a queasy feeling in the pit of her stomach as she got off the elevator and headed down the hall towards the room. A VCR, why would they need a VCR?

As she approached the room a part of her subconscious realized that the door was open. Carol could hear voices coming out into the hall but they didn't really register until she was about to enter the room.

She stopped dead. Lisa! It was Lisa's voice, how could—and then in a split second she realized what was happening. Just a visit from an old friend my ass, she started to go in again when another voice jolted her.

She could hear Nancy talking just inside the door, not two feet from where Carol stood in the hall. Lisa was reciting her lines in the background like some kind of strange jazz melody line.

A wall of déjà vu held her in place. Who was saying what? Was it Lisa or was it Nancy, or was it both of them?

"First of all," a voice said, "I'm really glad you're going to direct this project. It really means a lot to me. More than I can tell you."

"I'm not sure I'm going to do it yet."

In spite of the disclaimer Carol knew as sure as she was standing there that Taylor was lying. He had already made up his mind. Without even consulting me, without considering what effect it might have on us, on the DollHouse, he's decided to do it. Whatever it is that they want him to go back to that god awful place and do for them he's going to do. It's a fait accompli.

She clenched her hands into tight fists. Well, we'll see about that idea right now. She caught herself. If I go in there now we will have a fight. Look at me, I'm trembling with fury.

Get a grip woman—stomp in there and the result will be as predictable as rain. And it might well turn out to be a fight you can't win. Do it right. At least calm down for a minute and plan it out.

Maybe he hasn't decided, maybe I'm reading things into his voice, maybe he's just thinking it over.

"I know you must think I'm a royal bitch." The voices came back. "When you saw me that time with, uh, with Lisa I was having some problems. I was out of money and about to leave California to go home with my tail between my legs.

"In two years I got exactly two bit parts at cattle calls. Six lines was the entire scope of my acting performances. Then I get this role in a feature film with one of the hottest stars around. It was like a dream somehow come true.

"I was pretty overwhelmed by everything, and when Lisa took an interest in me I was really flattered. The next thing I knew I was loaded and, well, you saw the outcome..."

Taylor nodded, not knowing what to say.

"But that wasn't the only reason I acted so weird. I was really jealous..."

"Of Lisa—"

Nancy touched his nose with her finger. "No silly, of you. Well, I mean because of you. I thought you were this gorgeous man who seemed to be at Lisa's beck and call. Every guy I had met in California was either a total sleazeball or gay. Lisa was so rude to you, but there you were, Mr. Nice guy, writing for her, managing her, holding her act together.

"I was so jealous of the way you treated her. So I was rude. I've changed since then, Taylor. I've grown up and I really want to work with you to finish this film. It can be dynamite—and that's my little speech.

"Are we friends?"

"I can live with that idea," he answered.

"Good. Because I know you're going to do this and I am never wrong."

Was that line on the tape or in the room? Carol was having trouble keeping track of the source of the conversation.

"Oh, and Taylor, there is one other thing I need to tell you…"

Now, Carol thought. This little scene has played itself out. It's time for an entrance—but her legs didn't obey.

"What's that?"

"I've had a thing for you ever since I saw you and I still think you're one gorgeous guy." She stood on her toes and kissed him full on the mouth.

This time Carol forced her body to obey. She stepped into the room just in time to see Taylor drop his hands in order to slowly cup Nancy's hips and pull her body to his.

Something. I should do something. Scream. Scratch her eyes out. Instead she backed into the hall and then ran to the elevator.

As soon as she got home Carol took a bottle of Taylor's Scotch down from the shelf and poured herself a water glass full.

She grimaced as the odd tasting liquid registered on her taste buds. She felt like she was outside her own body, watching events happen but unable to exercise any control over their sequence.

She took a long swallow and tried to remember how she had gotten home. It was as if a movie she was watching had slowed down—she could pick out individual frames, frozen still life scenes devoid of any action—but she could not see the entire story. It refused to make sense.

I should be raving. I should be pulling my own hair out. I should have shot them both. But I don't have a gun. And I don't know how to shoot. Other than that, it would probably have worked out okay.

Is this what it all comes down to? I went through this once, am I supposed to be better equipped for the second go around? What is the matter with me? Why do I just feel numbed out… Have my feelings gone with everything else?

Do you suppose this is what depression is really like? She looked at the empty glass in surprise. Well, I guess I'll just get loaded and put off the inevitable until tomorrow. Take the chicken's way out…

Carol thought of Lisa's voice on the VCR, mocking her. What have you done Lisa? Did you ever have to face anything you didn't want to? Of course not, you always had a crutch...

Maybe that's the ticket. Some sort of crutch. Carol raced to the spare room and dug into the closet, pulling out a dusty suitcase full of Lisa's old possessions.

Come on Lisa, pay your debts, you owe me one for this, it's all your fault. She rummaged through the case, part of her amazed by the number of expensive outfits Lisa had left behind without a second thought.

Near the bottom she found what she was looking for: several plastic pill bottles.

Come on, Lisa, you had a least twelve varieties of mood adjusters in here. I'll settle for a single Valium. She shook each bottle in turn but there was no one home.

Damn it all anyway. How could she not have left a single goddam pill behind? Carol threw the last empty bottle at the vanity counter, where it shattered.

It wasn't empty after all. A small paper envelope fell out. Carol picked it up and slit it open with her fingernail, knowing what she would find inside. A little trail of sparkly white powder slid from the hole onto the tile. It really was quite pretty.

Idly Carol picked at it. Individual flakes lifted up and drifted on the air currents like tiny birds. She moistened the tip of her finger, dipped it into the pile and licked it.

The strong taste of the chemicals made her cringe. It tastes like a doctor's office smells, she thought.

Carol opened her purse and took out a credit card. I can't believe I'm doing this. She crunched the pile of crystals into a dull powder with the edge of the plastic just as she had seen Lisa do so many times. She laid out a tiny pile then rolled a $10 bill into a tube, leaned over the powder and inhaled.

It hit the inside of her nose and she sneezed abruptly, scattering the rest of the pile.

That was certainly stupid. God it hurts. She grabbed her nose to stop another sneeze. Why did I do that? Just because my life is falling apart...

And then it happened. It was as if she had inhaled a small bottle of champagne—tiny bubbles of pleasure reached up and grabbed her brain.

Things seemed suddenly clear and, at the same time, less serious. Damn, I feel good. I really feel good.

So Taylor's a jerk after all. Just another man out for what he can get, well I guess life goes on. At least I think so, maybe I need a little more Scotch. Then she looked at the tiny paper container still stuck half in the bottle. Life was buzzing like tiny bees swarming, and she felt ten years melt off her soul.

I deserve it. I deserve some enjoyment in my life. I deserve feeling like this.

Carol poured a larger pile of the coke out and began crushing it.

Just this once...